MRS. MUNCK

MRS. MUNCK

ELLA LEFFLAND

Graywolf Press

Saint Paul

First published by Houghton-Mifflin Co., 1970.
First Graywolf paperback edition, 1985.

Publication of this volume is made possible in part
by a grant from the National Endowment for the Arts.

ISBN 0-915308-70-3
Library of Congress Catalog Card Number 84-73373

Published by Graywolf Press
Post Office Box 75006
Saint Paul, Minnesota 55175

MRS. MUNCK

Prologue

I ALWAYS looked like a widow during my marriage. Now I am in my proper frame, so to speak.

Dying was too big for him — an enormous coat he could scarcely hold up to put on. When at the end his eyes fastened on the hospital window with a harsh love of light, and then began to drain of color, and his hand rose in a bitter gesture, then he was one with the moment, he'd got his arm in the coat sleeve; but a moment later he resumed his usual acrimonious expression, more suited to a trivial argument than the cessation of life; and with a sour smacking of lips he sank away.

All the solemnity that followed, from the respectful tolling of the bells to the long hushed interment — the sun even went creeping behind a cloud, as though to do the fitting thing — all this seemed to ask of him a weight he didn't have. And when I think of him now, lying in that immense darkness, I can't picture him stretched out at a proper length, but see him crowded like a scrap of paper into the foot of the coffin.

The funeral was held up the bay in Martinez, the town in

whose hospital he died (we have no hospital, funeral parlor, or cemetery here in Port Carquinez). A few of the old Italians and Portuguese from here attended the service, strictly out of respect, for Harley was an unconscionable bore, a cipher whom no one could regret seeing to rest. I wished to appear the normal figure of grief, to oil my way to acceptance with tears, but I could not; I looked at them with the eyes of a statue, and they looked back unhappily. Why they expected me to be fonder of Harley than they, I do not know, but somehow I wounded them in their deepest feelings.

I thought of this when I came back into the house that evening. As though in deference to them I sat down with lowered gaze and crossed my hands in my lap. But my fingers fidgeted, my eyes wandered. I took up my stationery and wrote to *Popular Mechanics*, stopping Harley's subscription. There was no trace of him in the room except for a crumpled pack of cigarettes and the magazines, which he never read. I threw the cigarettes into the stove and removed the magazines to the cellar. Then I made a bacon and tomato sandwich and read the paper.

I meant to say something kind about him, but I suppose this must stand. RIP.

It would be wrong to think that I have no qualms about death. My skin hangs dry as a cracker and cross-hatched with broken veins, submitting inch by inch to the arrangements of death. I am not old — forty-three — but I feel prematurely aged. And even the strongest of us reflects on death when he reaches this age.

I worry that just before the death rattle I will feel my mouth opening wide in a silent testimony to horror. I do not feel this horror, I only suspect it. It is as though I suffer at ten removes, as though my fear were under water, slow, deaf, somnambulistic. I am quite aware of this; I understand myself perfectly, but I am no longer interested.

And in this town, for instance, there is no one whose demise could startle or pain me. The old Italian and Portuguese families — the Ferreras, Gaudenzis, and Pompanos who sit on their weathered front porches and seldom stir — this handful of ancients has had its day, as I. I believe they are by nature shrewd, sensuous, religious, often implacable. Even now, with all their juices watered down by age, they are inspiring — not to me, but to anyone capable of inspiration. Still, they have had their day.

When they die I will regret only that the town will pass to the others. The others are not a new breed — they have been collecting here in California like flotsam for over twenty years, since the war — but they give the appearance of novelty because they are always on the move, shifting from town to town in search of cheap housing until they can afford better, and even after. No matter how old the house they move into, it immediately becomes older: the steps fall in, windows break and are stuffed with rags, limbless dolls and rusty automobile parts litter the yard. And yet they themselves always look new, in a raw, garish way. Perhaps it's the color of their clothes, which tends to chartreuse, shocking pink, and sign-painter's red — to me, a travesty on what are surely the internal colors of their owners: metallic gray, choleric yellow. Any of these people could die and I would nod with satisfaction.

It is only the town itself whose death I would regret. Every time a shed is torn down or a tree is blasted by a storm, I am bereft.

But I must correct myself. There is one death aside from the town's that would have an unwonted effect on me. This thought has been growing in me ever since I came back to the empty house after the funeral.

Unfortunately, it is a small house; you would be living in each other's pockets, staring into each other's face. Nor is the location advantageous. The house is set halfway up a steep hill, fronted by almost perpendicular wooden steps. But I have Harley's empty room, I have all the time in the world, and I have the will to dedicate myself. Why not?

I have finally sat down and written them, both Frank and Cathleen, offering to take care of the old man. There were some attractions I was able to mention; for instance, the view from the front window. You can see the trains coming and going, the foreign tankers breasting the waves on their way to the refinery. The view encompasses the whole Carquinez Strait and miles of the opposite shore where barren hills like great sand dunes stretch into the distance. The sunset is unforgettable from my window.

But can a view decide them? They must have faith in my ability to see to their father. Certainly I have no doubts myself, being capable and well organized and sincere. And they cannot help but see the sincerity, since I have offered to take him without recompense. The offer will come as a total surprise to them, since I have not seen or been in touch with them for twenty-three years; nor had Harley, whose cousins they are. Twenty-three years. Ever since we moved here. But every year, without fail, I have gone to San Francisco and visited old Aunt Monica, the gossip. Through her I have kept track of the family. Now the old man is partially paralyzed, living in a nursing home. I hope Frank and Cathleen will realize that a proper home with a relative, even a relative by marriage, is more salutary for an invalid than a nursing home run by professionals.

But I have a suspicion that will be the least of their reasons if they leave him with me. It must be terrible to grow old and discover that your children think of you only as a burden. It must be especially terrible for old Mr. Leary, or Uncle Patrick, as Harley called him; he always believed in his children's love. He has always had a special place in my memory.

A week has passed and they haven't answered. My interest waxes and wanes. Sometimes I am annoyed with them for their apparent indifference to my offer. Other times I think, what does it matter if I do or don't make this last gesture? And why do I speak of "last gesture," as though I had only a short time left? Most women my age are racing around in station wagons, attending plays, experimenting with new hair styles. But I have been isolated and unsociable for many years now. Even when Harley was alive I seldom conversed. Harley was a grumbler, a whiner, a gossip, but not a conversationalist. The house is silent now.

Frank finally replied and was definite. He and his sister discussed my suggestion with their father; they said he showed enthusiasm, and asked me to write and tell them when they could bring him. I have already answered, setting next Saturday afternoon as the time, and giving directions to the house.

All week I have scrubbed and swept. I asked the oldest Shotwell boy to fix the wobbly front steps. The Shotwells are my next door neighbors, noisy, unpleasant people. Fortunately there is a large empty lot between us. The boy came surly, sullen, in cleated boots and greasy Levi's, leaving a trail of gum wrappers and cigarette butts behind him. Although I always pay him well he looks as though he could bite me. But he's a thorough worker and the place now looks irreproachable.

Today I walked over to Martinez and bought new curtains,

bedspreads, and a bright rag rug for the empty bedroom. My house has always looked rather grim, but now it seems almost attractive. I have put flowers in every room and tacked splashy impressionist prints on the walls. I've drawn the curtains back from the front window so that they will have the full effect of the view when they arrive tomorrow.

Saturday dawned sullen with haze. By nine o'clock it was already hot. I walked outside with a pair of shears, breathing deeply of the dry grass and salt water. There was no sound from the Shotwell house. The parents had probably taken their brood on a screeching trip to some suburban supermarket. Steve, the oldest boy, had gone off on his motorcycle very early, splitting the sleepy air with his departure.

It was a delicious hour of the day, filled with morning potential. I walked up the wooden steps, their edges worn round with age and thickly overgrown with thistles. Reluctantly, I cut down the thistles, each like a purple gem set in a cluster of gold prongs. Mr. Leary could not be brought from below, it was too far to climb; they would have to bring him down from above. A disused dirt road ended at the top of the steps, and a gate stood there whose rusted lock I had removed the day before. They could park their car by the gate and carry him down the ten or twelve now-accessible steps without difficulty.

I straightened up from my work and went up the last few steps to a small clearing where I had long ago placed a wicker chair. I sat down and had a smoke, feeling nervous — something I had not felt for years — but gradually the familiar sights and sounds calmed me. A dog scratched around in the underbrush, its license jangling. Seagulls swooped down to the water, which looked shallow and thin, its current delicately shifting and crisscrossing, teasing a rowboat this way and that. A freight train roared along the water's edge — New York Central System, Northern Pacific Railway, Pennsylvania — and then was gone. The dry October leaves rustled in the warm breeze. I looked up the hill at my side, steep, wreathed with cow paths. They would be coming from around that hill. I got up and checked the gate again; it opened easily.

It was only ten. They were to arrive at two. Here and there the steps had caved in so that a path had been worn around them. At the foot of the steps I passed Felix's bait shop, a small whitewashed shack with a tin sign: FELIX's, with a star over the I, and underneath, the amateur profile of a fish with a smile. Wilting red-hot pokers grew in front, from a terrain of soft black dirt and cracked cement. Felix, in his old skipper's hat with dirty gold braid, and with his dog, Dave, at his side, sat outside on a backless kitchen chair, talking with a stranger. He nodded and the stranger stretched, looking past me to the water.

I went on, passing the old concrete warehouse (inside are housed the barbershop and grocery store), and crossed the gravel frontage glinting with Coca-Cola caps and little rings of broken glass. Then, stepping across the oil-blackened railroad ties, I stood at the edge of the water. It lapped below me, the color of cider. Silver fish heads with naked spines littered the ground, surrounded by quarreling gulls. The tops of the pilings were thick with dried, discolored fish entrails which gave off a piercing smell. I looked at the beached ferry, turned almost completely to moss; long feathery strands rose and fell with the waves. It was an honest, roughscuff scene. I wished nothing about it changed.

Today I did not linger and was soon back at the house. I took some pains with my appearance. I have tended to severity over the years, and I realized that this does not put people at their ease. Puffing out my hair and using a little makeup, I softened my face. Then I chose a dress I seldom wore, full sleeved, white, almost virginal, I thought, as I slipped it over my head.

I waited for them at the gate of the old road, telling myself that something had happened and they would not come. By the time they arrived — it was almost four o'clock — I was black with pessimism. There were only two people in the car, Frank and his father. I don't know why I had expected Frank's wife Louise as well, and his sister Cathleen and her husband, four people who might have to be impressed favorably with the house, dinner, myself. I was relieved, and opened the gate with a confident smile. Frank got out and walked over to me, a beefy man my age in slacks and a bright sports shirt.

"Well, Rose," he said, shaking my hand vigorously, "it's been a long time." When I last saw him he had been a nervous, brooding youth just testing the loud casualness that had apparently become second nature. But there was still something about him, a preoccupation, a hardness that took me back. "Rose," he said, nodding at the car, "I can't tell you how Dad appreciates this. Twin Oaks was getting him down. We'd love to have him at our place, Louise has been wanting to have him, but I can't let her, you know how sick she's been these last years."

"I know," I said, although I did not know, and did not believe it.

He paused. "I was very sorry to hear about Harley, Rose. I wish you'd gotten in touch with us when it happened."

I said nothing.

His hand was still in mine. He removed it now and squinted at the gate. "How do we get him to your place?"

"It's just a few feet down those steps," I said, pointing.

"It's certainly wonderful of you . . ." he threw back, walking to the car. "Dad's been complaining about that place for so long . . . and he always thought a lot of the Muncks, he was broken up when we told him about Harley . . ."

"When Harley died I felt I needed someone . . ."

"I know, Rose, it must be lonely." He was opening the car door now, reaching inside. A moment later he slammed the door shut with his foot and came toward me with Mr. Leary in his arms. He was an old, old man, wizened, bald, and he lay in his son's arms like a corpse. He looked terrified. "No, Frank," he protested in a thin voice with just a memory of its former gravelly quality.

"It's Rose," Frank told him, "Harley's wife. You remember Harley." He gave his father a little shake. "Harley?"

"Hello, Uncle Patrick," I whispered, trying to smile.

The old man swung his head back and forth. He looked senile.

Frank gave him a reassuring squeeze. "Look, Dad. What a fantastic view!" And he proceeded through the gate and down the steps. I followed, watching one of Mr. Leary's heavy black shoes waving feebly in the air. It must have been his left leg that was paralyzed.

Once inside the house Frank deposited him on the sofa. The left arm, too, I could see, was paralyzed. But the face was not. The old man blinked, frowned, wrinkled his nose, drew back his lips from his teeth, and began to weep. Frank took me aside.

"It's the change that's upsetting him. You know he hasn't been out of that place in five years."

"Yes," I said, "taking a person his age from familiar surroundings, even if he doesn't like them, can be a shock. Sometimes quite damaging."

"I have the greatest faith in you," he said shortly, adding, "We paid two hundred and fifty a month at Twin Oaks, we'd like to pay you the same."

"I wouldn't think of it," I said.

"But you don't know how much I appreciate your taking him. He was losing touch with everything at that place, turning into a vegetable."

"And you would like him to be? . . ."

"I've got to get back," he said, looking at his watch and walking over to his father.

"I'm not staying, Frank," Mr. Leary quavered, wiping his nose. "I liked it at Twin Oaks. I don't like this place, I don't like all those damn steps, I don't like her, and I don't like you either. Why are you doing this to me?"

Frank gave me a weary look. "I'll just go up and get his things."

I felt it was best to leave Mr. Leary alone, so I went into the kitchen to make the salad. I thought of all the trouble I had gone to — the mended stairs, the new curtains, the dinner — and I realized that of course Frank would have left his father here if it had been a cowshed.

Frank returned with a folded wheelchair and a suitcase. "Sorry I have to run off like this, Rose," he said, and took his father's good hand in his. "We'll be over to visit you, Dad."

I doubted that.

"How're you feeling? O.K.?" he asked. "Come on, Dad, you'll like it here."

"Don't leave me, Frank."

"I've got to go now. You'll like it here when you get settled in. I know you will." He squeezed the old hand and dropped it. "So long, Rose, I hope you'll get on all right. Just sock the old duffer if he makes trouble," and he threw his father a wink.

I closed the door after him and returned to Mr. Leary. He had worked his way to the edge of the sofa and sat there forsaken, sickly looking.

"You really don't recognize me?" I asked, sitting down next to him. He drew back and averted his watery eyes.

"You know it's Rose. Rose. Rose. Rose."

And I knew he had been feigning lack of recognition from the first moment, for without the slightest change in expression he clutched the sofa arm with his good hand, which was still surprisingly virile looking, square, ruddy, and covered with coarse black hair, and levered himself to a crouching position on his right foot, his eyes darting between my face and the door.

"You'd better not try to stand," I said.

He did not answer, but took a step forward and folded brittlely to the floor. I watched his fingers scratching the rug. "Now you'll have to manage to get back to the sofa," I told him. "In the meantime I'll finish dinner."

I went into the kitchen and continued tearing apart the lettuce. When I was finished with the salad and had taken the turkey from the oven I went back into the living room. He was crawling laboriously to the door. I went over to it and locked it from the inside with my key. He looked at me, spent. "Now get back on the sofa, Mr. Leary. I don't serve dinner on the floor."

Harley and I never ate in the living room. We always sat in the kitchen with the same two chipped plates and cheap knives and forks; we were as drearily informal as the crusted ketchup bottle neither of us ever used. That kind of living was for some reason repugnant to me now. Removing the table runner, I laid down a lace cloth and set two places with good silverware and china I never used. I pulled the table over to the sofa and brought the food in.

"This is a real occasion," I said. "I'm so pleased to have you here. I hope you'll find everything to your liking. Which do you prefer, white meat or dark? I forget." I began to sharpen the carving knife. I paused and walked over and knelt by him on the floor, balancing myself on the knife, whose tip pierced the rug by his fingers. For the first time I took a close look at his attire. He was wearing baggy, greenish trousers hoisted up to his chest, and a flannel shirt that was fluttering wildly over his heart. He tore his eyes away from the knife to my face.

"What's happened to your waist, Mr. Leary? It seems to have crept up to your neck. And your shoulders, where have they gone? You have the most pathetic shape, like a frog's. Like those frogs they dissect in biology classes."

I straightened up, swinging the knife between my fingers. "Why are you crying? Aren't you ashamed of yourself, crying in front of me?"

I went back to the table and sat down. "Whenever you're ready," I said, pouring the wine and helping myself to the food. I had a keen appetite. "You'd better be quick or there won't be anything left. No, that's not true, there's enough here for an army. You see, I expected Frank and Louise both, and Cathleen and her husband. I don't know why I thought they'd all come to look things over and see you settled in. I don't know why I assumed they'd be that concerned."

I put my fork down and looked over to the window, where I could see the sinking sun. I got up from the table, feeling curiously lost. "Get up!" I cried in a sudden passion. "You look grotesque lying there."

He did not move.

"All right, lie there. I'm going for a walk." I looked around the room. I had had the telephone disconnected. The windows were locked, the room was in fact stuffy. The carving knife was still on the table, but that was all right; if he wanted to cut his throat, let him. I went out the back door, locking it behind me. The thought struck me as I walked alongside the house that perhaps he was deaf, since he had not responded to one word I had said. I envisioned myself ramming a lead pipe through his eardrum and screaming through it; he must hear me, he must hear what I had to say. And I stopped by a side window and looked in. He was still on the floor, stroking his afflicted arm as though he were a father and it his child. I rapped my knuckles on the pane and my heart leaped as he turned his head in response.

A recklessness possessed me as I walked away. I remembered how, as a small child living on a isolated farm, I had almost burst with anticipation the few times visitors were expected, but how instead of waiting to welcome them I had fled across the fields, kicking up puffs of dust, honing my anticipation to the point of pain. I imagined how everything would be — they would seat me on their laps, let me talk, give me a trinket or two. I knew I could turn back and they would be there in the big bare front room, there in the flesh, waiting; but I kept running, breathless now, and tired, my face working with the scene I imagined. And when I did finally turn back I found they were the same as on previous visits: rawboned, improbably wrinkled people like my parents, worn down by the elements to a pure, dead worry. They spoke of crops, of loans, and when their eyes rested on me it was with a fleeting, preoccupied kindliness, like the flicker of a defective Christmas tree light.

Tonight I felt this old childhood urge to run madly into the horizon before the hoped-for moment. But this time my anticipation would be fulfilled. This guest would not ignore me.

I went swiftly down the steps in the setting sun. The longer I stayed away the better; the house would grow dark, the night wind would rise, making the trees moan and the windows rattle. I could picture him crawling inch by inch across the floor to the sofa, hoisting himself up and huddling there, trying to pierce the darkness with his small eyes.

Passing the Shotwell house, I threw a look back up at mine. Half paralyzed though he was, he might still somehow unlock a window and call out (I had fixed them so that they could be raised only a few inches) or even throw himself through the glass. When people were frightened they were capable of amazing feats of strength. And if anyone heard him they might investigate. Let them, I thought, passing on, going down to the tracks. My mind whirled with the complexities that might arise in my absence; my brain felt like a powerful and precise machine equipped to meet any crisis and anxious to prove it. When a train hurtled toward me through the dusk I leaped nimbly off the tracks, enjoying the danger.

Stopping now and then with a delicious restlessness to look across the water, I walked a mile or so along the tracks. No ocean could have smelled more pungently of space and freedom than the strait did that evening. As I started back the ground vibrated with an approaching train and a moment later the *City of San Francisco* roared by, the train that had left me in Port Carquinez on a summer evening in 1939 with Harley standing beside me. I had always hated that train, but tonight I felt a delight as I watched it, all lit up, rushing toward Port Carquinez, which it would pass without reducing its speed. Port Carquinez had been dropped as a station stop ten years before. With a kind of passive perversity, my little town grew steadily more isolated as the rest of the county mushroomed.

When I got back I saw Shotwell and another man coming down the steps. My pulse raced. Surely Mr. Leary had managed to catch their attention and they were looking for me. I paused with a forced smile on my lips, and as I stood there I could see that the lights of my house were blazing. I looked anxiously at their faces in the dark, Shotwell's mean-featured, dull of expression, the other man's heavy, observant — he was the same man I had seen talking with Felix earlier that day.

"Yes?" I said, waiting. But they were only pausing on the narrow steps for me to pass. They knew nothing of Mr. Leary. Relieved, I squeezed by, forgot them, trailed my fingers through the tall, dry grass as I climbed higher, stopping now and then to admire the lights of the town. I turned with an excited sigh to the gate and swung it open, looking up at the front window whose broad yellow beam fell at my feet. I smoothed the skirt of my white dress and went down the path to the back door.

"I'm back, Mr. Leary," I called from the back porch. "I see you found the light switch. Aren't you resourceful?"

In the living room I looked around for him but he was nowhere to be seen. Nor was he in the kitchen or the bedrooms, and I returned to the living room where I stood quite still, gratified that he was able to respond to his situation with some cunning. Then I noticed a bulge behind one of the drapes. As I watched, the bulge moved, and I knew that he had been sitting on the floor and was now vainly trying to rise smoothly and inconspicuously to a standing position. I sat down on the sofa and waited. After a while the bulge slid to the floor again. This happened three times in the next hour. Finally I walked over to the drape and pulled it aside. He was sitting on the floor with the carving knife in his lap.

"Why are you sitting behind this drape?" I asked. "Were you going to jump out at me waving that knife? One would think you had taken leave of your senses."

His face was white and cold looking.

"You could catch pneumonia sitting on that cold floor, Mr. Leary. Your lungs would fill up with water and you'd drown just as surely as if someone held you under in the bathtub. I'd take care if I were you." And I let the drape fall back.

I sat for a while longer on the sofa. I was restless, disappointed. Every human being has a tempo: Mr. Leary's was far too slow to suit me. All the anticipation that had built up during my walk now faded and I felt as I had those long years ago when I had come back across the fields to nothing. I turned out the light and went to my room, wiped the unfamiliar lipstick away and pulled off the white dress.

Putting on my pajamas, I got into bed, where I lay wide-awake. Very late I heard a noise I couldn't place at first; then it came to me that it was the doorknob, clicking faintly, turning by infinite degrees. I got up and tiptoed across the room, paused for an instant, then swung the door open to find Mr. Leary leaning precariously against the wall, a glazed, bewildered look on his face. The carving knife was in his hand, and as I watched he raised it above his head, where it trembled badly. And then something passed over his face, leaving his eyes clear and narrowed. He threw the weight of his whole body behind the knife, and as I jumped aside he drove it into the doorjamb, where it stuck, quivering. I could feel the force of the act in his thrashing arm as I pushed him back. He fell against the wall and, holding himself half erect, stared steadily at me.

"Now we understand each other," I whispered.

"Yes, we understand each other," he shot back in his thin, reedy voice, and as though the sound of it enraged him, he hit the wall with his fist.

I closed the door.

Chapter

1

UP IN THE MOST NORTHERN PART of the state, in the corner made by the Oregon and Nevada borders, is a country of rain-colored stubble broken at great intervals by a black barbed wire fence. My father tried to raise alfalfa here, failed worse with every year, died of a stroke while still young, and was buried in the ground that broke him. As a child I never understood why he didn't try some other kind of work. I supposed he had some kinship with the place, found satisfaction in the austere levelness and the great cloud cathedrals that moved over it, but it may have been only me who felt passionately about that grim landscape. When it was that I first wandered off the farm onto that plain — prairie, steppe, whatever you might call it — I don't remember; I seemed always to have been drawn there, and kept there by a deep excitement. There were no trees, and only some scattered sagebrush. For the most, it was just gray, rock-strewn earth stretching into a horizon as astoundingly long as half the circumference of the globe. The sky was greater, the wind more alive here than anywhere else, and they sent a rush of some unnamed joy through me. High overhead the clouds blew along, and beneath them with a silence that was profound, their shadows moved swiftly across the ground. Often I stayed so late that the stars emerged between me and the farm, a tiny handful of buildings at the other end of the naked plain.

I loved the farm, too, the dust and peeling paint, the animals. Often I ran off from my chores and hid in an old packing crate which was as large as a room. Hollyhocks grew around it, ivory, ruby, butter yellow. At the height of summer when the wind faded, the hollyhocks stood monumentally still, their fragile skins threaded with veins, their edges dry and slightly curled. Though they were shaped like bugles they never made a sound, but I half waited for one, gazing out through the torn-away slats, my eyes narrowed against the glare. Sometimes I was disturbed here — my mother or father came to fetch me back to the field — but sometimes my mother simply came and lingered, standing by the hollyhocks, smiling, waiting like a neighbor woman to be invited inside, a bony, sun-dried woman in a starched housedress and scuffed saddle shoes. "Did you want something?" I would ask curtly, and she would shake her head and walk away.

She was always busy, always urging me to be busy, to cook, to clean house, to sew. I might have shown more interest if she hadn't prefaced every lesson with, "Rose, when you marry you gotta have something to offer." She braided my hair with painful vehemence and tweaked my neck if it was dirty, not because I owed it to myself to look neat but because "no man wants a sloppy woman." I felt my entire personality was to be a dowry, as hers had been.

And looking at my father, I wondered why. There was something of a spurious lord about him, a fifth-rate aristocrat whose armpits stank with two weeks' accumulated sweat and

whose scopeless, bloodshot eyes took for granted the small
niceties — the carpet slippers, the filled pipe, the cherished old
crystal set tuned into his favorite station. When I was very small
I wondered if he always came first because he was sick. Every
evening when they returned from the fields he would accompany Ma into the kitchen and fall into a chair muttering bitter
things about the crop, and while she busied herself at the stove
he would hold up a blistered hand, indicate a dust speck in his
eye, or clutch his stringy neck and describe its soreness. She
would bandage the hand, remove the dust mote, or massage the
neck, making comforting sounds at the back of her throat that
filled me with a horror I could not define.

There was a time, in 1931, when Pa considered abandoning
the farm. He talked about it for weeks — it was the only time he
talked to her for more than five minutes at once — and she would
always shake her head in the same gentle way and murmur the
same words, that he knew nothing but farming and that life was
hard enough without plunging into something new. He seemed
lacerated by indecision, developed an agonizing crop of boils
that she doctored, and finally, lying under her hands one evening
while she stroked on a soothing balm, he agreed with her that
this farm was his life, he would make it pay yet, and the ragged
subject was closed. After which he flung himself away from her
and went outside alone.

But if the question of abandoning the farm was closed, his
squalid battle with alfalfa remained his sole subject. With this
exception: once in a great while he would speak of a "musical
evening" he had once attended as a boy, some kind of concert.
He did not speak of this to my mother, just as he would not have
spoken of it to his pipe or his plow, but he must have thought of
me as a kind of stranger, and strangers have the reputation of

being good listeners. At these moments my resentment of him stepped back; nervously, studiously, my eyes glued to his, I would try to follow his words — the memory seemed a thick, troubling one for him. And I would respond as children do, with questions, a mistake whose only alternative was a hopeful silence, also a mistake. For whichever I did his eyes drifted away, he entered himself again, a tall rawboned man whose long unshaven face was already fissured into the mosaic of old age and whose sun-slit eyes searched only for refuge, even in me, even in a scrap of a child. I was, I supposed, at these moments, to get up and massage his neck or make little sounds in the back of my throat.

I sat across the room from them in the evenings after the chores were done, and in the summer the evenings were long, sticky. The rusty fan went round and round, clicking. We sweat. I read a book. The voice of Dude Martin issued from the crystal set. My mother knitted or sewed without looking at her fingers; her eyes were on Pa, waiting; she was ready to bring him lemonade (half a lemon squeezed into a quart jar of water), to open a window, close it, to switch off the radio, scratch his back. He sat in the comfortable chair, with his pipe and his slippers, his mulish face in a kind of half repose. And fight it as I would, I could not keep from falling into a shameless reverie. I was inside Pa's shirt pocket where I heard his muffled heartbeat, strong and regular. This simple thought filled me with an almost divine relief that welled up in my chest like a fountain of tears. When the fantasy passed, leaving me strangely lighthearted, I would study him, growing at once disappointed. He was deep in his own thoughts, relaxed in his chair. His eyes — hard, deep brown — were closed in drowsy meditation. His lips were shut, his shirt pocket securely buttoned. Dude Martin twanged on.

(There was a bottomless gulf between Dude Martin and the "musical evening" Pa tried to describe. I thought it strange; he could have heard music similar to that of his famous evening if he had wanted to, but he rigorously confined himself to the farm news and the interminable Dude. And of course I had no say in the matter, because the radio was his and I was not to touch it. But one day when I was alone in the house I threw caution to the winds and turned it on, finding some music of the sort he always switched off or ordered Ma to switch off before a bar was ever completed. My head jerked down to the speaker; I pressed my ear to it, bug-eyed, shakened to see the hollyhocks bugling to the heavens, and the heavens cascading across the plain. I jumped up, only to crouch hurriedly again, turning the volume up and opening my mouth to hear better. "Gloria!" the voices sang out. "Gloria in excelsis Deo! Gloria in excelsis! Gloria in excelsis! . . . Gloria . . . (a sustained, heartstopping flight) . . . in excelsis! In excelsis Deo!" Then someone slammed into the house and a voice yelled, "What's the matter with you all of a sudden? You don't *touch* that!" He switched the sound off — wrenched it off — his eyes wide with outrage. "My wireless! Turned up full blast! I wonder it's not broke!" He seemed galvanized by anger, but it was not me, I felt with surprise, that he was angry at. He ran his hands agitatedly through his hair, then slammed back out; it was a good twenty minutes before he went on down to the barn and I was free to turn the radio on again, this time low. But all that was left was the announcer giving the title of the music, which I repeated to myself until I had it memorized, the "Gloria" from Bach's *Mass in A Major*. The words were as new to me as the music. That night, not anxious to return to the subject of my misdemeanor, but unable to control myself, I asked him excitedly, "Who's Bock? What's a mass in a major? What does 'Gloria in excelsis Deo' mean?" He did not answer. He was filling his pipe. I said, "It's what they were singing on the radio." Still he did not answer me. He never answered me. "Is that the kind of music you mean when you talk about that night when you were a boy?" I persisted. He smashed his thumb into the bowl of his pipe. "You just better forget about fussing with my wireless!")

Click click — mother's knitting needles. A yellow jacket buzzed between her and Pa; she swatted it. The kerosene lamp flickered; she refilled it. She gave the appearance of walking on tiptoes, her head carefully thrust forward. She had a large but unfleshed brown body, with surprisingly dainty feet and fine-boned hands that somehow made me sad. Her and Pa's faces had grown to resemble each other, both narrow and lined, with big underslung jaws; her eyes, too, were slitted from the sun, but they were bright blue, like the crockery she once admitted she had a hankering for but as sure as she breathed could do without.

I attended a country school two miles from a small town called Alturas. When I was twelve I discovered that if I played hooky in the afternoon I had plenty of time to walk into town and read in the little library there and then return to catch the school bus back to the farm. I told the teacher I was seeing a dentist in town and forged a letter from my mother to that effect, going so far as to explain that I had seventeen cavities.

The library was wedged between a linen shop and (I was happy to discover) a dentist's office. Jasper O. O'Hara, D.D.S. It salved my conscience that first day to stand under Dr. O'Hara's black and gold sign, to touch my teeth as though they throbbed, and walk away with a stoic sigh. I had soon conjured up a picture of him and was able to increase the validity of my story by telling my teachers, "Dr. O'Hara wears five rings on his fingers. He discusses your zodiac sign with you." Every time I passed his office I strained my eyes for a glimpse of him.

The books in the library had been haphazardly arranged along "popular fiction" and "other things" lines. Bashkirtseff stood next to "Baby Care" and Plato next to "Petroleum Mining." I proceeded to read everything with a sense of urgency, peering over my shoulder for the truant officer. The first thing I learned was the translation of Gloria in excelsis Deo, but it was a cold illumination and I sank back into my chair with disappointment. It meant Glory to God in the highest. God lived some eleven miles down the road from the farm, in the True Gospel Church where our nearest neighbors, the Hobergs, chugged to and fro in their old truck three nights a week plus Sunday. He frowned on the repeal of Prohibition, and to judge by the Hobergs, inflicted His followers with bad breath and melancholy. That was all I knew about Him. And so it seemed to me that the translation was faulty. I printed the phrase on a piece of paper, and after some minutes of thought, erased the word "God," and wrote in its place "me."

One morning my teacher took me aside and said, "Rose, let me see your teeth. I think you've made this dentist up out of whole cloth." And she pulled my mouth open to find two rows of perfect, untouched teeth. "Seventeen fillings," she whispered, "you unholy little liar. You tell your parents I'm writing them a letter, and you'd better be ready for a thrashing."

I waited two days for the letter to reach the farm, anxious for the thrashing, yearning for it. Not just a slap or a cuff — that was everyday — but a real thrashing that they would put their souls into, because it would mean that they had finally seen me, not as somebody who did the chores, or as a female offspring to be married off in due course, but as me, Rose, a free spirit, who did strange, terrible things on her own. The letter arrived. I gritted my teeth happily, and submitted to the whippings. Ma's was energetic enough, but Pa's was short, offhand, almost mechanical, no more caring than his silence, and in sorrow and rage I tried to bite his hand, but he didn't notice.

I had been inspired by Marie Bashkirtseff, that beautiful, spoiled young Russian who had been beloved by everyone, and I started a diary of my own, using a brown school notebook. I remember the first entry clearly: "I am exactly thirteen years old today, feeling extremely fine, and am glad to begin the undertaking of this project, namely, to record everything. Good luck to Rose Davies!" And I described the plain, the wind, the clouds, the farm, every wrinkle on my parents' faces. Bashkirtseff had died at twenty-three; I pressed my forehead, wondering if I had only a decade left. All winter I wrote with a passion, filling one notebook after another. Troikas, gargoyles, oceans, ballrooms, battlefields flickered before my eyes — all that I had stumbled upon in the library. I wrote about them to Jasper O. O'Hara, D.D.S., long letters I never mailed.

My mother wanted to know what was the matter with me. "What is it?" she demanded. "You been looking so peculiar." And I would clutch my temples and turn away.

"Are you sick?" she kept asking.

She believed that "it" was happening to me.

"It? It?" I said angrily, "What do you mean?"

A closed gratified look came over her face. Every day she scanned my expression for some sign that "it" was upon me. I grew self-conscious, as though I were on display at a fair. I began to feel that my body was something alien if it could put a trick over on me. "If you dare," I told it at night in bed, "I won't belong to you anymore." But nothing happened. Winter wore on, spring arrived. Something gentle stirred inside me and a vision of a tiered garden rose before my eyes. For some reason I placed this garden in Bulgaria. In such a garden you would have to be cultivated, full of integrity and high ideals. You could not kick things or brag. That was all right, that was as it should be. Dr. O'Hara would be there. We would walk together. And all around us would be cheerful, lighthearted people with eyes that shone with affection.

And then one night as I got up to go to bed, my father nodded to my mother and she took me firmly to their room and closed the door.

"Rose," she said, embarrassed, but stolidly thrilled, "any day now you're gonna get what we call a period."

"I know all about it," I said, making for the door.

"You started?" she asked eagerly, blocking my way.

"Naw!"

"You heard about it from the other kids at school. Don't listen to them, they make it out dirty. It's not dirty if you look at it the right way. A period means your seed's ready. It's like a seed you got inside that's gotta be fertilized . . ."

"Like alfalfa and manure!"

"Don't make it out dirty," she warned.

"I don't want to hear more."

"Naw, you don't want to hear more," she said, crossing her arms. "You want to keep running around shirking your chores and acting like a crazy-head. What sort of a life will you have if you go on like that? You gotta face things. Don't worry, I can see how you've tried to ignore this big change that's commencing in you . . ."

"It hasn't commenced!"

"It *will!*"

"Not if I don't want it to."

"Goddam!" she shouted, and it was the only time I ever heard her swear.

"You can't be a kid forever," she went on in lowered tones. "Maybe a woman's life isn't the best, but you gotta accept it. A woman's got everything cut out for her and that's all there is to it. You can't go traipsing around like a crazy-head. You've got a man and a house and kids to look after and that's that. So you better face it. Join the club." She stood back.

"Isn't there anything *good* about it?" I asked.

"Good?" she cried. "Of course it's good! The whole thing's good! It's how it is! It's how we're made!" And suddenly she looked so bitter and lost that I blinked at the sight of it.

"There, now," she said with a broken sigh, pulling me into an unaccustomed embrace, her bitterness sinking under a smooth conviction, "it's nothing so awful, you just gotta get used to it. Me, for instance, there's a whole lot I don't like but I put up with. See, it's them that does the things that count, and it's us that's gotta make it easier for them. That's all you got to remember, Rose."

"I don't understand," I said, sensing something I didn't like.

"You can't expect them to pay any heed to you, so you learn to forget yourself, that's all I mean. You do what you gotta do. Stand behind and help." She stroked my hair with her small, rough hand. "That's the best way. It's the only way. It can't be no different."

"It's a shrunk-up idea!" I cried, tearing away from her. "Shrunk-up! You bug!" My eyelids twitched with the fear of a blow, but I backed through the door before she could overcome her hurt and surprise enough to move.

For several days she kept a glacial silence, but the scene was never referred to. As it happened, our discussion was a whole year premature. When the change did occur — and by that time I had grown used to the idea, had bowed, almost gracefully, to the inevitable — I was careful to keep it a secret from my mother. But that was not difficult, for by that time she had given up all hope of the smallest intimacy.

Chapter

2

I STAYED on the farm until I was sixteen, a loose-jointed creature with thick, swollen features (cheek and chin one pudgy plane), timid, blindly arrogant, ultrafastidious and sweepingly coarse. I was mortified when a boy in class used the word "bathroom" but told and listened to witless jokes using bathroom nomenclature. I stooped like a hunchback to hide the inconsequential line of my bust but sprawled when I sat and never thought to pull my skirt over my knees.

I went to school, did my chores, and in the summer worked alongside my parents in the alfalfa. With them everything seemed strangely fruitless and wearing. At least, I thought, if they would exchange a warm look just once, or stroke old Tommy, the plowhorse, and enjoy as little as that. Yet, there were moments when I felt an overwhelming oneness with them. It was when the setting sun rushed up against me like a tidal wave, and I would turn and find that they, too, were enveloped in its glow.

Each harvest the alfalfa crop was smaller, the blossoms paler. Everything was in a state of disrepair. The barn and house were on their last legs, the fences sagged, the road was deeply rutted, even the animals were thin and scruffy. Even I, disinterested in farming as I was, could see that the ground was finished, sucked dry by my father's stubborn, unintelligent methods. Every day he went out and stabbed at the poor earth, crippling it further, and came back at night with my mother, both of them stamped with weariness, and she saw to his comfort though her back was as sore as his; saw to it as though he were a holy gift entrusted to her.

But not so with her house. There was not one personal touch in it, not one picture on the wall, save for a faded and severe tintype of a man with a handlebar mustache which had been there when my parents moved in. Not a vase or a doily or a potted plant. But it was clean, scrubbed raw with scouring powder, the curtains limp and bone-white from Clorox, the kerosene lamp innocent of the slightest trace of grime. She didn't believe in tablecloths or knitted potholders — the table was bare and the potholders were boiled scraps of underwear. Yet she knitted, she knitted for him — socks, mufflers, sweaters — but nothing for herself, nothing for me, for the house. The house was to work in. Her tongue between her teeth, she would take a chicken or hare and cut it up on the table, hack away, as the blood spread out and dripped to the floor. Then afterwards she was a human fury of scrubbing until everything was as before, only more hacked.

One afternoon I was sitting inside the packing crate, looking out, and my parents walked past with Tommy. My father stopped and lifted his hand up for my mother to see. I could make out a small smear of blood on the palm; it looked as though a blister had broken and been abraded by the plow handle. Dropping Tommy's reins with a little cry, my mother took the bleeding hand in her own two hands and bent her head over it. "Oh, Melvin," she said, raising her eyes, "it must hurt."

"Of course it hurts," he said, grimacing as he flexed the fingers, then thrusting the hand back at her. "It's like a crater."

She gave the palm a maternal peck. "You have no luck, no luck in the world, my poor boy. But I'll make it better, I'll put some salve on it."

Placated, he shuffled on, the hand cradled against his chest, and my mother picked up the reins. She stood there for a moment regarding his back with a look that astonished me, a look of unspeakable contempt. Then, the look vanishing, she started off behind him with her dogged, sinewy field walk, her head stretched before her like a turtle's. I knew she would outlast Pa and that she knew this, and that somewhere down inside her, where the look of contempt had gone, she was very glad. I got to my feet, intending to go after her, to give her a special look, touch her hand, do something to show that I now understood. But I sat down again, knowing that she would never admit hatred to me; she would not even admit it to herself. She was a lie. Plow her under I breathed, as she disappeared into the barn. And him, too, the soft, lesioned dog. Plow them both under.

I told them that I intended to quit school in June and go away. I was not much use on the farm, I explained, so I was no good to them. My father said I lacked gratitude. My mother sat at the table, her fingers rubbing furiously against each other, her eyes filled with a staring, unbelieving light. I would escape, join those free souls she so bitterly condemned, those unnatural females who blighted the world with their silly antics. She had no idea that I wished to abolish **war** and write poems of **grave beauty.**

"Don't worry," I told her reassuringly, "I'm a serious person."

"Pah!" she exploded. "You're a freak."

But they put up little opposition. It was decided that I would go to Alturas and there I would find a live-in housekeeping job. I agreed to this in order to get away. I planned to stay there exactly two months, by which time I would have saved enough money to get to San Francisco, which was to be the first stop on my journey. What I was going to do was to go around the world.

When the time came for me to leave, my father arranged for Hoberg to take me with him when he drove his produce into Alturas. Saturday, June 27, 1936. It was a clear, stone-quiet morning. I awoke at four, dressed, packed my notebooks and an extra dress into a tin suitcase, and sat on the bed in the darkness, immobile with fear. As it grew lighter I studied the little room I was leaving. There was the imperiously large bureau with scuff marks and gashes showing white against the dark stain. In its drawers had lain my notebooks, stones from the plain, dried foxglove. In its old warped mirror my face had always been reflected as from a barrel of brown water. The curtain fluttered in the summer breeze. At five o'clock I heard my parents stir and I went downstairs to the kitchen with my suitcase.

"You don't look so good," my mother said.

"I woke up too early."

"Pity you couldn't of done that before now."

When Pa came into the kitchen I waited for him to say something, perhaps something terrible, but he did not mark the occasion with more than a sharp glance when he finished breakfast. "Be careful," he said, going to the back door.

"Won't you be coming back before I go?" I asked.

"Maybe. We'll see," and the door slammed.

I helped Ma with the dishes. When we finished she wrote down the address of a friend of hers in Alturas whom I was going to stay with until I found work. "You'll be lucky if you find anything in times like these," she remarked. Then she cleaned the cooler.

At seven o'clock I saw Hoberg's truck sending up a cloud of dust in the distance. I grabbed my suitcase, standing like a petrified soldier. "He's coming!" I said.

She looked out the window. "Won't be here for another five minutes. Sit down."

But I ran down to the barn, instead, touching the old crate and the hollyhocks. Pa was working in the field; he gave the approaching truck a peremptory wave, wiping his face with the tail end of the gesture, and went back to work. I ran around the barn, skidding to a stop to look once more at the only tree on the farm, a little willow squeezed into a shadowed cleft between the barn and plowshed. Anyway, I told it, when the barn falls down you'll get some light. Then the truck was driving into the yard, its horn blasting. "Hurry up," my mother called from the porch. "Once his motor stops you know he can't start it again."

"I'm going then, Ma," I said, pushing my face against hers and glancing down to the field to see if Pa was coming back.

"You take care, Rose," she said.

"I hear her dying," Hoberg yelled. "Let's go."

I picked up my suitcase and climbed up into the cab. The truck backfired and lurched over the gray dirt in a big semicircle, then pitched forward down the road. I hung my head out the window. Tying a kerchief around her head, my mother started down to the field where Pa was still working. Beyond them stretched the immense plain under a sky blue as watered ink.

I pulled my head back in. Oh God, how unhappy I am, I thought.

After a while the sun climbed up into the sky and Hoberg passed me an orange.

Chapter

3

WITHIN THE FIRST WEEK I found a housekeeping job with an elderly couple who offered a slightly larger wage than I had expected. I wrote this news home, but did not add that I was seriously ill — stricken by a severe case of loneliness that constricted my chest and destroyed my appetite. Nothing helped except the little library I had escaped to four years ago; at least it was a distraction. I went back very much aware of the sophistication I had acquired in the interim. I knew, for instance, that God had a more impressive tradition than I had inferred from the Hobergs, and that to erase His name and put "me" in its place might be considered presumptuous. However, I stood by this action. For He was just a name someone else had thought up, an agreed-upon term, something outside yourself. If when the wind rushed up against me I said, "This is God," it would be like putting on someone else's clothes, intrusive, unnecessary. I was there, the wind was there. It was enough. It was much more than enough — the "Gloria" had described what it was. But even the "Gloria," the little I could remember, did not assuage my homesickness. Nor did books. In two weeks I read both *War and Peace* and *The Red and the Black*, sitting up every night and stumbling through the day, but still the agony gnawed away inside. The farm, the plain, the sky—I had left them. It was as simple as that. And only something as simple as time closed the wound: toward the end of the second month I realized I was feeling much better. I began to notice the shade trees, the small bustle of the town, the scent of honeysuckle that drifted through my window at night. With a burst of enthusiasm I counted the money I had saved. I had enough for my train ticket and a little left over. I had no idea that one gave notice; telling the surprised old couple that I would be on my way, I thanked them for their kindness and walked down the steps with my suitcase.

But before going to the depot I gathered my courage together and carried out a plan that had been growing inside me. I went to Dr. O'Hara's office. "If I could see Dr. O'Hara right away," I told his nurse in a rush, afraid she would say yes, afraid she would say no. "I have a toothache like the fire of Hades, it shoots up into my cerebrum and down to my clavicle and never relents." I had practiced that beforehand.

After regarding me for a moment she went into the inner office, returning to tell me to go in. Inside, I stared at the floor, afraid to look at him. "Sit down," he said, "we'll have a look at that tooth."

I opened my mouth, swinging my eyes wildly to his face. He was a man of about thirty, in no way unusual, but with keen blue eyes. "Which one is it?" he asked, his hand resting warm and reassuring on my jaw.

I touched one of my teeth at random, and very gently he tapped it. "Does that hurt?" He removed his finger so I could speak.

"Like the fire of Hades. It shoots up into my cerebrum and down to my clavicle and never relents."

He raised his eyebrows and probed around some more. "How long has it been paining you?"

"About ten days," I ventured.

"Ten days?"

I nodded, my eyes dropping to the pocket of his white coat.

"I don't know," he mused, "it looks like a healthy tooth, but if it's as bad as you say it should come out."

I had not anticipated this — I had thought no farther than penetrating his inner office and seeing him. Saying that I would come back some other time, I scrambled out of the chair and made for the door. But there I turned. "I suppose," I said shyly, "you do a lot of reading, what with the library next door."

A smile broke across his face, such a kind, sympathetic smile that I blushed in agony and fled from the room. An hour later as the train pulled out of the station, I twisted around in my seat and stared back at what I was leaving. Dr. O'Hara. With whom I had so often walked in the Bulgarian garden. We would never meet again. Still, I had seen him and he had touched me. I put my hand to my face where his fingers had lain, and felt with interest the softness and smoothness of my skin. It was possible that my skin had given him the same pleasure his touch had given me. Glancing around the carriage from under my lids, I breathed deeply, sternly through my nostrils, filled with pride and confusion.

Later on I remembered the letter I had received from my mother that morning, which I had not had time to open. It was the first communication from her since I had left home.

"Melvin (crossed out) your Father went yesterday of a brain hemrage, he went quick, it was a mercy, he was out in the field, I ran all the way to the Hobergs for them to get the dr but it was no use, I sat alone with his body all night and was out of my mind, he will be beried here at home tomorrow, you wont get this in time for it, but you must come home now, we only got each other now, your Mother."

I put the letter down. The train was clattering across a railroad bridge high above a river. I could picture her sitting through the night with the body, vaguely troubled that he had gone quickly, that he had not lain for months with a cancer she could have ministered to, watching it eat him up under her eyes, and — but here her mind would balk, horrified — at the end coolly eluding his hands which for the first time sought her with true urgency. But he had cheated her, and perhaps in that second when a small crunch in his brain sent his hands groping wildly in the air and he dropped, finished, to the ground — perhaps in that moment, alone, away from her, he recaptured his pride.

But she had not found hers. It may be, I think now, that there are more folk myths between a woman and self-truth than between a man and self-truth and that she could not help what she was. But I did not see that then, and when the train stopped in Horse Lake I bought a picture post card and scrawled: "I got your letter saying Pa is dead. You'll pretend your grief is real. I wouldn't come home to see that even if I could, which I can't. Rose." After mailing the card I climbed back on the train and sat down again by the window, my hands unaccountably cold. I remembered Pa as he described his muddy, haunting "musical evening," his deep brown squinting eyes, his groping words and sigh of frustration; and I thought of her, too, not as she hacked up a hare or pinched my gray neck, but as she stood by the packing crate, fingering the hollyhocks, waiting like a neighbor woman to be invited in. I thought with a stab: maybe I acted wrong to them.

Chapter

4

IN THE MORNING when we got off the train in Oakland I was pulled from my thoughts by the prospect of my first sea voyage, a ferryboat ride to San Francisco. The whole crossing I hung over the rail; a light mist hovered overhead but the sun shone luminously through and lay in scattered glimmerings across the water; it was a beautiful new world, and there was even music, carried by the wind, faint and eerie, yet dimly resolute, like a triumphal march. The closer we came to the city the steadier it grew, and when at last we disembarked at the Ferry Building I rushed down the ramp with my tin suitcase banging against my side and ran into the street which was choked with crowds.

I had come upon the largest Labor Day parade in the city's history. Plunging around clanging streetcars into the mob, I fought my way to the curb; smartly uniformed men struck their drums and flourished their trumpets; open black automobiles drove slowly by, filled with important personages; behind them marched long columns of ordinary men and women, not even in step, just walking along. "There's the power," someone cried, "the unions!"

"Hurrah!" I yelled, hurrying along the curb after the parade, leaving lower Market Street with its derelicts and flophouses and pressing into the heart of the city, where I looked up through thick networks of cables to towering buildings, sooty and splendid. The march ended in a public square, and when the noise died away the speakers gathered on a flag-draped platform and through sputtering microphones spoke of the New Deal, the Wagner Act, the CIO. My head raced with visions of revolutions and utopias, and I wandered through the crowd happy and excited. Suddenly, in late afternoon, the crowd dispersed, leaving me to myself. A light drizzle had begun to fall.

I turned my coat collar up and started off to look for a room, passing from streets of dreary wooden buildings to wealthy areas where Victorian mansions sat with solid grace on well-kept grounds, and then back again to the shabby streets. In a run-down, nondescript neighborhood I turned into a building with a "For Rent" sign. Though it was still light outside, an electric bulb burned in the dark passageway. I was shown a room on the second floor whose window looked out on a backyard of green bushes, making up for the lack of cheer inside. I took it. It was bare except for a washstand, table, gas ring, and a bed with a rash of black metal sores. A mirror hung on the door, the first full-length mirror I had ever seen, and throwing off my coat, I looked up and down the figure reflected in it. It was short, lightweight, half lost in a long brown dress of coarse backwoods material. Its lips and cheeks blared across the room at me, a rustic, indelicate red. But the thick adolescent pudginess had receded. The brows were dark, straight, like two definite crayon lines, and the hair, reddish and unruly, hung over one shoulder in a thick braid that ended in a frizz of curls. I unbraided it, twisted it in a coil, and pinned it haphazardly on top of my head. I spun around, feeling like a peeled grape, every nerve exposed to whatever lay before me. The rain pattered lightly against the window, the room was filled with a watery golden light. I flung open my suitcase, stacked my notebooks on the table, and hung my extra dress up. Then I dropped to the bed and clasped my hands together expectantly.

The next day a blond, rosy youth stopped me in the passageway and introduced himself, speaking with gentle, sculpted articulation and looking into my face with a strange, candid pleasure. He had the room next to mine. Would I care to join him that evening for a glass of wine with his friends?

I prepared thoroughly for the call, scrubbing my face, cleaning my fingernails, and rubbing my shoes with newspaper. There was something about this boy, whose name was Paul, that struck me as out of place here, as though years of well-balanced meals, supervised study, and carefree play had left him with a sheen his shabby clothes and surroundings could not dim. Pinning my hair up as neatly as possible, I took a deep breath and went to his door.

His friends were a bony, vociferous writer named Levine, and his betrothed, Dora. Levine actually used the dated word "betrothed" in a bitter, sarcastic manner. They were both in their late thirties, she as thin and nervous as he, with a hard, stubborn, worn look that darkened as she listened to the ceaseless talk.

"Hemingway's a semaphorist, is that style?" Paul put to his friend.

"Style!" Levine exclaimed. "What's style? Oh, if you knew how it torments me not to know!"

I sipped my wine with excitement.

"Well, if you don't know, don't worry about it," Paul said

kindly. "Do you suppose Shakespeare worried about it?"

"Shakespeare!" Levine gasped. "Dora, he brings in Shakespeare!"

"So he brings in Shakespeare."

"Forget Shakespeare," Levine rushed on, "it's me I'm talking about, Levine. Levine has no style."

"Let's get back to Hemingway," Paul said.

And now, gripping my wineglass, I made my debut, leaning forward with a pounding heart and saying very carefully, "You call him a semaphorist. Is this because he does not use metaphors?"

Paul smiled at me but kept his eyes on Levine, who was busy shredding the butt of his cigarette to pieces.

"They don't hear you, darling," Dora told me. "Do like me. I sit and wait. Maybe I'll wait right into my coffin."

Though worn, she was a handsome woman in her way, bold featured, with thick hair drawn into a knot low on her neck — long black skirt, severe middy blouse. Suddenly aware of the silence, I made a second attempt to be heard. "I recently read *The Sun Also Rises*," I stated loudly.

"A fine book," Levine said in a subdued voice.

"But it's anti-Semitic," Paul said with a gentle frown.

Levine shrugged.

"And what's worse, you never get a feeling of the oppression in Spain, the poverty . . ."

"It's not that kind of book," said Levine.

"Bah!"

I had never heard anyone say "bah" before, and sat up straighter, as though in the presence of an academic tradition.

"I liked the part where . . ." I began, but Paul cut me off.

"After all, it's terribly limited," he said to Levine.

I looked at them both with narrowed eyes, disappointed and insulted.

When the couple took their leave Dora said bitterly over her shoulder, "Thank you, Paul. I always remember you in my prayers."

"Good night, Dora," he replied softly.

"They're extremely unusual people," I conceded grudgingly as the door closed. "She looks like an anarchist."

"Dora? She's a waitress in one of those Russian holes that pass for being picturesque. I'll take you there someday."

He had chosen me as his friend, then. It eased my anger a little.

"But Levine," he went on, "Levine is writing the novel of the century."

"Oh! Is he a genius?"

"He'd better be. Otherwise his sacrifices are too great." He sat down opposite me and for the first time that evening gave me his attention. "You are incredibly beautiful," he said, almost in a whisper.

"Incredibly what? . . . Excuse me?"

He nodded, staring at me with a kind of sadness. "I'd like you to read these," he said, giving me a folder. "It's my work. It's me."

In my room, I opened the folder, which contained ten poems. I read each one waiting for a jolt of enthusiasm, and put each one down with a sigh. Pulling at my lips, I wondered how I could find a tactful way of telling him that I found his work stupid. But I needn't have worried, for when I returned them he did not ask my opinion, but just assumed that an intimacy had now been established and kissed me on the lips, a chaste kiss, like the touch of a moth's wings. Though it was my first kiss, it did not move me, it was so quick and light. But a moment later something dropped through my body like a firebrand. He had twisted around in his chair for his cigarettes, and his shirt stretched tightly across his shoulders, revealing broad, rock-hard muscles. I found my eyes boring through the shirt, and when he turned back I looked up to his face with embarrassed compulsion as I saw him in a new, searing light. I had never before been aware of the quality of maleness.

"What's the matter?" he asked.

"Nothing!"

Dropping my eyes to the floor, I waited anxiously for him to kiss me again, and when at last he did, I instinctively pressed my lips more firmly against his so that his lost their cool respect for a moment. But from the look in his eyes as he drew back I felt I was doing something low and unwomanly. "I respect you, Rose," he said. "Maybe other men haven't, but I do."

"There haven't been any others," I said wonderingly. Was it possible that my cheap clothes and bitten fingernails pointed to an internal baseness of which I was unaware? I hid my fingernails in my fists and thrust them behind my back, shamed to the soles of my feet, yet at the same time resenting him. But he was now regarding me with a pleasant, serious expression and talking about his work in progress, of which the poems I had read were but a small part.

He was dedicated. A blond stubble covered his cheeks, and his fingers were stained with ink and nicotine. All day he wrote, and in the evening he took a walk and had a bowl of chop suey at a neighborhood restaurant where the tables were covered with newspapers. He wore the same outfit every day, a pair of soiled black trousers and a workman's blue shirt frayed at the cuffs.

Levine, on the other hand, was a dresser. He always wore a

suit with vest and tie, threadbare but clean. It seemed like a gesture of pride. He was very much concerned with his pride. "If you don't have pride you have nothing!" he would spit out of the blue. This was so true, I thought, that it wasn't worth saying. But each time he said it Dora would respond harshly, "Pride you bring up! You, a leech!" And a new battle would ensue.

"They're a peculiar pair," I remarked to Paul about two weeks after I had moved in.

"She can't understand his dedication to his book," he replied, tapping the latest chapter which the author had left for his criticism. "She wants him to settle down and marry her. It's the old story. You women are all like that."

"I'm not."

"Of course you are."

I looked at him, surprised. "I am not," I said, narrowing my eyes.

He smiled wisely.

"I'm very independent," I said. "In fact tomorrow I start my first real job. It's with an insurance company, Paul. You can't imagine how relieved I am, I was down to my last nickel. I told them I was eighteen and they believed me and they hired me — I'm going to be a file clerk."

He was absorbed in the chapter lying on his knees.

"May I look at Levine's manuscript?" I asked sullenly.

He thought for a moment, then nodded and handed it to me. I sat back and read the chapter intently. It was eminently controlled, quite the opposite of the author's spoken words, but it was nothing more, and as I closed the folder I felt sorry for Levine. It kept me from saying anything.

But Paul was not waiting for a comment. He pulled me gently to him.

"I don't think it's very good," I said after all.

"It's a man's book," he murmured, the moth's wings fluttering across my lips. "I wouldn't expect you to like it."

I yanked away and jumped to my feet. "I don't know!" I exclaimed, searching for words. "It's like you make me into a foreigner, it's like you can't understand anything I say."

He took my hand in his, he stroked it, kissed it. It was love, it was some sort of love. But there was no passion in it. I looked at him gloomily.

" 'A woman moved,' " he whispered, " 'is like a fountain troubled, muddy, ill-seeming, bereft of beauty; and while she is so, none so dry or thirsty will deign to sip or touch one drop of it.' "

I snatched my hands from his and went to my room. With all respect to Shakespeare — a public drinking fountain! But I was less angry than I was tired, flat, as though I had been stumbling around in a mist since I came. It was the opposite of everything I had expected when I had first stood here with my hair swept wildly up on my head and my hands clasped together almost in a gesture of thanks for having arrived.

I went to bed early, but lay awake for a long time listening to Paul's muffled voice through the wall as he read his work aloud to himself. As lonely as I had been in Alturas, I thought of the farm. The next morning I got up exhausted to face my first day with Kiernan & Co., insurance brokers.

At once I disliked the cramped atmosphere, the deadly routine, the sense of waiting for your master's voice. The executives all had glass-walled offices to themselves and we in the outer office could watch them swinging around in their swivel chairs talking on the phone, lighting cigars, buzzing for their secretaries. All day I fetched and carried gray folders, trying to divide my attention between this empty task and the Trans-

Siberian Railway, for I had decided that I would go first to Russia, by way of the Orient. In the evening when I went home the gray folders and the gray faces of my fellow clerks dropped from my mind as though they had never existed.

As time went on I learned from Paul that he was supporting Levine. Paul received a monthly allowance from home; this he shared with his friend. It was just barely enough to keep Levine going. "It's the least I can do for someone with his gift," Paul said, "and it's nothing, really. I wish I could do more. The cards are stacked against him. He's frail, he's not young, and then, he's Jewish. Jews need to feel they're accepted."

Sometimes through my wall I heard Levine's voice rise in a crescendo of unhappiness: "The book's no good! I should give it up, look for a job like Dora says."

"Dora," Paul's voice came across with faint contempt.

"But she loves me! And I love her. Paul, I have no pride living like this, I'm a weak man, I let you carry me. Oh, if you knew how it torments me!"

"The book's the important thing."

"I don't fool myself, how do I fool you, an educated man?

But Paul would argue him out of his pessimism, and the chapters accumulated.

The clerks in the office were something like Levine. Young or old, they had pasty indoor faces and wore sober suits and dismal green visors. They were like broken-spirited dogs in a kennel, and I wished they would throw their pens to the floor and try to find work on the docks or in the lumberyard. But it was as if they had no control over their destinies.

There was one executive who, whenever he emerged from his

office, caused the clerks to exchange looks. This was Patrick
Leary. He was at that time fifty-one years old. He was short,
no taller than I, but his figure appeared hard and compact under
his well-tailored gray or chocolate brown suits. He wore an
old-fashioned high collar, and this gave him the look of an elder
statesman. His voice was as well bred as his collar; though it
was gravelly, it was never raised, its words were formally
spaced, and their messages took the form of suggestions rather
than demands. He belonged to the family that had founded the
firm.

One afternoon when I had been there about a month I was
called into this executive's office. He told me to sit down. He
smiled. He had thin hard lips and his chin protruded like a bulldog's; but his smile was cocky and his teeth looked as though
they were still his own.

"Miss Davis," he began, "some of the other members of this
firm have expressed a certain dissatisfaction with your work, and
I feel it incumbent upon me to tell you that you'll have to try to
give us just a little more of your attention." He spread his hands
out on the dark polished wood of his desk and gazed at them.
Noticing a speck under a fingernail, he took a gold file from his
pocket and cleaned it. His hands were well shaped, strong, and
covered with dark wiry hair. The fingernails were smooth and
pink, each with a large white half-moon at its base. "Of course,"
he went on, "I realize that a young lady as attractive as you has
many other things to think of besides the dreary duties of this
office. There's probably some lucky young man who takes up
your thoughts, and believe me, I understand that. I certainly do.
Still and all, we do pay you for the help you give us, and we do
expect just a tiny bit more efficiency. Now, I hope I haven't
offended you . . ."

"Oh no!" I cried, prepared to sacrifice my very life for the concern.

"Fine," he said, taking up his work again. As I rose he looked at me and his eyes flashed. "To be candid, Miss Davis, my colleagues asked me to fire you. But I want to give you a second chance."

I went out thinking that it was strange no one else had complained about my work, but knowing that it was a lucky fluke to have gotten the job at all I now began to make a greater effort. I grew more aware of Mr. Leary. He was different from the other elderly executives: his step was springier, his back straighter, his face more tanned, and another thing, he did much less work. Though he was forever calling for files, he seemed only to spread them out on his desk and yawn over them.

The clerks, although they seemed to hold Mr. Leary in special regard, did not discuss him among themselves and the reason was that one of them, Harley Munck, was his nephew. Harley was the palest and most dedicated of the clerks, mild and considerate, ordinary looking except for his strangely shaped ears which were like small wax crullers pressed so tightly against his skull that you longed to pry them loose and relieve the pressure. I ate my lunch in a nearby park and soon Harley took up this habit, asking with a shy frown if I minded if he shared my bench. At first we ate in silence, but in time we grew used to each other and began to talk. He was from a family of "limited means" (he never used the word "poor") but his mother, née Leary, had never allowed him to accept favors. Nevertheless, when she died the year before he had at once accepted his uncle's offer to work in his firm. "I know she wouldn't have approved," he told me, "but pumping gas didn't have much future in it."

"It was nice of him to give you the job," I remarked.

"He told my mother while she was dying that he'd look after me. And believe it or not, she leaned halfway out of the bed, dying though she was, and pointed her thumb at the door. She was a rare one, she didn't say much but she could pack a lot into the twitch of her eyebrow."

"Was she demented?"

"Of course not. Or maybe she was about Uncle Patrick, couldn't abide him, her own brother."

I told Harley about my plans to travel. "I want to get as far as Vladivostok on the first lap, but I don't mind if I land in Australia."

"Good luck," he said dubiously.

One evening at quitting time I was again summoned into Mr. Leary's office. He congratulated me on the improvement in my work. "You see," he said with a smile, "there's still time to think about your young man without doing it at the office."

I nodded.

"If you have any plans to marry and quit us I hope you'll tell us well in advance."

"I don't have."

"Just as well. In my youth I made mistakes, I had no one to guide me. When I see young people like yourself, starry-eyed, impractical — if you'll forgive me — I just want to hold out my hand and say, 'Whoa there, look before you leap' . . ." He leaned back and crossed his legs, lighting a cigar. The office had emptied. "Won't you have dinner with me?" he beamed. "We'll celebrate my gaining an indispensable employee."

I hesitated, looking down at my dress.

"No, don't argue," he said, holding up his hand, "you look as though you could use a good meal."

He took me to an expensive restaurant off Union Square. Nervously smoothing my skirt, I drank in my surroundings — plush red rugs, glittering chandeliers, vases of roses. "Hold on," my escort murmured as we were shown to a table and I pulled out a chair. I recoiled, and with a smile like a madonna's the waiter glided around me, laid his fingers on the back of the chair, and nodded. I sat down. He gave a gentle, futile push. Mr. Leary indicated that I should raise myself a little; I did so, leaning heavily on the table, and I could feel the chair sliding in, touching the backs of my knees. I lowered myself with a grim smile and clenched my hands in my lap, determined to be cool-headed. Enormous vocabulary words floated to my lips like life preservers. "This brumal weather is unprecedented, don't you think?" I asked. "It's been pretty cold," he said, looking at the menu. He ordered for both of us without consulting me, and I put the menu down with a sigh of relief, since it was all in French. The ordering seemed endless; every time the waiter nodded, increased his smile, and turned from the table, Mr. Leary called him back with more instructions. "Be sure to serve the sauce separately, Gustave," or, "Only turn the fish once," until Gustave's smile trembled. When he finally went off, half the evening seemed over already.

"Tell me a little about yourself," Mr. Leary said.

"Well, I come from Modoc County, I've been here about six weeks, and by this time next year I'll be on a trip around the world."

"A trip around the world?" he said, amused.

"I'm saving my money. I'll manage it."

"What places are you most interested in seeing?" he asked.

"I haven't decided." I didn't want to share my plans with him. I liked him, but not that well.

"What do you do for amusement?" he asked.

"Oh, I like to read." And I added archly, "I'm what is known as a voracious reader." The conversation lapsed. Every once in a while our eyes would meet and he gave me a warm, reassuring smile.

When the food was brought he sent back the fish, saying that it was overdone. Gustave smiled, took back the fish, and returned much later, hovering over Mr. Leary solicitously. "All right, it'll do," Mr. Leary said, and Gustave nodded with his ghastly, strained smile.

My escort's table manners were beautiful. I shied away from the finger bowl but he flicked his fingertips into the water with a casual gesture that thrilled me. He did not take great pleasure in the food, as I did, but chewed mechanically, his eyes moving leisurely around the room, their expression reflective and faintly contemptuous. Even in the soft light of the chandelier his face looked hard and crude. His large nose seemed to have been broken several times, his chin was firm and pugnacious, his small brown eyes were narrowed to slits, as though he were shadowboxing. By this time of day his whole jaw was the color of slate except for a handful of small white scars where the whiskers wouldn't grow. The only thing that sustained his judicious, cultured look was his hair, straight, black, still thick, but very much receded and touched by white at the temples. His face was ravaged by lines; a chasm sat between his narrowed eyes and deep furrows flanked his compressed lips. Behind those features was a rough power, the raw material from which the even-toned confidence derived. He was not the sort to cast a woman in alabaster; when he kissed his wife she probably knew it.

Afterwards, as we were drinking our coffee, he saw some

people he knew and waved them over to our table. "My niece from Chicago," he said, patting my hand.

"How is Chicago these days?" the man asked. His wife plucked at his sleeve. "We've got to go," she said coolly. "Give Beatrice our regards."

"Why did you say I was your niece?" I asked when they had gone.

"Against company rules to associate with the office staff after hours."

"I think that's rotten."

"It is, dear. It's one rule I always try to break. People are people, no matter what position they hold in life."

"But couldn't you have just said I was a friend?"

He laughed heartily at this. "You have a clean mind. I have a clean mind. But not everybody has a clean mind. Let's just leave it at that." He gave a gentlemanly yawn, his fingers over his mouth. "Shall we go?" he suggested, dropping a ten dollar bill by his plate. "Now just stay where you are until I pull your chair out for you." Instead of being mortified by this command I was put at my ease. I rose graciously, I hoped, and walked out of the restaurant with him. Because of his aplomb and his age I admired him as a picture out of the *National Geographic*, something rare and wonderful but of another world. But when he took me home in a taxi and we stood on the steps of my rooming house he suddenly rested his hand with familiarity on my shoulder. I jerked away.

"What's the matter?" he asked.

"Well — you're so old," I explained, annoyed that he was ruining the pleasant evening.

He lit a cigar and it trembled in his fingers. "If you would like . . . if you would like to keep your job . . ."

"What?" I asked, astonished.

"Then . . . then you'd better learn some manners and not insult people when they're only expressing a desire to help you. I hope to God my own daughter would never misjudge a man as badly as you have."

I blushed to the roots of my hair. "I don't know what to say," I stammered.

He took the cigar from his mouth, his fingers still trembling. "I'm very disappointed. I'm very disappointed."

"I'm really sorry!"

"Good night, Miss Davis."

"Davies," I murmured. "Thank you for the dinner."

Chapter

5

THE NEXT MORNING I woke up aching in every bone. It was influenza, and I was in bed a week. Harley had never been to my room but one evening he poked his head timidly through the door and entered with awkward pleasure, his hands stuck with forced casualness in his pockets. He pulled a chair up to the bed and sat down.

"How's everything at the office?" I asked.

"Oh. All right."

"How's your sister?"

"Oh. She's all right."

He supported a younger sister who pestered him for money, cultivated a fast crowd, and threatened him with running away. Weak and softhearted, he gave in to her, let his clothes grow shabby, and swallowed the scraps of food she burnt for him. He could not get angry. Poor Harley, he accepted life with a smile. In his mind everything was simple and good. And it was not just youthful idealism, it was a kind of divine idiocy, flowering in the face of his late mother's cynicism and his sister's selfishness.

He looked at me happily. "Your face is flushed. Like a red

rose." Inspired, he leaned forward. "Rose, you are a rose."

I smiled, but my head was throbbing, and the sight of Harley's tight ears made it worse. I wished I could loosen them.

The room was filled with silence.

At last he said, "I know this isn't the right time . . ." His face began to work, as though he had a tic. His shining eyes were locked in a staring gaze like someone about to fall down in a dead faint. "I want to ask you to marry me," he gasped. We had never before so much as held hands, but now he took my hand in his and we sat that way for a long time.

"Well, I think you're very nice, Harley," I said at length, "and I'm very honored that you've asked me, but I'm not even going to think about marriage for a long time yet."

He nodded and pressed my hand and left the room.

Every afternoon Paul took a break from his work and came in to read me what he had written. "You're a captive audience," he joked, but it was true. I had no desire to hear his poems, I only wanted to sleep. Sometimes, feeling feverish and drugged, I would break into his reading with some reference to my trip, and he would pause until I had finished, and then go on. But finally he put his folder down and said, "You could save your money for something more sensible than a trip through Siberia . . ."

"Sensible!" I muttered, wrinkling my nose.

"You could rent a decent room. Buy some clothes. Take time to be a woman."

"Oh that," I shrugged, and added, "maybe I don't know what you mean."

"Well, you'd better learn before it's too late."

"Is there a deadline or something? That's a very ominous remark."

"You really don't understand, do you?" he asked with a kindliness that cut me to the bone. "You work at a boring job, at night you empty a can of stew into a pot and eat alone and dream of some unrealistic trip around the world . . . that's no life for a woman, Rose."

"I don't intend to live in a furnished room forever . . . for heaven's sake, I just turned seventeen, I've got lots of time . . . and for your information, I get a lot out of my life . . ."

"You think you do."

"Who the hell are you to tell me . . ."

"Oh, I'm tired of this," he said, pulling at his chin, and then he leaned forward as though forced by some urgent conviction: "I'm tired of you taking yourself so seriously . . . books . . . trips around the world . . . you don't *need* them. You're complete as you are. Dammit, I consider woman God's highest creation!"

"Why!" I raised myself on my elbow.

"Because she's the light-bearer for man."

The blood rushed to my heart with a clap. Everything fell into place. An almost rapturous fury took me. "I see it! I see why I've felt so at odds with myself . . . all dimmed and cramped up, as though I were stuffed into a box. It's that you won't see me, you twist me into something for your own use. It's as though I wanted . . . a French cavalry officer with spurs . . . and I said, Paul, you're a French cavalry officer with spurs, and *all men* are French cavalry officers with spurs, and I won't tolerate any pretentious talk about you being Paul, so don't open your mouth . . . Don't you see how blind and cruel that is? It's like a rape!" I smashed the pillow with my fist. "I'm a dumbell! A lousy dumbell! All this time you've been raping me and *I've* been feeling guilty, as though I didn't measure up, as though something was wrong with me . . ."

He gazed at me with surprise and disgust. At last he said, "I

paid you a compliment. All I was saying was that I need someone to believe in me . . . I write for you, Rose."

"I wanted you to be something *to* me, not *for* me. But it's too
late now."

"Don't be melodramatic."

"You mean I'm melodramatic because I take you seriously? I
should just shrug you off? But you're part of life, aren't you?
You mean something, don't you? And to me your meaning
offends life."

"You're talking gibberish . . . it's the fever . . ."

At that moment Dora and Levine knocked on the door and
came in. I gave some response to their commiserations, but I
was thinking: he uses people against their will. With all that
idealism and soft talk he uses them like a rapist. And suddenly I
knew it was good to be a person of my nature — extreme in everything, somehow merciless if touched wrong — but to be a
woman, too; that was always going to be hard. Because all
around you, in the very air, was the expectation that you lose
yourself in the desires of others, and to deny this was considered
a terrible kind of irresponsibility, almost — to judge by Paul's
look of disgust — a crime against nature. But all the same, it was
good that I was as I was.

Noticing how quiet I had become, my visitors left. I lay still,
thinking with smoothness and clarity.

A while later Levine returned to my room alone.

"Don't tell me you left Dora and Paul together," I remarked.

"God forbid," he replied, sitting down by the bed. "No,
Dora's gone off in a huff somewhere, and Paul's gone out to
eat." He kneaded his thin hands together, and said again, with a
sigh, "Yes, he's gone out to eat." Suddenly he grimaced. "The
things I've done to that boy. I have no faith, I'm vicious . . . do you know what I do, Rose? I follow him. Yes,

I follow him like a cur full of spite. Three times a week he goes home and eats a big meal with his family. It gnaws at me, it eats away at me that he won't admit it. I stand there in the bushes and watch them through the window. They eat like with flood-lights in a store window, the schmucks! God forgive me, why shouldn't he go home for a foursquare meal? But it's that he won't admit it! And tell me what's so terrible about my want-ing to marry Dora. But he makes me feel ashamed, as though I'm not a man. And yet, I swear he loves me like a brother. He does, Rose! He's kindness itself. Oh, what I'd give for that boy's kindness — I could break the world's spine with it!" He swung his head around and glanced guiltily at the door. "And I sit here and talk like this, behind his back. If only you knew . . ."

"He lies to you about the book," I said briefly, but in a loud voice.

He plunged abruptly into silence. At last he said, "Well, I know that . . . and yet, he really does think . . ."

"It's what *you* think."

"What do you know? You're only a child," he said, getting up and going to the door. "Good night . . . I'm sorry . . . forget my nonsense . . ."

"It isn't nonsense, Levine!" I yelled after him as he softly closed the door. Restlessly, I turned the pages of a book, then took a stapler and some clothes that needed mending and, sitting up in bed, began stapling together the raveled seam of a slip. When Paul came back to my room after eating, I said immedi-ately, "We're no longer friends. I don't want to see you again. And tell Levine to give up his book. You know it's no good."

"And you should probably take your temperature again, you must be at the crisis."

"I'm not delirious," I told him, and said again, "It isn't good, is it?"

He didn't reply.

"Is it?" I shouted.

Speaking softly, as though trying to calm me, he said, "Maybe not, but Levine needs to believe in it, he has nothing else."

"What a filthy lie the whole thing is!" And I pressed the stapler with angry force. He looked at what I was doing, turned away, but immediately turned back again, unable to contain himself. "That's abnormal," he stated, "using the stapler."

"Faster than sewing. All the girls in the office use one."

"I don't know what's wrong with them," he replied with such distaste that I snorted. "All right," he said, "you can laugh, but you and your office friends act like freaks, not like women at all . . ."

"Oh God, I'm so sick of hearing you spout off about women. Get out of here! Take all those useless muscles of yours out of here!"

Turning on his heel, he started for the door, but stopped to give me a long bitter look. Then to my astonishment he pulled me from the pillow and kissed me very hard for once, coldly, as though draining from my lips all the cruelty he saw there, probably for some future poem. I slapped him vigorously across the face and he nodded, as though I had destroyed any lingering doubt in his mind: only a slut would hit a poet in the face. Still nodding, with his fingers pressed to his flaming cheekbone, he left the room. I threw my head back on the pillow, ecstatic. Humming "Gloria in excelsis Deo," I fell into a good sleep.

The next day the landlady knocked on my door and said someone wanted me on the pay phone. Pulling a robe around me, I went into the passageway and picked up the receiver.

"What's this about our indispensable employee being ill?" a low, gravelly voice asked.

"Mr. Leary?" I said, surprised.

"I hope it wasn't the dinner I gave you?" he joked, but there was an edge to his voice. Maybe he thought I was staying away because of what had happened at the door.

"Oh no, it's the flu," I told him, pulling the lapels of the robe together in the draft. "I should get back to bed."

"Yes, yes, you take care of yourself," he said warmly.

"Thank you for calling," I said, hanging up, relieved that he didn't harbor any ill feelings about that evening.

I slept off and on all day, reading a little in between. Late in the evening — it was past ten — a military knock sounded at the door and Mr. Leary came in, carrying a paper bag dark with grease. "Eat something," he said, gazing around the room. "No wonder you get sick, living in a hole like this." He extracted a hamburger thick with nauseous relish and put it in my hands, his eyes resting on the safety pin that held my pajama top together.

"Go on, eat it."

I shook my head, looking up at him. Some of the relish fell on my chest.

"Never mind," he said, "but you've made a mess of it." He withdrew a white handkerchief from his breast pocket and leaned over me. I tensed with embarrassment, but he dabbed the relish off with gentle fastidiousness, then laid a cool hand on my forehead. "Here's a get well present for you," he said, taking from his pocket a little box daintily wrapped in gold paper. Opening it, I found a small bottle of perfume.

"Thank you," I said hesitatingly, wishing he would go away.

"Now, don't you feel nervous about my being here, don't try to talk. I'll just sit here awhile and read one of your intellectual books and you get some rest." He tucked the covers around me and picked up *Zuleika Dobson* from a pile of secondhand books on the floor and sat down in a chair.

I watched him as he put on a pair of spectacles and leaned back with the book, opening it with a serious frown. My eyes drooped, but I was too uneasy to give in to sleep, and continued to watch him from under my heavy lids. But he was so quiet, so absorbed, that gradually, reassured and comforted by the figure sitting there, I dropped off, allowing myself the luxury of feeling watched over.

When I woke again the light was out and something lay around me warm and solid and with a definite aroma — cigar smoke, and more faintly, a wild wood smell. I sat up with a start, his hands following me, trembling on my waist. "Don't go all to pieces, dear," he whispered, "you wouldn't want an old man to sit up in a straight-back chair all night, would you?"

"You've got to go," I stammered. "You're my boss, Mr. Leary."

"I didn't know you were so conventional," he said, gently pulling me back. "You know what's wrong with conventional people? I'll tell you what's wrong with them. They have no trust. Show me a conventional person and I'll show you a suspicious person. We're above that, aren't we?"

I nodded, though what he said was stupid. I lay back. What an overwhelming joy it was to find a warm muscular arm under my head. For all the uncertainties of the moment, it was one I would not have traded for anything. The weave of his coat jacket, the sense of dark coziness there in the crook of his arm, the knowledge that he was actually watching me as I closed my eyes — as though I could be so interesting, so important — and the wood smell, hair lotion, I supposed, which made me think of the Russian birch groves where Bashkirtseff had walked: all this made me sure that Bashkirtseff could never have been more content than I at this moment.

The next time I woke the window shade was pale with morning light and his hands were on my bare stomach under my pajamas. I was confronted by a steady, alien, sovereign thrill and I lay perfectly still, shivering in the cold, as he removed the pajamas, throwing them to the floor with a little plop. Then he scrambled off the bed and I heard the window shade rattling up, sunshine filled the room, and he came back and sat still. I felt his eyes moving over my body in the sunlight like the tips of two soldering irons, this body that no one had ever seen before. He was still fully clothed; his hands slowly kneaded his thighs while his parted lips formed a few silent words. Suddenly he leaned over me and my eyes flew shut. His lips bore down hard on mine and thrust their tongue inside my mouth. After a while I opened my eyes uncertainly, moved my tongue, and clasped my hands around his neck where the short hairs prickled against my wrists. He made a low noise as though to say "good," then broke away and began to pull off his clothes. I closed my eyes again and crossed my legs tightly but a moment later he pulled them apart, at the same time lying down on top of me with a crushing weight, putting his shaking hand over my lips. Our faces were close together; I looked into his eyes, which were hard, and began to cry with pain, the tears collecting along his hand and dripping down his wrist. I felt nothing but the ripping pain between my legs and the smaller crushing pain of his hand on my mouth. Suddenly with a cry he dropped his head next to mine and his hand relaxed its grip, the thumb playing tiredly on my bruised lips.

"How do you feel?" he asked after a while.

I crushed the pillow over my face as though to obliterate myself.

"Don't give me any hysterics," he warned, pulling the pillow off. "You weren't any little virgin, you know."

"I was! I was!" I cried, and though I knew how childish it must sound, I kept repeating it. "I was! I was!" Adding with new despair, "And what if you've made me pregnant?"

"I was wearing something, for God's sake," he answered and got out of bed and began to dress. He had a good-sized paunch covered with black fuzz; underneath this his testicles hung elongated with age. His shoulders were narrow, his arms hard but stringy and his thick red neck loose skinned under the chin. I turned away, unable to understand that this apparition stood here in my room.

"I smell like a whorehouse," he muttered.

Again the tears burst through. After a while he sat down next to me. He took his handkerchief and dried my eyes. He looked fine in his clothes, like Mr. Leary from the office; his eyes were compassionate and his words were soft. "And I was really the first one?" he asked. "You never had anybody before?"

"Never!" I said bitterly, realizing that this was my first act of love and I would have to carry the memory of it with me the rest of my life.

"Is there blood on the sheet?" he asked.

I stared at him with astonishment.

"I'm sorry," he said, "but you don't know what it means to a man my age . . . I say that in all humbleness . . ." He got up and gave me a long look. "God!" he said bitingly, his teeth clamped together, "God, I love you." Picking up his hat and straightening his tie, he was ready to go.

"I'm quitting my job," I said.

"On account of this? Don't be silly. Stay home a few more days, rest up, get rid of that cough. Then we'll have a nice dinner somewhere . . ."

"No."

He kissed me on the forehead and for the second time tucked the blankets around me. "And as for *Zuleika Dobson*," he said as he went out, "if that's literature I'll eat my hat." I could tell that he felt like a million dollars.

I got up and went to the mirror. My face looked tired, my unloosed hair was matted with a week's sweat, and my lip was swollen from the pressure of his hand. But, I realized, dispassionately staring at myself, I did have beauty. I hadn't really believed it before, but it was true. I was sorry I had not paid more attention to this, taken some pleasure and confidence from it when it might have meant something, since it couldn't mean anything from now on.

I pulled the blood-flecked sheet off the bed, and noticing a greasy spot on the pillowcase where Mr. Leary's head had lain, I tore it from the pillow and dropped it with the sheet on the floor, kicking them both into a corner. I wanted a bath more than anything. I would scrub my body with Dutch Cleanser, burn myself with cigarettes as a penance, quit my job, move to another room where Mr. Leary could not find me, never get close to a man again, and lead a pure and studious and even more frugal life until I could climb aboard my ship and sail away.

I looked at the books on the floor and in the orange crate bookcase. He had thought them pretentious, had insulted them. I picked up *Zuleika Dobson* and wiped it gently with my hand. It was a fine little book and I had been happy reading it. Books were better than life. Opening the door, I tiptoed down the passageway to the bathroom, filled the tub with scalding water, and submerged myself in it like a bundle of dirty clothes. Then standing up, I sprinkled Dutch Cleanser over every inch of my body and began to scour myself with a stiff brush. As I worked I noticed that my cough and fever were gone, probably shocked out of my system during the night. My skin was raw when I was finished and I felt better.

I went back to my room and with a rush of guilt and gratitude toward my old friends, the blue-lined notebook and yellow pencil, I began reworking an old poem, "In Bulgarian Gardens." They were built high, these gardens, like vineyards I had seen pictures of, sloping along hills in tiers of green and gold and crisscrossed by paths of pale sand. Dr. O'Hara's face appeared before me. The pencil slipped from my fingers. All day I sat motionless at the table. When I finally stirred I saw that it had grown dark already. There was a sound outside the door and once more Mr. Leary walked in.

He looked at me apologetically and removed his hat. "I want to tell you how much I regret last night," he said quietly.

"Get out of here."

"I have to be home in twenty minutes, please let me have that little time to make amends."

"No. It's my room. I have a right . . ."

"Rose," he said, calling me that for the first time, "it's true I'm years older than you and that we come from different walks of life, but there's a bond between us. You can deny it if you want to, but it's there. It always will be."

"No," I said, nervous and somehow shocked.

"You couldn't have done what you did last night if there weren't. You're not that kind of girl."

"I didn't know what I was doing."

"Yes you did," he said gently, adding, "once or twice in a lifetime this kind of thing happens, this strange powerful attraction. As though it were predestined. And there's nothing you can do about it."

I nodded in agreement, saying inwardly: "But not with you," and shook myself as though covered with lice. To be tied by destiny to that thing, old and wrinkled and full of lies — and what right had he to speak of destiny and eternal bonds, impinging on poetry, he who was so calculating and pedestrian that in *Zuleika Dobson* he saw only a stupid ungraspable joke? "There is no bond," I said stubbornly.

And yet he was still standing there. I could shout for the landlady or throw a book at his head, yet I did neither. I suddenly remembered a starving dog that had shown up one day at the farm, creeping up the stairs and whining at the door. When my father opened the door the creature lifted its head no farther than the feet, which were motionless and which must have seemed encouraging; but if it had looked up it would have seen that the face with its impatient scowl had nothing to do with its seemingly well-disposed feet. A moment later when the kick came the poor thing let out a yelp of astonishment; but it was the animal's own fault, it should have looked farther.

Mr. Leary was moving toward the table. I ran ahead of him and slapped the open notebook shut. He put his hands on my shoulders. "I admire you for studying in your spare time," he said.

"Not studying. Writing. I'm a poet."

"That's even more admirable," he said without the laugh in his voice I listened for. "There aren't many poets in the world. We need all we can get. I'm not the artistic type myself, but maybe that's why I have such a high regard for those who are."

"I thought you scorned books and things."

"Me? It's what attracted me to you in the first place, that look you had of knowing another world. Oh, I've met my share of writers and painters — my wife likes to entertain them — but they've already arrived, they've got the stamp of the world on them. I've never known anyone burning with their first fire. You give me — I don't know, something I can't describe. I want to protect that fire."

He had crossed his hands around my waist. He stopped talking. The room was dark with evening. He drew me to the stripped-down bed, and as we sank down on it the thought flashed through my mind that I had been had for a cheap compliment, but my mind was dropping away. Afterwards, he lay back and pulled my head onto his chest. His chest was hairy, it was like lying safe in a thicket, and his hand holding mine was hard, the pulse still throbbing with the authority of his passion. This time it had not been so painful.

He left very late. I lay on the bare mattress with my eyes closed, frightened beyond anything. This was the other side of the plain, and it was not a fuming underworld like Doré's illustrations of Hell that I had come across in the Alturas library. It was just a squalid corner. I seemed to watch myself from a distance, as though a part of me had split away.

I returned to the office the next day. In the evenings Mr. Leary came to my room.

Chapter

6

PAUL MOVED OUT of the building soon after. One night Levine phoned, tense with excitement. He and Dora were moving to Los Angeles, they were going to be married, he had broken with Paul. "You've got a clear head on you for such a kid," he concluded in a rush. "I give my thanks."

"What did I say?" I asked him fiercely, "What was I like?"

"What do you mean?"

"I don't know! I don't know . . ."

Mr. Leary — and he was Mr. Leary to the end — spent two or three nights a week in my room.

"Doesn't your family wonder?" I asked.

He nodded, almost with satisfaction.

"What if your wife found out and came here and insulted me?"

"She wouldn't. But what if she did? You've got some insults coming, haven't you?"

"You bastard."

"Oh, what a word for an intellectual to use."

His profound admiration had not lasted long. He was always saying, "Don't talk like a book." I don't think he had ever read a book in his life, and it was reflected in his conversation. Except for a really impressive number of highflown phrases he had picked up over the years, he spoke a strangely threadbare, tautological language.

One day, passing an empty lot, I saw a discarded Chinese screen, tattered and broken but of good quality. I took it home, patched it up with tape and was very pleased with it. The only place I had room for it was in front of my orange crate bookcase, so I put it there. When Mr. Leary came that evening he looked at it with a frown. "It takes up too much room," he said, and folded it together and leaned it against the wall, glancing at the books as though relieved that they were still there. And wondering at his simpleness, I saw that though he scorned books they gave me a certain prestige in his eyes.

I continued my office friendship with Harley, and inevitably he began asking me to see him outside the office. I told him I was dating someone else and that it wouldn't be fair. But he had a persistence that didn't fit his personality — or perhaps it was only that he was persistent in situations where he knew he was already beaten — at any rate, he said, "I don't see why we can't just go to a show once in a while like two friends." Mr. Leary, on the infrequent occasions that he took me out, chose formal places where we always bumped into friends of his and his wife's. I yearned for a casual, guiltless date with someone my own age. I began going out with Harley on the nights I knew Mr. Leary wasn't coming, sometimes to a movie, sometimes just for a walk. Harley never tried to kiss me, though once or twice he made a feeble attempt to hold my hand.

One evening when Mr. Leary came to my room he said, "I didn't know you knew my nephew."

"Well, of course I know Harley. I work with him."

"I mean intimately."

"I don't."

"I came over here last night and you two were standing on the front porch together. Eleven o'clock at night."

"So I went to the show with him. I knew him before I knew you, Mr. Leary, I can't just drop him like a hot potato. He's a nice, decent fellow . . ."

"A moron!"

"He's your own nephew, how can you call him that?"

"I'll call him whatever I want." He pulled off his high collar and flung it on the bed. "He makes me sick." I sensed that if he had found me with someone more prepossessing than Harley he would not have been so offended.

"There's nothing between us," I said. "He's just a friend . . ."

"We won't talk about it any more."

The next day just before quitting time Harley came out of his uncle's office and without a glance at anyone walked out the door.

"He quit," Mr. Leary told me that night. "Said he couldn't keep up . . ." He was interrupted by the phone in the passageway. It was Harley, calling from his house. Like a bolt out of the blue, he said, his uncle had fired him.

"It wasn't a bolt out of the blue," Mr. Leary countered when I repeated the conversation to him. "I'd told him before that his work didn't measure up. There are certain standards, Rose. Certain standards. And Harley didn't meet them."

When I visited Harley the next week I knew I had cost him

his job and I spoke in a hushed, funereal voice that must have made him uneasy. He lived in a little alley in the Mission District, in a tiny, cramped apartment. His sister wasn't home and he had made the dinner himself, a strange concoction of fried catfish and sweet potatoes. He was like a broken man as he discussed his position; he would never again be given an opportunity like the one he had; he possessed only one influential uncle, his uncle had only one favor, and it had been lost. He had already given up looking for another job in an office and had returned to the gas station around the corner.

"You could work yourself up to manager someday," I said hopefully.

He nodded without enthusiasm.

As I was leaving his sister came in, a girl my age garish with makeup and already blowzy, who walked past us as though we weren't there. A couple of weeks later she ran off with a married man and Harley moved into a room with cooking privileges. Gathering up his spirits a little, he spent his evenings studying accounting.

Why couldn't I fall in love with Harley, I sometimes asked myself. He might not be stimulating, but he was open and kind. But he was also weak, lusterless, and he was young. Young men were timid, respectful; they made you feel like a heavy marble statue; their clear, bright eyes somehow never saw you. Mr. Leary's bull-like neck and ravaged face, the power and complexities of age, seemed to hold out something immensely more compelling.

I was not especially clumsy, but I always found myself bumping against my lover, spilling coffee or Coke or cigarette ashes in his lap, scratching or jostling him when I put my arm around his neck. Once I even dealt him a sharp blow on the jaw with my elbow as I got up from beside him. "Sometimes I think you don't like me," he said with innocent humor as he rubbed his jaw.

"It will pass, it will," I told myself whenever I sat with an unread book in my lap, waiting for his footstep. And to precipitate its passing I tortured myself with unpleasant memories and visions. There was, for instance, the way his son treated him. Frank was eighteen or nineteen then, a small but hulking youth, rather shy, but already learning to cover up with a breezy arrogance. From the little Harley said about his cousin, Frank was a brooding, restless sort, had already flunked out of college, was extremely fond of his mother and worried about her — why, Harley didn't know, for his aunt impressed him as a charming, well-liked woman. At present Frank worked in an office around the corner from his father's, and sometimes dropped in to meet him for lunch. Mr. Leary beamed at him, squeezed his arm, smiled his alluring, cocky smile, and the boy responded with the coldest look I had ever seen. Mr. Leary seemed not to notice. His son loved and admired him because sons did. Mr. Leary was a great believer in every cliché he ever heard; they appealed to him because they were easy to remember, and if they were sentimental, so much the better, for he cherished himself as a softhearted, beloved man. (I saw the softness of his heart reflected in his eyes when he told me he had gone to bat for me and gotten me a raise. Later I learned that it was an automatic raise. "You lied to me," I told him bluntly, and he lied about the lie with such elliptical complexity that when he was finished he had certainly persuaded himself if he hadn't me.)

Another unpleasant image I tortured myself with was that of

him and his wife preparing for bed. Old, faded, both of them, they would undress in silence, removing the fine clothes that gave shape to their shapeless bodies. With dull familiarity they would pull back the covers of the bed and deposit their false teeth in two glasses on the night table (for I had discovered, probing around his mouth with my finger, that though lifelike, his teeth were not his own). Toothless and wordless, they would lie there like two old shoes.

And then the knock would sound at the door and I would push these scenes aside and jump up with my heart beating in my mouth.

The smell of his leather belt intoxicated me; his shoes, into which I would slip my feet, thrilled me with their warm roominess. The hardness of his coat buttons pressing against my chest; his hair, sleek, all of a piece, like a black helmet — everything about him that was solid and polished and mellow satisfied a deep hunger.

Sometimes he would ask me to read from one of my "serious" books. Then he would sit there like a sincere immigrant, interrupting now and then with a raised finger as though to say: I must remember that phrase. It annoyed me that he exposed his ignorance in all its nakedness, but soon after we began our affair he had stopped trying to impress me. He lapsed into Mission Street slang, used obscenities, and even ate sloppily when we were alone. I did not feel that this was simply because he felt comfortable with me; it was his way of spilling ashes in my lap.

Hardly a week passed that he didn't accuse me of sharing my bed with other men. "Don't give me that intellectual verdiage," he would bark with his cocky smile frozen to his face. "I know what you are. I know what you are. Why don't you cut out all the verdiage . . ."

"Verbiage!"

". . . You think you've got some blind old fool you can cheat on . . ."

"You're crazy, crazy!" I shouted, and at those times I thought he was.

"Who do you think you are, anyway? Christ, you still smell of manure, and living in this hole . . . when I think of the other broads I could get . . ."

"Get them then," I cried. "Get them, but would they want *you?*"

He stared at me, pale. "You always hit below the belt, Rose. You know what's wrong with you? I'll tell you what's wrong with you. You don't know what kindness is."

And he would stay away for a week or ten days, ignoring me at the office. I would breathe a sigh of relief at first, but inside a day my chest would tighten, I couldn't eat or sleep, and my mouth grew dry as sand. Then, having punished me, he would return cool and unsmiling, willing to give me one more chance.

He never told me I was pretty, and I wanted a tender word. I retaliated by taunting him with his age.

"What was it like in the olden days?" I would ask.

"Whaddya mean, olden days?"

"I mean before you got old."

"Whaddya mean? I've got more sperm in me than my own kid."

When I grimaced at this kind of talk, he would say, "Oh, mustn't offend Miss Davies, the prominent file clerk. Come on, Rosie, move your ass over here."

And I would lunge at him, trying to smash his face, but he managed to defend himself and squeeze my wrists to a pulp at the same time.

"You old thing," I would cry, "you unspeakably old geezer!"

And if I said it long enough his hands would begin to tremble as though in involuntary agreement, and I would watch them with savage satisfaction.

But at the beginning we got along fairly well. I told him everything about myself, all the things I had hoarded for years, knowing he wasn't the one to tell, yet unable to contain myself as I lay in the crook of his arm. At first he absorbed it all with such comments as "That's interesting," and "Is that so?" but gradually he began to taunt me because my big plans had come to nothing.

"I haven't failed," I said. "Nobody's a failure at my age."

"You'll be a failure all your life." And he would lie back with his cocky smile.

He told me very little about himself. Aside from a few things that Harley had passed on I knew only what the other clerks said. His wife held a controlling interest in the firm and he had been given his job through her influence shortly after they were married. No one knew exactly what his job consisted of, but the consensus of opinion was that he did nothing. The newer clerks thought him decent enough, though reserved. The older clerks, those who had been there many years, considered him vicious. I asked one of these veterans why this was so, but he only said that Leary had a mania for firing people. It was a point of honor with him; if you didn't fawn he thought you rebellious, unreliable, out of place in a serious office.

"It doesn't seem possible that he could have so much say-so," I argued. "He's just one man, after all."

"They keep him from making any big noises by humoring him in small issues," the clerk explained. "What are a couple of clerks now and then?"

"And his wife? Why doesn't she put her foot down?"

"She's not interested in the office, it's just a place that keeps him out of her hair. She knows it's his hunting grounds for girls, but at this point I guess she's used to it. By the way, Rose, you're too smart to bite, but a word of advice — don't be taken in by him, he tries with every girl who comes in."

"Does he have much luck?" I asked lightly, masking the humiliated racing of my pulse.

"He's such a big bag of wind, who'd take him seriously?"

"Oh, I know," I said, wild to break off with him.

"No one else wants him," I said to myself despairingly. "I have a lover no one likes or takes seriously or wants." But beneath my chagrin I felt a gratifying surge of security. "I'll give him the heave-ho," I told myself. I was so much better than him, I did not need him. The weeks went on. Months accumulated. A year passed.

At night I would awaken with a sensation that made my mouth taste of metal. Something was sitting heavily on my chest, a presence without shape, the incarnation of all lonely hours, terrible catastrophes and designed cruelty. Its hands were dry as dead hands, though it had no hands. After a while I would realize that nothing was there but I would remain awake, staring at the space in front of me.

When I looked in the mirror it was as though I saw the face of someone I had cheated and humiliated and who had reacted to my abuse with obscenely eager compliance. I had lost myself as palpably as if the marrow had been drained from my bones.

And the more strongly I felt this, the more urgently I turned to him for enlightenment. Squeezing and pressing his hands, looking into his eyes, I would silently ask how I had gotten here, and how I could go back. "Show me . . ." I once began aloud.

"Show you what?"

"Myself."

And with a grin he brought his face close to mine, until I saw myself reflected in his small black pupils.

I read, but I wrote nothing and stuffed my notebooks into my tin suitcase in the closet. Mechanically, I continued to save my money, aiming for five hundred dollars, almost twice the amount that after eighteen months of working I now had.

And finally — it seemed I had waited a lifetime — I felt Eros cracking down the middle like a cheap statue. With my abiding complicity Mr. Leary gave the final tap.

I stood still in the darkness while he groped his way to a lamp and turned it on with a little click. It was a small lamp with a fluted shade of transluscent bone the same warm pink gold you find on the underside of some seashells. It threw its corner of the room into a soft rosiness, leaving the rest dim and somehow very still, as at twilight. On the walls in gold frames hung several paintings of flowers, skillfully wrought but with a certain melancholy in the dark backgrounds into which the heavy reds and golds of the petals were drawn.

"Who painted these?" I asked.

"Her. One of her hobbies."

There were real flowers in the room, too, though wilted:

vases of drooping roses and baby's breath, no doubt gathered from the garden a week ago before the family had left. They were spending ten days in the country. Mr. Leary was staying at his club downtown.

The French Provincial furniture stood on a soft rug which Mr. Leary defined with pride as an Aubusson. The bed was narrow and covered with a plain white but rich looking material. Above it on the wall hung a white crucifix.

Mr. Leary, somewhat nervous, crossed the room to the windows and pulled the velvet drapes together where they hung long, elegant, slightly worn, framing him for a moment in their somber, raisin-colored depths. He moved away, picking up a framed photograph from the mantelpiece. It was a picture of him and his wife taken many years before; he was swarthy, coarser looking than he was now, but his smile radiated a vital, compelling charm and was obviously not lost on his wife, whose face I scrutinized, taking the picture from his hand. She was pretty, even under the unbecoming prewar hairstyle; small, dark. He put the picture back and kicked a dead coal into the fireplace.

"Well, what do you think of it?" he asked jovially, his eyes wavering for an instant at a distant sound, then resuming their satisfied tour of the room.

I examined a shelf of worn books. Ronsard, Belloc, Chesterton. "Good taste," I said.

"Ah!" he grunted.

I moved over to the vanity, glancing at the cut glass decanter of rose water, the blue enamel hairpin tray, the old fashioned mortar for loose hair. A tangle of dark hair lay in it. I was suddenly chilled and pulled the collar of my coat up. "I want to go now. I didn't want to come in the first place."

"Not much you didn't. It was your idea."

"I only said I'd like to see that zillion-watt chandelier you're always bragging about. But you've taken me straight up to her room. I feel cheap."

He sat down on the bed, smoothing the bedspread with nervous, tentative fingers. "It's not her room," he said, "it's the maid's."

"The maid's?"

"Bea sleeps downstairs, she can't take the stairs. She hasn't been up here for years. Come on, sit down." He drew me down beside him with a sudden burst of nervous energy that I realized had been building up ever since we entered the room.

"No, it's her room."

Pushing me back, he covered my face with ardent, furious kisses, as though half wishing to bite. "Oh baby . . . oh baby!" he cried in a ragged voice, shattering the exquisite room. With a blind, preoccupied bitterness he yanked up my skirt, straining one hand toward his fly and holding my head down roughly with the other while hairpins slipped from my head to the bedspread in a little patter.

"Not on her bed!"

"Yes, yes, on her bed," he groaned.

"Let me go . . . they've come back . . . I hear something . . ."

"Nobody's here." His eyes had closed in a spasm of anticipation, but suddenly they blinked open. He scrambled off the bed.

"Patrick?" someone was calling from downstairs.

"The coat," he breathed. When we came in he had thrown his topcoat across one of the chairs in the entrance.

"Are you home?" the voice called, its owner moving up the staircase. Other voices floated up from the entrance.

He clutched his temples, and with a little cry dove to the bed, swept up the hairpins with shaking fingers and thrust them into his pocket. "Get out of here!" he hissed. There were tears in his eyes, they swam in a brightness of utter chaos; then they cleared and he pushed me under the bed with such force that my head struck the frame painfully. I lay in a ball, my teeth clamped into my hand.

He stepped to the door and swung it open. "Bea?" he said in a soft voice, so soft that its tremor was masked.

"Oh. What're you doing in there?" Her tone was flat, polite, mildly curious.

"I heard one of the windows rattling," he replied, still softly. "I could hardly close it, it was stuck."

"I thought I'd closed them before leaving. What are you doing home?"

"Some papers I had to pick up." Then, his voice slipping into a low, rich gear of affection, he said, "But what about you? Why are you back so soon, giving me the nicest surprise of my . . ."

"The weather turned cold, we decided to leave. I'm tired, Patrick. I'm going to bed."

"Come downstairs and have a bite first," he cajoled. "Just you and me alone. Like old times."

She gave a short laugh, dropping her coat on the bed.

"Please, Bea."

"You're tiresome."

He stood at the door — I could see his feet — until she closed it on him. Then I heard her moving around the room, undressing, taking the hairpins from her hair and dropping them into the enamel tray. Presently, she, too, left the room. I crawled out from under the bed and opened the door to a crack to find her disappearing into a large white bathroom down the hall. Her husband stood by the stairway like a man on a strange street, looking first in one direction, then in another. His son and daughter had started up the stairs, I could hear their voices. His face twisted into a white grimace and his arm shot out, pointing to the right. I fled blindly to the door he indicated, threw it open, and found myself on the backstairs. A moment later I heard muffled greetings in the hall I had just vacated, Mr. Leary's voice high and jolly with relief, and with something else: pride. I began the long unlighted descent, knocking over a mop on the first landing and treading on the tail of a sleeping cat when I had attained the moonlit kitchen. I let myself out the back door.

"Then, that's the end," I said as I lay down on my bed. My stomach was churning even more than it had been lately. I tossed on the bed. Early in the morning — it must have been two o'clock — the phone in the passageway began to ring. It was Mr. Leary, speaking in a low voice still keen with the enthusiasm of his narrow escape. "How are you?" he asked conversationally, and I could picture his shrewd eyes and slight smile, one ready to blot out the other according to my response.

"Disgusted," I said.

"Oh? Why?"

"Oh, Christ, if you don't know. I felt like the lowest . . . Her room. Her bed. You've got to hit her as low as possible. I'm finished."

"You certainly are. Don't report to work tomorrow." He hung up the receiver with a click.

❀

Chapter

7

FROM OUTSIDE came the sound of the landlady watering the shrubbery in the backyard. The splashing water sounded so beautiful that I got up and rushed to the window and opened it wide with gratitude. I had been suffering from a lassitude that I felt had now been vanquished as I leaned over the sill. It was an unusually warm February morning. The shrubbery glistened a vivid, upsurging green and on the fence a sparrow filled the air with its scolding. I turned from the window, leaving it open so that the curtains billowed, and went directly to the closet, dragged out my suitcase, and flung it open. Pulling out the most recent notebook, I wrote in a headlong scribble: "When something ends, something else begins. A person must learn to forgive himself . . ." Suddenly I scrambled to the basin and vomited in it. As I rinsed my mouth I stopped and stood stone still.

The following day I went to a doctor.

"No need for a test," he said after his examination, "you're about three months pregnant."

"I want an abortion," I snapped. "I hate the father, I don't want his . . ."

"You should have thought about that when you . . ."

"Don't give me any sermons."

I was ushered out of the office. I walked home, ferociously kicking over a newsstand and pinching the flesh of my arm to keep from breaking into tears on the street. In my room I flung myself down on the bed, thinking: "It's his. Part of vile Mr. Leary inside me. I won't allow it!" I fell back in an impotent rage, my whole body, my whole life imprisoned by a microscopic particle he had left behind. What would a mother do on the Trans-Siberian Railway? What would a mother do, anywhere? It wasn't right. I wouldn't be one.

I got a nickel from my purse and went out to the phone in the passageway and called Mr. Leary's office.

"I have been sterile for the past fifteen years," he replied in a hushed, controlled voice to my statement.

"Why did you always use protection, then?" I whispered. "It's not true. You've got to help me. I'm telling the truth, you can check with the doctor." And I gave him the name.

"I have been sterile for the past fifteen years," he repeated, "and I should warn you that my brother-in-law is Francis Kiernan, the attorney, and if you approach me again he'll have you in court for extortion so fast it'll make your head spin."

I hung up the receiver. The landlady hovered at the end of the passageway; I glanced at her hesitatingly. Several times during the course of my affair with Mr. Leary she had made an attempt at intimacy, saying in a joking, innocent voice, "That guy with the collar, what is he, your uncle or something?" or "Where'd you meet him anyway, is he your boss?" I had always responded with a shrug, but now I felt myself turning to her. Checking the impulse, I walked back to my room.

That evening I was surprised by a visit from Francis Kiernan.

He studied both me and my surroundings carefully, with large melancholy eyes, before getting down to business. Then he said, "My client says that although he is not responsible for your condition he will extend you a sum to terminate it."

"He's a liar."

The lawyer said nothing.

"Would he extend me a sum to raise the thing?" I asked angrily. "No, of course not. This is easy for him. Why didn't he come in person? The dirty coward. Cover it all up. Lie about it. Just a few dollars out the window." I thrust my hand out and he gave me a hundred and fifty dollars in twenty-dollar bills and a piece of paper with a name and address on it.

"I'm very sorry about this," he said in a quiet, hesitant voice, going to the door, "believe me, I am."

The doctor whose name I had been given refused to take the risk since I was more than three months along. Dazed, I left his office, the seed still growing inside me like a fungus. I threw myself down on the curb and with blind rage tore the money to shreds and kicked it down the sewer grating. "Nothing of his!" I cried aloud, "Nothing of his!" and running home, I gathered together everything that belonged to him — the little perfume bottle, a comb he had once forgotten, a half-empty fifth of Scotch and an old cigar butt — and threw them into the garbage can in the backyard. While I stood there I racked my brain for bits and pieces from novels and whispered conversations and I walked to the top of the backstairs and jumped off, rejoicing in the hard jolt as I hit the ground. I did this five times, then dragged myself back upstairs, filled the bathtub with scalding water, and lowered myself into it with a sharp gasp. After that, in my room, I jabbed at my stomach with the handle of my hair brush. Finally, unable to recall anything else, I drank a bottle of

ink, which came up immediately. The next morning I awoke
sore in every bone, my stomach bruised, my tongue black, but
otherwise unchanged.

Every morning I would look fearfully at myself in the
mirror. "It's drinking up my vital juices," I said to myself. I
was sure that the other roomers could hear me retch into the
basin, and soon, with a protruding stomach, everyone would
know: the landlady, the grocery store clerk, the children who
played on the street. They would look at me with contemptuous pity, a hulking, trapped piece of flesh. I wanted to move
away but I felt so sluggish and nauseated that I stayed where I
was.

On occasional evening walks I usually found myself ending up
in a section of large homes whose lofty windows threw long
shafts of gold across the flower beds. I would stand on the pavement before one of them — a fine three-story building with large,
well-kept grounds — and in a spirit of dull malevolence wait for a
glimpse of Mr. Leary. One evening I saw him and his son walking up the street to the house. I stepped into the shadow of the
hedge, prepared to step out in front of them with an accusation
that would shred the man's dignity to bits before his son. But
my nerve failed and they passed, Mr. Leary's face sharply delin-
eated by the streetlamp: the vivid touch of white at the temples, the energetic squint of his eyes. "Do it!" I whispered to
myself and ran after them, grabbing Mr. Leary by the shoulder
and pulling him around. "You brought me into your house here,
and wanted to go to bed with me in your wife's room, it was the
night she came back from the country." I turned to Frank.
"You talked to him in the hall, remember? And I had just run
down the backstairs. Now I'm pregnant and he's sent his law-

yer to me with money for an abortion and still pretends he's not responsible . . ."

The boy stood smoldering and silent, looking steadily at me. His father's face expressed nothing. "Nutty kid from the office," he said to the boy. "Jackson fired her . . . she's tracked down every man in the office with these accusations." Turning to me, he said gently, "You'll have the police after you if you keep running around like this." The boy had turned and walked on. His father's face was suddenly haggard, his fingers pressing his forehead nervously. He breathed an obscenity at me and hurried after his son.

Chapter

8

I HAD no plan. Weeks passed. I lay in my room thinking of how my Trans-Siberian money was being nibbled away and half expecting my condition to magically disappear. Whenever Harley telephoned I was cool and untalkative, and at last he stopped calling. I no longer took my evening walks. I lacked even the energy to wash my hair or change my clothes, and felt self-conscious and awkward at the corner store where I bought my groceries. When I began to show, I faced the clerk and customers with a shamed, defiant silence.

In May I paid my rent, as usual, on the first day of the month. The landlady glanced at the ten-dollar bill and said, "The rent's been raised to fifty."

"Fifty!"

She nodded.

"Then I'll pay fifty!"

"Oh no you won't. Look, a long time ago I tried to be nice to you, I tried to give you some advice, but you couldn't be bothered. O.K., that's the way you want it, fine, wonderful, but I can't have you here. There are places for people like you. Go to one of those homes for girls who get in your condition. That's where you belong."

A few days later I packed my suitcase, and leaving my secondhand books scattered across the floor under a film of dust, I took the streetcar across town to the Mary Stone Home for Unwed Mothers.

We were like patients sitting in a waiting room; our duties were only a way to kill time. The days crept by, our bodies grew gross and alien to us. We were slow moving, full of small complaints, kind enough to each other but sarcastic about ourselves, as though each one pretended she were caught in a stupid joke that must be treated with a light, scornful touch. Almost none of them kept their babies.

"If you kept it what would you name it?" one of the girls asked me toward the end of my term.

"Gargantua."

"Was that your boyfriend's last name?"

"He was no boyfriend. He was an old man."

"Ugh," she said. Her boyfriend, as she, was fifteen. She was a dull girl, and very plain, with carroty hair and a mass of freckles. She said she would rather be pregnant than go to school. She was the only one who died in childbirth. As we heard it, the fetus had grown into the pelvic bone.

When my time came I had a sensation of dark solitude such as I had never experienced before, and I knew that this encroaching loneliness was the vestibule of death. "What if it's grown into the pelvic bone?" I asked the nurse, touching her hand.

"Don't be silly."

The phrase jarred me. It was so normal, so innocent.

Gradually the pain increased to something I had no concept

of, and I fought against it with all my strength. "That will never do," soothed the nurse. "Go *with* the pain, go *with* it . . ."

"I will never . . . go with it," I gasped, finally angry. Such pain had no right to invade me, it was cruel, unbelievably cruel, and all my anger fastened on God, who appeared to me as he had when I was a child, the Hobergs' pinched, bilious God. He should be publicly denounced . . . I would do it . . . I would burn down all the churches . . . burn Mr. Leary . . . burn everything . . .

"There, it's over. Your Dr. O'Hara's ears must be ringing."

I was exhausted, cold with sweat, at peace with myself. Mr. Leary's festering seed was gone, my stomach was flat again, I was myself, myself alone. I watched something being carried by, a scrap of pink flesh. "Let me see," I murmured, though I knew the rule was not to show the mother her baby if she meant to give it up. "I was the one who had it! Let me at least see, dammit!" But the door swung to.

The next day I told them I had decided not to give it up, and they finally let me see. There was something secret and hard earned about this baby, like the poems in my notebook. And I felt sorry, for her, she was so new, and had no place in the world and she cried so much, looked so confused and almost desperate. There was not an atom of Mr. Leary in her, of that I was sure, otherwise she would have perished when I tried so hard to do away with her. Nature would have seen to it. But she was not like him and she was meant to be born. To think that something conceived without love, carried in anger could touch me so deeply. I named her Gloria.

I had only enough money for two weeks more at the Home.

I was advised to give her up to find a job and then come back to the Home to get her. That might take weeks and I was too impatient to consider it. Any minute, I feared, she would be taken away from me "for her own good," since it was plain that the staff thought me a flighty, irresponsible parent. Formulas and diapers did not interest me. I only wanted to hold and play with her, and that seemed fine with her.

I did what seemed the only natural thing under the circumstances. I took her and went away. Late at night I once more packed my suitcase, slipped down to the nursery, gathered her up in a blanket, and left. The street was empty, lit by a thin moon. I scuffed hurriedly along in my old loafers, glancing up as the moon went behind a mountain of rain clouds; a moment later they broke and the rain came down in a waterfall. Hastily I pulled the blanket over Gloria's head, my steps faltering as I saw the injustice of taking her into such a night. Sorrowfully, it seemed, she began to howl, and I was stopped short by the sudden awareness that she was now entirely dependent on me. "And look what I'm doing to you!" I thought, watching the blanket grow sodden. I started to walk again, faster — there were no busses this time of night — and it was a full hour later that we arrived at the Ferry Building. I dried her briskly and sat back with my eyes closed to wait for morning. When it came we took the first ferry to Oakland.

I found a cheap room and a few days later was able to start part-time work as a waitress. Mrs. Catania was the reason. She was a widow of seventy who lived down the hall, a lonely old Italian woman who still wore the black of her peasant forbears and wrapped a shawl around her when she went out. She told me she would be glad to take care of Gloria any time I needed her.

She bought nightgowns, booties, blankets, and frilly caps at the Salvation Army store; prepared an exact formula for the bottles, testing the heat of the milk on her arm with a look of great concern; she bought a secondhand crib and threw out the clothesbasket I had dragged in from the back porch; she washed out diapers with fervor until I insisted she stop. When I got my first paycheck I paid her for all she had bought and she promptly purchased an elderly, battered English baby carriage, huge and elaborate, like a movable shrine, with wheels whose grinding squeak could be heard a full block away. With Gloria gleaming from the depths of this ornate vehicle, Mrs. Catania walked all over the neighborhood, proud and content, pausing by the cafe where I worked so that I could glance out and be reassured that all was well.

She was much more efficient than I was and Gloria thrived in her care, but I felt no jealousy toward the old woman. She had round, pale brown eyes and there was always something pleased, innocent yet wise in her expression. Sometimes when we were together in my room — I would spread a blanket on the floor and play with Gloria, kissing her while I danced her on the floor — I would feel a look of gentle inquiry from my friend. One day she said tentatively, "It's too much, Rosie, always you and the little one alone in this room."

"It's what I want," I said. I felt I had managed extremely well. Gloria was sturdy, rosy, pretty, with a perfect miniature widow's peak and long eyelashes that lay like fans across her cheek when she slept. We were safe, we had enough to eat, we were together.

That winter was wet and cold. In February Gloria came down with colic, and the broken sleep I got left me tired and run-down. In the hot crowded cafe customers sprayed the air with winter sneezes and I caught a nagging chest cold that developed into pneumonia. I was in the county hospital for two weeks during which time Mrs. Catania took care of Gloria, but I was afraid my job wouldn't be held for me, and when I came out I found I had been right. I was told by the landlord that I had two weeks to pay up or get out, but, still bedridden, I could not look for another job.

A stale disorder possessed the room. The bed was rumpled and dirty, used dishes stood with baby bottles, hairbrushes, and the gas burner on the dusty bureau. Dust covered everything not in daily use. Mrs. Catania, invigorated at first by her sense of usefulness, was now exhausted from taking care of both Gloria and me. The rain came down, swelling her arthritic joints until it was all she could do to take care of herself.

I turned and turned in my bed, filled with the rage that mounted each morning when I woke to find my bones still leaden, the rain still pouring, and Gloria crawling energetically around her crib, anxious to be put on the floor where she pursued her great adventures. Everywhere she crawled it was dirty, and I hated to see her pick up a ball of dust and look at it as though it were a flower. But I couldn't imagine what worse surroundings she would find herself in if we were kicked out. I felt that if only I could get back on my feet, clean up the mess in the room, find another job, then everything would be all right again. "It's not that I'm asking for so much!" I said, hitting the pillow. I could probably go to Public Welfare, but I was certain that they would take Gloria away when they saw how we lived. There was only one thing to do, and I crawled out of bed and dressed and went down to the public phone booth in the corner drugstore.

"Mr. Leary, please," I said when I got the number.

A moment later I heard his special office voice, precise, almost British, very courteous and yet a trifle pressed.

"It's Rose," I said, "don't hang up or you'll be sorry."

"Why should I hang up? What can I do for you, Miss Davies?"

"First of all, I didn't go through with you know what . . . what you gave me the money for . . ."

"I don't know what you're talking about."

"The fact is, I had the baby . . ."

"Congratulations, Miss Davies. And please extend my congratulations to the father."

"Oh Christ," I murmured. I gripped the receiver with both hands. "I didn't want to ask you for anything more, but the baby comes first so I have to. I need fifty dollars. I've been in the hospital and I lost my job and I need this money to get me back on my feet. You'll get every cent back, I don't want to keep anything of yours."

"Well," he said, and paused for a good minute. "It seems to me I already gave you a tidy little sum to get you out of a jam with another fellow, Miss Davies. I can't go on forever paying for your mistakes because we once happened to be friends."

"All right, you can expect your wife to receive a phone call from me."

"My wife is dead," he said.

It was not one of his outrageous prevarications; he had said it with too much sincere satisfaction.

"For God's sake, you old fool, I'm only asking for fifty dollars . . . send it to me and that's the end of your responsibility."

"I have no responsibility toward this baby of yours. I have been sterile for the past fifteen years."

"That check had better be in my mailbox in two days or I'll go to Kiernan and slap a paternity suit on you." I gave him my address. "Write it down, Mr. Leary," I said, "don't lose it. It's all you've got between you and a lot of trouble."

Chapter

9

ALL THE NEXT DAY it rained with renewed fury, but the following morning, Saturday, I woke to a stillness. A few drops fell from the eaves to the pavement below where the neighborhood St. Patrick's Day parade was gathering. It seemed a good omen: St. Patrick's Day. Patrick. The two would connect. I would get the check today. The mail was usually delivered around ten o'clock; I had half an hour to worry and hope. I had taken Gloria into bed with me at six and given her her bottle, and we had fallen back to sleep together. She was still asleep; the pale sunlight fell through the curtains and touched her eyelashes so that the tips were golden. A vein in her forehead throbbed lightly and I lay my finger on it, feeling the little pulse. Her mouth was open and she was snoring like a small woods animal. I wanted a cigarette badly.

Shortly before ten Mrs. Catania stuck her head in the door and said she was going out to watch the parade. A few minutes later the door opened and Mr. Leary walked in, his face flushed the color of raw bacon, his eyes taking in everything with one dangerous, severe glance. I put my hand on Gloria. As he came closer, I slipped the cover over her head. "I don't want you to see her, or her to see you," I said, climbing out of bed and pulling on my robe. It was worn and soiled and I knotted the sash with a nervous attempt at confidence. "Why did you come here? All you had to do was to send the check."

"And start a habit? Every two weeks you'd be putting the bite on me. No, Rose. No." He leaned forward on a silver-tipped walking stick and whispered roundly, "No." The walking stick was something new. He had grown finer since his wife's death, almost opulent. His overcoat sported a large beaver collar that all but obscured his shoulders, and two enormous, clumsy mother-of-pearl cuff links gleamed from his wrists.

"You look like a prosperous bookie," I couldn't help saying. He brushed a piece of lint from his sleeve and looked around the room again. "Great little place you've got here, great place to raise a kid, doing her a real favor."

"Are you going to give me the money or not? If not, get out."

He sat down in a chair and planted his feet firmly on the floor. "You're suffocating the kid," he commented.

I removed the blanket from Gloria's head. She was awake and fretful. Holding her close to me, I put her back in the crib where she immediately set up a howl.

"What's the matter?" he shouted over her cries. "Afraid to let me see her because she looks like the father? Mulatto, maybe? Or squint-eyed?"

"You bastard," I shouted back.

"No, you've got me and her mixed up."

I picked her up again, shouting over my shoulder for him to leave, and tried to soothe her. She strained toward the floor and hopefully I let her down. She lay there for a moment, and then, in the way of all infants, seemed to forget whatever terror had possessed her the minute before, and began to inch across the floor — thankfully not in his direction. He said nothing. His eyes rested not on her face but on the dingy nightshirt and yellowed diapers and her grimy little hands and feet. His expression was one of censure and pity. "How can you live in such a dump?" he asked. "Don't you have any pride? Don't you care about her?"

"Someday I'll kill you."

This seemed to please him. Underneath his social objection to me as a bad parent he was warming to the game; on some deeper level maybe he was even congratulating himself on his fatherhood. He settled more firmly into his chair as though he intended to remain for some time. I stood by the crib uncertainly. All I had to do was to take Gloria into Mrs. Catania's room and wait for him to leave. But despite my controlled voice I was consumed by a hatred so passionate that my only wish, blotting out everything else, was to keep him there and to find a way to hurt him badly, cripple him — no, to destroy him completely.

"If you killed me you wouldn't get a cent out of me," he said at length in his soft, gravelly voice, as though making a chess move.

"You're enjoying this," I said, still coolly.

"Far from it. I'm sorry to see you like this, and dragging this little child down with you." Gloria had turned and was now crawling toward him. He moved his feet, but could not help observing in a curt, informative aside: "Kids always take to me." I picked her up and turned her in the other direction.

"O.K.," I said, "what about the fifty dollars? Do you leave it behind when you've finished with your insults and lectures and games? Or do I take my case to . . ."

"Case? What case have you got? Look, I came here strictly to protect myself from any further approaches from you. I won't be exploited by some cheap little lay who sees a patsy in me because I once happened to be good to her."

"Good? Good?"

"Yes, good! What about the restaurants I took you to and the raises I got for you and the liquor I brought over to your place and that hundred and fifty bucks when you were in trouble? Apparently somebody's got a short memory. A short memory. And I mean I was generous in other ways, too, ways you apparently haven't realized yet, generous with my experience, Christ, you didn't know what fork to use when I met you. I scraped the manure off, or at least I tried!" By this time his voice had risen, partly from emotion and partly against the approaching blare of the St. Patrick's Day parade. "All I've gotten in return are a lot of trumped-up accusations. Sterile. That's what I am . . ." Suddenly I realized he had come to believe everything he was saying, and in his mind he was being cruelly persecuted. No wonder he was loathe to part with a sum that would have been inconsequential to him. It was a matter of principle. "Sterile," he repeated, "for the past fifteen years. Nothing can change that fact. You were cheating on me all the time. No, don't give me that face, I knew about it, there was talk in the office . . ."

"What talk?" I yelled. "What insane thing now?"

"*Talk*, that's all. I don't know which guy it was, maybe that jerk with the nose, maybe Harley, how do I know, or some crummy elevator operator in the building. Reverting to type. Reverting to type! Well, I've had enough of you for the rest of my life, and I'm telling you . . ." He shook his walking stick at me, his face suffused with blood. He was as outraged as I.

". . . I'm telling you Kiernan's one of the best lawyers on the coast, and if you have any ideas about going to him with your crazy story don't be surprised if he throws you out. I warn you, Rose, we'll have the authorities take the kid away. It should have been done a long time ago, you're an unfit mother, a selfish, sloppy, dirty little nothing, and we'll see to it, you just bet your sweet little life, we'll see to it . . ."

My eyes, as though the muscles had been severed, brought me a vision of blurred, whirling furniture in which one thing, the coffeepot, stood out like a bright star each time it passed. I rushed to it, and rejoicing in its heavy lethalness, threw it with all my force at his head. Whether it struck him or not I never knew.

In a second his arms were pushing me back to the bureau so that its edge bit into my spine, and his face was straining over mine, his lips stricken dumb by the ultimate abuse. For a moment we stared into each other's eyes, then I pulled an arm free and grabbed for some object on the bureau to hit him with, missing my mark and feeling the blow of his fist on my arm. I twisted around and we struggled silently, knocking plates, hairbrushes, and even the gas burner to the floor in an earsplitting cascade. With a final effort he managed to pinion my arms behind my back, panting, almost growling. Then I felt his hands drop away. Grabbing his walking stick he ran from the room without a word, in his haste kicking the coffeepot which clattered across the floorboards, spilling out a long, twisted brown puddle. The parade was still marching by, the hearty boom of the drums throbbing through the window. Gradually my breath came back and I moved from the bureau, but as I did I felt a foreboding. Hurtling around the bureau, I saw Gloria lying on her side in the debris, the gas burner obscuring her head. I fell to my knees and tried to remove the burner, but my hand came back each time I extended it, and it was sometime later — the fact of her stillness had become a long-standing one, like an historical fact, and the food bits she lay among had slowly assumed the magnified texture of an art photo — that I finally removed the heavy object from her head, which was a pulp. My own head had become steadily packed by a shattering noise, like an amplification of tissue paper being torn wildly apart, and I saw that the room, the building, everything, was sliding down a crevasse and out the other side of the earth into darkness. My hands flew back from her, I scrambled to the center of the room, facing away from her, and the noise stopped. I felt suddenly light and at peace and I walked outside, barefoot, still in my bathrobe.

Someone touched my shoulder. I looked up and saw that it was evening. I was sitting in the tall weeds of an empty lot, under a light drizzle. The man who had touched my shoulder was a stranger to me, but he seemed to know me, and he brought me back to the room where I found two more strange men and Mrs. Catania.

I went to the crib, looking for Gloria, seeing from the corner of my eye a large stain by the bureau which stirred some memory that I quickly blocked out, going then to the bed. There my hand closed around a hard object between the covers. I pulled it out, the bottle I had fed her with that morning. But she was nowhere in the room and I could make nothing of it.

Chapter

10

THAT NIGHT I slept with Mrs. Catania on her narrow bed. I huddled against the wall and didn't answer when she spoke. There was something about her I could not bear; she was so old and frail and had so little. I was alone in a snowstorm. I plunged through snow up to my waist and the moon shone down in a frozen wash of white. I counted every step I took, pulling first my right foot from the heavy drifts, then my left, methodically and endlessly. By the time the room was gray with morning I had counted thousands and thousands of steps. Mrs. Catania was awake. I don't think she had slept all night, either.

"They said the hearing will be next week," she told me. "You stay here with me. I'll be good to you."

I was told to see a public defender, but instead I took the ferry to San Francisco and went to Mr. Kiernan's office. I didn't remember him clearly from his visit to my room but I had received a favorable impression, and now as I spoke to him I searched his face to see if I had been right. As I did so he gave a sigh. "I can't represent you at the hearing, Miss Davies. I'm very sorry."

"Are you?" I asked, but I did not mind deeply. At his first words I had already drawn back into my snowstorm and his voice now came to me as from a distance.

"But," he continued, "neither will I represent Patrick. For family reasons, I want nothing to do with the case." He paused for a moment and went on. "But I'll get you a lawyer." He paused again. "I feel I should warn you that Patrick has two things on his side, an unshakable belief in his own innocence, and witnesses who will support him despite evidence to the contrary."

"The two things don't fit together," I observed from my great distance.

"Well, you know the man, Miss Davies, perhaps better than anyone else. Which is a mystery in itself."

"Yes, it's a mystery," I agreed.

"In any case, all you can do is tell the lawyer the truth and hope for the best. A great deal will depend on the judge who hears the case, but I think that under any circumstances the decision must be involuntary manslaughter."

"I can't pay a lawyer, you know," I told him.

"That doesn't matter." He shook hands with me, looking at my face with his kind, melancholy eyes.

Mr. Venning, the lawyer Mr. Kiernan chose for me, was a squat young man with sharp blue eyes that overlooked nothing. He took me to my room and had me reenact the scene, which I did with a wooden objectivity, as though following a script. I watched him search for anything Mr. Leary might have left behind, but he didn't come up with as much as a cigar butt. And we could not trace his automobile, though I knew he owned a 1936 Buick which he must have parked in the neighborhood. Nor had anyone seen him; owing to the parade the tenants had all been outside, where there had been such a crowd that no one would have noticed a resplendently dressed stranger.

"His filthy luck, as usual," I said.

"You'd better not talk that way at the hearing," Mr. Venning suggested. I could tell that he considered me a discouraging client. I had been fired from my job, had tried to get an abortion, had been known as an irresponsible mother at the Mary Stone Home, had run away from there and moved with the baby to a slum where by my own admission I had allowed someone else to do most of the work in taking care of her. I was indifferently groomed and spoke listlessly. Everything I told him cut the ground from under me, and yet I was certain that the hearing would go my way. "He was here with me," I said dogmatically. "He'll be punished."

"You can't even prove that you knew him outside the office."

"Plenty of people knew. Mr. Kiernan himself. He gave me the money for the abortion."

"I think we'll forget about that," Mr. Venning said shortly. "I think that's something you've misconstrued entirely. Mr. Kiernan isn't involved in this."

"He came to my room, he gave me a hundred and fifty dollars."

"I think you should remember that it's due to Mr. Kiernan's kindness that you've got a lawyer. I think you should remember that. You owe him something. Now, put him out of your mind and just let me handle the case as I see fit. What about the people who saw you and this man Leary together?"

"There was my landlady for one," I said sullenly. "And the

waiters at the restaurants, and lots of his acquaintances, only I don't know their names."

"Count the waiters out, and the acquaintances. But I'll check the landlady." He dropped his professional tone and asked, "What do you really want out of this, Rose? I get the feeling that you want to indict this man for no less than murder and go free yourself."

I nodded, taking out a cigarette. "I want that."

"It's not going to happen."

I nodded again. "It will happen. He did it. I didn't."

"Did what?"

I wanted to say: He was the one who pushed the burner off the bureau and killed Gloria, but I could not phrase the words for fear that they would bring life to the scene I had managed to deaden. I shrugged my shoulders. "It was him. It wasn't me."

He rose to go.

"I want . . ." I said, "I want the judge to know what he is. I want everybody to know."

"That's not important," he said emphatically. "It's not healthy. It's yourself you should be thinking about, your future."

He returned a couple of days later. Mrs. Catania and I were eating. He had spoken to my landlady who said that I had associated with some young men but she had never seen me with anyone fitting Mr. Leary's description.

"But she was always asking questions about him," I said.

"She's evidently been prevailed on to change her mind. But what about these young men?"

"She must have meant Paul, he used to live there. And Harley Munck from work, Mr. Leary's nephew. He took me to a show once in a while."

"Did you have sexual intercourse with either of them?"

Mrs. Catania grimaced and put her hands to her ears.

"No. Only with Mr. Leary."

"Only with him," he said, shaking his head. "For over a year. A man old enough to be your father, whom you say you hated. A man you shared no interests with, who never gave you anything outside of a dinner now and then."

"Are you doubting me?"

"No. Only you present a strange picture, Rose. You're not easy to understand."

"She's a good girl," Mrs. Catania said, patting my hand.

The hearing was held at the Hall of Justice. My clothes had been painstakingly washed, mended, and ironed by Mrs. Catania, my shoes were resoled and polished, my hair neatly braided and wound up in a coil. Earlier Mr. Venning had given me a pair of girlish white gloves to carry — not to wear, for he had also given me a wedding ring to show that I cared about appearances and to make me look pathetic. I had never owned a pair of gloves and I carried them stiffly before me like a bouquet. It seemed I was scrubbed clean of all feeling, from everything around me; so complete was my insulation that as I entered the lobby with Mrs. Catania I wondered for a moment what I was doing there. But I was brought abruptly to a sense of my surroundings: in a dark, sober suit and his high collar, Mr. Leary was standing by the stairs with another man. "What is it?" Mrs. Catania asked as I drew back. Not trusting myself to reply, I walked on as Mr. Leary nodded courteously. Upstairs Mrs. Catania sat down in the outer office and I went into the judge's chambers where Mr. Venning was already seated.

A few minutes later Mr. Leary and his lawyer came in, and now, against my will my eyes swung to his face. He returned my look with an impersonal but not unfriendly reflectiveness, and then gave a patient, courteous smile. I looked away, the edges of my breathing already ragged, and for the first time since that day I heard again the shredding, tearing noise, which seemed to emanate from inside me. At the same time I was startled by the light in the room. The sun from the window blinded me, and my hands seemed unbearably alive. I lifted them and studied them, thin, too white, yet astonishingly alive, with the veins running blue and long to the sharp knuckles.

"Put your hands down," Mr. Venning whispered. "Don't make an issue of the ring."

I stared at Mr. Venning's face in the light, its familiar vagueness falling away like a veil, revealing every pore, every individual hair at the temple; his eyes, pierced by the light from the window, looked deep and swarming with life, like oceans. I dropped my hands, shattered by a sudden, clear memory of Gloria's eyes.

I felt Mr. Venning's hand on my arm, gently prodding me. I became aware of the judge's voice; he was asking me the manner in which the child had been killed. I moved my lips tentatively, the words coming out so faintly that I was asked to repeat them. When the same question was put to Mr. Leary he said he knew nothing about it. I twisted around in my chair, barely keeping a cry back.

"The police report," the judge said to me, "indicates that you were gone for more than five hours after the child died. Where did you go?"

"I don't remember," I said, fighting to control my voice. "They found me in a vacant lot."

"Is it possible you went to the quarters of the man you had the fight with, to wait for him?"

My control vanished, I pointed with my whole arm at Mr. Leary. "He's the man I fought with, I didn't go to anybody's quarters."

"Miss Davies," the judge said, "will you please tell us what your relationship with Mr. Leary has been?"

"Yes. I'll tell you." I leaned sharply forward, my eyes clamped into the face of my enemy. He had put on a pair of spectacles, and now, pushing them a trifle down the bridge of his nose, peered over them with an expression of candid interest. I plunged, describing our affair fully, leaving no detail out, but when I concluded it was on a low note, for I was sure I smelled opprobrium in the air like a subtle stench. After all, night after night I had slept with this specimen I had just finished reviling. It was reason enough for the deepest contempt. Mr. Leary was scratching his temple. The judge now nodded at him for his comments.

"Your Honor," he began, removing the spectacles with a frown, "I knew Miss Davies as a file clerk in my office, and as my nephew's girl friend. He also worked in my office. I was, naturally, friendly to her in the course of our work, and she may have misinterpreted this . . . anyway, after she left the office she began to telephone me with all sorts of irrational charges she had thought up. I went to my nephew. He said he had broken off with her because he had found her to be, what shall I say — well, I won't mince matters — mental."

"What?" I cried.

"Well, the calls stopped for a long while," he went on. "Then they resumed. I discussed the situation with my wife and we decided not to go to the authorities but to ignore the calls. My wife . . ." He paused and looked at me for the first time with reproach, "My wife was very ill at the time, and in fact passed away only three weeks ago. Miss Davies's calls were very trying, to say the least, coming just then. In any case, just after her child's death Miss Davies called me again, this time demanding a sum of money . . ."

"What was the sum?" the judge asked.

"It was one thousand dollars. I told her, of course, that I refused, and she then said she would implicate me in the child's death, and this is what has happened."

Mr. Venning stood up, his face flushed. "You've accused my client of blackmail."

"No," Mr. Leary responded, putting on his spectacles, "no, this is a very young, very unstable girl with overwhelming problems, I don't think she knew what she was doing. I have only sympathy for her."

"I don't care about your sympathy, you've accused her of blackmail."

Mr. Leary lifted his hands and shrugged helplessly.

"Mr. Leary," the judge asked briskly, "were you present when the child died?"

He said he had been with an old friend who had just bought a new automobile. They had taken a ride down the peninsula. He was still shaken by his wife's death and wanted to get out into the country. His lawyer, speaking for the first time, said that the witness was available for questioning.

"Were you the child's father?" the judge asked Mr. Leary.

"I have here," the lawyer said, handing him a piece of paper, "a statement by Dr. R. V. Harris testifying that my client has been sterile for the past fifteen years due to a hydrocelic condition." The judge read it and handed it back.

"Would you agree to have your client examined by another doctor?" Mr. Venning asked, and I strained forward in my chair, knowing already that the statement would hold, that the hearing was over.

"Rotten, lying bastard!" I managed to shout before Mr. Venning cut me off.

"There is no necessity for a second examination," the judge answered Mr. Venning, ignoring my outburst, and in the same breath he said briefly, "I don't consider that the evidence I've heard here constitutes grounds for a court trial. This is clearly a case of involuntary manslaughter, and as such requires no further proceedings." That was all. He stood up from the table with an imperceptible sigh.

"Judge O'Connor!" Mr. Venning said in an outraged voice. The judge picked up his papers. Mr. Venning stared at him for a moment, then with an angry shrug turned away.

"How did it go?" Mrs. Catania whispered to me in the outer office. "They didn't give you a jail sentence, did they?"

I nodded, my eyes following Mr. Leary as he walked out the door. It was the last I saw of him for twenty-three years.

Mrs. Catania looked tired and ill. Every day I said, "I should get up and find a job and let you get some rest." But when I finally got up I stayed in my bathrobe, leafed through my friend's Italian newspaper or just sat in a chair, not thinking. I was pained when I looked at the old woman, and I would look away; I could not bear to see her grief.

Sometimes I thought of Gloria, of Mr. Leary, but they were curiously unmoving memories, for I saw them as though from a height of miles and they were so tiny and distant that they were unrelated to me as I sat in the chair in my bathrobe. Whenever

Mrs. Catania spoke of Gloria I hushed her. Gradually she stopped referring to her.

One day she went to the doctor and came home with some pills, saying she was sure she would feel better soon. But as she stood at the stove that evening preparing our meal I was shocked; her face was sallow, her eyes and mouth sunken, and the thin arthritic hands were already stamped with a terrible inner stillness. The next day when she went shopping I packed my suitcase and walked away. It would have hurt me to see her death.

I had walked several miles, almost to Berkeley, when I realized that my feet were burning and that I had no place to go. A bus came roaring down the street and it occurred to me that I could step forward and bow down under its wheels and find a permanent, peaceful place for myself, and I watched its approach with a pleased, dreamy smile. I stepped out into the street, but far too slowly, for the bus came to a shuddering halt just in front of my toes. Annoyed by the open-mouthed faces pressed to the bus's windows, I walked slowly away, my feet still burning. I took my shoes off and felt better. The shadows were lengthening, the spring air had a sharp edge. I longed for a warm bed. Going through my purse, I came up with a nickel and went into a phone booth and rang up the gas station where Harley Munck worked. He was astonished to hear from me, where had I been all this time, why hadn't I written? I brushed his questions aside and arranged to meet him the following day in Union Square.

I slept that night at the Oakland depot and in the morning took the ferry once more to San Francisco. I had plenty of time to kill when I got there and since it had come to me that I looked crumpled and shabby I went into a crowded department store, found a smart blue coat on the rack, and walked down the backstairs with it, stuffing my old coat into a trash can on the way. It was a simple and graceful thing to do and I felt soothed by it. That afternoon I met Harley as planned and in the evening he found a room for me. It was a few days before he got up the nerve to sleep with me, but once he did he was mine. A week later we were married at City Hall.

Harley was radiant for the first and last time in his life. I watched him indifferently as he introduced me to his room with apology and pride. He had tried to make it homey for me; it was cluttered with vases of daisies and the broken ,divan was draped with a garish shawl. "But you're so quiet," he said when I had looked around. I smiled and kissed him. It was enough for him, it stopped his voice.

A wedding present arrived — a check for a hundred dollars from Mr. Leary, mailed on the eve of a trip to Hawaii.

"That was swell of Uncle Patrick," Harley said, "remembering us, with Aunt Bea passing on last month and all."

"What was she like?" I asked sharply.

"Aunt Bea?" he said, thinking back. "I don't know. She was a lady."

"Is that all?"

"No. I don't know. My cousins were crazy about her; for instance, I don't think Frank, especially, will ever get over her dying."

"You liked her too, didn't you?"

He nodded. "You know why? Because she always made me feel at home in her house when I was a kid."

"Is that all?"

"It's a lot. It's like somebody takes time for you."

I looked at his long pale face and tight ears all bathed in a naked glow of sincerity. "You're like that, too," I observed, and his eyes shone with pleasure.

"We're not going to stay in this dump," he said with sudden vitality. I nodded, but I wasn't interested. How strange it was that I was Mr. Leary's niece by marriage. I would always have him at my fingertips, so to speak, and I had time — mountain ranges of time, such as the dead have — to decide what to do with the proximity.

Harley's family was very small. There was only Mr. Leary, his cousins Frank and Cathleen, and his Aunt Monica, Mr. Leary's sister. Aunt Monica was an indigent spinster who attended funerals and pestered her relatives shamelessly for their company. She visited us almost every day and the strain began to tell on me. I explained to Harley that the city made me nervous. It was not difficult to persuade him to leave his job at the gas station and move. He felt that with me he had luck on his side. First we moved to San Jose — I found it too big — then to Richmond — still too big — and finally we came to Port Carquinez and moved into the little house on Railroad Hill where there was nothing to hear but the wind in the trees and the occasional cry of a freight train. Harley got a job at the brickworks down the tracks and by degrees gave up his accounting course. My nerves repaired in my new surroundings. I slept a great deal, read books, and took long solitary walks. At the end of the first year I saw with surprise that a bloom of decay had already sprouted on Harley. I put my arms around him with sudden tearing regret, and then the moment passed and never returned.

Chapter

11

AND NOW I closed the door on Mr. Leary's thin, enraged voice and the carving knife still vibrating in the wall. Though my movements were steady my body was feverish with excitement, and lying down on top of the covers, I pulled off my pajamas and threw them to the floor. Neither daring to sleep nor able to, I tossed and turned through the rest of the night, quieting only when the sun began streaming through the window to lie warm across my naked body. It was midmorning when I got up. I had not stayed in bed so late for years; usually I was up at dawn, and watched the scrub oaks and towering windbreaks of eucalypti catch the sun on one side, casting long violet shadows down the hill to the town below, where the streets were still cool with night. At that early hour you could smell so sharply the saltiness of the water and the dewed flowers and old wood. I always loved that hour, for I felt I possessed the town then. But by midmorning it was everyone's. Through the window I saw Shotwell in his backyard with Felix and some other man, sitting on the old discarded chesterfield whose stuffings hung to the ground. Nearby, Steve, Shotwell's oldest boy, gunned his motorcycle, somehow maliciously. The stranger was the man I had seen with Shotwell the night before. He was wearing sharply creased khaki trousers and a white shirt whose sleeves were rolled up to the elbows, and he looked out of place in the littered yard with old Felix and Shotwell, a slovenly boor. As I watched I saw them get up and go to the gate. The stranger walked with a couched vigor.

I stretched luxuriously. It was a beautiful morning, the strait turquoise, the hills white gold. The day seemed long, as all the days to come seemed, immeasurable and filled with promise. All these years I had known somewhere in the back of my mind how it would be: my nearest neighbors separated from me by an empty lot, no visitors, no one and nothing but us two, Mr. Leary and me. I had never feared that he would die of simple old age in the meantime; he was like an animal that always finds a hole to hide in, and outlives the whole jungle to sit with blind satisfaction in the last rays of the sun. But there was no hole for him to hide in now.

I was curious to find where he would be, perhaps behind the drapes again or hiding in some corner, but I doubted it; I had struck his cringing tearfulness from him like a mold. The thought excited me; I began to dress. My face felt different, swollen, as though the blood underneath were turgid. I sensed my body keenly and stroked my arm, felt the tickling of the scatter rug under my bare feet. I have narrow, well-formed feet, very white, but for some reason the thought of them troubled me, the thought of my body troubled me. I put on my dress with a feeling of annoyance; I should get some new dresses.

When I opened the door I pulled it back sharply, in case he

was waiting there with the knife. He was stronger than I had believed. His weak point was his balance.

But he wasn't there, nor was the knife. He was sitting on the sofa in the living room, without the knife, haggard but composed. The change in him from the day before was astonishing.

He looked at me coldly. "Frank left my wheelchair here. Open it up for me."

"Do it yourself."

His look changed to one of fury. Of course he couldn't do it himself.

"Are you able to attend to yourself?" I asked casually, savoring the words. "You understand what I mean?"

For a moment I thought he would cry out in helplessness and rage, but he only said, "If you think you can get at me by reminding me I'm old, you're simpleminded. This place has made you stupid."

"On the contrary. It's preserved my singleness of purpose."

"What do you do here all day?" he asked loudly. "I'm sorry for you, living in a dump like this. I'm really sorry for you. What the hell do you do?"

"Our concern is what you will do, Mr. Leary. What are you used to doing in that old people's home? Crocheting? Polishing your false teeth?"

"Christ," he said with disgust.

I made breakfast, setting two places on the table which I drew up to the sofa. He ate like a beast; I never knew an old man could have such an appetite. His manners had grown very shabby; he stuffed the food into his mouth and some of it fell on his shirtfront.

"You've changed from what you were, Uncle. You were proud of yourself in those days. Look at you now." He made no reply, but continued to stuff himself. "Are you finished?" I asked abruptly. "Good, I'll just clear up," and I pulled the table away from the sofa, leaving him sitting there with his fork in his hand.

"I wasn't finished!"

"Then you must learn to eat faster, Uncle."

"Uncle!" he shouted. "I was Harley's uncle, not yours, never yours, you low bitch! Don't call me uncle!"

I was fascinated —he pulled at his hair, at the few strands that decorated his blue-veined temples, and his knobby fingers shook. Then his hand slipped down to his eyes and he sat like that for a long time.

Later I went back to the living room and sat down at the sewing machine, having decided to brush up on my sewing in order to make myself some dresses. The machine was next to the sofa where Mr. Leary still sat, not having moved an inch since breakfast. He was slumped back, his eyes closed, asleep. I bent over the material and grew absorbed in my work when suddenly the sound of a frenzied leap jolted me; the next second he had my neck in the crook of his good arm and was squeezing with all his strength, pressing my eyeballs into a throbbing stare that took in the hairy grottos of his nostrils. Struggling to my feet, it took me a while to break free; my windpipe felt broken; I stared at him and tried to laugh, my hands trembling on my hips, and without a word between us I sat down at the sewing machine again and took up my work. We were both breathing in diminishing gasps, like lovers after the final spasm.

It was a long time before I knew my voice would be steady. When it was, I said, "Are you concerned about your future? Are you taking into account the complications that would arise if you managed to pull off the sort of thing you just tried?"

I didn't want to discourage him; I was honestly curious.

"I could ask you the same question," he answered almost courteously, almost hopefully, and I realized that he would willingly exchange our battle for a shallow discussion that might clear the air of all but a little workaday dislike. Already he was tired. He was an old man with an old man's small lecheries for quiet corners and quilts and cups of broth, and more than that, he was depthless, always had been. If I began to treat him as an elderly boarder, no more, no less, he would with relief forget everything else; his husbanded strength would collapse. Nothing went deep in him, nothing. The only thing capable of stirring him was fear. He was a treasure house of fear. I must keep my hand plunged into those riches.

"I could ask you the same thing," he repeated stubbornly, but still mild and courteous.

"You mean how will I go about killing you," I said, "without arousing suspicion? I won't have any difficulty. I'm intelligent, Mr. Leary. You aren't. You never were. If you hadn't married into money you'd have wound up one of those stupefied derelicts with cardboard in their shoes. Even with money, you didn't accomplish anything." I knew that when his wife died she had left everything to her children, and he had invested the money he had in a burst of mindless grandioseness that had eventually forced him to move into a modest flat on upper Market. In the years since, he had turned to his children for loans, but without marked success.

"Isn't it odd," I went on, "that no one wanted you when you got old, that no one ever came to visit you at Twin Oaks, that to all intents and purposes you were dead, your life had been a waste?"

He said nothing, though I could see his mouth working. Finally the words came out in a feeble yet triumphant rush. "You're the failure. You were going to be so much, and look at you, you poor old spinster."

"Spinster?" I asked, amused. "I admit Harley wasn't much, but . . ."

"No, he wasn't much, but he was enough for you. And what do you know about me? You haven't seen me in God knows how many years, *you* don't know who came to visit me at Twin Oaks . . ."

I shriveled at his transparency. If he was going to lie, let him do it well, as he had in the past.

"Don't you know that Aunt Monica and I are friends?" I asked. That was all I had to say. Old Aunt Monica was the only visitor he ever had at Twin Oaks except at Christmas and Easter when Frank or Cathleen came by for a few minutes.

He stroked his left hand reflectively. Suddenly he flashed, "She'll be coming over here to visit me. She's my sister, after all, you can't keep her away."

"She's just as old and feeble as you. She'll soon die."

"Frank will come."

"Frank will not come."

"He will!"

"Why should he? You're nothing to him."

"Nothing to Frank, my own son?" His face went red with anger and his mouth began to work again.

"Don't overexcite yourself," I said, "or you'll have an accident. I really think you should let me help you into the bathroom now."

"No, get my wheelchair," he commanded.

"That's for you to do," I replied, offering him my arm, alert for any sudden movement on his part. And finally, after a long while, he moved, rising with my help, and I half carried him into the bathroom. "You must have a marvelous bladder," I remarked, letting go of him as he sat down on the rim of the bathtub. "Just call if you need me."

He was in there at least half an hour after the toilet flushed, apparently fighting the need to be helped back. At last I heard a resentful call and I returned. But as I took his arm I heard a sound that made me stop short, at a loss for the first time. No one ever came to see me, no one from town, no door-to-door salesmen; the steep steps were too much bother. I looked at Mr. Leary, but he dared not cry out; and suddenly the knocking stopped, and I could hear footsteps crossing the porch and going down the steps. Through the bathroom window I caught a glimpse of the man I had seen with Shotwell and Felix.

The rest of the day Mr. Leary spent lying on the sofa, his eyes open, his mind apparently clicking away. When it grew dark and he asked me to help him to his room, I did so without a moment's hesitation, concealing my wariness, and locked the door behind him.

I awoke refreshed by a good night's sleep and went to my guest's room to wake him. I had created a charming little nook from the hole Harley had inhabited. I had even waxed the floor, and now it reflected the sunlight cheerfully. Mr. Leary lay on the bed like a sore. His clothes were wrinkled — he had slept in them — and a gray stubble covered his cheeks, his eyes looked inflamed, his wisps of hair stood on end.

"Bad night?" I asked, getting him off the bed into a chair. He seemed weak and spiritless. I noticed that the wood around the doorknob was gouged raw. That accounted for his weariness;

he had been at it with the knife all night. "It won't work," I told him. "The wood's too strong. Well, we must certainly give you a shave, you look reprehensible. But first we'll eat."

I had just gone into the kitchen when once again I was drawn up by the sound of knocking.

"Somebody at the door! Somebody at the door!" Mr. Leary screamed at the top of his lungs, "Hang on! Don't go away!"

I slammed the door of his room shut and, because he had made it necessary, answered the front door. It was the same man who had come the day before.

"Mrs. Munck?" he asked, glancing behind me to the place where the cries had emanated from, then looking back at me. "My name is Husar. Vincent Husar. I represent Jason Enterprises. You're probably acquainted with some of our work in the area, the Rio del Sol Marina . . ."

"Yes," I said sharply, "I've been there."

"I'd appreciate very much if I could talk with you for a few minutes," he continued in a breezy, direct manner, and then his eyes narrowed. Following his gaze, I turned around. Mr. Leary was crawling into the living room with the carving knife between his teeth, his eyes lifted in a wild look of supplication and triumph. Now he let the knife fall from his teeth and cried, "You there! Help me!"

I forced myself to turn my back on him. "It's my uncle," I explained. "If you'll excuse me, I must get that knife away from him. I don't know where he got hold of it, I try to keep everything sharp out of his reach . . ."

Mr. Leary had replaced the knife between his teeth and was crawling toward us like a maimed insect. I walked over to him and pried the knife out from between his teeth, saying over my shoulder, "Mr. Husar, we'll have to postpone our talk."

"Call my son Frank Leary, San Francisco!" the old man screamed. "He's in the phone book. Call him, tell him I have to defend myself with a knife. Call the police! The police!"

I hovered over him uncertainly. "He's never been so wrought up," I told my visitor nervously. I could not make out the man's expression through the screen door. Now the door snapped sharply as he pulled it and found it locked. "I'll help you," he said, but I could not tell if he was addressing Mr. Leary or me.

"I can handle him best alone, strangers upset him," I ventured, and waited.

"I'll come back this afternoon, then," he said. "Is that convenient for you?"

"Yes, that's fine," I said, not showing my relief in my voice.

Mr. Leary remained where he was on the floor, exhausted, and I went back to the kitchen to make breakfast, furious to have been intruded upon, after all these years, just when Mr. Leary had finally arrived. When I brought the breakfast in, he had gotten up on the sofa and now he looked pleased, almost smug, reassured by our visitor's promise to return. I set the food on the table and then pulled it three feet away from him and began to eat. There grew a look of vast longing on his face. Every once in a while his eyes would move from the food to my face with a reproachful look, and I could sense his salivary glands working. Food was of vital importance to him, for it gave him whatever strength he had. Finally he slid stiffly off the sofa and crawled to the table. He tried several times to stand up but it was impossible, so he sat on the floor, half under the table, and reached blindly over its top with his veiny old hand and drew bits of food down to his mouth.

"That's right," I said, "do it that way or you won't get anything."

He munched on toast, on a strip of bacon, he even pulled down a handful of scrambled eggs.

"Pig," I said.

"Pig yourself," he countered dully. His heart wasn't in it.

I threw a napkin down into his lap. "Use it. If you leave one crumb on the rug I'll eat alone from now on and you won't get a bite."

He picked up all the little crumbs between his horny fingernails and laid them in the napkin.

After breakfast I went into his room and opened his suitcase. I took out a clean shirt and his shaving things and brought them into the living room where he was sitting on the floor, leaning against the sofa. "We must clean you up for our visitor," I told him.

He was docile when I spread the lather over his bristles; but when I fixed a new razor in the holder his eyes grew suddenly frightened. But I had no intention of cutting him, for it would draw Mr. Husar's suspicion to me, especially in the light of the claims the old man was sure to make. "Don't worry," I said, "I'll be careful." I stretched the sagging skin of his cheek and drew the razor across it. The temptation was too much; his small eyes peered apprehensively down his face to the gash where the blood streamed boldly onto his shirtfront. "So much blood," I said nervously, but with gratification. By the time I had finished — cutting him only twice more — the first gash had stopped bleeding. I got some rubbing alcohol from the bathroom and rubbed it into the cut, murmuring, "It hurts, doesn't it? Have you ever been hurt before?" His eyes streamed, his old lips bumped together, but he made no sound. I wiped his face off with a towel, then I combed his sparse hair down and stepped back. His face looked like that of an aged fetus, a dead smooth whiteness hanging from the skull in thick folds. Only the cuts had any color. I unbuttoned the bloody shirt and pulled it off him, and then removed the undershirt. His caved-in thorax was covered with long white hairs under which the two mounds of his breasts sagged down to the mound of his belly. I threw the clean shirt on his lap.

He struggled with the shirt, and when it was finally on he dragged himself onto the sofa, the pain forgotten, an almost unbearable anticipation in his eyes. I too was excited. I was feeding on some new substance, some wondrously nourishing, highly charged stuff to which I was already addicted. And I had handled the unexpected difficulties so smoothly that I was now actually thankful to Mr. Husar for having given me the opportunity to grasp the dimensions of my resourcefulness.

As we waited, I thought back to the only visitors Harley and I had ever had. One was Felix, who came around one spring evening many years ago looking for his pup, Dave. The other was the doctor, whom I called for Harley when he got sick. (A week later Harley developed complications — an accomplishment in itself for him — and in another week he was dead.)

Mr. Husar did not arrive until four o'clock. By that time Mr. Leary was sick with nervousness, but when the knock finally sounded he smiled broadly, almost sweetly, as though his future was secured.

Chapter

12

I ANSWERED the door and ushered Mr. Husar in, and even before I had finished introducing the two men, Mr. Leary had drawn the stranger close and was whispering into his ear.

"Uncle Patrick," I admonished, "none of that. You promised."

But the old man, now bold as brass, said aloud to our visitor, "Did you hear me? Do you understand?"

Mr. Husar frowned in my direction.

"I'm sorry," I said, "he persists in grabbing people . . ."

"It doesn't matter. Now, what I'd like to discuss with you . . ."

"Sit down!" Mr. Leary insisted, "next to me."

Mr. Husar seated himself and began in a loud voice: "Mrs. Munck, you probably know that my firm, Jason Enterprises, has been interested in Port Carquinez for some time now as the site for a marina . . ."

"This is an unlikely spot for anything but exactly what it is," I said sharply. "It's a backwater. There must be such places."

"Why?" he asked, sitting back and lighting a cigarette with a flashy-looking lighter. His voice was rather high-pitched, metallic.

"Did you understand what I told you?" Mr. Leary broke in. Then, showing some strain, he went on in a respectful tone, "I know you've got other things on your mind, Mr. Husar, but this is terrible . . ." He gave me a glance and plunged on, "A terrible situation. I wish you'd give me your attention."

Our guest looked at me again with a frown, but then the expression flopped over to one of jolly anticipation, and he puffed on his cigarette quite at ease.

Mr. Leary pointed to the cuts on his face. "She did this, cut me purposely while she shaved me. Would I cut myself so deeply?"

Mr. Husar put the question to me with a lift of his eyebrows.

"Go on, Uncle Patrick, Mr. Husar doesn't have all day."

"She won't unfold the wheelchair for me. I have to crawl on the floor. That's right, you saw me. And eat off the floor, too, like an animal. Listen here, do I sound like a raving lunatic or do I sound like a reasonable man?"

There was no response from Mr. Husar. He had quickly grown bored and preoccupied. His expression, his whole personality seemed highly equivocal, as did his physical appearance. He was heavyset, almost stout, yet he carried his bulk with a breezy lightness, a bounce and vigor that was in accord with the casual, collegiate khaki trousers and the white shirt with its rolled up sleeves. His face was that of a man of about forty, crude featured, with a high color. The lips were V-shaped, sensual, loose, slightly teasing, but at moments compressed to a grim line; the thrusting nose was at a glance majestic, but close up revealed pits, as though it had once been the site of a tedious case of acne; and the quick, alert eyes — which were a shade of gray that flashed from slate to silver — were overhung by heavy lids that now seemed razor-shrewd, now lethargic. His hands were well formed, and the color his florid face should have been, amber, sun-warmed. They were restless, but sometimes sat solidly on his lap in two strong fists.

"Call the place where I used to live," Mr. Leary went on, his voice rising, "Twin Oaks Nursing Home, San Francisco, and ask them if I'm not of sound mind. Call my son, Frank Leary, San Francisco!" he demanded. "Call my daughter, Cathleen Price, San Rafael. Ask them. You've got a pen, write down their names and call them for God's sake and tell them that Rose Munck is going to kill me! Take that pen out of your pocket, damn you, and write!"

Mr. Husar bounced to his feet. "Sorry," he said to the old man, and turning to me, "May I see you on the front porch for a minute?"

"Take that pen out of your pocket!" Mr. Leary shrieked, at which our guest went outside. I followed him, closing the door on the noise. It gratified me to see this man's purpose obstructed by the scene. I had come across his type in books (I have probably read every book in the public library, walking six miles along the tracks to Martinez twice a week and lugging back as many volumes as will fit into my big net bag) and now, after having read about him as one reads about the Huns or Romans, I was looking at a Land Developer in the flesh, here, in lost, cinder-swept Port Carquinez. It pleased me that he squinted irritably at the door and then at his watch. His eyes shone like tinfoil from his fleshy face.

"It'll be a week before I'll be back from the city," he said. "We'll have to talk then."

"No. You've made me very anxious, Mr. Husar. Port

Carquinez has been my home for almost twenty-five years. Tell me what you want."

A few minutes later I slammed the door behind me and leaned against it. They were buying up the land along the waterfront for a marina. All the other homes on the hill had already been purchased. The frontage had been leased from the Southern Pacific. They would give me a good price for my house. None of this was in the future, it was here, now, an irrevocable fact. I pressed my hands to my face in sudden bereavement and my sense of ruin was turned like a landslide on the old man; I wanted to kill him, savagely, now, this moment, and he knew it. His face drained of color as I started toward him. "Rose," he said without moving his lips, and then with a superhuman effort he grabbed a nearby stool and sent it crashing through the front window.

The next moment Mr. Husar's astonished face appeared, framed by the remaining glass. "What the hell's wrong with him?" he demanded, and receiving no reply, he picked up the stool. "Open the door."

I did as he said, frantically trying to gather my wits together and glancing at Mr. Leary, whose head was pulled down into his shoulders like an animal preparing for the last leap. As soon as Mr. Husar was at his side the old man was all over him and the color flowed back into his cheeks. "Promise you won't leave without me," he cried. "You've got to take me with you."

Mr. Husar gave a sigh and turned away, but the old man grabbed his hand. "Hear me out," he said frantically, casting me a wild look. "I was at Twin Oaks, a nursing home, I liked it there, I didn't want to come here, it was her idea, she wants me here. Listen . . . listen . . . she was in love with me . . ." And frightened as he was, there was pride in his voice; I could see him in some cobwebbed chamber of his memory, touching all the old furniture of his allure. Then it passed and he looked worriedly at his listener.

"I take it that was some time ago?" Mr. Husar said with such seriousness that my eyes jerked to his face. But he was looking with restrained amusement at the old man.

"Oh God, yes," Mr. Leary replied, "twenty-five years ago. But there was more to it than that." Now his lips beat soundlessly together. He was afraid to go on. Suddenly he began to cry, wantonly, as though all were lost.

"Maybe you ought to call a doctor," Mr. Husar suggested.

"The doctor is coming tomorrow," I lied.

"She's lying," Mr. Leary accused through his tears.

"Do you want to sit in your wheelchair now?" Mr. Husar asked him. "Is that all right?" he asked me.

"Of course," I said, and he unfolded it and helped him into a comfortable position.

"Are you going?" Mr. Leary asked, wiping his streaming eyes.

"I'll drop in on you again," Mr. Husar said, giving him a casual pat on the shoulder.

"Please do," Mr. Leary whispered. "Please do, if I'm still alive."

"I'm sure you will be," Mr. Husar said, glancing at his watch and going to the door. I walked him to the gate, but suddenly I hung back, sickened by his closeness. What a horror human beings were, with their penetrating eyes, their busy tongues and hands and shifting feet . . . for a second I could visualize a milling crowd where the quiet frontage lay. "I must go in," I said.

"We'll have our talk next week then."

I nodded.

"And in the meantime, just a suggestion . . . maybe

you should think about putting him into a hospital."

"He just came out of a hospital, Mr. Husar," I retorted, offended by his familiarity. "His family left him with me for a little personal care and affection to offset the dehumanizing effect of his confinement." I realized what I had said was ridiculously stilted and affected, but he suddenly looked at me with admiration and beamed me a smile, a token of the expansive energy that seemed to bring such healthy color to his crude face. And swinging the gate open, he started down the steps, the smile already gone. He looked now, I thought, like a Cossack, with his large nose, grim mouth, and heavy-lidded eyes, and I watched him slipping away into the world of mercenary councils of war and coups d'état. At the bottom of the steps he climbed into a low-slung sports car and roared away, leaving a cloud of gravel dust behind him.

I went back inside. Mr. Leary looked exhausted but his wheelchair lent him some confidence.

"I want to lock you in your room for a while," I told him. He looked carefully at my face, saw that I was calm and preoccupied, and wheeled himself to his room. He was skillful in the wheelchair and took pride in it. "I'll be back soon," I said, and as I started to close his door I caught sight of the tip of the carving knife protruding from under the mattress. I wondered if, in just the short space of time I had stood with Mr. Husar at the gate, the old man had started some new project with the knife, and seeing that one of his shirts was draped most artfully across the windowsill, I went over and picked it up. Sure enough, beneath it the wood was gashed white. "No matter," I said, glancing at his tense face and carelessly dropping the shirt back. Before his arrival I had made sure to hammer that particular window fast from the outside.

Walking down the steps, I trailed my fingers through the tall dry grass, listening to the familiar sound of my feet on the old wood. I knew each step individually; this one leaned to the right, this one to the left, this one was cracked down the middle, the next five were sturdy, but the sixth you must skip. At the bottom I saw Felix sitting in the sinking sun before his bait shop, and I hurried by, unable to face so much as a nod from another human being. Sal's grocery store was empty except for Sal, sitting behind the scarred counter watching television. I remembered how Harley had spent most of his nights at the Railroad Bar up the street, nursing a beer through endless television programs, coming home late to speak of personalities I had never heard of, almost as though they were dear friends. I went to the public phone in the corner without speaking to Sal. The beauty of having lived in a place for twenty-odd years was that people came to accept you as you were and did not ask for the amenities. I called the glaziers in Martinez and they said they would come the next morning. Slamming the screen door hard behind me — sometimes Sal irritated me with his big, accepting but curious eyes — I walked down toward the water, noticing that Felix had gotten up and with old Dave was following me. I stopped and faced him, incensed that people kept forcing themselves on me.

"Guess you had a visitor today, Mrs. Munck," he said, as Dave sniffed around my feet.

"Yes."

"He's been hanging around, talking to people. Wondered when he'd get to you. Saved you for last, I guess. We told him you'd never sell."

"And you. You've sold."

He pulled thoughtfully at his lips. "Yas, I have."

"How could you?"

"Well, I told him them people on water skis wouldn't want to come to Port Carq, they wouldn't like the place, it's too old-fashioned. But he said they'd love it, they'd get more out of it than we do. So listen here, Mrs. Munck, what's so bad about exchanging the Shotwells for a boat crowd? They'd be cleaner, anyway. And I'd kind of like to see some spanking new speed-boats zipping around out there, flags flying . . ."

"And everyone has done what you have? Everyone has sold?"

"I guess you wouldn't know about it, you don't mix much, but that's right, everybody's sold. Guy who owns the Shot-wells' and Piggotts' places, he sold before the words was out of Husar's mouth. And Shotwell, he's pestering Husar to get him on as foreman when construction starts. Foreman, and that poor fool couldn't supervise a thumbtack being stuck in a wall."

"I don't understand any of it," I said, walking away. The sky was growing dark. I crossed the tracks and stood on the rocks at the water's edge. The wind was strong now, whipping the water into points. Nearby a cat, gray as the hour, lifted its paw as though to command light, then ran silently across the beach into the decayed ferry, and the moon rose. I felt forlorn and started back.

Perhaps I was wrong, and Port Carquinez should be brought back to life. For half a century it had been like this, a whistle-stop, but once it was a rough, lively grain port and railroad town, with twelve or fifteen saloons, some of which still stood, wooden shells where a child sneaked now and then to look for mystery. Maybe the town would welcome crowds and noise again. I had been to the marina in Rio del Sol once, a few months ago, the time Harley bought the car. (For twenty-three years he wanted a car but always gave in to my hatred of owning one, until about a month or two before his death. One morning he walked out of the house without a word and drove back that night in a 1950 Ford, twelve years old and ready for the scrap heap. A few weeks later it fell apart. That seemed to break what spirit he had, and it was soon after that he became ill.) But during the time the car lasted we drove up to Rio del Sol, a river town with low rolling hills, pear orchards, and masses of acacia trees. The marina had just been completed, concrete, immense. The new parking lot was jammed and a sleek restaurant with blue glass doors was doing a great trade. The human form was to be seen everywhere, shaking a child, slamming a car door, hauling provisions. And over it all hung the human voice, shouting directions. One boat would slip into the congested water, then another, the voices merging with the whine of motors and the wailing of transistor radios as each boat idled in its footage of liquid.

No, I thought now, walking back up the steps, there is a difference between a lusty, youthful town and a carnival like that. Maybe Port Carquinez looked back with longing on the crowds that tramped off the railroad ferry, and missed the clank and grind of the great turntable (only a circular depression in the frontage now) and the all-night loading of the ocean-going vessels, and the saloon fights and busy jailhouse — but nothing could make it confuse that purposeful bustle and riotous relaxation with the piddling, gear-strapped amusement drive of Mr. Husar's public. Only the real thing or nothing at all. Let him construct his marina on some isolated beach that had no basis for comparison.

But it was too late, I remembered, standing still. Then let me have just a week's grace, and draw my shades and lock my doors and do what I had to do.

Chapter

13

THE GLAZIERS came the next morning and replaced the broken windowpane. When they were finished I closed the door on them with a sense of finality and leaned against it, suddenly dazzled by the prospect of time and privacy. My interruptions were behind me, I had a solid week before the next one when Husar returned. Husar. A crossness shot through my well-being — those warm amber hands busy tearing down houses like mine, all that energy misused on raping the countryside. When he came back I would be much ruder than I had been, for I would not be caught off guard due to Mr. Leary; by then I would have done what I had set out to do.

Mr. Leary was locked into his bedroom and lightly bound and gagged against a repeat performance of yesterday with the glaziers. The house held stillness in its arms like a fragrant bouquet, and I sank to the couch with a deep intake of breath, imminence racing in my chest like a motor. A contrived accident might be best, but there were other ways, too, and as my mind soared and a smile spread across my face I saw flickering before me a picture of his body in the death throes. It was wonderful that outwardly I could always appear so calm. I knew that no one who saw me — not Felix or Sal or the glaziers, not Mr. Husar — had any idea of the towering contrast between what I felt and what I showed. It was the signet of my strength.

But as I sank voluptuously into my plans, my eyes were roaming around the room as though by their own volition. The gray threadbare carpet, the walls with their slapdash waiting room green paint, the cheap knickknack shelf bare except for a chunk of petrified wood — it was a desolate house, a sad envelope for a human being. Harley had always complained about it, in his half-whining, elliptical way. Yet I had kept it spotless, and it was snug enough. Not like some of the places I had lived. One room in particular — where? — a stale compound of gray dimness, cold, and disorder. There had been someone who tried to bring light to it; a wave of memory broke across my mind — a thin old woman in black pushing a broom across the floor, and by her feet an infant holding up a ball of dust — and disappeared as quickly as it had come. I twisted around, enraged, to stare at Mr. Leary's door. Even silent, locked into his room, he managed to work his malice on me, his very proximity cracking the chains on images that had lain immobile for years.

The sweetness of the silence had faded along with the smooth anticipation, and my thoughts ran jerkily from the carving knife to a ball of dust, from Harley's tight ears to a fly buzzing madly against the new pane. I jumped to my feet, rolled up a newspaper, and smashed the insect against the glass. Flinging myself back on the sofa, I sat with my hands clenched in my lap for the rest of the day.

Toward evening I went into the bathroom, undressed, turned on the shower, and stepped under the pounding water. I looked down at my body. Some of the smooth, youthful lines were

gone, replaced by small bulges; the breasts did not thrust up-
wards but were settled comfortably on the rib cage; here and
there on the skin were broken veins like tiny clusters of violet
threads, and intertwined wrinkles at the points where I had bent
in repose over the years. But by and large the lines were still
firm; it was a body unclogged by fat, the body of a walker.
Stepping out of the shower and going to the mirror, I studied my
face. The forehead was lined, but the rest of the face was
strangely unmarked, almost as though it had never expressed
anything. I had skinned my hair back into a knot for twenty
years and it had lost its original unruliness; I unloosed the knot
and shook my head, and it fell straight and heavy to my shoulders, still a rich auburn, untouched by gray.

Back in my room I pulled a housedress from the closet and
looked at it with dissatisfaction, then I cut off the sleeves and
shortened the hem, securing it with safety pins, and slipped it
on. Clumsily, I plucked my eyebrows, then renewed the lipstick
I had begun to use the last few days. I brushed my hair one hundred, two hundred, three hundred times. Lastly, having no mas-
cara or eyeliner, I applied a ballpoint pen to my eyelids, outlin-
ing them as artfully as I could. My hands were shaking.

Throwing open the door, I went into the living room where I
walked around aimlessly. It was almost dark. The silence of the
house was absolute. "What in God's name will I do with
myself?" I asked, and turning on my heel, I strode to Mr.
Leary's door and unlocked it. He was still lying on the bed in
his long johns, a scarf wrapped around his jaw and his good hand
bound to his useless one. Grabbing one of Harley's neckties
from the closet and holding it out like a garrote, I rushed toward
him as his eyes grew bright with terror. "Get dressed," I said,
dropping the necktie and setting him free.

"But why?" he faltered. "It's almost night." But he was obediently sitting up, his eyes fastened nervously on mine. I looked down at his underwear — there is something about long underwear, with its yellow cast, its bare, round neck, its bagginess that suggests decrepitude, and in this case the man inside completed the picture. I stared at him, comparing him to the man I had first known — the bearing of alert benevolence, the small eyes a deep, puissant brown, the skin a healthy nut brown. In those days the first sunlamps had just come out and every morning Mr. Leary stuck his head under the rays of the most expensive edition, so that even in the gloomiest San Francisco weather his face shone with Mediterranean splendor. Now it was a relief map of crusted trivia, the eyes like two dim raisins half lost in an avalanche of dry skin, all authority, drive, passion, vanished. Where was the man I wanted to kill?

"Get dressed," I said again, going out.

He wheeled into the living room a while later, wearing an old robe of Harley's, his hair slicked down, a polite, nervous look on his face. I had picked up my work at the sewing machine, having decided what kind of dress I wanted. It would be orange, in the straight slim style I saw in the newspapers but never in Port Carquinez, sleeveless, with a high neckline. Suddenly, I wanted it very badly; over and over I ran the needle across the scraps of practice material, my spine tingling. I glanced restlessly at Mr. Leary. "Say something," I demanded.

He thought for a moment, then ventured, "I'm hungry."

"Say something real!"

"Hunger is real."

I leaned back against the sewing machine. "I'm not going to do anything to you tonight," I said shortly, and I saw him relax a jot. "You have my word and my word is good. So you can say what you want and I won't touch you."

His eyes lit up a little. "Then," he said, "I'd like something to eat. I haven't eaten since breakfast."

Grudgingly I went into the kitchen and made him a sandwich and poured him a glass of Coca-Cola. He ate quickly, but his manners were not as primitive as they had been. Afterwards, he smacked his lips and looked me over, as though he had just now noticed my altered appearance. I felt my eyes, my ears, even my nostrils sharpen their perceptions, like an animal's.

"Trying to recapture your youth?"

"Not at all," I answered casually. "Just getting back into my ordinary grooming habits. Since you came I haven't had time to iron a dress or comb my hair properly."

"You've had time to do anything you wanted. But if you think I take up so much time, why keep me?"

Without even having prepared for it I had brought us to a crucial moment. "Would you like me to tell you?" I asked, pronouncing each word with significant clarity. "Would you like to discuss it?"

He blotted his mouth carefully, folded the napkin, and laid it beside his plate.

"I asked you a question!" I said. "Do you or do you not wish to discuss my motives in bringing you here?"

Again he picked up the napkin and patted his lips. "I do not," he replied.

"No, of course not," I breathed, "you stinking poltroon."

"That's a word I don't know," he said with a faint smile. "I admit it, Rose, I've got a small vocabulary compared to yours . . ."

"To anyone's!"

". . . I was always your mental inferior," he went on, the smile growing more confident, "I admit it, Rose, you're a genius, sensitive, talented; while I'm just a common, ordinary . . ."

"Never common, never ordinary, oh never. Less, much less!"

"All right, a much less than common, ordinary sort. So I'm sorry if I don't always follow you . . ." He gave a small, gentlemanly burp and wheeled to the front window where he looked down at the emerging lights of the town. I followed him. I looked, too, at the lights. They danced before my eyes, they filled me with a painful brightness. "Say something, for God's sake!"

He looked up at me. "I may. In time."

Somehow I had allowed him to gain control of the situation; it was as though *he* were playing with *me*. But at least he smacked more of his old self.

"Do you intend," he enquired, "to stand over me all night to see that I don't break your new window?"

I forced myself to walk away. I stood looking at him from across the room, seeing, not him, but a slice of time from the past — my thoughts were blown back to the little room with its blurred figures of the old woman and the child. I put my hand to my mouth and pressed my teeth into it.

Still looking out the window, he said in a casual, soft voice, "Frank knows. About you and me. I told him everything." He turned around, shooting me a sly, triumphant glance. "If anything happened to me, he'd know enough to put his finger on you."

My hand fell from my mouth as I burst into a paroxysm of laughter. It was the first laugh I had had in years and it shattered the air like an explosive. With tears streaming from my eyes, I gasped, "And he left you with me? Do you find that odd!"

"He thought it would do me good to be in the country," he returned crisply.

"Does that make any sense, you idiot? Oh, Frank knows. I'm certain he knows. Part of it, anyway. But not through you. He remembers that night outside your house. He's not stupid. And that's why he brought you here. He hates you as much as I do."

"Ah!" he spat. "My own son?"

"Your own son."

"I'm a good man!" he cried sharply, as though in spite of himself, and the veins stood out on his forehead. For the first time I saw something like pain in his eyes. A warmth spread through me like wine.

"Go to bed," I said.

❁

Chapter

14

As I UNDRESSED for bed I returned to the plans I had entertained that morning. Already I had one day less. Tomorrow I would go to Martinez. I would go straight to the library and find a book on poisons — that seemed a good start — and then I would buy some material for my new dress.

But Mr. Leary could not be left by himself. Left alone so long, even locked into his room, he might manage some way of getting out or attracting attention. Alone with a stranger I was certain he would try to be as disarming and docile as possible. I could see him greeting his savior in quiet tones, searching his mind for every felicitous phrase he had ever overheard, trying to appear the respectable, retired gentleman. Then, when his visitor had been properly impressed (poor Mr. Leary, he didn't know it was impossible to impress my neighbors), he would cough judiciously, and — his tongue perhaps curling with the seeming absurdity of his words — begin to describe his peculiar captivity, the entire effect being nothing as he was regarded with the same final look Mr. Husar had given him. The thought titillated me. Who, I wondered, should be the recipient of all this?

Only twice had I so much as stepped inside one of my fellow townsmen's houses.

During the war there was a little life in Port Carquinez; bored servicemen from nearby Camp Stoneman climbed off the train and wandered around the dusty dead-end streets, finally congregating at Felix's to drink beer. One early evening I found my path playfully blocked by a husky young soldier as I was returning from Sal's with a bag of groceries. He had dark eyes like overripe cherries and white teeth that gleamed in the dusk.

Coolly, I turned my back on him and walked away. As I went up Locust Street I saw the old Italians on their porches, bathed in the apricot light of the streetlamps; here and there I was bedazzled by a spray of water from a garden hose held by some dim figures among the geraniums. I was wearing huarachos, I remember, and between their slap and the footfall behind me I could hear sounds from the porches: floorboards creaking, drifts of foreign conversation, the click click of a dog's nails as it wandered among the chairs. I might have stopped at any one of these houses and complained that I was being followed, but I walked on at a normal pace, and eventually the houses were left behind and I stood on a little wooden bridge. The night was filled with the hollow roar of crickets.

He arrived a few moments later, looking behind him, and with no hesitation softly laid his hand on my shoulder. I did not move, but looked down at the dry creekbed which was so dark that it seemed a ravine; then I carefully set my groceries down and turned to him. His fingers curled around my upper arm, urging me off the bridge. As we climbed down the bank the crickets all at once hushed.

I dropped to my knees in a pile of dry leaves, drawing him down with me, and threw my head back, looking straight into the sky through the trees. My dress buttoned all the way down the front; I undid every button and at last we burrowed into the leaves, sounding like big animals moving in the underbrush. Then, as we came together I suddenly fought and pushed him away; but a moment later a heat like sunlight poured through me and I felt myself giving in, pulling him to me, forgetting the sound of my name and the feel of my feet on the old steps, so powerfully sodden with desire that a few minutes later, for the first time in my life, my cry burst out unrestrained, deep and carrying.

As we lay there afterwards the crickets started in again.

I had grown terrified, for no reason that I knew. I rolled quickly away from him and started to dress.

Shrugging, he felt around the darkness for his trousers.

And I knew that when Lazarus was raised from the dead, the sunlight must have burnt his body like acid. Perhaps if he had not had an encouraging audience, he too would have pulled the lid of his coffin back over him.

Hastily buttoning my dress, I climbed back up to the bridge. Down from the frontage came the roar and clangor of a train stopping and pulling out. "Missed the last one," the soldier said, joining me. "I guess I'll have to hitch a ride. Any cars ever go by on that road up there?"

"Not many. I hope you won't get into trouble."

"It was worth it."

"I won't be seeing you again," I said briefly.

"Why not?"

I looked at him coldly.

He shrugged again and walked off in the direction of the Snake Road, pausing to light a cigarette. In the flare of the light his round young face shone out strong and rosy. When he was gone I stooped down and picked up the burnt match he had thrown away, and forgetting the groceries, walked off with scalding eyes. By the time I reached the row of houses I had passed earlier the tears were streaming, and through them I saw the figure of a woman standing before me, Mrs. Amelia Pompano, I learned subsequently, an elderly soul of great amplitude, with a nose like a potato and a neatly clipped mustache. She asked me what had happened, why I was crying; she had seen me walk by earlier, and then the soldier. Had he chased me, the no-good son of a bitch? Where was he, which direction had he run off in?

"He just scared me," I managed to say, "nothing happened."

"You come inside and have a glass of wine to calm you down," she said, taking me by the arm and leading me into her house. She poured me a glass of red wine and we sat down. I took stock of myself. I had misbuttoned my dress, so that one side of it hung three buttons lower than the other. My face flamed and I took a big gulp of wine, noticing as I did so that a few skeletal leaves were sticking out from my bangs. I brushed them away and they fell in brittle bits to the floor.

Mrs. Pompano's eyes rested thoughtfully on the particles and the strangely buttoned dress. Turning away, she brought out photographs of her husband who had died in 1928, and of her sons and daughters. "They don't stay in Port Carq, the young ones, they move away."

"But there are new people moving in all the time, since the war started," I said, trying to appear at ease.

"Sons of bitches. They make a mess. Their houses cave in, they hang blankets in the windows, their children never say good morning. My children, I smashed them if they didn't say good morning to their neighbors. Do you have children?"

"No."

"They're a big trouble, they leave you old, but it's worth all. Are you Catholic?"

"No." I belonged to no church, but I said at random, "I'm Methodist."

"Well, it's something, anyway," she replied dubiously, adding, "Does the wine relieve you? You're a nervous type girl, you should have a glass of wine every night before you go to bed, it builds up the blood and calms the nerves."

"I feel much better now, thank you. I think I'd better get home."

She told me her name and I told her mine. "You come back sometime and we can visit again," she said, seeing me to the door.

I thanked her once more, and went back down the street to the bridge where I retrieved my groceries and walked home. I filled the bathtub and pulled off my clothes. Shards of leaves filigreed the creases of my body; they floated out into the water and went down the drain with it. Afterwards I dropped the dress in the clothes hamper, first removing the soldier's burnt match from the pocket. I turned it in my fingers for a long while, then I opened the back door and threw it into the night.

The second time I entered a house in Port Carquinez it was also by accident, and it happened a short time later. I had returned one night from my yearly trip to San Francisco, sharing a coach with a crowd of noisy soldiers. The blackout shades were down, making the smoke-filled coach claustrophobic, and I glued my nose to my book, trying to forget where I was. When I got off the train I had a headache, I felt out of sorts, and I was annoyed to find that the tule fog lay so thick around me that I could see nothing. I made my way slowly across the frontage and found the steps and began to climb, counting, for I knew there were exactly fifty-six steps to my gate. At one point a cat flashed across my feet, making me lose count, but I turned in at what I thought was my gate, put the key in the door, giving it a little push at the same time and finding it unlocked. I went thankfully into the dimly-lit living room, noticing a strange couple that rose as one from a sofa chair. One of the figures was Hazel Something. To myself I had always called her Hazel Something (not even Hazel Someone, for she looked somehow subhuman) because every night a different soldier would cry "G'night Hazel!" as he hurried down the steps.

She was an old blonde hung somewhere between menopause and dotage, cheesy with decay on the inside, I felt, and all hardness on the outside, with one of those polished walnut faces much more darkly pigmented than the peroxide-tormented hemp falling around it. She smelled of poverty; it was in her decrepit house, her frayed, garish clothes. She was a far cry from a thriving lady of the night, but seemed more like one of those elbowing doxies from Hogarth's time, leaning tiredly against a tavern wall giving tuppenny's worth of usage, more concerned with the pain in her back and the fire in her feet than the gymnastics of her partner, and always dirty, always old.

I saw that her house was as ugly inside as it was out, damp, somehow sorrowful, with a heavy smell of liquor and grease. And I, in the powder blue coat I had been married in, and a proper white hat, holding my book, Bury's *History of Greece*, in my hands. She stormed toward me, all bared teeth and lancelike cigarette, ashes cascading down her flowered blouse rotting under the armpits. She had a twitch, and she pulled on her liverish cheek as though to hold it still, yelling, "Who the hell are you walking in my door? Get out of my house, I'll call the cops, this is *my* house, *my* house!" She was drunk, but not staggeringly; her eyes were clear enough, and frightening. She hit me hard, between the shoulder and chest. I dared not turn around, so I backed out, and she followed, hissing, "*My* house, *my* house," spitting her cigarette out onto the floor, holding her face with both hands, making vicious kicks at my ankles. The door slammed in my face.

Seeing her afterwards, she appeared as sane as before; tough, bitter, eminently cool, as though those ugly, monkeylike hands had her sordid little world well under control. From that time on I always nodded hello to her, and she responded with the contemptuous, distrustful hint of a nod with which she responded to everyone. I nodded not because I approved of her, but because there was such admirable effort in that controlled, disdainful glance. I knew that behind that cool look sores festered and suppurated in a dim sorrow like that of the room I had walked into. I felt one must salute those hard, puffy, restrained eyes — cold locks on the doors to Bedlam.

And that was the history of my social essays into Port Carquinez society. This, my last visit, to Hazel (she moved a few years later; the house fell into other, equally indifferent hands, and was now occupied by a family of Piggotts who were related by blood as well as type to the Shotwells), this visit took place in 1944, almost twenty years ago. Both Mrs. Pompano and Hazel were gone. There was not a living soul in the town whose house I had ever entered.

Chapter

15

"GET UP, I'm going to town today," I said to Mr. Leary. "I'll get someone to stay with you."

Astonished, he jerked his head from the pillow and stared at me. While he dressed I prepared breakfast, going to my bedroom several times to check my appearance in the mirror. My face was carefully made up, and I had coiled my hair loosely on top of my head, the way I had worn it as a girl. I was satisfied. My eyes sparkled from between the lines of the ballpoint pen.

Mr. Leary wheeled into the kitchen, wearing his good trousers and a white shirt with an unknotted tie around his neck. He asked me to tie it, and when I had, his face grew stern, arrogant, vain; he moved his neck around like a cat stretching with satisfaction.

"Such splendor," I said. "Why today?"

"I don't want to discredit you when your neighbor or whoever it is comes. I was looking pretty sloppy."

"No sloppier than my neighbors." I picked up my coat and purse. "I'll skip breakfast, I want to go now."

He was trying to appear disinterested in my exit, but I knew that his heart was thumping with excitement.

"Somebody will come soon," I called over my shoulder as I let myself out the door, wondering as I said it if I could find anyone.

It was the Shotwell gate I turned into; they were, after all, my closest neighbors. But as soon as I knocked my legs grew weak.

The door was opened by a boy in food-stained pajamas. "Mom!" he yelled, and Mrs. Shotwell came, chewing regularly on a piece of gum as her eyes, surprised but noncommittal, roamed freely around my face.

"My uncle is staying with me, Mrs. Shotwell," I said slowly, afraid I might stammer. "I wonder if you know of someone who could stay with him for a few hours while I'm in Martinez? I'd be willing to pay two dollars an hour."

"Shut up!" she cried at her children, who were fighting around the television set. She had been my neighbor for over a year but I had never spoken with her, or even looked at her except with a careless glance. I had not noticed her eyes, which were large, dark, with heavy, haughty lids. She might have been the subject of a Spanish painter, one of those ugly damsels with magnificent eyes who look out at the world half aware of what they see, lost in visions of passion and pomp. "Cut it out!" she shouted again, adding in her midwestern drawl, "I'll take the job." A child of four or five was hitting her thigh, trying to squeeze out the door. "Come on in," Mrs. Shotwell said to me, "and you get out, Chlorinda," this with a push that landed the child on its posterior on the porch. "In the kitchen," she directed, banging through a swinging door. I followed tensely.

Mrs. Piggott, who lived in the next house, sat at the kitchen table chipping polish from her nails. "Hi," she said pleasantly enough, but with an expression of such surprise that I might have come through the door walking on my hands.

"She says her uncle has to be sat with, I'm going up," Mrs. Shotwell told her, sweeping bread crusts from a chair and offering me a seat. I accepted, fighting down a compulsion to flee. "Hear he bashed in your front window," my hostess remarked, pouring me a cup of coffee.

"Yes, he did," I replied after a moment's hesitation. "It was an accident."

"He might do Darlene in," Mrs. Piggott suggested with an animated frown but Mrs. Shotwell made a disgusted gesture; she was tall, bigboned, with arms like jackknives and a neck thick as a man's.

"I suppose it was Mr. Husar who mentioned the window?" I said carefully to Mrs. Shotwell.

"Husar? No, Steve was up there with his gun looking for jackrabbits. He saw this old guy through the window . . ."

"Why was he looking through my window?" I asked sharply, and smiled — a moment too late.

"He just happened to look over your way and saw this old guy through the window pick up this chair and throw it. He don't pry, Mrs. Munck. He don't give a damn who bashes out your window."

Steve was her oldest boy, the one who fixed my porch steps. I had never liked him, with his sullen look and noisy motorcycle, but I was pleased that he had already acquainted his mother with Mr. Leary's strangeness. "My uncle is up in the age," I told her. "He's quite a handful. Well, you can imagine, throwing a chair through a window."

"What is he, soft in the head?" enquired Mrs. Piggott.

"Soft as an omelet," I said with a smile that trembled. I tried to pick up my cup of coffee but my hand shook and I put it down. "Speaking of my uncle, he'll be growing anxious," I said.

"I'll go on up," Mrs. Shotwell yawned.

"I'll be back around one o'clock I think. I'm really very grateful to you, Mrs. Shotwell."

"Dar*lene*," she corrected, unfolding her long torso and looking around the kitchen for a moment. Garbage overflowed from paper bags on the floor, unwashed dishes stood high in the sink. And Darlene, in the midst of it, looked terribly, reluctantly, in her element, wearing a pair of soiled brick-red pedal pushers and a torn aqua blouse. She was about forty. Her hair was already streaked with gray and hung to her shoulders.

"O.K.," she said, wiping her hands on her pedal pushers, "let's go." And I rose, thankful to escape, yet aware of a feeling of craven gratitude.

Leaving the children to fend for themselves, she led me and Mrs. Piggott out of the house. The bounced child had removed all her clothes and was swinging back and forth on the gate under a sky of puckered mauve clouds. She was touchingly thin, with shoulder blades sharp and light as two fish scales. At the sound of her mother's voice ("Where's your common sense?") she dashed through the yard, hopping over the debris like a deer, and disappeared behind the house.

"She'll catch pneumonia," her mother remarked, passing through the swinging gate. I glanced back and saw the child's face peering around the house, all wind-blown hair and round eyes electric with the glorious dangers of her fancied world. How could Darlene visit the ugly name "Chlorinda" on such a beautiful elf, push her onto the porch, neglect her? If she were mine, I would know how to play with her.

"Wouldn't it be nice to run around like that again?" Mrs. Piggott said.

"Huh!" said Darlene, stopping in her tracks. "It's nice 'til they get slivers or runny noses. Nothing comes free. Why, each one of those kids was a payment for a natural pleasure among Royal and me, it never seemed fair. You always pay. And anyway, if you ran around like Chlorinda there, they'd call the cops, or some louse would jump over the fence and rape you."

"Oh, come on, Darlene," said Mrs. Piggott. "Don't take everything so serious."

"There's no pleasure without pain, that's all I know." Darlene's eyes blazed with this pronouncement.

"And yet there is pain without pleasure," I said.

She shook her head, finished with philosophy. "Two dollars an hour, you say? It's going on nine now." And with an emphatic chew she started up the steps. I watched her ascent, suddenly apprehensive. Nervously, I turned my attention to Mrs. Piggott — or Bobby, as she had asked me to call her — who had been talking steadily in my ear. ". . . and fixed up the old jailhouse. He lives there."

The honest ruddy face made me want to run. The curious round eyes clung to mine, which I now shaded with my hand. Yet I didn't wish to offend her. "What jailhouse?" I asked.

"The *jail*house. He fixed it up and moved himself in. Husar."

"In the jailhouse?" I asked incredulously.

"Well, come and take a look," she said, and led the way. It was up by the Italian section, where I had not been for years.

A good part of the front wall had been knocked out for a large window, but other than that the building looked unchanged. It had been erected in 1858, a gray wooden building that might have passed for a bank or post office except for its small barred windows. It had not been used for fifty years, but had not caved in as so many of the old structures had. I always visualized the interior as a grimy wood and iron warren, permeated with the moldering tang of slop pots; a silent, sunless hotel for rats whose tails left thin paths in the rusty carpet of dust.

"He always keeps the drapes drawn," Bobby said, "because people stare inside. What does he expect?"

"It's very strange. I had no idea he actually lived in town."

"And who could care? But Darlene's gone back to her second childhood, wants a hero." She began to speak angrily. "Royal's a pain in the ass, sleeps all day, always going on about raw deals, well, he's a pain, but he's better than Husar, and she better remember it."

"I have to leave now," I said. "I'm going over to Martinez."

"I'll come with you," she said at once.

"I'll be walking along the tracks." I waited for her to smirk, but she didn't; only shrugged, disappointed. Whether due to some remarkable largeness of spirit or to stupidity she was entering the first stages of a friendship with me. I began to walk faster.

She accompanied me all the way to the tracks, as though I were catching a train. "See you," she said, shielding her hair from the wind, and it seemed to me that modern-day people never said goodbye; as though afraid of tempting the ultimate departure; they used such timid phrases as "take care," "so long," " 'bye for now," sophisticates even indulging in "ciao, baby."

"Goodbye," I said.

As she turned and waved, I noted the care with which she dressed. Her vivid green stretch pants clung to her legs and hips, and above them, like an overflowing wastebasket, was a white blouse whose starched ruffles stuck out in every direction. She had arranged her dyed orangeade hair in a towering bouffant, prepossessing from the front, but from the side sticking up like the false front of a store. On her feet, making her walk with a nervous, erratic gait, were a pair of blood-red stiletto heels. I remarked to myself that if she had appeared on the street in this outfit twenty years ago she would have been thought insane.

Chapter

16

IT WAS a relief to be alone, walking as usual along the tracks. But as I passed below the cemetery — a Garden of Babylon high in the hills, tier upon tier of wild rose bushes, tangled acacia trees, and soaring black cypresses — it was with a new and uncomfortable feeling that I looked up at it, as though the Harley who lay up there was a pale young clerk in a green visor, his eyes mild and hopeful. Then it was behind me, the hills unfolded barren and gold, and Martinez came into sight, fruit cannery to the left, oily trucking compound to the right, yellow train depot ahead. A cutting moisture had gathered in the air and I hurried down a side street and darted into Penney's just as the skies opened.

I felt oppressed, horribly nervous. I should not have left Mr. Leary with another person; it was as though I were working against myself, shattering all my plans before I had crystallized them — and even if I had been so foolish as to leave him, how could I waste precious time buying material for a dress? But a great indiscriminate jumble — dresses, eyeliners, green visors, high collars, balls of dust, coffins, and summer suns — had spouted up through a sudden crack in a thick, time hardened crust; and overwhelmed and frightened, I made my way to the yardage counter.

It's too late in the year for a summer dress, a cold voice inside me said. "No, it isn't!" I argued aloud, rummaging through the material as a saleswoman glided up to me with a look of such rude curiosity that I checked myself in a nearby mirror, discovering that the ballpoint pen had run pathetically. I rushed into the ladies' room and washed the idiotic smears away, and with dampened enthusiasm I went back and chose three yards of orange material and a pattern.

On the way out I paused again — again! — at the cosmetics counter and asked for an eyeliner. "Liquid or pencil?" the salesgirl demanded, and I knew she was thinking: what does she want it for, the freak? And indeed, I thought grayly, how could so long and intense a solitude be hidden simply by pinning up the hem of a dress and putting on some lipstick? "Liquid," I stated nevertheless, as though giving an experienced preference, and I was sure I saw her smirk. She would not smirk at Darlene or Bobby — oh no, not at them: sleazy, grammatically unsound; part of the sleazy unsound world everyone knew and understood and communicated through. But oddly enough, the thought of the two women calmed me: I had had coffee with my neighbors — what an unbelievable thing! I paid for my purchase and took it from the salesgirl with a quick, tentative look of being within my rights.

Outside the shower had already passed and a burst of sunlight illuminated the wet sidewalks. I hurried down the street to the library. Pressing my lips tightly together, I went to the section where I might find the sort of book I had in mind, and a tendril of pleasure curled through my anxiety as I pictured page after page bursting with lethal lore — how, with a dash of cleaning fluid and the scrapings of a moldy onion you could turn a healthy man's stomach into a death chamber in three minutes . . . But of course I found nothing like that. Looking around, I walked over to a huge dictionary and turned to "arsenic," the simplest and most time-honored of all solutions, but when someone walked by I jumped as though shot and slapped the dictionary shut. It was hopeless. The trip had been a mistake. I must return home at once. I went to the door.

"Mrs. Munck."

I whirled around, my eyes starting from my head. It was the librarian, a faded quiet woman I had seen for twenty-three years but had never spoken with except to say hello and goodbye.

"Aren't you checking out any books today?" she asked, and I seemed to hear an unwonted warmth, a liveliness in her voice that was matched by her look. Was it because I had moved around the library so quickly, so purposefully; because my face communicated some strange animation?

"I was just looking something up . . ." I faltered.

She smiled. It seemed to me a radiant smile, touched by affection, and I pushed the door open and hastened out. A weight had descended upon me, the weight of Darlene and Bobby and now the librarian; I was laden with pleasantries and hospitable looks. I felt lost, rudderless. "But you'll kill Mr. Leary," I reminded myself, and it steadied me.

An hour later I was back at the frontage. I climbed the steps to my house, and arriving without another breath in my body, discovered the front door standing wide open.

They had taken the wheelchair. On the kitchen table stood the remains of lunch: bread, sandwich spread, two untouched cups of coffee. I could see the old man, his eyes dripping gratitude as strapping Darlene plunked down the pimento cheese spread under his nose . . . "You don't know what it's like, living with Mrs. Munck, no, you don't, Mrs. Shotwell, but I'll tell you . . ." And Darlene would chew her gum more and more slowly, listening with all her ears, and then before her coffee had cooled she would, like a charioteer, have raced him out of the house in his wheelchair, delivering him with clattering dispatch from these rooms whose walls echoed some nebulous testimony to hatred . . .

Looking frantically around from the porch, I saw something on the old road above that moved like a procession. I was at the top of the steps in thirty seconds. It was Mr. Leary, all right, like a king on a movable throne. Darlene was there, puffing, shouting at her children who were fastened to the wheelchair like flies, pushing it gleefully.

At first my voice would not work. I swallowed, coughed, and tried again: "Where have you been? I was worried."

"Took him for a ride in his roller chair," Darlene gasped. "God, I never knew what this old road was like, all ups and downs."

I was so relieved that it was all I could do not to burst into hysterical laughter. Instead, I looked with elaborate concern at the clot of children straining up the last few yards of the hill. "I hope they haven't jogged him too much. I don't know if he's up to an outing like this."

"*Loved* it. You don't understand the old guy. He, well, sort of doesn't live the way you do. I mean he likes having people around, especially kids."

"Kids?"

"He's got seven grandchildren."

"I'm aware of that. Nevertheless, he is not fond of children."

"That's what I mean, Mrs. Munck — don't take me the wrong

way — but you don't understand him. You only got to look at him to see he's nuts about kids. And they're nuts about him."

"About his wheelchair."

She threw me a glance. "I know it's none of my business, but if you don't like him you shouldn't keep him."

I returned her look with coldness. We need be friendly no longer, even though we had drunk coffee together. "It was wrong of you to take him out like this," I said sharply. "He has a heart condition."

"He does? He said he was in perfect health except for the paralysis."

"I imagine he said a lot of foolish things." I looked at him. Under his jollity lay a current of desperation. It flickered through his hands as he neared me; they forgot their head patting, their scenic pointing, their contented lap repose, and the fingers crept nervously together. So he had told her. And she had not quite bitten. And he didn't know which way the wind would blow.

"Thank you, children, for being so thoughtful to my uncle," I told his retinue, and received a collective glance of disappointment. They were loathe to part with the wheelchair. I watched with interest.

"*Don't* you push Mr. Leary!" Darlene yelled. "That's *his* roller chair. Earl! Luster! Bonnie!"

I smiled at him. He was trying to be gallant and fatherly and amused, and shot Darlene little looks of would-be enjoyment. How good to see him tormented by children. I moved in through them and pushed him alone the rest of the way to the top of the steps, thinking over and over: just to get him back into the house, back into the house. My hands were slippery with perspiration.

"Darlene?" he called nervously.

"Listen," she said, striding over to me, "he said he realizes he's too much trouble for you, especially with Mr. Munck just passing and everything. I've got a big place, and it wouldn't be no trouble for me to take him. I mean if that would suit you."

"It wouldn't. I'm responsible for him."

"If you want me to come with you now, Darlene," he said tremulously, "why, I don't mind."

"Come, Uncle Patrick," I said, "let's get you down these steps."

"Six bucks," Darlene broke in, "three hours, two bucks an hour."

"My purse is in the house," I said, trying to lift him out of the wheelchair.

She helped me, taking one of his arms as I took the other. "If you ride in that there roller chair I'll smash your heads together," she shouted back at her children, and together we struggled down the steps with him. He was awkward as a bag of groceries and his body trembled. "Look at him," Darlene said suddenly. "Look how trembly he is. He's a nervous wreck. Half the time he talks wacky."

"I don't talk wacky!" he denied.

"What have you been telling Mrs. Shotwell?" I asked.

". . . Only that I wanted to go back to Twin Oaks," he replied anxiously.

"Well, I don't consider that wacky," I said to Darlene. "He misses his elderly friends there. That's very natural. Do you think that sounds wacky?"

"No," she said shortly. "Open the gate. I'll hang on to him."

"Don't drop him. He's brittle."

On the porch he let his weight go dead. "I would like to visit you and your family, Darlene," he pleaded. "You invited me and I'm accepting."

"It's up to Mrs. Munck here," she said, looking at me.

"Later, perhaps. For a short visit. But right now peace and quiet, as the doctor said."

"Doctor!" he cried. "You haven't had a doctor to see me!"

"He's going into one of his paranoic phases," I told Darlene. "He'll start yelling about someone trying to brain him with a tire iron. I'll get your money."

She took the money and stood by the door a moment. "Maybe I'll come up and see you tomorrow, Leary," she finally said.

"Yes, tomorrow. Come tomorrow, Darlene," he entreated.

She nodded and went back up the steps to get her children. I hoped they had run his wheelchair into a tree.

He was exhausted, but I was almost wild with relief. I wrung my hands and turned to him. "This was your big opportunity, and you bungled it."

"Maybe I didn't," he said uncertainly, "she's coming back to-morrow."

"You may not be around by tomorrow."

"It would be stupid to do something now," he said anxiously, "just after I've talked with her."

"Why? What did you tell her?"

"I don't have to tell you that," he murmured.

"Anyway, she thinks you're wacky."

"She was surprised by what I told her, who wouldn't be? But she thinks I'm a pretty sharp guy."

"Of course, she's an ignorant woman."

"Sure, she's ignorant!" he spat, suddenly aroused. "But she's not deranged. She's not going to wind up in an asylum for the criminally insane. She'll be ignorant but free while you're quoting poetry to yourself in a padded cell . . ."

I whirled around and slapped him with violent force, once, twice, three times; it was a wild, private nihilism of the sort that starved wolves must feel when they finally turn upon each other, and when I brought my hand back, the palm red and stinging, I felt indeed as if I had just eaten raw meat. "What you say may be right," I whispered, suddenly remembering Hazel's mad eyes. "So much the worse for you."

But he heard nothing. He was undergoing a series of deep shudders, his eyes closed. "Will you get my wheelchair?" he finally asked in a broken voice.

I retrieved it from the road and put it in the center of the room for him to crawl to; then dismissing him from my mind I unwrapped my dress material. When he finally spoke it was to tell me again that my hands were now tied, that Darlene was too well informed. "That guy Husar, too," he added, "if you did something now you'd have an inquest on your hands so fast your head would spin."

"Shut up," I muttered. The only thing I wanted at that moment was to walk along the beach in this orange dress with the sun spilling down on me. Only that. Mr. Leary had faded to the periphery of my consciousness; but even as I grew absorbed in laying out the pattern I sensed that he was the axle from which this new spoke of sartorial passion sprang, and that if he had not been here I would never have opened the sewing machine.

I worked all afternoon and most of the night, and finally, the completed dress folded over my arm, I went to my room and tried it on before the mirror. It was stylish, it fit well. I smiled at myself, and hoping that the morning would be a sunny one, I sat down to wait for it.

THE SKY lightened to verdigris, here and there deepening to a glassy bottle green matched by the strait; on the hills the wind blew gently through the dry grass in long waves of pale sunlight. I combed my hair, put on the new dress, and went out, but just in that short time the sky had begun to dull and the wind to rise.

The frontage was still damp from yesterday's rain and I tried to walk across it lightly since I was wearing my best shoes, but my feet sank in and my soggy footsteps were loud in my ears. I stopped; there was no sound to be heard except for a foghorn up the bay. Going on, I crossed the tracks and finally stood before the darkening water. The wind drove the dress unbecomingly between my thighs and stung cinders into my face, but there was nothing to do but to walk as I had planned, and so I did, squinting in the wind, rubbing my goose-pimpled arms, looking in vain for the sun. Finally, feeling foolish and stone-hearted, I turned on my heel and went back up the steps.

Throwing myself down on the bed, I closed my eyes and gave

way to fatigue, only to be jolted awake by the sight of myself walking down the shore under a blazing sun — it was no longer an indistinct scene, but brilliantly defined: the narrow shale beach was transfigured into an isle set apart from a world whose culmination was the tubers, the night crawlers, and the sun was rushing up against me like a tidal wave, lifting and burning me without pain or decrement . . . Scrambling off the bed, I wheeled around to be rid of this sight, a monstrous sight, cruel in a way I could not seize, as though it flouted the room I stood in, these cold hands that clutched each other . . . And at last it retreated, but as it did a final flicker of light was trajected into the past, where it hung over the old rock-strewn plain.

Mr. Leary waited all day for Darlene. Every time I stood up he said hastily, "You'd better not try anything, not with Darlene coming."

"Why do you speak in the abstract?" I finally asked. "Why don't you use the word 'kill'?"

He cringed, staring at the floor.

"Kill," I said.

"Except," he said faintly, "except now, with Darlene, with Husar . . ."

"Why should it matter to me if I sat here or in a cell the next twenty years?"

"No . . . not even you . . . I don't believe that." But there was no conviction in his voice. He seemed to be fighting down panic. He wheeled rapidly to the window, pulled back the curtain, and looked down at the Shotwell house.

"If the whole town comes trooping in here today it won't change anything," I told him. "I'll kill you. Today. Tomorrow. The next day."

His hand crushed the curtain, the blue veins stood out like ropes.

"Come away from the window," I said. "Entertain yourself, do a crossword puzzle."

Obediently, as though in a daze, he took his glasses from his pocket, found a pencil, and awkwardly folded the newspaper to the puzzle section. But he did not fill in any of the squares.

The afternoon brightened a little just before dusk and I went to the window and looked out. There was no one to be seen down below but an old Italian woman dressed, as all of them, in black from head to toe. I thought of Mrs. Pompano, the bulbous nose and kind eyes, the hands swelled with arthritis . . . no, her hands weren't arthritic, it was someone else's hands that were, someone not large like Mrs. Pompano, but frail . . . I dropped the curtain and strode into the kitchen to make dinner, bustling and clattering around . . . but she came back, a frail old figure with arthritic hands, a painful question in her eyes. What was her name? Catavo. Catano. Catania. Mrs. Catania. I knew now that her presence had never left me all these years, but had been like a haze, assimilated in the deepest, blindest part of me. But what was I making for dinner, I suddenly thought, seeing one hand holding a pear, the other a spatula. It was so hard to concentrate on what I was doing. Tears stood in my eyes, old tears that had lain unused for years. But something infinitely worse was to come, and I pressed my face into my shoulder as the other figure formed behind the first, a child with a face utterly laid waste.

Mr. Leary wheeled up to the kitchen door. "What's a Sitwell?" he asked politely. I took a deep breath and tried to expel it slowly so that my voice would be even. But the two figures were still there; it was as if I could hear them breathing in the room.

"It says a Sitwell," he explained, "eleven letters."

"Sacheverell," I said, and spelled it for him, turning around. He caught my eye with a look of self-mockery for his ignorance, trying to please me, to cajole me. I bent down and lit the oven, looking hopelessly into the flame as the two ghosts gathered at its blue center. He had ripped them from their gauze by his presence, and as long as he was with me, they, with their soft grievous breathing, would be with me.

Chapter

18

"Go to bed," I said. All evening I had sat staring at the floor in a kind of stupor. Now it was late.

"I think I'll just sit up tonight," he replied in his strained, courteous voice. "I'm not really sleepy, I'll just sit here and read, or finish this crossword puzzle."

"Can you still be expecting Darlene?" I asked contemptuously.

He shook his head with a smile, but I knew her failure to appear had been a bitter blow. "Or are you afraid of being killed in your sleep?" I asked.

Again the smile, this time thinner. And now he caught my eye once more with that forced look of merry self-deprecation: "Not that I'm very good at these crossword puzzles, I can see how stupid I am . . ."

"I said go to bed."

He wheeled heavily to his room. I locked the door after him and went outside for the night air, climbing the steps to my wicker chair in the little clearing. It was much better outdoors. I felt alone. It had been days, I realized, since I had felt alone;

and it had not just been Mr. Leary, and callers, but those re-kindled memories. Those I could not be rid of by walking off alone, but at least out here in the darkness they were easier to bear. The strait lay below me a serpentine moon-washed gray; the wind was cool and now and again rose high to beat through the trees. Somewhere nearby a dog moved in the underbrush with a sporadic crackling; or so I thought until a voice stung the silence, a man's, loosing a curse. A crash followed, and a female laugh; then a girl ran quickly down the steps. It was silent again. I wondered if the man would also go away or if he would walk into the clearing, and I rubbed my cold arms thinking that I should leave; but presently a figure stumbled into sight. It was Steve Shotwell. I was faintly disappointed.

He walked over and lit a cigarette. Leaves were stuck to his clothes; apparently the girl had pushed him into the underbrush. He stood looking at me with the cigarette dangling gangster fashion from his lips, a big well-developed boy with high cheek-bones and narrow amber eyes and a straight blunt nose that seemed suited to the sneer that always wrinkled it. Only his teeth marred his appearance: badly decayed, almost black. We had never conversed; on the occasions that I paid him to perform chores my silence was always matched by his. But to-night he was drunk; I caught the whiff of beer on his breath as he leaned forward. "What're you doing up here?" he asked.

"I sit here because I choose to."

"You look different."

In spite of myself I glanced down at my new dress, pleased.

He was moving his lower jaw back and forth theatrically. Frustrated by the girl, he was now rerouting his sixteen-year-old lust in my direction. Abruptly, though tentatively, he laid his hand on my arm.

"Are you insane?" I asked.

Just as abruptly he removed it and shuffled away, but my arm was warm where he had touched it, and it bloomed in me that I liked the feel of that rough young hand, and that — my eyes blinked in the dark with embarrassment — I would like to see his body unclothed. All the times I had looked at him and never been struck by the fact of his body . . . strange; for it was the only thing I was struck by now. His body, bubbling with youthful juices. I would like to feel it pressed down on mine. It was a desire of astounding novelty, and I moved uncomfortably in my chair.

He was leaning against a tree, looking out at the strait.

At length I said casually, "Was that your girlfriend?"

He shrugged, picking up a stone and throwing it down the hill. "You know Felix?" he asked suddenly, the glowing ember of his cigarette moving up and down in the dark. "He said when you moved here you used to run around these hills like you had a devil on your tail."

"I beg your pardon?" I said after a pause.

". . . Like somebody out of a book," he said.

"Why does Felix discuss me?" I asked sharply.

"He don't discuss you. I asked him."

"Why?"

And flinging another stone as hard as he could, he muttered, "I don't know," and slouched down the steps.

I left a while later, mildly amused and flattered by the boy's unexpected interest. Going into the house, I curled up on the sofa with a book, hoping to dull the persisting sensuousness by reading.

I woke late in the morning, the book still in my lap, the lights still burning. Someone was rapping on the door and Mr. Leary was yelling from his room, "Rose! The door! The door!"

I stumbled to my feet and unlocked the old man's door for appearance's sake and then, still dazed by sleep and wildly confused, I answered the front door. It was Husar, wearing a bright red shirt and a brilliant smile that together almost blinded me. "You . . . you said. a week," I stammered, but my mind was rapidly calculating. It had been almost a week, six days. My period of grace was over.

"Well, Mr. Husar!" Mr. Leary exclaimed heartily behind me, "Come in, come in. Where are your manners, Rose? Ask the gentleman in." He was disheveled, drawn, wearing the same clothes he had worn yesterday; he must have sat up in the wheelchair all night. But his eyes were bright and alert. "Well!" he said again as Husar entered. "How have you been? Excuse my appearance, I was just going to change. How have you been?"

"Fine," Husar answered, surprised by the old man's poise, and looking at me with a lift of his thick eyebrows.

He had come to finish our talk, and the old man swiftly seized this opportunity for his own ends. "You just sit down and have your talk," he said, "and I'll go on down to Mrs. Shotwell's. She asked me over today."

"You misunderstood her, Uncle Patrick," I said, my spine stiffening.

"No I didn't. Yesterday she said, 'You come on down tomorrow and let Mrs. Munck have a day to herself.' You heard her yourself, Rose." He looked at Husar. "You wouldn't mind giving me a hand down there, would you?"

"No," Husar said agreeably.

"But it's out of the question!" I snapped, my heart pounding.

"Why?" the old man asked quietly. "Why are you making

such a big fuss about it? You're acting very strange. Anybody would think you didn't want to let me out of this house."

"Oh, for heaven's take, then go if you must!" I threw Husar a bright, put-upon smile, but my lips were like ice.

"Fine, let me just change my shirt," Mr. Leary said, and I followed him to his room.

"Help me off with this shirt," he demanded, all yesterday's craven politeness stripped from his voice. Reluctantly, I pulled it off and helped him into a clean one. "Now, a tie," he said, thrusting his chin out, and I ground my fingernails like a serrated bottle cap into the jaw before obeying. Then he wheeled off to wash his face. I leaned, distraught, by the closet door, which stood open. All Harley's clothes still hung there, his shapeless gray slacks, his work clothes still covered with brick dust, his old striped bathrobe. A thousand times he had wrapped that robe around him to sit down at the breakfast table, talking, talking, talking, though I never listened. The day before he was taken to the hospital he had gotten out of his sickbed to come into the kitchen where I was eating breakfast. He wanted company, he wanted to talk. I still remembered shreds of his conversation . . . Mrs. Piggott, whose husband had brought another woman into their house . . . the big carp someone had caught by the brickworks . . . something about the old jail being fixed up. That was his life, the life of others, and as usual I only vaguely listened, comparing him in his dirty old robe to the neat young man he had once been. I had walked out of the room in the middle of his words, and when I returned he had crept back to bed where he lay with his square calloused hand over his eyes.

I shut the closet door. Why should I keep thinking of Harley, why now, when I had such important things to concentrate on? Mr. Leary wheeled through the hall, his face washed and his

fringe of hair combed. He looked crisp, almost natty. "O.K.,"
he said, joining Husar, who bent down to help him out of the
wheelchair. I walked over to them, trying to appear natural, but
my face felt like granite. He would be as good as a thousand
miles away from me, free, with access to a telephone, and I
would be stuck up here. I said suddenly to Husar, "I'd like to
get outdoors for a while. We could have our talk while we
walked . . . I'll just get my sweater." And I ran to my room,
throwing a glance at the mirror and stopping dead in my tracks.
I wriggled out of my crumpled orange dress and looked desperately for something to wear, finally yanking on my white dress.
But it was wrong for a stroll, all my clothes were wrong for a
simple stroll! I clutched my face, unable to move beyond this
crushing fact. My God, to think all these years I had tramped
along the tracks and over the hills in long print dresses like a lunatic woman. And this frilly white dress! Idiotic! I looked like
an old child bride. I would have given anything for Darlene's
faded pedal pushers, anything to make me look less eccentric.
Hurriedly, I ran a comb through my hair, dashed on some lipstick, and picking up my sweater I joined the two men, picturing
the fashionable women that thronged the streets of San Francisco where Husar had just come from.

Carrying the folded wheelchair, I followed them down the
steps to the Shotwell house. Darlene answered Husar's knock,
filling the air with surprised pleasure at the sight of him; but
seeing me, the light in her great eyes went out. "Uncle Patrick
wanted to visit," I told her, "but I'm sure you'd rather he came
some other time . . ."

"No, no, it's fine," she said, her eyes resting again on Husar,
then moving to the beaming Mr. Leary who lay in his arms.
Her husband, Royal, was asleep on the discarded sofa in the

backyard, a tall juiceless man, all creases and creaking joints, with a thatch of hair the color of old ivory. Maybe, I thought hopefully, he would reject the elderly intruder. But I doubted it. Darlene was too intent on having him. I suspected her interest sprang from more than his morbid description of his confinement. I suspected he had told her I was being paid handsomely for keeping him, and that it would be to her advantage to take over the job. And now that he had cracked his isolation, he could use this opportunity to call his relatives, perhaps even the police.

A moment later the door closed and he was beyond my reach. Looking back over my shoulder as I walked away, I condemned myself for my ineptitude, yet quite apart from what was happening with Mr. Leary I felt a strange buoyancy. The day was mild, the birds sang, and I was alive. Still alive, and walking along with another person — there was something quietly astonishing about it; it had the spacious simplicity of a good dream. A pepper tree stirred in the wind, a cat stretched and rolled luxuriously in the dust before us, and the dust settled, softly. Everything was fresh, luminous, enduring.

"This place is a junkyard," my companion said.

The buoyancy sank.

"It's a pigsty of welfare cases," he added, "a slum in the country."

We sat down on a log by the water.

"Oh yes," I admitted, "the houses have gone to pot, but the scenery is wonderful."

"The scenery's great," he agreed, but I caught an element of practicality in his enthusiasm. I studied him as he looked back across the town. His heavy lips were for a moment curved into a smile; his thick dark hair, gray at the temples, was cut short like a military man's and was unmoved by the breeze. "You live here in Port Carquinez, don't you?" I asked. "It surprised me. Why do you live here?"

"I live in the city, but I've got business here so I stay on now and then."

"Do you enjoy staying here?"

"It's a change."

"Then why do you want to mutilate the very atmosphere you enjoy?"

"Not mutilate, Mrs. Munck. Enhance."

"Enhance with concrete and crowds? Ridiculous!" But I could not bring my whole mind to bear on the conversation. It kept returning to Mr. Leary back there with the Shotwells, and it was pleasantly aware of the soft wind on my face, and unpleasantly aware of my silly dress. And it was far too aware of Husar, of his restless gray eyes, which had dropped once to my breasts and legs. "Perhaps you'd better tell me exactly what your company wants," I said abruptly. "What would you want with my house if I were to sell it?"

He sat forward eagerly.

"Don't jump to conclusions," I warned him, "I won't sell." Just then a figure in fluorescent pink started picking its way toward us along the tracks, waving languidly. It was Bobby Piggott, who, when she arrived, dropped down on the log between us with a grunt. "Haven't seen you around lately, Husar," she said at once. "Where've you been?"

"In the city." His voice was breezy, yet familiar. "You're looking very good, Bobby. New hairdo?" He gave the orange edifice an appreciative look and her eyes brightened. How odd, I thought. There was no real warmth or interest in his tone; why did he bother? Already he was lighting a cigarette with his usual look of preoccupation.

"I'm tired of fishing," Bobby sighed from between us. "God

am I tired of fishing." Her eyes were resting on two figures down the beach. One I recognized as her husband. He was fishing with one hand and holding a woman around the waist with the other. I recalled what Harley had said about a ménage à trois.

"Well, what do you do?" she whispered to me. "So I fish with them."

Husar got abruptly to his feet and suggested we be on our way, and Bobby joined us, hobbling along in her high heels, waving to her husband. At the frontage Husar turned to her. "O.K., Bobby, see you later. Her face fell, but she nodded. "Take care, doll," he added, giving her arm a squeeze.

"I think her feelings were hurt," I said as he and I began walking up Locust Street.

"She's a drag. Christ!" And the smile that followed was meant to show that he felt very differently about me. Nervous and embarrassed, I looked away.

I had not seen Mrs. Pompano's house for years, and now as we passed it I glanced at her porch and could envisage the old woman sweeping down the stairs with lumpy majesty to avenge some lost soul deceived by the night. The house, boarded up for the twenty years since her death, was all but lost under vines and bushes.

"See," said Husar, "even here, the stable part of town — Little Italy, isn't that what it's called? — everything's falling apart."

"So let it fall apart. What does it matter to you? Anyway, will you please tell me what you want with my house?"

"We've got a motel and restaurant in mind for that hill you're on," he said. "That should give you some indication of how valuable your property is. I could quote figures . . ."

"Don't bother. I'm not selling."

"Then you'd better anticipate living cheek and jowl with a motel. You've got a vacant lot between you and your nearest neighbor, but if we build we'll build within an inch of your fence. As for the other side of the hill, across from those wooden steps, we intend to sheer it off and build a swimming pool at the bottom. Of course you'll still have your view, but . . ."

"You're sadistic," I said, stopping in my tracks.

"Not so sadistic that I want to see you run over," he laughed, taking my arm. Suddenly I could not bear his glaring red shirt and casual talk about motels and swimming pools, and I pulled away, half sensing that it was also his touch I was squirming from.

"To be honest, Mrs. Munck," he went on, "isn't a clean motel preferable to a dump like the Shotwells'?"

"It's not just a motel! It's a marina and a restaurant and a swimming pool and a crowd of rubbernecks milling around. It's the whole idea!"

"Times change," he murmured, looking down at Tule Lake which lay below us. It had once been a swimming hole but the water had receded over the years until it was now nothing but a rank quagmire. I scrambled down to the old footbridge all grown over with reeds. This pond is mine, I said angrily to myself, the town is mine, that fool is an alien. I half hoped as he started to follow me that he would trip over his own feet and plunge into the tule. "Hey," he called in a warning, "you're not dressed for a hike."

"Who cares?" I returned contemptuously, and glancing back I was surprised by the expression of admiration on his face. Pressing on, I quickly reached the other side where I began to climb the steep hill that rose above the pond. I didn't stop until

I had reached the top. My body was pleasantly tired, and the sensual promptings that had disturbed it earlier now seemed calmed. When he caught up with me, sometime later, there was a wide stripe of sweat down the back of his shirt, his suede shoes were muddy, and he was breathing like a bellows. "What was that all about?" he gasped.

"This isn't your land, Mr. Husar. Maybe you can buy it but it will never belong to you."

He gave a breathless laugh. "You're an unusual woman."

"How would you know?"

"You were born and raised here, I take it?" he asked, sitting down beside me, still catching his breath.

"No, I wasn't."

"May I ask why you moved here?"

"My husband's work."

He was silent for a moment. Then he said softly, "I know your husband passed away not long ago, Mrs. Munck. I'm sorry all this business has come right on the heels of your loss."

It sounded like a phrase he had got up beforehand. To each what she seemed to want: flattery for Bobby, respect for Mrs. Munck. I got up and walked across the hill toward the Snake Road and he rose and followed, still puffing. "I suppose your job doesn't provide you with much exercise, does it?" I asked. He didn't reply. "Do you like your kind of work?"

"It's a job."

"It's a swindle. Everyone knows land development is a swindle."

"I wanted to talk to you about your house," he said with an edge of honest anger in his voice. "If you want to trade insults I'm sorry."

At once I liked him better, and when he stepped onto the road and continued walking away from town I made no objection, though I was anxious to stay near the Shotwells'. He was tall beside me; his feet were large and they trod the old road with a solid, masculine rhythm that was soothing.

"I've seen an old cemetery from my car," he said after a while, squinting across the hills. "It's really wild."

"Yes, it's very overgrown."

"No, I mean wild. You know, far-out. I'd like to look around it."

"It's two miles away."

"Are you game?"

I thought of Mr. Leary, but what difference did it make if I was one mile or three miles away from him? And the cemetery was a worthwhile place.

When we got there Husar gazed around with his hands on his hips. The Snake Road ran straight through, separating the Catholic side from the Protestant. "Here," I said, "I'll show you the Catholic side." It was a bald plateau overlooking a sewage plant by the tracks. Its gate always ajar, it invited every vandal in the county: rubbish littered the graves, the headstones were toppled. I was sure Frank and Cathleen would leave the funeral arrangements to me. This is where Mr. Leary would be buried.

My companion crossed the road to the other side where the tree-jeweled hill rose up almost perpendicular. Following him to the stone steps, I waited there, leaning against the retaining wall with its garlands of bougainvillaea. I had been there a thousand times and had always derived a serenity from the old tombstones under which all sorrow and worry was ended. Silence always lay like a film over every blade of grass. Often at dusk deer came down, sometimes even in broad daylight. Now, suddenly, a flock of white birds appeared overhead, and like the elegant gesture of a white hand, they described an arc and disappeared beyond the trees, their cry filling my ears. I threw down a leaf I had been shredding and ran up the stone steps, taking a path to the left.

The mound of dirt was still swollen. The headstone was small, the cheapest I had been able to purchase.

Harley S. Munck

1917–1962

That was all. Not even the intaglio of a dove. Actions could be shuffled over in retrospect, in private, but the shabby enduring testimonials were unalterable.

Husar had walked up behind me. "I'm sorry," he said, "I didn't think when I suggested coming up here."

"It's quite all right," I replied, looking at the withered wreaths from the funeral. "Since preparing for my uncle's visit I haven't had a chance to get up here. I'm glad to have the opportunity." Crouching down, I picked some pale pink wildflowers that stood out vividly from the shady ground. Harley would have been grateful. Even at his worst, when he was sour and querulous, there was a place where offerings could be made.

But the gesture by its very tardiness rang false. I threw down the flowers and walked back down the steps. Husar followed silently.

"Don't be embarrassed," I told him as we neared the town. "You must know that there are marriages and marriages."

Chapter

19

INSIDE THE SHOTWELL HOUSE the children quarreled around the television set, two lean hounds growled in a corner, Bobby shouted over the telephone, and Royal lay sound asleep on the sofa, his feet mashed up against a welter of orange peels and newspapers. In the middle of all this Mr. Leary sat in his wheelchair, his good hand clasped over his paunch, the picture of contentment. Clothes, torn magazines, beer cans, and empty glasses littered the tables and chairs, which were haphazardly arranged on the bare floor, so that you felt these people never sat together to eat or talk, never sat down at all except to crane their necks at the television or to tie a shoe. There was a feeling in the room of perpetual movement like that found in the most benighted savages who, not knowing how to work or play, peregrinate through life poking at the soil for roots, and die where they fall.

Darlene, coming from the kitchen, looked tired and irritable. She switched off the television. The children turned it on again. She shrugged and resigned herself to conversing in a shout, assuming, I suppose, that it was more ladylike to yell than to punch the children. Royal snored on. And now, at last, Mr.

Leary wheeled through the mess to my side. I stiffened, waiting for his words. He was back in his elder statesman role, quiet, self-confident. "You missed a marvelous meal," he told us with a smile. "Mrs. Shotwell has talents a Waldorf chef might envy."

But Darlene didn't hear. She seemed worried; her eyes kept wandering to Bobby, who had been on the phone since we arrived but who now slammed the receiver down and looked at us with her face screwed into a knot. As we watched, the knot came apart, and running from the room she gave vent to a loud sob.

"Damn," Darlene sighed, "I'll be back in a minute. You come with me, Mrs. Munck."

I cringed at the request but I could not refuse with so many eyes on me, and I hurried after her down the hall to a dark bedroom where Bobby had thrown herself across a rumpled bed and lay weeping. With one long arm Darlene flipped her friend over on her back and the unmuffled sobs rang through the room. "Will you shut up?" she said, and after a moment's hesitation slapped her hard across the face. "Roll up the shade," she told me, looking uneasily at her palm.

I did as she asked, finding myself in a surpassingly chaotic room whose closet door stood open, revealing the figure of Chlorinda curled up on the floor with a strip of mangy fur.

"Get out," her mother said in an aside, and the child slipped from the room, looking back with wide but unfrightened eyes. "You all right now?" Darlene asked Bobby.

"Give me a cigarette," she said, "I'm all right. What'd you hit me for?"

"Because I'm sick of your crying and whining. No, don't go, Mrs. Munck. I want you to talk to her."

My fingers rose nervously to my throat. "Why me?"

"You talk to her!" And the door closed, leaving me panic stricken.

Minutes passed. Finally Bobby let out a long sigh. "I guess I brood too much."

I searched my mind for something to say. "Would it help if you had more to do?" I finally asked.

"Hell, I've always worked. During the season, over at the Martinez cannery."

I tried again. "Sometimes, adopting a child . . ."

"When I've already raised my own?"

"I didn't know. You seem so young to have grown children."

"They're both married now. They married young, like me . . . I married Rob at fifteen . . ."

I gave a deep inward groan, no longer nervous but bored and impatient.

"Robert and Roberta . . ." she went on. "When he used to come home at night it was like we were two Siamese twins who'd been cut apart all day." She jerked her head in the direction of her house. "You think it was him who got tired of me? That it was him who stopped feeling like Robert and Roberta? He *never* stopped feeling that way, and I swear he never will! No, it was me. A long time ago. I admit it, I started playing around, I'm still playing around, but nobody ever lit me up like Rob did, and I always come back to him." She looked at me angrily. "You think I'm a slob? That's the word she used, this broad he moves into our house under my own nose. Who's she to come between us? It's *him* and *me!* And always will be! But now they're moving to Crockett together as soon as they can. He told me that a couple hours ago. And when I made a fuss — Jesus Christ, who wouldn't? — he locks me out of my own house. And won't say anything on the phone except that it's all settled." Her voice dropped. "I know I don't deserve anything else, but I never meant to hurt him. I always liked him better than all the others rolled together."

"I see," I murmured. "But how could he know that?"

"And it's not just losing Rob," she pursued with a ragged sigh, "it's this feeling I get of wasting thirty-seven whole years. I look back and all I see is time going by and none of it meaning anything . . . sometimes I get this nutty idea — I never told anybody — what if somewhere there was a street named after me? Just a very short street, even? I even had a dream about it once. I was walking through this strange town and suddenly there in front of me was this big sign that said Roberta Piggott Boulevard."

"Well," I said, "if you want a boulevard named after you, you had better go somewhere else, start over again, do something."

"Do what?"

"I don't know. I am not God."

She took a deep breath. "As long as we're here I think I ought to tell you something. You know last spring? . . ." She stopped, took another breath and went on. "I was driving over to Martinez and I saw your husband walking along the Snake Road with his fishing pole and I give him a lift. Well, to make a long story short, we had a couple of beers in Martinez and afterwards we drove to this friend of mine's house who wasn't home but I had the key." She looked at me anxiously.

My heart was pounding, not with jealousy, but with the shocking strangeness of the scene. "Harley and I led separate lives," I said in a calm tone. "This is no concern of mine."

She nodded, relieved. "I got that feeling. I mean that you led separate lives. He was a very lonesome type guy."

I remembered the spring in question. Yes, he had been terribly restless, and terribly kind to me. Poor man, to suffer such pangs of conscience over something that would have meant nothing to me. I had often wished, in fact, that he had someone on the side to drain off the trickle of passion with which he occasionally bothered me, but he was a dull, sour-mouthed man whose lack of vigor or charm had all but obscured his gender, and always I knew no one would want him.

"Did you find Harley attractive?" I asked, curious.

"Oh, I don't know. I guess I'm not very particular."

I could have slapped her, for his sake; instead I turned away, thinking again of Tule Lake. In the beginning, when Harley came home from work we would slip on our bathing suits and go down for a dip before it got dark. All around the water grew a mass of yellow bushes that seemed almost tropical, and beneath them lay the beach, white dirt, velvet to the touch. I loved to swim; I never felt freer than when I was in the water, even with Harley beside me. Somehow, in the water we got along fine. And when we crawled out, dripping, and looked at each other through matted eyelashes, we smiled in a way that would have embarrassed me at any other time. I would lie back against him and stare up the side of the steep hill, blue with summer haze. Hawks soared lazily, our eyes closed, and we slept. We would wake late; it was still warm, but the shadows had lengthened and all the colors, so pale and dusty a while ago, were deep and cool except for the leaves of the bushes, burning like hammered gold in the low sun. It would not have hurt me to put those wildflowers on his grave, even if it was too late.

I went to the door. I wanted to dislike her, but I couldn't. She was not malicious, only stupid. She got up from the bed now, a shy smile on her lips. "Could I come and visit you sometime? I wouldn't stay long." She paused reflectively. "See, it's like I go along doing these things I mentioned and I don't know why. I want to say: maybe I will and maybe I won't, and make a choice. Maybe you could help me."

"The whole point of making a choice," I said, "is making it yourself."

"But I could drop in for a minute, maybe?"

I shrugged, closing the door, annoyed that I could not be harsh with her. Darlene took me immediately aside. "I hope you told her to straighten up and fly right," she said. "See, what I want is for her to move away now. It's a bad situation. She ought to go somewhere else."

"I should think so. It must be very dull in this town for someone with her inclinations."

"Oh, it's not all that dull. There's plenty guys here she can shack up with and has. She's even given Steve the eye. And you've noticed how she acts around Husar. I don't like her undressing him with her eyes, it looks bad, she's my own sister-in-law," and her great eyes filled with sullen, jealous heat. "You ought to persuade her to leave now. She thinks you're smart, she'd listen to you . . ."

"It should be her own decision," I said impatiently, looking toward the living room. "I must decline your request."

"Ah, why don't you stop talking like a book?" she said ungraciously, leading me back to the other room where I found Mr. Leary smiling, looking very sure of himself. But he was coming back with us; Husar was wheeling him to the door. I almost closed my eyes with relief.

Royal had progressed from the couch to a chair where he sat, chin in hand, dully following the roaring antics of a cartoon character on the television screen while the children roughhoused around him. It was a clamor, but an empty one; something in the emptiness of it seemed kin to the soul of my own house, and this surprised me, for I had always thought these people suffered from something I could not understand.

As we went to the door Darlene looked with mounting rancor not only at Husar and me leaving together, but at the room we were leaving her to. "It's always nice to see my favorite people," Husar said with a roguish smile, and her coarse neck reddened with pleasure. Then he lifted Mr. Leary into his arms and I folded the wheelchair and followed them outside. It was almost dark now, and through the gloom I saw that Steve was coming through the gate. Husar asked the boy to carry the wheelchair for me, and he took it from me, not looking at my face.

We had almost reached my house before he spoke, then he said in a low tone, gruffly, "I was stoned last night."

"It doesn't matter. I enjoyed our conversation."

He sighed, as though relieved, and a moment later allowed something pent up to burst out in an angry exclamation. "You know what they're doing, don't you? They're sending her away!"

"You mean Bobby?"

"Bobby?" he echoed impatiently. "Hell no . . ." We had joined the others at the gate. He handed me the wheelchair and started back down, but slowly, looking back over his shoulder. And I felt that whether I wanted it or not here was another one, like Bobby, who would be showing up one day with a woeful appeal in his eyes. Leave me alone! I cried under my breath.

I unlocked the door and we went inside. I felt drained; it seemed I had done nothing but talk all day — more talk in one day than I had indulged in for months at a time. But Mr. Leary was in rare spirits and wanted us all to have a drink. Husar declined, saying he had work to do. "Look," he said to me at the door, "let me put it to you this way: you'd get a lot more for this house than it's worth. The place has had it, it's practically sliding off its foundation. You'd have to move in a few years anyway. If you sold now you'd make a tremendous profit on a worthless house."

"I'm not interested in a profit."

Again I saw the admiring look touch his face. I thought suddenly, with a pang that startled me: why does he have to represent an ugly enterprise? Why can't he just be a private person?

"Come around again, Mr. Husar," Mr. Leary called from his wheelchair, giving a snappy salute. "Always a pleasure to see you." As soon as the door closed he turned to me, and I waited for his words with a foreboding. "I had an interesting conversation on the phone while you were gone," he informed me.

"Did you really? With whom?"

"With Frank."

I said nothing. His face was bursting with triumph. "Yes," he said, "yes, I spoke to Frank. Spoke with Louise, too. Monica was visiting, but I didn't get to talk with her. Didn't get to talk with the kids, they were out . . ."

"Get to the point."

"Frank is driving over here tomorrow. He and Louise and the kids. The whole family. They're coming to get me."

"Coming to get you?" I repeated tonelessly. "Frank said so?"

"Well, how in God's name do you *think* he'd react after what I told him?"

"What did you tell him?"

"I told him exactly what was happening. He was horrified."

I lowered myself into a chair. I was sure he wasn't lying; he had always been able to pretend outrage, but never satisfaction.

It was unbelievable that I had misjudged Frank so badly.

"Still," I said, so tired I could scarcely form the words, "you'll just go back to the nursing home. You'll just turn into a vegetable again. It's no future."

"I tell you, Rose," he said exuberantly, "I want something — a flat of my own again, I want to see people, I want to do things. I told Frank that."

I looked at him with unconcealed hatred and wondered how, probably for the hundredth time in his life, he had managed to come out on top. Any other old man taken from a nursing home and put into the hands of someone intent on destroying him would have shriveled up and died; but he had merely profited by the change.

"And what about you?" he asked. "What are your plans for the future?"

"Maybe I have some plans for you tonight."

"It wouldn't be wise, old girl. No, it wouldn't be wise. Not after what I told Frank. You really had me going at the start, I thought you didn't care about consequences. But you're as anxious to live out the rest of your life as anybody else. That's why you won't take any chances. That's why you won't do anything tonight."

I looked away. It was true.

"Well," he said, "what about a little drink? It's still early."

"Mix it yourself."

"Too much trouble. Too awkward with this useless old arm of mine. You know what it's like having an arm and leg like this? It's like carrying a lot of junk you can't use. That's why I never moved around at Twin Oaks. They wanted to give me therapy but I let 'em know it wasn't for me. But I tell you, I'd like a go at some therapy now. Wouldn't need anybody to show me how, either. I saw the others doing it. I know the exercises. You flex. You try to flex. And you try and you try, and lo and behold, a muscle finally moves." With his good hand he laid the paralyzed arm on his thigh and looked at it with smiling patience. "You can't expect results right off the bat. It takes time. I've got an idea the thumb and forefinger will be the first to move. They've always been different from the other fingers. I get twinges in them now and then."

"Why don't you go to bed?"

"No, I want to have a serious chat with you, Rose. About your future. Now, what about this Husar? Think you've got a chance with him? Think you know how to act around a normal man after twenty-five years of Harley?"

"Shut up about Harley."

"Shut *up* about him? *Somebody* ought to talk about him. Here he is, not even cold in his grave and it's like he never existed. Poor Harley. Poor old Harley. What'd you do it for? Marry a poor fart like that? Louse up your whole future, and his too. Because he'd have been all right with some ordinary little broad who didn't have delusions of grandeur, somebody who'd have given him a couple of kids and a pat on the back once in a while. That's all he wanted."

I moved my tongue hesitantly. "He could have left me."

"But he *loved* you. Jesus Christ, Rose, don't you realize the poor man loved you?"

"How do you know?" I flared. "How would you know anything about it?"

"Because I know what he was like. The soul of slobbering gratitude. Besides, Monica told me how crazy he was about you." He wheeled slowly to his bedroom. At the door he stopped. "How come you two never had any kids? You should have, Rose. You'd have been a great mother. As long as you didn't drop something on them."

He wheeled hastily inside and shut the door. He would probably extricate the knife from under the mattress or wherever he had now secreted it, and lay it across his lap in case I came screaming in. But he had assessed my mood shrewdly; it was one of defeat. My eyes rested on my limp hands. She used to take my fingers and try to pull each one straight, always surprised and delighted when she was finished that I had curled them up again. I could feel the touch of that small hand like a live coal.

Too exhausted to get up and go to bed, I remained in the chair I was sitting in, and when toward morning I fell asleep, I dreamed of her. She did not appear in this dream as an infant, but as a child of four or five. She stood on a deserted road waiting for me, and as I hurried toward her — thinking in the natural, unsurprised way of dreams: there she is, she's been lost for over an hour, but I see her now, waiting for me — everything was bathed in a glow from the familiar reddish sheen of that hair. But when I reached her and stretched out my arms, I saw with horror, but again without surprise, that her face was deeply crushed and had been sealed up with something hard, like cement.

Chapter

20

"WE'LL HAVE an early breakfast," Mr. Leary said the next morning. "They'll probably be here before noon."

There will be a tomorrow, I thought, looking at him, and he will be gone. This quarter-century void will have been for nothing. I had no appetite, but I put some bread in the toaster and made fresh coffee. He sat working on his hand. "I got the thumb to quiver last night," he remarked. "Here, watch," and he concentrated on the thumb, glancing proudly at me with his small, intense eyes.

"Go to hell."

"Soften up, baby, you'll never get anywhere being nasty." He buttered the toast as well as he could with one hand and took a big bite. Swallowing, he said, "Tell me something, I've always been curious: did you keep it from Harley that you had a kid and what happened to it?"

My eyes widened in a frozen stare. Why couldn't I grab a paring knife from the drawer and plunge it into his neck, right there where the loose flesh rose like accordion pleats from under his collar, since in this long week I hadn't found some graceful, nonincriminating way of ending his life?

"Or did you let him in on it?" he continued. "Is that why he stayed with you? Felt sorry for you?" He leaned back, snapping his fingers. "I've got it. You told him about it, and that's why he never wanted any kids. Afraid you'd sweep 'em off the front porch, or run 'em through the wringer with the wash . . ."

Throwing myself across the table, I tore at his face with my fingernails, but he fought back with a new vigor, banging away with his knotted fist at my head and finally pushing himself back from the table and spinning around in the middle of the floor. "Cut it out!" he warned, wheeling swiftly into the living room where he pulled back the curtain from the window and looked out. His face relaxed, he grinned and waved in a beckoning arc. "Two kids sitting on the steps," he muttered curtly to me, still smiling at them. "They see me, you better leave off." A moment later he added, "The boy's coming up."

I went to the door and flung it open. It was Steve. "He doesn't want anything, he was just waving to you," I told him shortly.

"I wanted to talk to you anyway," he said, his face closed with gloom and anger.

"Some other time!" I said harshly, and he stepped back, almost flinching. I looked again at him. "Only for a minute, then," I said with impatience. He glanced down the steps at Chlorinda, who was draped around one of the hounds, and followed me inside.

"We want to talk privately," I told Mr. Leary. "Go to your room."

"I'll go out on the front porch and wait," he replied cheerfully. "Fog's dried off already, looks like it'll be a fine day."

As soon as the front door closed Steve flung himself down on the sofa. "They're taking Chlorinda away," he said bitterly. "Up to Sonoma, this nuthouse for retarded children."

"But why?" I asked.

"Because she's a moron!" he said loudly, cracking his knuckles. "Jesus Christ, she's ten years old."

"Ten? I thought she was four or five." I reflected for a moment. "But in that case, perhaps it's for the best."

"Why?" he asked, even more loudly, leaning forward. "She's not hurting anybody. Mom don't want to be bothered with her, that's all."

"Wait just a moment. There are six or seven of you children, aren't there? Your mother has a great deal of work, not much money, perhaps little moral support from your father . . ."

"I know all that crap. I live there! I know what she's like. The place is a rat nest, and she and him are the big rats and all the kids are gonna grow up into rats like them . . ."

I was startled by his vehemence, but I said hopefully, "Then be thankful Chlorinda's getting away."

"Ah, Chlorinda's safe. She's crazy. They could never get to her. Besides, I always looked out for her. She's O.K." His face was hard with restrained sorrow and with the tough boy's shame for such feelings. I wanted to touch his hand, but could not find it in me to do it. "I'm sorry," I said, "it's hard to part with a child you care about."

"I'm leaving, too," he said abruptly.

"Won't your parents worry if you run away?"

"I thought you had more brains!"

"Don't be impertinent."

"There's nobody in this dump I'm telling except you, and you talk to me like one of those welfare workers."

"All right. It's quite possible your parents won't be at all upset if you run away. Where are you going?"

"Sacramento. I know a guy up there can get me a job in a motorcycle repair shop." He cracked his knuckles again, working something over in his mind. At last he put his hands on his knees. "She and him always said you were a screwball, but anybody who'd pay a mind to them would be a screwball himself. When I come up here and worked in your yard it always got to me there was something else. I mean something besides . . . I don't know, besides all that." He gestured in the direction of his house. "I don't know. You didn't have to say anything."

But he wanted me to say something now. I looked at him, unsure. "I knew there was something else, too, when I was your age. I was young, too, when I left home."

"What'd you want?" he asked.

"Want?" My mind reeled back twenty-five years, and the burst of words that followed could not have startled him more than it did me. "I had an idea about taking a ship somewhere. To feel the ocean under me . . . and I wanted to get off somewhere where I'd never been before, and not know what would happen next. I wanted to see everything . . . the Russian steppes . . . the gargoyles on Notre Dame . . . I wanted to walk in old gardens, and I wanted to write poetry . . ." I broke off, mortified.

"Did you?"

"What?" I asked, trying to regain my composure.

"Did you do those things?"

I looked at his serious, intent eyes. "Yes," I lied.

He stood up and went to the window. "I never had a thing about going overseas like that. My thing was always panning for gold. I always wanted to get some gear together and go up into the Sierras all alone and camp along one of them big flat rivers. I seen it on TV." He looked gloomy again. "Those crumby bastards," he muttered, staring down at his house where his mother, in an old housecoat, was picking up the paper from the front porch. "I better go," he said. He shook my hand roughly, smiling his tight smile to conceal his ugly teeth.

"Try not to worry about Chlorinda," I said, going to the door with him. "She'll find new friends where she's going. And Steve . . ." I cleared my throat, feeling very awkward, "you be true to yourself."

He nodded and walked down the steps to Chlorinda with a short wave to Mr. Leary, who ignored him. "There's Frank's car!" the old man said excitedly, pointing to the frontage where a blue sedan had just pulled up. I went out on the porch and watched stonily as the car door opened, but it was a man with fishing equipment who stepped out. "Well, it's still early," Mr. Leary said, squinting up at the sun.

The sun climbed steadily into the sky. At noon he called for a glass of water and drank it with short preoccupied sips, his attention divided between the frontage and the old road above. In the early afternoon he wheeled inside to use the bathroom and wheeled directly out again, unbuttoning his collar. By four o'clock I could hear the heavy, pleading roll of the wheelchair on the old boards of the porch.

A deep sense of relief had been growing in me all day. I had not misjudged Frank after all. I had been given another chance. And I knew now what I would do — it had come to me in the space of a second, in a clear, radiant vision: I would buy an automobile, and I would arrange an accident in such a way that no suspicion would be aroused. It would have to be done on some isolated road, on the cliffs along the ocean, or up in the mountains around Lake Tahoe. I had once read a newspaper account of a car that had plunged off a promontory up there by the lake and had hit the bottom with such force that when it was discovered days later a special emergency crew had had to cut it apart to scrape the people out. The account had horrified me at the time, but now I could almost see myself jumping out at just the right moment and rolling along the ground while the car swooped off the edge into the air, hanging for an instant like a ball that has been thrown high and stands still before plummeting back down; then falling, falling, very straight, like a bomb, its tremendous momentum flattening the old man like paper against the back of the seat until — perhaps eons later by his reckoning — there was the ground before him, and all the chrome and metal and upholstery and bones and muscles were one fuming tissue.

I blotted my hands on my dress. First thing in the morning I would walk to Martinez and make my purchase. All the diffused energies and desires of the last week had converged in one searing point.

Just before the sun went down he wheeled slowly in, his face whitened by the evening chill.

"Well?" I said.

"He must have meant tomorrow."

"Do you really believe that?"

Tears stood in his eyes. Lowering his head, he wheeled into his room and would not come out again, not even for supper.

Chapter

21

IT SUITED ME that he wished to stay in his room. I locked his door and went down to Sal's to telephone Frank myself, for if there was the slightest possibility that he meant to come for his father I must know at once. But though I let the phone ring ten or eleven times no one answered. Thoughtfully, I hung up the receiver and went over to the counter to buy some cigarettes. "You're looking very good these days," Sal said, his eyes not meeting mine, perhaps afraid of such intimacy after all the years of monosyllables. "Thank you," I replied, my eyes lingering on my hand, rather square, but smooth and slim fingered, and went out the screen door to be met by a familiar explosion. It was Steve, in his silver-studded black leather jacket, a blue canvas suitcase strapped behind him, roaring down alongside the steps from his house. His hand shot up in farewell as he saw me, then he was careening up Locust Street, his red taillight diminishing over the ruts. Several people had gathered in his wake — Darlene, Royal, Bobby, some of the children — and stood staring at each other almost in a parody of bewilderment. Well, I thought, he's made his escape in the grand style. And in order to avoid the little group I went the other way, slowing as I saw Husar come out from the Railroad Bar. "What's happening over there?" he asked, indicating the group.

"It's Steve. He's just left home for good." I felt very happy, with the sound of the motorcycle now reaching my ears from the Snake Road.

"Left home? Why?" he asked, walking beside me.

"He was afraid of becoming a rat in a pile of beer cans. Don't tell his family that. They're not supposed to know."

"You talked with him?"

"Yes, I encouraged him to leave." The words sounded strange in my ears. I, Mrs. Munck — friend and confidante?

"You encouraged a kid that age . . ."

"He'd already felt the mold growing on him. When you feel that, there's nothing to do but make a change. It doesn't matter if you're sixteen or sixty."

Again I saw the admiring glance. Now the roar of the motorcycle was cut off as the boy put the first hill behind him, and the night was quiet again. We were passing the jailhouse.

He nodded his head toward it. "Come and see what's become of one of your historical monuments." His voice dropped with faint suggestiveness, "If propriety allows." The jolt of response I felt almost made me decline, but I was curious to see the interior of the jailhouse whose abandoned cells had crawled in and out of my imagination for so many years. It was a relief to find the door opening on a spacious room where not a trace of dark punishment remained. "You've done quite a job," I said.

"Not really. The room's only half the size of the building." He tapped the inner wall with his knuckles. "This is just a partition, the other side's untouched. It would have cost a small fortune to renovate the whole thing." Turning, he indicated a chair. "Sit down, make yourself comfortable. Care for a drink?"

"Oh no, thank you so much. I can't stay." I forced my eyes away from him and looked around. "I wonder you chose this building. So very old."

"It was a challenge. Creative."

I had to grant that he had created light from darkness, but such an anonymous light. It might have been an expensive motel room. There hung the bold abstract, there squatted the low, elongated furniture, there lay the wall-to-wall mauve rug. I looked around for some sign of my host's personality but found none. Kneeling by his phonograph, I looked at his records, Broadway hits interlarded with the *Sorcerer's Apprentice*, highlights from *Carmen*, Ravel's *Bolero*.

"My taste in music's pretty crumby," he said. "I never seem to have the time to sit down and listen to anything really creative."

"How often do you stay here?" It was hard to picture him at all in the hundred-year-old jailhouse of a yawning whistlestop.

"Couple nights a week. It's a change."

"From what?"

"Traffic. Phones. Slamming elevators. It's great to suddenly look up from what you're doing at three in the morning and know you're the only person in town still awake."

"Sometimes I'm awake then," I said, and felt my face reddening. I went to the door.

"Like it?" he asked, walking outside with me.

"Do you want an honest answer? No. It lacks flavor. Even an unpleasant flavor."

He accompanied me back down Locust Street. "I have to go in here," I said at Sal's. He rocked back on his heels, his eyes on the dark sky. "You ever wonder . . ." He stopped, his eyes swinging to my face, "how long you've got left?"

I put my hand on Sal's door. "I have to go in here," I repeated.

He started off back down the street toward the Railroad Bar. I hesitated a moment, then went after him. "I'm thinking of buying a car," I said when I caught up with him, "but I don't know much about them . . ."

"I'd be glad to go along with you," he offered at once.

"Oh no, that would be too much of an imposition. But do you think you could look it over for me after I get it?"

"Sure, just let me know when."

I thanked him and returned to Sal's where I called Frank's number again without success. I started back, shivering in the cold. Autumn was coming early this year. Soon the tule fog would settle around the house like a dripping screen, lifting in the afternoons only to disclose a leaden strait and sky. Then the rain would come; it would slant silently into the strait day after day, and sprawling brown puddles would cover the frontage and the railroad ties would turn a sodden black. It was at the year's end that I especially liked to walk across the hills, sloshing through the withered grass with my head bared to the rain. Coming home with my feet numb and my hair plastered to my cheeks, I would sink into a hot bath and feel momentarily happy. But now this held no enticement for me. I had outgrown such solitary pleasures.

Exhausted from my night in the chair, I went to bed early and slept for more than twelve hours, waking with a burst of enthusiasm. I unlocked Mr. Leary's door and threw together a late breakfast, but he would not come to the table. He wheeled sullenly to the window, instead. It was a raw, windy day; the pane rattled noisily. "They'll come today," he assured me, picking nervously at his chin. He had not had a shave since the first time when he had been nicked so badly, and the white bristles were growing long. "I think Frank said Sunday. I'm sure he did."

"Oh, well," I said, going for my coat, "if in the face of all reason you wish to believe . . ."

But he was whipping the curtain aside and flattening his nose against the pane. I strode over to him and followed his gaze. Martinez' only taxicab had pulled up on the frontage and the driver was helping old Aunt Monica out.

"It's Monica! Why, it's Monica!" he cried, and in his excitement the thumb and forefinger of his good hand were going up and down like a vibrating machine. He began slapping the window, shouting, "Monica! Up here!" and then he wheeled furiously to the door to fumble with the knob. I bashed his hand down and stood between him and the door until several minutes later when the knock sounded.

"Monica!" he breathed as she came in, wrapping his good arm around her waist and gazing up at her face. He didn't have far to look. She was tiny as a child and quite bent. Exhausted from her climb, she stood catching her breath; then she said in her frail, powdery voice, "You're looking pretty good, Pat," and her eyes consumed the room with one curious swoop that came to a full stop at my face. "You, too, Rose. What happened?"

"What do you mean?"

"You look ten years younger . . . you look absolutely grand. Why, I thought you'd be so cast down by poor Harley's death."

"Please sit down," I said. "I assume you've come on an errand."

She sat, her legs in their heavy chocolate colored stockings not quite reaching the floor, and removed the hatpin from her little hat, looking all at once surprised at herself. I knew that she had not been out of San Francisco since the spring of 1916 when she attended a wedding in Petaluma. What could have possessed her, I wondered, to take a bus to Oakland, climb aboard the train there, rattle for thirty miles to Martinez, and search the streets for a taxi that swung her around the curves of the Snake Road and finally deposited her in an isolated village with her stomach churning and her wallet flat, only to toil up a flight of steps steeper than Jacob's ladder? I waited inhospitably, the smell of defeat curling uncertainly in my nostrils.

"Wonderful to see you!" her brother was saying over and over, having wheeled as close to her as possible. "Absolutely wonderful! Although I did expect Frank . . ."

"Oh, he was too busy," she said. "He's been called out of town."

"Called out of town? Is that why he didn't come yesterday like he promised?"

"Oh, did he say he was going to come yesterday?"

"Of course," he said impatiently. "I talked to him on the phone Friday. Well, you were there when I called." He threw me a significant look. "I had to call from a neighbor's house. There's no phone *here*. Rose had it disconnected when I came."

"It was a luxury item," I explained to his sister. "I couldn't afford it."

"You?" she said, leaning forward to bite into a subject close to her heart. "A houseowner? And with a husband who had steady work? You're well off! I've *never* been able to afford a telephone."

"I know you're very poor, Aunt Monica."

"I am not poor," she said, her face going hard. "You can't measure wealth by money."

Nevertheless, despite the reckless spirit that had moved her to come this great distance at such an expense, her hands rested on her worn purse with a certain regret.

"Where did he go?" Mr. Leary was asking.

"Who?" said Aunt Monica.

"Frank."

"How could he go anywhere? He's home sick in bed."

Surely, I thought, she was not senile. Though eighty-three, she was more alert and articulate than some people fifty years her junior. I watched her with curiosity as she efficiently tucked the windblown strands of her hair back into her bun. "Yes, he's sick in bed," she repeated.

"You just said he was called out of town," Mr. Leary accused.

"Did I? May I take off my coat, Rose? I got awfully hot climbing all those stairs."

I did not dislike her altogether at that moment. "Would you like some coffee?" I asked, taking her coat. "Some lunch?" With an enthusiastic nod she followed me into the kitchen, saying that she had always wanted to see my little house, and adding that she was sorry Harley wasn't here and that I had certainly been slow enough in letting the family know of his passing. "He was still a young man," she said sadly. "It was such a pity."

"Yes," I said.

Mr. Leary wheeled in behind her, his eyes boring balefully into her back. "When is Frank coming?" he asked.

"Harley was such a quiet child," she said, ignoring him. "He took after his dad. Munck was one of those squarehead types, you know, German or Dutch, never let his hair down. But Harley was sweet, he had the smile of a little angel. I think Teresa was hard on him, wanted him to be a leader. But poor Harley just wanted to be himself . . ."

"I asked you about Frank," Mr. Leary persisted.

Now she turned and looked at him. "Harley was wild about you when he was little. You know, you had a way about you then, Pat. And that's what Harley needed, somebody to sparkle him up. Only you never really cared, did you?"

"I asked you about Frank."

"Oh, Frank. You'd think you cared any more about Frank than you did Harley. Or anybody else."

"I want to know about Frank," he demanded. "I want to know what happened to him."

"What happened to him is that he has always been a very unhappy man."

"What are you talking about? Shut up!"

"Sparkle, sparkle. See, Rose, he's got his sparkle back. He never used to talk that way when I visited him at the nursing home."

"Your visits," he said sourly. "You don't know how often I begged the nurses to tell you I was asleep so I'd be spared your goddam visits. You got a big kick out of seeing me flat on my back."

"Considering how few people came to visit you, you should have been thankful to see me."

"I hope to God my family had better things to do than hang around a nursing home!"

"God granted you your wish," she said gaily. "They certainly did have better things to do. They still have."

"Why don't you shut that asshole mouth?"

"Oh Lord, how I hate him," she whispered, turning away. "You'd never know he used to belong to a good club. I don't know how they stood him."

"Asshole!" he shouted.

She clapped her hands to her ears and shouted in her turn, to me, "It's just like when we were small. I was such a nervous child and all he had to say was 'There's a monkey in the closet' and I'd cry. He caught on fast, he loved to terrify me. It was like he'd been born to it, it was such a talent!"

"Stop that goddam racket, Monica," he snapped.

"Even when he was grown up," she went on, "he had everything while I groveled in my furnished room, and could he afford to be kind? No, whenever he came — and I can tell you it wasn't very often — he had to leave his mark. I'll never forget the time in 1942 I took out my best cup to serve him coffee — it was a little cup commemorating King George's coronation — and wouldn't you know he dropped and broke it, never apologized, just said, 'What's an Irishwoman want with a cup like that, anyway?' Some Irishman he is, hasn't been to Mass for fifty years! And I loved that little cup . . ."

"Come, Aunt Monica," I said as I put coffee, muffins, and some ham on a tray and brought it into the other room. We had never been close, but as she sat down she caught my eye and held it with hers, an eye still damp with her lamentation, but steady and angry, and we exchanged a look of approval.

Her brother wheeled to a stop before her and laid his good hand on her knee. She jerked away as though pawed by a masher. "Monica," he said, hastily withdrawing the hand, "we may have had our differences over the years but we've always been good friends underneath, haven't we? I thought you'd be glad to find me better than when you last saw me." And he flexed the muscles of his good arm with a small, almost shy smile. "Why, when I saw you coming up the steps my first thought was: what a fine surprise for Monica!"

At this point Aunt Monica's eyes held an expression of mirth unusual to them. She lifted her cup to her lips just as a queen would, her little finger extended, her color tastefully heightened. "Pat," she said, smacking her pendulous lips and putting the cup down, "you are a perfectly healthy paralytic. I always thought so when I visited you. You just needed a little encouragement . . ."

"Hell," he scoffed, "puny. Puny was the word you used. Every time. 'Pat, how puny you're getting."

"Only because you were. You let them do everything for you like a sick cat . . ."

"And you loved it!"

"Bosh. I wanted to see you back among the living. That, of course," she said in a clear, penetrating voice, "is what we all wanted."

"All right," he said after a moment. "You're glad I've improved. Now tell me what you're here for."

"I love your view, Rose," she said, looking at the window.

"I'm going out on the porch," Mr. Leary declared angrily. I got up and opened the door for him. "Screw her," he muttered, as he wheeled out.

An hour or two rolled by calmly. Mr. Leary stayed on the porch, wheeling by the window every now and then to glare at us, and Aunt Monica unburdened herself of a year's gossip about her friends and our mutual relatives. Due to Harley's death I had not made my annual visit, and she had much catching up to do. None of it interested me. She visited people in hospitals and she went to funerals. As for her family — she had moaned to me more than once: oh why, when it was a commonplace that the Irish spawned broods, should she have but one sister, dead, and one brother, Pat? And she would appear uninvited at Frank's house, stay till all hours, remaining patient when they conversed with one another as though she weren't present, or left her to herself in the room. Although a word of censure never crossed her lips I knew she was resentful. In the white light from the window her wrinkles were sharply defined. They were not deep, but they were many, a lacework of slights and small disappointments. I wondered all at once if she had come simply to gossip.

The wind rose and battered the house, forcing Mr. Leary inside. He wheeled into the kitchen and clumsily mixed a drink — whether to steady his nerves or to irritate Aunt Monica, who was a fanatic teetotaler, I did not know — and retired to his room, slamming the door shut.

I brought Aunt Monica more food — she had the ravenous appetite of the undernourished — and she downed sandwiches and cupcakes and more coffee with a raptness that curtailed her talk. But now it was growing late. Her eye lit on the clock. "I told the taxi to come back at three," she said, turning to me with a fixed look. "Why did you take him, Rose?"

I was startled by the question but relieved that she had finally gotten to the point. "I have my reasons," I said.

"But such work," she probed. "Such work, taking care of an invalid."

"I haven't put myself out."

She nodded approvingly and leaned toward me. "The family doesn't think you'll do well by him."

"What have they said?" I asked.

"It's hard for me to put into words . . . it's something in their voices when they mention him. Which isn't often, Rose, not often at all. But Friday when he phoned them — I was there — well, I heard things. Well, it was more than just a feeling that I got."

"I don't understand."

"It doesn't matter," she said, sitting back. "I don't want to say too much. I don't like to gossip."

I had to smile. She raised her eyebrows. "You think I'm an old fool."

"There are times when I did. But I like you better today than ever before. I like you very much."

She nodded thoughtfully. "It's as though we had a bond." She looked away for a long while, as though going back into the past, and said slowly, "Teresa never liked him."

"No, I gathered that. And you never did, either."

"Why should I?" she asked with sudden passion. "Hasn't he been a bleeding sore of a brother and husband and father all his life? What has he ever done for anyone but Pat? Oh I could tell you things. Teresa washed her hands of him for good, and she wouldn't have done that if she didn't have reason. Teresa had the ideals in the family. And the brains. She was a grand person, my sister. Pat liked her, but even with her he couldn't be straight. And when she finally washed her hands of him I *knew* he was a lost cause." She moved closer to me and spoke in a whisper. "Just before he met Beatrice he got a girlfriend of mine into trouble. He'd given her an engagement ring but after she got pregnant he dropped her flat, and she went to Teresa, Teresa being someone you could rely on. Teresa told Pat he must marry her, or at least stand by her, but he was already taken up with Beatrice, so that was that. That's when Teresa told him never to set foot in her house again — and do you know, he visited her and Munck more often after that, just to prove nobody could tell him what to do! But Teresa never again addressed one word to him. That's how she was. My girlfriend, Polly was her name, dropped out of sight, but years later she moved back into the neighborhood. She had kept the child, it was a boy, born with a dislocated hip, or without a hip socket at all, I can't remember. Anyway, his walk was something to see.

And one day Pat came to see me and she was there. 'Polly, after all these years, you're looking grand, filled out a little, haven't you, well it suits you,' etcetera, etcetera. That's what he said. She withered up like a leaf and left without a word. 'Did you see the boy playing downstairs?' I asked him. 'The crooked boy? That's Polly's son.' All he did was shrug. '*Your* son,' I said. 'Not mine,' he told me, and a minute later was smiling and talking about something else. That's Pat. He can forget anything he wants to. And the things he says about people!" She gave me a sidelong glance. "He accused you of shocking things on the phone, Rose. I was on the extension — don't let that get back to Frank and Louise, it would sound awful — anyway, I got the impression, well, I felt that maybe you had an ax of your own to grind . . ."

"Forgive me, Aunt Monica, if I don't wish to discuss anything. I'm very sorry, since you came so far."

"Oh, there's no need to discuss, that's not why I came," she said, smoothing her thin hair with an almost voluptuous gesture and turning a pair of glowing eyes on her brother's door. "I came to say goodbye to him."

I glanced at the clock. "Aunt Monica is leaving!" I called.

He wheeled out, coming to an abrupt stop before his sister. "I want to know when Frank's coming," he said emphatically, "and I want to know what he said about my proposition. Don't worry about Rose's feelings. She knows I'm not staying here permanently."

"Your proposition?" she repeated, pulling at her lips. "Well, let's see. You said you wanted to have a flat of your own in the city and a male nurse to look in on you and drive you places." She smiled broadly, exposing the yellow gums of her plates. "Well, Pat, Frank said you were where you ought to be. He said he'd get an unlisted number so you'd stop pestering him."

"Frank?" he said in a whisper.

"Your son Frank." She eased her dangling feet to the floor and walked behind the wheelchair, her cheeks mottled. "He's not sick in bed and he's not out of town. He's well and busy and he has no time for you. Pat dear, if he had wanted to come after all those shocking things you told him, he would have come. He doesn't care what happens to you."

Mr. Leary sat stiff as a board, his thumb and forefinger twitching spasmodically. Suddenly he grabbed the wheel of his chair and the vehicle spun wildly around, almost spilling him out. "You senile old cunt!" he cried. "You tell him to come!"

She picked up her coat and hat and made her way rapidly to the door, where she stood for a moment burning his face into her memory. "Goodbye, Pat, God be with you until the end."

He stared at her, his face white, then rolled thunderously across the room, but she was already out the door. I grabbed my purse and went after her, slamming the door and locking it.

"I am so tired," she said as we started down the steps, "and I spent so much money. But it was the best day of my life."

God pity you, I thought, almost fearfully.

"It got to him," she added, looking back at the window through which he was staring at her. "That it did."

I took fifteen dollars from my purse and she accepted it with a feeble protest. Presently she said, "Try to forget about this visit. It shames me."

The taxi was already parked on the frontage. "Come visit me afterwards, Rose," she said, climbing inside and slowly leaning back under the weight of her triumph.

When I returned to the house he was in the kitchen trying to mix another whiskey and soda and making a mess of it. "Take me down to Darlene's," he said, shoving the bottle aside.

"Frank's got an unlisted number now. Didn't you hear Aunt Monica?"

"My God, the woman's deteriorated. Senile, and only six years older than me."

"You don't believe what she said about Frank, do you?" I asked.

"Are you joking? Of course not."

"But he didn't come for you."

"I think the only thing she said that was true was that he was sick. I think he's been taken ill all of a sudden."

His confidence was rolling back, his brain was ticking away.

"Mix this thing for me," he commanded, handing me the bottle.

"I had my reasons for bringing you here," I said, putting the bottle back, "and it wasn't to do for you."

He grabbed the glass and downed what was in it, sloshing the liquid onto his shirt front, his eyes blazing over the rim of the glass into mine. Finishing the drink, he looked down at his thigh where his thumb and forefinger stretched and quivered like two birds straining from the ground, until, with a burst of will that shook his face, the hand jerked forward a fraction of an inch.

"Your strength may be coming back," I said, "but not fast enough to help you."

As soon as he was finished with breakfast the next morning I wheeled him back to his room, locked him in, and started off for Martinez, breaking my pace only once, at the bottom of the steps to look in my mailbox. I pulled out an envelope with Frank's return address on it and tore it open. It contained a check for two hundred and fifty dollars, nothing else.

The used car lot in Martinez intimidated me with its whipping plastic flags and blood-red signs, but as I hovered by the entrance a small, scholarly-looking man approached me with a welcoming smile.

"These automobiles all appear so new and expensive," I said. "Don't you have something quite used but in first-rate condition? Something about twenty years old?"

"You wouldn't want a car that old," he assured me.

"Yes, I'm afraid I would," I countered, but even as I spoke my eye caught a small contemporary car painted a rich maroon that gave the effect of having been glazed over and over by a Flemish master. Peering through the window, I noted a neat black dashboard and spotless cream-colored upholstery. I stood back. "That's the one I want," I said, my throat closing with exhilaration.

"A lovely little model," the salesman said, beaming at me, and opened the door.

"How much is it?" I asked.

"Six years old and as good as new . . ."

"How much is it?"

"Perfect condition, hardly been used . . . six hundred ninety-nine dollars and ninety-nine cents and a steal. Let me drive you around the block."

I climbed inside, troubled by the price. I could afford it — Harley and I had had a solid savings account we seldom drew on — but it was a great deal of money to pay for a car I would be using for such a short while. "I'll take it," I announced before he had turned the first corner and before I had allowed myself to think too long. "Just give me time to go to the bank. And where do I apply for a learner's permit?"

An hour later I was back with a money order in my purse and a booklet of driving instructions in my hand, already studying it. I signed the papers and was driven along the Snake Road to Port Carquinez, watching with impatience and envy as the salesman maneuvered the wheel and pressed his foot on the pedal. As soon as I learned to drive — someone would have to teach me, but it should not take longer than a week or two — I would be sitting behind that wheel as powerful and confident as this man, and far more zestful. One flick of the wrist and I would zoom up mountainsides wreathed in mists or down to beaches where the waves crashed green and white, and all the windows would be open for the wind to fill my lungs, and I would be doing ninety if that's how the mood took me; I saw myself starting out in the spreading salmon pink of the dawn and all day winging over every avenue of the unknown, pressing into the heart of night with the headlights glowing like the eyes of a great ruby dragonfly.

"Just park it at the bottom of the steps," I told him when we arrived, my voice skidding. When I was alone I stood back to feast my eyes on this extraordinary acquisition. But before I could taste full satisfaction the Shotwell gate swung open and Darlene and Bobby walked into view, sending a groan of impatience through me. I turned away, seeking an escape, and a moment later I was standing in Felix's bait shop. I had never been inside before and the suddenness with which I had arrived rattled me; at the same time, I was glad, and felt I had undertaken a new adventure. The room was empty except for Felix, who sat close to a kerosene stove in the corner. It was a small room, holding only a counter and a few chairs and the stove. On the walls hung yellowed Coca-Cola signs from the thirties surrounded by a mass of old calendars and fishing notices. It was a warm, snug atmosphere, and the smell of kerosene and tobacco was pleasant. I smiled at Felix but he did not greet me. My good spirits offended, I seated myself at the littered counter and ordered a Coke. Perhaps women did not come in here alone, it occurred to me, and I bristled with the unfairness of it as Felix got reluctantly, rudely to his feet, walking around a mat covered with dog hairs.

"Where's Dave?" I asked sullenly.

"Buried him out back," he said with a cold abruptness.

I felt a small shock. "When?"

"Just finished," he said, still shortly, but the hard voice broke and he went into the other room where I heard him heavily pacing back and forth. He came out a few minutes later, stuffing a handkerchief into his pocket. "I better close up today," he said in an undertone, going to the door and turning the sign around with fumbling slowness. "I don't feel up to it."

"I'm sorry, Felix," I said, touching his shoulder, and I went out as unobtrusively as possible, adding up in my head that he had had Dave for sixteen years. Sixteen years. Always together, lolling tongue by shuffling foot. There would be no obituary in the paper; no one would send flowers; the idea was grotesque, and yet our customs were narrow, I thought, remembering the old man pacing the floor so heavily.

My spirits had seeped away; I leaned against the bait shop. There was the truth behind me, bereavement, soundless chaos and there up ahead where the Shotwell gate swung back and forth in the wind, creaking: the child is gone, the child is gone. My eyes lunged fiercely away from the gate, only to break against an old woman coming down from Little Italy, knobbed hands clutching a black shawl in the wind, as though everything in the world were combining to grind me into the deaths of my past.

Across the frontage the strait lay a deep brown, and above it the sky hung thick with clouds all folded into each other like a dark batter, the sun hinted at by a small round bruise of pearl. Mountain peaks and oceans were only landslides of the senses; it was the impassive sky that seemed to hold the final truth, to make one bow before it, as though it were a force, a friend, a father that said: I will protect you from illusion until the daily death merges with the final one, holding away all landslides, all scorching music, all passionate, pathetic jerkings of the nerve ends . . . Now as my eyes rested on the car, it had the cold gleam of a capable tool. Darlene and Bobby had walked up to it. "This yours?" Bobby shouted.

I nodded.

"Let's take it for a spin," Darlene suggested, though she looked neither friendly nor enthusiastic, but badly dejected.

"Where's the little girl?" I asked with sudden malice, again remembering the child kicked out on the porch. "The one who took her clothes off?"

"Gone away," she sighed, her great eyes growing darker. "You want to take this thing out for a little spin?"

"I don't know how to drive yet," I said, starting up the steps.

"I'll teach you," she called after me. "I wouldn't charge much. Dollar an hour."

"No thanks."

She started up the steps behind me. "How's your uncle?"

"Fine."

"I want to say hello to him."

"He's resting today. He's not receiving visitors."

"The hell you say. You keep him locked up in there like he was a prisoner."

"Really?" I said lightly, though I was vexed enough to kick her down the steps. "It may interest you to know that he was utterly exhausted after his visit to your house and is still recuperating."

Bobby clattered up between us in her stiletto heels, an improvement noticeable in her spirits since her watery monologue three nights ago. Her husband's paramour, I was informed, had been dispatched to the hospital Saturday night with a broken big toe, and this had cheered Bobby greatly. "What a night!" she exclaimed. "First Rob rushes that thing to the doctor with a broken toe, then Steve tells us he's leaving and not coming back and roars off like a bat out of hell . . ."

"Shut up with all that," Darlene broke in. "I'm trying to talk to her, I'm trying to tell her that old guy needs company or he's gonna be ready for the nuthouse, or dead. You break a guy that old's spirit, and that's it."

"You're insufferably rude," I said, "and absurd."

"Maybe I'm rude but I'm not absurd. Maybe the authorities should take a look in on him."

It was unthinkable that an innocent person should have to bend under such crude intimidation, but I was not innocent, and I bent, for I sensed that to turn her away at this moment might result in more complications than if I allowed her to see him now. "My uncle's welfare is my first concern, Mrs. Shotwell," I told her levelly. "What you cannot seem to understand is that he's not the best judge of his own strength. You're welcome to speak to him if you wish, but your visit may do him more harm than good."

"It'll do him good," she stated flatly.

As we climbed the rest of the steps I concentrated on what I must do when we came into the house, and I reached into my purse and secreted the key to Mr. Leary's door in my hand. Once inside, I asked the two women into the kitchen for a glass of beer, and following them, swiftly unlocked Mr. Leary's door as I passed it. A moment later he wheeled out. "Oh, you've awakened," I said, opening the pantry and taking out some dusty bottles of beer from Harley's time.

He was overjoyed to see his friends, but he was very angry with me. "It's a great thing when a man's always locked up like a prisoner . . ."

"The door was unlocked, it's always unlocked," I said patiently. "Otherwise you wouldn't be here talking with us, would you?"

"The hell with it." He turned his attention to his visitors.

"You don't know how glad I am to see you. I haven't changed my mind about anything, Darlene. This witch is driving me to my grave."

Darlene cast me a weighty look from under her lids.

"Do me a favor," he asked her, wheeling out for a moment and returning with my stationery in his lap. "If I write a letter will you mail it for me?"

"Sure," she said, and spreading her hands flat on the table, she addressed me: "Look, let's talk about this thing straightforward. There's something about you, Mrs. Munck — no offense meant — just something, I don't know what, that scares him . . ."

Mr. Leary had laid a sheet of paper on the table and was scribbling away. He glanced up now and reinforced her words with a stern, self-righteous look.

"It's bad for his health," she went on, "for his heart. You said yourself he has a bad heart . . ."

He was addressing the envelope now, and reading it upside down, I deciphered: Martinez Police Station, Martinez, California.

"Well," I murmured, finding it hard to attend to what she was saying, "his family wants him here, it's their wish."

"O.K.," she said. "What's wrong with my writing and telling them how much he wants to stay with Royal and me? You couldn't mind that if your heart was in the right place. It's for his own welfare."

"Do, by all means," I concurred, knowing she would never receive an answer.

He wrote down Frank's address and held it out to her with the letter. "As for that," I said, extracting the envelope from his hand, "I cannot have you writing for all those magazine subscriptions. You've already subscribed to *Time, Life, True* . . ."

I ignored his incredulous look. "You'll have me in the poor-house, Uncle Patrick, enough's enough." I tore the letter up and dropped it in the ashtray. "Anyway, now that we have a car you won't have to be inside so much. We'll be going to Martinez for your therapy treatments and we'll be taking some nice drives."

"What car?" he asked, lifting his eyes from the ashtray. "What therapy?"

"You remember we discussed your having therapy over at the Community Hospital. And so I've bought a car. A very nice car. Maroon."

"An old clunk," Darlene said, getting to her feet and putting the address away. "Listen, I'll write your son, then, Leary. He'll see your side of it, wait and see."

I indulged in a smile. He wanted to live with the Shotwells about as much as he wanted to live with me. He had only started that line of thought in Darlene's mind in order to get into her house and contact Frank. But since his phone call had come to nothing he would start supporting her maneuvers with everything he had, and indeed, he now shook her hand with a military, man-to-man earnestness.

In the other room Bobby had grown deeply absorbed in something through the window. "Is someone harming my car?" I called, going to her side. But it was Husar she was watching, crossing the frontage with his fishing rod. "I guess I'll toddle off," she said, throwing Mr. Leary her limpid wave and clattering out the door. Darlene followed with her heavy tread, leaving more cheerfully than she had arrived. I watched them through the window. Though the wind was high the water looked unruffled, strangely still. Coming to the bottom of the steps, the two women started across the frontage, Darlene now in the lead, loping along like a stag, her gray hair streaming in the wind, while Bobby wobbled behind her as fast as she could, her arms sticking out on either side for balance, like an airplane about to leave the ground. How grotesquely they pursued the man, I thought; they could not be more obvious, more crude if they had tried to knock each other down. Reaching him at last, they crowded close to him and stood like that for some time, until Bobby finally detached herself and stumbled back across the gravel with short, hard steps, like a sulky child. Darlene remained for a while, her big head tossing with animation, but eventually she too wandered back to her house. The frontage was deserted except for Husar. His arm shot the line out, then he stood motionless.

"Where's that car you bought?" asked Mr. Leary from the other window, his irascibility dimmed by the tapestry stillness of the scene.

"That's it down there, the maroon one."

"How come you bought it?"

"I want to see a little of the world."

A long pause, then, "What about me?"

"You'll be coming with me." And as I said this I realized that my plan would require a whole new approach; he would have to be made tractable and agreeable. I did not know if I was capable of that much restraint.

He dropped the curtain and looked steadily at me: "I thought you had other plans for me."

Ignoring him, I went back into the kitchen to clean up. He wheeled in after me and continued to look at me, for a long, long while, until I raised my eyebrows. The fingers of his good hand tapped the arm of the wheelchair once and then stroked it gently, as a faint, almost beautiful smile formed on his lips. "All this murder talk, it's just a game, isn't it? You'd just like to keep me here until I died of old age."

"You'll never die of old age."

"You're damn right I won't," he said with a rich quietness. "I'm sound as a rock."

"I mean you'll die by my hand." I could not lie to him about his death. That was the one thing I could not do.

But in spite of my words a great weight seemed to be falling from his shoulders; his withered body seemed to grow fuller. He lifted a blunt finger and pointed it at me. "The joke's wearing thin, Rose. You don't like me but you're no Lizzie Borden, so don't pretend you are. Hell, you've had plenty of time, and you've had plenty of rages, and I'm still here. You're playing some game, some psychological thing."

Rubbing the finger along his bulldog's jaw, he continued in a voice of quiet resolve: "You've had me coming and going. Coming and going. But it's not going to work anymore. No, it's not going to work anymore. Sure, I don't like it here, I admit that." He looked up with a squint of resentment, "I don't like the house — like a tomb, no TV, not even a radio or phonograph — I don't like being locked up in my room, I don't like those sadistic tricks you pull, I don't even like your cooking, and I can't stand your stinking hillbilly friends, and maybe enough of that could drive me nuts. But I'm not going to be here that long."

He began kneading his dead hand in the vigorous, mechanical way he had taken up of late, and went on in rising tones: "You'd better get that through your head. And while I *am* here I won't be led around by the nose by those goofy threats of yours. That's right, Rose. That's right!" Breaking off and wheeling to his room, he returned a moment later with the carving knife which he threw in a drawer. "That's where it belongs. I feel like a fool for keeping that thing under my mattress."

"Nevertheless, you should leave it there."

"Don't tell me what to do anymore, all right, dear heart?" he asked with a smile of sugary sarcasm, head thrust forward, brows lifted. He sat back. "And you start treating me like other people. For instance, you served beer to those two jackasses but none to me. That's bad manners, Rose, very bad manners. Shameful manners. I want a glass of beer."

"That beer is as flat as a pancake."

"Then mix me a whiskey and soda," he said carefully.

"Just because I serve you a drink it won't mean anything," I told him, knowing that I would have to do it.

"You mix it. I'll tell you how."

I did as he asked, but I could not bear his false assumptions. "I've only got one thing to say," I stated. "My plans haven't changed. I'm telling you again in order to maintain some truth between us. Since you came here you learned to live with the truth, at least for a little while. Don't cheat yourself now."

He looked over the rim of his glass with good humor.

"I've told you something important. Nothing has changed. If you think, for instance, that what I said about therapy treatments was true, you're mistaken. You should know by now that what I say in front of others is for their edification alone and has nothing to do with you. I don't lie to you."

"I know that was said for Darlene's sake," he laughed. "But I don't care if you persuaded her that you chewed my food for me and sang me to sleep on the harp every night, she wouldn't leave off trying to get me down there. That broad's so money-hungry she'd pick her own pocket, and for pure stinking gall she's got no match. You've got a real enemy there, Rose, and if you think she's going to be turned away, you're wrong. It's just a toss-up who gets me out of here first, her or Frank."

"That reminds me," I said, and I got my purse and took the check out. I held it up before him. "Payment for the first month."

He unfolded his glasses and put them on with a studious frown. "Must have been sent before I talked to him on the phone Friday," he said, sitting back.

"It was signed Saturday."

"People postdate their checks all the time."

"Then look at the date on the envelope. It's postmarked Saturday."

"So? I talked to him about five o'clock, when he'd just come home from work. He probably made out that check just before he left the office and put it with his business letters for his secretary to mail and she got them out late."

"Your mind is an extraordinary device," I said wonderingly. "I suppose it can also work its magic on the fact that he has neither come himself nor sent someone in his place."

"He's been taken sick, poor fellow. I hope it's not his heart."

"It is his heart. His heart has been damaged."

He leaned forward with surprise and concern.

"Oh, not the way you think," I said, "but part of his heart was bruised a long time ago."

"Did Monica tell you that?" he asked intently.

"Of course not! I told you he's well. He's as well as I am." I got up and went to my room, where I sat at the window, watching Husar fish.

Mr. Leary was apparently busy for the next hour or so. When I came out of my room he had given himself a shave of sorts and changed his shirt, and was stretched out on the sofa, a quilt tucked around his feet, the newspaper in his hand, and his old ebony cigar holder clamped between his teeth. Gone was every trace of the prisoner; he was a man taking his ease at a resort. He gestured at my shelf of books. "All your books are dry as dust. And I've read this paper clear through a dozen times."

My eyes were drawn to the cigar holder between his teeth. I remembered it from the old days, stubbed into my tin ashtray as he stepped out of his pants, and fitted with a new red ember as he made his cheery departure. "How many other items of junk do you carry around in that suitcase?" I asked. "Have you got your high collar in there, too?"

"I was looking around for some cigars," he said, taking the holder from his mouth, "but I guess Harley didn't smoke them. How about getting me some tomorrow? And listen, have you ever thought of renting a TV?"

"TV. Cigars. You could become an expensive guest."

"And all those magazine subscriptions, and the doctor's visits, and the therapy, don't forget them." He smiled cozily, almost conspiratorially, his eyes glowing with the fact that I had allowed him visitors, had mixed his drink, had told him we would be driving places. Surely it bore out the idea of a game, which, by the nature of games, bowed before practicalities, external demands, moods. I could not shake his belief; the knife remained in the drawer.

"I'll say it just once more," I told him. "My plans haven't changed."

He gave an understanding nod.

"Just because you float along on a flimsy cloud of cowardice and lies, don't think I do," I said.

"Mind that tongue, dear," he scolded, shooting me a humorous look from his small shining eyes. "It couldn't have been your sweetness that attracted me." He added with mock awe, "No, it was that noble soul blazing away with youth and poetry . . ."

I raised a hand in warning.

But he was in a nostalgic mood. "Kidding aside, you had something in those days, Rose, some wild thing, like a mustang."

"What unfortunate imagery," I sneered.

"Like a mustang," he insisted, "with a white flower in its mane."

"It gets worse!" I scoffed again, but my voice came hollow.

"But it wasn't just that . . . I guess you were the most beautiful kid I ever laid eyes on."

I stared down at him in a silence of welling bitterness, remembering how swiftly the night had descended on that first glow of youth. Turning without a word, I went to my room and sank down before the dresser. After a while I took my nail polish out and spread my hand on the table. The cuticles were not so ragged as they had been, the nails were growing out, the fingers were beginning to look long and elegant.

The door swung open and he wheeled in.

"How dare you come in here!"

"Well, I get lonesome out there! Anyway, you ought to be glad somebody wants your company." He looked around the room, his eyes running eloquently up a rusty streak on the wall, wafting down to the old lampshade where the bulb had burned against it leaving a mahogany spot the size of a tennis ball, and finally coming to rest on the windowsill whose paint had been slathered on years ago, forming lumps over the dirt and spattering long drops against the glass. "I'm sorry for you," he said, gratification filling his eyes, dampening them as though with tears. I remembered the days when his thrusts were hard, somehow impersonal, as though issuing from an abstract principle of abused felicity; now they had grown spongy with pleasure; but they were the same at bottom, they had only aged along with the rest of him. "Please leave my room," I said with weary irritation, glancing in the mirror at him. Even the mirror in this room was dismal, yellowish, and the embroidered scarf beneath it seemed pitiful in its attempt at finery.

"Poor Rose. Only this. No husband. No kids. No future. No wonder you need somebody to stay with you."

"Leave my room," I said again, capping the bottle with an unsteady hand.

"Look at yourself in the mirror," he told me. "Look at the ugliness in your face. It's all there, big as life, the ugliness and the craziness, and you move like a corpse, you always will, you can't change that. A new dress, a new car, a new friend or two — they won't help. You're finished."

"I will not be forced to leave my own room!" I said with a harsh stammer that made me jerk my head back as though I had struck myself. I went to the door and flung it open.

"You know," he said, reluctantly turning the wheelchair around and slowly heading for the door, his voice still brisk and cheerful, "I was always going to give you money for college or a business course or something. I wish I had. You could have become a schoolteacher or a secretary, you'd have had something now, some kind of future."

I shut the door and leaned against it for a moment. Then, going back to the mirror, I raised my eyes fearfully to my face. And though I had thought I was feeling something new these last few days, a thin struggling shadow of the spirit I once possessed in abundance, I saw before me now only dead bone and bitter eye, blinding me like the glare from ice. "He's wrong!" I whispered frantically, grabbing my brush and tearing it distractedly through my hair, brushing, brushing, until at last I felt soothed and my hair hung bright and smooth around my face. "He's very wrong," I muttered, clipping on a pair of earrings, "I will have something greater than survival, scraps in a corner . . ."

"I'll be gone awhile," I told him, coming out with my coat, and I added in an offhand tone, "You've persuaded yourself that I've lowered my guns, and I see clearly enough that you've lowered yours. I've given you warning but if that's the way you want to play the last act it's all right with me. I won't lock you into your room any longer. You may have free run of the house." I might as well use his self-deception to my own advantage; there was no point in locking him up and causing further strife. I let myself out of the house, giving him a last glance. He was trying to appear indifferent to his new freedom, but his eyes were snapping with victory.

❁

Chapter

24

"THE DOOR'S OPEN," Husar responded in a shout to my knock. He had dropped his fishing gear in the middle of the floor, switched on the television, and sunk into a chair, from which he now rose with a surprised smile. "Sit down," he said, turning off the sound of the television, and I nervously seated myself on the edge of the sofa. This time much of my host's personality was present in the room: bottles of liquor and a half-empty glass stood on the simulated marble coffee table alongside an open carton of desiccated chop suey and a dirty plate; clothes drabbled to the floor from chairs, and the hide-a-bed was an eyesore of twisted bedclothes. The gray light of the afternoon merged with the dust that lay in a film on every surface. "I hope I haven't disturbed you . . ."

"No, no, not at all," he said with a disgusted wave at the room.

"You see, my uncle is coming along very well now . . ."

"Are you keeping him permanently?" he broke in with a note of concern that sent a wave of gratitude through me.

"Oh, no, no." I smoothed my hair. "His son is building an

extra room onto his house for him, I'm just keeping him until it's finished. We all thought it would do him a world of good to spend some time in the country first. And since I want to take him over to Martinez for therapy treatments, I've bought that car I mentioned. Did you notice that little maroon one at the bottom of the steps?"

"You mean that fifty-six Dodge?"

"Yes, that's mine. I just bought it this morning. And that's why I've dropped by. Do you think — if it wouldn't be too much trouble — that you could just take a look at it and tell me if I got a good buy?"

He nodded agreeably.

"You see, I know nothing about cars. I don't even know how to drive yet."

"I could teach you," he offered. "I've taken some time off work."

I felt a little explosion of joy, but I said quietly, "Could you really? I would be so grateful."

"Yes," he went on, "I've taken time off . . . my work's getting me down . . ." He stood up, going into the kitchenette and returning with two glasses. "What would you like to drink?"

I hesitated a moment. "I guess I'll have what you have."

He filled the glasses with the same whiskey and soda my guest was so fond of and dropped back into his chair. Watching him, I drank steadily, just as he did, disguising my reaction to the unpleasant taste. He was staring moodily ahead of him.

My eyes wandered to the television set where a herd of buffaloes stampeded silently across the screen, then to a paperback book on the coffee table, entitled, *Trade Your Bouquet of Thorns for a Golden Rose: Creativity Through Commitment.*

"I've just been sitting here thinking," he said slowly, in a voice that had slid down from its usual high youthful pitch. "I think I took the wrong direction . . . but I wouldn't want to bore you with that."

"It wouldn't bore me," I assured him, "and if it did I'd tell you. I'm very direct."

"Yes, you're direct." The familiar look of admiration momentarily lightened his heavy expression. "It's a stupid job, that's all. Driving around, bargaining. What's to show for it in the end?"

"The marina?"

"Oh, the marina's not a bad idea. After all, the town's rotting away . . ."

I forced myself to say nothing.

"There are people who could use the place like it should be used," he went on. "They'd bring some life in . . ."

They'd bring some money in, I thought to myself.

"They'd add something very real, very authentic in its own way . . . but the point is, the point is, the marina, sure, it's great, but my end of it — the bargaining, the driving around — there's no fulfillment, no ultimate meaning in it . . ."

I had never heard anyone use such words in conversation and I was faintly embarrassed, but I knew it was probably one of the changes in social intercourse that had taken place in recent times. "Haven't you ever done any other kind of work?" I asked.

"I was a used car salesman for ten years."

In spite of myself I smiled.

"I didn't like it," he said defensively, refilling his glass. "At least what I'm doing now is more . . ."

"Lucrative?"

He shook his head with a frustrated sigh, but gave me a

friendly glance. "You're so absolutely blunt. It's fantastic." He took a long swallow and set the glass down, "A guy reaches forty, it's corny enough . . . a couple divorces behind him . . . a job that's just a merry-go-round . . ." Getting up, he picked something off his desk and put it in my hands. It was a small wooden carving of an animal.

"Oh," I said, "a cat. Did you carve it?"

"A dog." He took it back and frowned at it. "It's not finished. Not worth finishing, I guess. But I've never worked at anything with my hands before. I need to get back to the elementary things." He turned it musingly in his fingers. "I've got to have a breathing spell."

"Are you ill?" I asked all at once. "The other night you said an odd thing, about wondering how much time you had left."

"Jesus," he laughed, putting the carving down, "do I look like a terminal case? No, it's just that time goes by, and all of a sudden there you are in the middle of your life . . ."

"The middle? Three-quarters of the way through . . ."

He looked uneasy. "It's so quiet here. I can't get used to it."

"I thought you wanted quiet."

"I did. Had the walls soundproofed, all except the partition." He gave it a glance of ironic satisfaction. "Only noise I ever get is the rats on the other side."

I listened, and heard a faint scraping. My arms roughened with gooseflesh.

"It can be blotted out," he told me. "What's your taste in music? Probably nothing I've got — Christ, I should get some decent records."

"What about *Carmen*? I haven't heard that for a while." A while. Twenty years. When our radio broke down in the forties I refused to let Harley have it repaired, although he was a grateful follower of a dozen programs. But I had never liked the radio. It wasn't Harley's programs I minded, but the music I sometimes inadvertently heard. "But could you play it very low?" I asked anxiously.

He put the record on and a moment later a robust but deeply muted melody filled the room. Finishing my drink, I looked at him sleepily. "You were married twice?"

He held up three fingers.

"My word, three times . . . what were they like, your wives?"

"Like roommates that didn't work out," he said, sinking back into his chair. "We didn't relate to each other. They weren't meaningful involvements." With a rueful smile, he held up the three fingers again and bent them back one by one as he spoke. "I married the first time when I was a kid, because the girl was gorgeous. A knockout. Fantastic. People turned around on the streets, even women. The second time it was because she was a gourmet cook. No, honestly, I'm not kidding. She literally drugged me with her cooking, it was like an addiction. And she kept house like nobody, but nobody; even ironed the dustrags. The third time it was because we had our work in common. Real estate woman, highly successful, very dedicated . . ."

People had grown freer since the time I had been among them; no doubt intimate disclosures of this nature were the usual thing. But I could think of no comment to make.

"Each time it seemed like a great idea," he concluded musingly.

And somehow I could clearly picture his proposal each time: a snap-of-the-finger inspiration, a drink to give him courage, and a non-stop drive to Reno. "You had children?" I asked.

"Never had time for them then. Afraid of any real commitment, I guess." He leaned over and refilled my glass, spilling some of the liquor on the pink-veined table top. "What about you?"

"Oh, I . . . we did have a child. That was so long ago."

"Where is he now? Or is it a she?"

"There was an accident . . . an accident."

"I'm sorry," he said in a grieved voice. "I didn't mean to get so personal," he sighed. "It's just that life can really be a funny thing . . . for all I've done with mine it wouldn't have mattered if I'd died as a kid . . ."

I found him repulsive at that moment, soggy with drink and self-pity, but he caught himself deftly; he seemed to contract, and his eyes cleared. "I'll tell you something terrible," he said suddenly. "Those three marriages, they didn't make me suffer."

"You wanted to suffer?"

"Hell no, I didn't want to suffer. I wanted to be happy. But if they didn't make me happy, they should at least have made me suffer. At least that. But instead, nothing. Just nothing."

"To want to suffer," I said, closing my eyes with sleepiness. "It's for youngsters of twenty — no, sixteen — before they know anything."

"Ah, well, you can say that," he replied respectfully, "you've already gone through it, I can tell. It's shoved out everything trivial and half-baked and empty."

I thought of the long fetid trivia of my life. "I wish that were true, Mr. Husar."

"Vincent," he corrected, leaning his face heavily in his hands so that the skin under the gray eyes was pushed into two fleshy capsules and he looked like an angry merchant who is being cheated. "My name's Vincent. I'm tired of being called Husar. Even my wives called me Husar."

"You sound like Bluebeard," I laughed. "How many did you have?"

"You asked me that before."

"So I did." I put my drink down, trying to get his face in focus, but it had been blurred for some time. I wanted to sleep. "Would you like to live here for good?" I asked with a sigh that was surprisingly loud and abandoned.

"Oddly enough, I've given it some thought, actually."

I let my eyelids fall, and when I opened them he was sitting next to me, the V of his collar in line with my drowsy vision. I observed the hair that grew there, not too thick, like a mat, nor too sparse; but pleasingly right. Then he was lifting my chin, so that my eyes climbed slowly to his, and I observed the black lines that radiated through the irises, which had darkened. A tang of after shave lotion hung keenly before me; I no longer felt drunk, but alert as the night I had sat on the wicker chair talking to Steve and first acknowledged the old, time-choked prodding. This time I was not afraid of it. "You would never hurt me," I stated, as though in explanation, surprised that my tongue moved clumsily. The dim strains from the phonograph drew to a close, a click followed, and the room was silent.

"Of course not."

"I mean, you *couldn*'t hurt me." I lowered my voice to take the sting from what I now said: "Because I don't approve of you."

"Ah, the marina," he smiled, putting his hand on my head and slowly bunching up my hair.

"Broadly speaking, yes," I nodded. "Broadly speaking."

He did not pursue the subject. Looking at me as though to judge what my response would be, he seemed to find encouragement in my face, circled me with his arm, and pressed his mouth to mine. Unfamiliarity still hung like a sheet of cellophane between us and gave the moment a frantic pain of excitement as it was torn away. I rubbed my face against his jaw, dropping my eyes, suddenly aware of his crotch where the trousers bunched and creased over his warm heavy sex, provocatively secret. Glancing at the closed drapes, he started unbuttoning his shirt.

I downed the rest of my drink. Turning instinctively sideways, I gathered my dress up over my head where it stuck for a moment, locking me in suffocation and sudden despair and forcing a nervous laugh from my throat; but at last I was free of it, and in a furtive glance at Husar I saw a pale torso covered with a symmetrical pattern of dark hair. I tried vainly to think of something to say, then abandoning the idea of speech I applied myself to the task of removing the rest of my clothes, overcome by a cold sensation of never having been with a man before. Finished, I sat with my head bowed, staring at the floor with a dark, gathering sense of the unknown; then to my dismay I felt him reach over and unclip my earrings, removing my last bonds to formality. I fastened my eyes on his face — the eyes a moist silver beneath the heavy lids, the full lips slightly parted — a face movingly familiar in contrast to the body that sat beside me enormously naked and foreign. "Relax," he soothed, drawing me closer but not moving in any other way, and by degrees his body lost its strangeness — the chest with its rough hair, the smooth skin of the back — until I felt a rush of well-being; and at once this feeling drew together and intensified, like sunlight flooding down on a glass, concentrating, and burning out the other side. "That's better," he murmured, and spoke no more, except once — later — a sound rather than a word, a surging note of pleasure.

At length we moved apart; a filament of spittle drew itself out between our lips, hung for a moment like a fragile bridge, and broke.

"Wow," he said, sitting up and pouring out two drinks. On the screen a newscaster looked earnestly up from his papers and began delivering a soundless report. "We had an audience," Husar smiled, handing me my drink. "But we deserved one." He rested the glass on his stomach and tipped it back and forth, daring the liquid to spill over the edge. "Well, life's full of surprises. You come on like a nun, and then . . ."

"Like a nun?"

"Well, maybe more like a priest. Something formal, anyway, like in a procession." The liquid darted over the side of the glass and lay in droplets by his matted naval. "But baby, you are barbaric."

"Barbaric?"

"Pagan? I don't know, I'm not good with words." He glanced at a crescent of red teeth marks on his shoulder and smiled at me. "What's the word I want?"

"I'm sure I don't know." But I was pleased.

"You know," he said all at once, "I don't even know your first name."

"It's Rose. You must have heard my uncle calling me that."

"That's right. Rose. Nice name. It fits you."

"Really?" I smiled. "I should think a barbarian would be called Oombaloo or Wori-Wori or something." I rested my head next to his, breathing in the dark, heavy scent of his hair. And then he was asleep, the gaiety seeping rapidly from his features. I rescued the glass from his stomach, marveling at the swiftness with which he had dropped off, and feeling alone. My body was calm now; it made me think of a great fish that leaps high out of the water, wriggling and glistening in the air, and then dives back into the depths until the next flashing emergence.

A muffled scratching sounded through the partition by my head; I quickly extricated myself from his arm and crawled over to my clothes. He stirred and looked at me.

"I have to go. Uncle Patrick's alone."

"Send him back where he came from," he muttered, dropping off again.

"What a cruel thing to say." I smiled, going to the bathroom and leisurely washing and dressing. Coming back out, I strolled around the room, my stockinged feet sinking into the deep nap of the rug. It was assuredly a desolate place, modern in the most pejorative sense of the word, but if only because of that it should be easier to keep — just drag the vacuum around once a week and dust a little. And suppose you wanted to add rooms, it was large enough that you could build a couple of partitions and still have plenty of space left. And it was peaceful. The dim light that seeped through the drapes now had a steely cast, like evening light; but then, I thought, it must indeed be almost evening. I had been here a long time, it was as though I belonged. Husar's form gleamed large, pale and motionless from across the room. Then his arm rose slowly and he beckoned me.

"That was very good," he said.

"Husar . . ." I began, thinking of the old man's words in my bedroom.

He gave a groan.

"I mean Vincent. Do you really like me?"

"You weren't satisfied?" he asked quickly.

"Of course! I don't mean that. I mean — do you consider me strange?"

"Don't be silly," he laughed. "But you're different. I'll say that." He gave my shoulder a squeeze. "But I like it, baby. And I need it."

"It?"

He moved the arm and clasped his hands behind his head. "Purpose. Discipline. Integrity."

"I see," I said with disappointment, and yet I didn't really know what I had wanted him to say. "I must go now, Uncle Patrick will be getting worried."

"Uncle's a nice old guy," he yawned, sitting up and pulling on his trousers, "but also a pain in the ass."

"Well, he's very old."

"A very old pain in the ass."

"Must you use that word?"

"I'm sorry, baby." He stretched mightily, throwing out his bronzed arms.

"From your face and arms," I said, looking at him with a combined sense of past and future pleasure, "I thought you'd be swarthy all over. But you're really quite fair."

"Disappointed?"

"No, of course not. I wish you'd stop implying that."

"Don't think I have been," he answered, giving his head a zestful scratching. "I'd be nuts to. I feel terrific." He strode into the kitchenette and threw open the refrigerator door, returning with his teeth sunk into a chicken leg. "Want something to eat?" he asked, tearing the entire glove of meat off with his teeth and turning up the sound of the television.

"No thanks."

"Got to cut down on these in-between snacks," he muttered, slapping his stomach, and I reflected that he had better catch himself soon or he would go over the edge into fat, and I felt that no matter how strongly he willed otherwise, his exercise would always be limited to strolling five blocks to the frontage with his fishing pole, or slouching over his desk with his carving and a glass of liquor. Rubbing his chest, he went to the window and drew back the drapes with the vigor of someone parting a stage curtain, and stood there squinting out. The tenderness he had shown earlier seemed to have vanished, and almost wondering if he had forgotten me I wandered over to the coffee table and picked up my earrings, hating to leave this room which I realized had changed from a box into an intimate hideaway. But I had been presumptuous, I thought, looking with resignation at his back.

At that moment he turned, fixing me with a look of the greatest intensity. "I'm going to start all over again."

"What do you mean?"

"It's all going to change. You said yourself, if you're sixteen or sixty you've got to change when you start feeling the mold grow."

"I'm not sure I understand."

"You ought to," he said significantly. "You're the reason behind it."

"I don't really understand."

"Don't you?" He smiled. "I think I'm a very lucky guy."

I looked down, wincing at the tinny phrase, yet dissolved by an almost demeaning gratitude.

"Come back tomorrow?" he asked. "Late, when you can stay longer?"

"I think . . . I think I might manage it."

"Great. Wait a minute, I'll walk you back."

"No, it's less conspicuous if you don't." But I was pleased that he had suggested it. I was pleased by everything and I turned quickly to the door, afraid to stay a moment longer lest it all collapse.

"And in the morning," he called after me, "we'll go out for that driving lesson. You can even bring Uncle along."

Chapter

25

HUSAR CLOSED THE HOOD with a slap and pronounced the car in fair shape. It was ten o'clock in the morning, another dark day shot through with light. We had helped Mr. Leary down the steps and gotten him into the back seat, and there he sat chewing with restrained exuberance on his cigar holder as Husar climbed in beside me. With the sound and jostle of Husar's body settling so close to mine I felt a heady recapitulation of yesterday, but fearing an unpleasant response from Mr. Leary, I tried to appear formal. It was with growing uneasiness that I realized Husar's voice and expression could leave no doubt in the old man's mind that we were no longer casual friends.

"Car's worth about four hundred," Husar said as we drove off, "even with the fancy paint job."

"I paid seven hundred."

"You were robbed!" Mr. Leary said gaily, giving the back of my head a vicious poke of his thick finger. Fortunately, he was too absorbed in the advent of the drive to offer more than this for the time being; glancing back, I saw his small eyes drink in everything as though he had never been outdoors before. My uneasiness subsided; riding smoothly over the Snake Road, the wind flowing through my opened window, a hectic excitement took hold of me, and I found it hard to wait until we reached the highway outside Martinez to get behind the wheel.

Mr. Leary burst into a rapture that was not to cease for the next ten miles; pressing his flabby cheek against the window, he began a vivacious account of the plane trips he used to take — how free one felt, how unbelievably free — while above him the clouds now gathered like storming armies, dragging fire behind them. "Nothing like the great outdoors!" he interrupted himself feelingly, and was still going on when we drove down the hills into Martinez. But though he was annoying — and might become more than that — it was essential that he grow used to being with me in the car by the time we took our trip to the mountains.

We drove a mile or two through streets of old frame houses and stucco bungalows overhung by shade trees, and then we were in the outskirts. Only once had I ever walked this far, and I had been impressed by the walnut and pear orchards that stretched in every direction as far as the eye could see. But now a world of pillboxes had erupted from the earth, and this strange, flat, uniform congestion showed no sign of ending, for when I looked with relief at the last row of houses I realized with disappointment that they had tossed their seed into the field beside them, for there sprouted a sea of stakes with fluttering flags. Even worse was a metropolis of sorts sitting solid and already soiled on the nude ground, a warren of cubicle supermarkets, Laundromats, bowling alleys, and pizza stands, all riveted together, it seemed, by the innumerable nuts and bolts of parked automobiles.

"My God," I breathed, and was just going to be thankful that

Port Carquinez had been spared this when I caught myself. There would be a snarl of thrashing bodies in a chlorinated swimming pool, a concrete harbor of whining motor boats and dogged water skiers — and above them on my hill with its cow paths and eucalypti I could picture a dirt-eating bulldozer clearing the way for a string of pastel boxes. "Could they ever build on the hills around Port Carquinez?" I asked Husar, overriding Mr. Leary's nostalgic description of the position he had held with Kiernan and Company.

He didn't reply. "Here," he said, turning onto the highway and stopping the car. The lesson had begun. Despite my anxiety about the hills, I felt a keen thrill as I slid into the driver's seat and took hold of the wheel.

"If you can teach an old dog like her, you'll be doing pretty good," said Mr. Leary from the back seat. "She's a regular Rip Van Winkle." But a note of boredom dulled his voice at the prospect of the lesson, and he fell asleep for the hour or more that I stopped, started, stopped, started, perspired, laughed with pleasure, and grew increasingly impatient. "Take it easy," Husar said, one hand resting on my shoulder. "Now," he told me at last, "don't stop this time, just keep going, keep to the side of the road." And I was actually driving, the car and I were working together, Husar was smiling. I turned and darted him a kiss.

"Don't embarrass the teacher, old girl," said Mr. Leary in the phlegmed voice of the just-awakened.

"You keep quiet now, Uncle Patrick," I said in a hopefully light tone, "or you'll make me nervous." But although I was disconcerted by his remarks, I was not nervous about my driving. In fact, I was feeling a profound sense of power and confidence. Gone was the bitter coldness the car seemed to have emanated yesterday when I came out of the bait shop — once more it filled me with affection. I drove past a short stretch of orchards, only to come upon another rash of tract houses. "We're out in the country," I said, "but where's the country? Is it like this all the way to Oakland, God forbid?"

Husar gave a faint nod. Then, "Don't pass that car! Keep it at thirty!"

But I had crushed my foot down on the gas pedal, and with a shiver that traveled the whole length of my spine, I had passed my first car, and once again had an unimpeded view before me.

"Don't do that again," he warned. "I think you've had enough for today."

"Good," said Mr. Leary, "now let's go for a real ride."

We did, driving some twenty miles east, through more tract-slashed country, and returning by way of the Suisun Bay which flows into the strait. "See," said Husar through the old man's talk, "plenty of land here along the water, just like it was fifty years ago."

"But for how long?" I asked. "With that gluttonous enterprise of yours eyeing it?"

"Sharp tongue," commented Mr. Leary. "Sharp nasty tongue. Don't let her cut you up, Mr. Husar."

As we drove back through Martinez I asked Husar if he would stop for a moment while I picked something up at Penney's. Dashing inside, I bought a pair of slacks, a pullover sweater, and a simple sheath dress, and while they were being wrapped I blew myself to a necklace of amber beads, comparing this visit with the last one, when I had stood here with a dragging heart, my eyes outlined by a ballpoint pen.

"Hey, you've bought out the store," Mr. Leary cried as I returned. He was puffing away on a cigar and held a box of Dutch Masters on his lap. "You owe Vince six bucks," he said cheerfully.

"It's on the house," said Husar, starting the motor, but I caught the lack of enthusiasm in his voice, and I realized that his friendliness toward the old man had waned steadily during the trip.

The first thing that met our eyes when we turned onto the frontage was a pipe-laden truck whose burden was being lowered to the ground. They were pipes of such enormity that a child could have walked through them upright.

"Already," I said.

"Not really," replied Husar, parking the car. "The plans have been underway for almost a year, you know."

"I never knew!" But it was my own fault, sealing myself off from everything, ignoring Harley's talk. Furious — most of all with my own self-perpetuated sense of abeyance — I gathered my packages together and followed the two men up the steps. "You'd better park the car at the top of the steps next time," the old man suggested from Husar's arms, "so it'll be easier getting me to it." But neither of us paid any attention to him; we kept looking back at the frontage, and I knew Husar was anxious to talk to the men who were unloading. At the door he took me aside and asked if I was coming to his place later, then he went back down to the ugly spawn of steel.

In my room I glanced out the window to the metallic glare below, and then back to the packages in my arms, torn between anger and pleasure. Finally I pulled the shade down and turned on the lamp. I tried the clothes on, pleased that they fit so well, and leaving on the dark green velvet slacks, the gold sweater and amber necklace, I hung the new dress in the closet where it stood out vividly from among the faded prints. How I hated those dresses, I thought, taking them from their hangers and tossing them in the back of the closet. They reminded me of skinned hares being hacked up for the pot, of a pair of small but rough, hard hands.

"Who're you supposed to be now?" enquired Mr. Leary as I came out in my new ensemble. "Some movie queen at home?"

"If that's how it strikes you."

"Haw!" he laughed. "Joan Crawford — wardrobe by J. C. Penney's. You're such a hick, Rose. You must really amuse Husar."

I sat down, ignoring the remark.

"Just get a load of all that stuff down there," he said, looking out the window. "It's going to turn into a big mess around here. You're really going to have to hole up in this shack. And it is a shack. You're like a homing pigeon, always finding another Okie dump like the one you were born in. Hell, you could have all the money in the world, and you'd still live like a crumb. You're such a crumb, Rose, and you spout such a big line."

"It is truly fascinating," I replied, "to witness the spontaneous generation of your remarks. The palest, most trivial comment is sure of becoming the ancestor of a robust aspersion in a matter of seconds."

"Ah, can the verdiage. Still taking yourself very seriously. As far as I'm concerned, you're just a nut that doesn't have anything better to do than harangue an old man." He picked up the newspaper and began reading in loud, ringing tones.

"Must you always read the paper aloud?"

" '*And*,' " he read on, puffing vigorously at his cigar, " 'Khrushchev's statement yesterday concerning this aspect of the

Cuban crisis has caused President Kennedy to repeat that the United States will not . . .' "

The ride had not made him more amenable, I thought, as I escaped to my room, but had only increased his self-confidence and the sharpness of his tongue. Unless I wanted to be goaded into a rage that might lay my plan in ruins, I would have to do something very quickly to deflect his bullying.

It was long before night fell and longer before I heard him wheel to his room and go to bed. Then I reached far back into a drawer for my old diaphragm: although we had been careless the first time, Husar and I had agreed that this would not continue. As my hand closed over the object I was electrified by the idea of grabbing a pin and pricking holes in it; I thought of all the children I had seen in this town — they grew as easily and beautifully as flowers, they thrived, wading, fishing with their fathers, shrieking with laughter. I started to search wildly for a pin, but my eyes closed with defeat; it would be a wretched, underhand thing to do.

At eleven, with a glance at Mr. Leary's door, I crept through the living room and let myself out of the house. When I entered Husar's room it was vibrating with a television comedy whose strident tones he thankfully lowered. Drink in one hand, a new wood carving in the other, he looked appreciatively from my outfit to my face. He put the carving in my hand. It was a half-finished head.

"Recognize it?" he asked.

"Benjamin Franklin?"

"You!"

"Me? But how kind of you . . . how nice . . ."

"But lousy. If it looks like Ben Franklin."

"Oh well, you want immediate results, Vincent. You must have patience."

"That's what I need you to remind me of, baby. You've got to say: slow down, be thorough, be disciplined." He mixed me a drink but I only took a sip of it, no longer in need of its courage. "Vincent," I said, in spite of my resolve to avoid the subject, "what happens with all those pipes?"

He shrugged, drawing me down with him before the television.

"I mean, what next?" I pursued.

"Oh, they'll get under way sometime in the future. Just the frontage section, not your hill for months to come. Don't worry."

"Sometime in the future?" I repeated. "When's that? Tomorrow?"

"Maybe."

"Tomorrow then. I wish you could be straight about it."

"That's your province, baby," he said irritably.

"I thought you wanted some honesty and integrity," I returned with uncertain sarcasm.

"Look, it's going to be built. Stop riding me about it. Anyway, it'll be very picturesque."

"Profitable, you mean!"

"I'm trying to hear this!" he said, staring at the program.

"And I came to see you, not to watch a bunch of cretins."

For a moment his eyes sharpened with anger, then his good nature flowed through, along with a spark of resolution. "You're right. It's trash. It's a habit I want to break." He turned the set off.

"I don't mean to be imperious . . ."

"Well, you are," he said cheerfully, "but I like your starch.

Come over here." He got up and sat down on the bed.

As I followed him I said casually, "We don't have anything to worry about tonight." And I added, as though driven to pursue the subject, "Of course it wasn't a great chance we took yesterday, since it wasn't the fertile time of the month, but you can't rely on that. I mean you can't really rely on that. We did take a chance." I waited anxiously for some indication of his attitude. It came with great explicitness. "Hell," he said, "I'd like a kid."

Exhilaration spilled through me as I sat down beside him, but it was with a cautious warmth that I moved my hand to his.

"Ever known a man my age who didn't? Natural thing as time goes on."

I nodded, thinking of Harley, who had always wanted a child.

"Ah, well," he said, "I must be talking off the top of my head. What would I do with a kid?"

"It isn't a question of you alone," I replied softly. "There are usually two people involved, you know."

The lines around his mouth deepened with a smile. "I have nothing against getting involved," he said, "I'm all for commitment."

Later, as we lay beside each other, my thoughts clustered around him as a father. Certainly he had the makings of a good one, with his enthusiasms and his basic kindness. And a good father was a beautiful thought, perhaps the most beautiful thought there was. Sleepily, I wondered if women felt so strongly for their children because they themselves sought the father's special touch; if women were so often religious because of God the Father; if it was a sort of longing they could never be rid of, the small unspoken need to be encouraged and consoled, they from whom it was always expected. Slowly, I wafted through a haze of images — there, a face, whose? Metal and porcelain and whiteness all around, and a warm reassuring pressure on my jaw, BULGARIA in large letters above a garden, O O O Oha O'Hara, from what unbelievable distance in time, with keen blue eyes that expanded into a sky under which Husar walked in a white Panama suit, his hand holding a tin suitcase, which became, not surprisingly, a stalk of hollyhocks, which became, not surprisingly, the hand of a child, small feet sinking into the sand of the frontage, no longer gravel but sand, pale apricot hue and soft as bath powder, with all the mammoth pipes standing upright and swaying like palm trees, their green fronds rustling, while in the sky white boats darted like swooning stars . . .

"Husar!" I said, waking with a start, "will Jason plant palm trees?"

He mumbled something.

"Palm trees!"

Sleepily he tightened his arm around me; drifted off again. And closing my eyes, I tried to recapture the marina I had just seen.

❀

Chapter

26

LOOKING OVER HIS MORNING COFFEE, Mr. Leary said rather merrily, "Went down there to his place last night, didn't you? I heard you leave."

"Last night? I went for a walk."

"Aw, come off it. But I hope you know what a big fool you're making of yourself, no better than those other two jackasses. He's got this charisma you dames lap up" — he pronounced it *sharisma*. "But be honest, Rose, what would he want with a hag like you, except for another screw when he's hard up? That, and the house. He'll drop you as soon as it gets through to him you won't sell."

I got up and cleared the table.

"You're letting yourself in for a big disappointment," he went on, now the darkly gratified spokesman for the hard facts of life. "He's not your type. He's a social, outgoing guy, and you're a fossil. I don't care what you put on your face or if you wear velvet pants, you're on the way out."

A spontaneous accusation of jealousy rose in my throat, but I held it back. "Some of what you say may be true," I acquiesced, much to his surprise, "though of course you exaggerate." And I terminated the conversation by switching to the subject of this afternoon's drive. I would have preferred that he not accompany us today, but I didn't dare leave him behind.

In the afternoon I went down to wait for Husar by the car. Work had not yet begun on the frontage; the pipes lay in huge silent neglect, deserted except for Felix, who was wandering among them with a small mongrel at his heels.

"Is he yours?" I called, and he walked over to me, his hands thrust gloomily into his pockets. "Didn't belong to nobody," he explained as the dog flopped down at his feet. "I give him some scraps and he's stuck to me like a burr."

"Have you named him?" I asked, waving to Husar who was coming down Locust Street.

"Spot. It's good enough for him." Grudgingly, he bent down and patted the dog's head, a look of restrained sympathy and interest in his eyes. Perhaps, I thought, watching him, it would eventually grow into something deeper; I was sure it would.

Husar greeted me warmly and turned to Felix. "You haven't met Rose's uncle yet, have you, Felix? He's staying with her, gets kind of bored, I was thinking maybe you'd enjoy a chat with him, we could bring him down to your place. A fine elderly gentleman . . ."

"Don't have no use for elderly gentlemen. Busy anyway." And he wandered back to the bait shop, the mongrel trailing behind.

I turned apologetically to Husar. "I know you'd rather Uncle Patrick didn't come with us."

"If he'd shut up once in a while . . ."

"Oh, I know how difficult it is to put up with someone so old and erratic. But can't we just ignore his carrying on? He does so enjoy getting out. Please, Vincent, for my sake. You know how concerned I am about him."

I cringed inside at this simulation of the selfless woman, and longed for the moment the old man would be gone from my life, taking with him all the lies and subterfuges he forced me into. But I was glad for this opportunity to stress his irrationality again, for I was afraid of what he might say on this trip.

But he seemed merely happy to be going out again, and bubbled away, holding forth on football and politics, commenting on the sights, passing into the unpredictability of the weather, for it was sharp and clear today. As we drove along a stretch of the Snake Road that clung precariously to the edge of a towering cliff — though doubtless puny in comparison to Tahoe's — I foreglimpsed the moment when the old man's voice would be cut off by a deafening extinction, and the anticipation so absorbed me that it was with a jolt that I was brought back to reality as Mr. Leary's voice dropped from its conversational pitch to a note of deep concern: "She doesn't get around much, Vince, never did, even when I knew her years ago in the city. Very grateful for a little company." His voice rose on a lordly note. "You be careful of her feelings. I don't want to see her hurt."

I clamped my lip between my teeth, looking away from Husar. But it was only the beginning. Throughout the whole lesson the old man indulged himself shrewdly, never including Husar in his remarks, coating each one with warm solicitude, and even spacing them in such a way that for once he could not be taken to task for garrulity. "Good to see you doing this, you can get out more, you've grown old before your time cooped up in that house . . . Thought you'd be nervous with a stranger teaching you, you always seem so terrified of new people . . .

Nice little car, but I wonder why you didn't buy a new one. You deserve something new for once, Rose . . ."

I was anxious to return home as quickly as possible when the lesson was over, but as we came around the hill that brought Port Carquinez into sight Husar stopped the car for the view, one of the finest in the area. It was a favorite spot of mine when I took my walks, and it was strange — somehow grown-up and like everybody else — to sit here in a car with other people, instead of standing in the dry grass, hands thrust into the pockets of my old sweater, a solitary figure in the wind. Once before, it was true, I had stopped here in a car, Harley's car, and Harley had looked through the window of his doomed, failing vehicle and spoken with liveliness for the first time in years. We had gotten into a rut, he said, but now that we had the car we'd take trips, things would change. He had known, if only for a short time, the same freedom I had felt for the last hour as my hands maneuvered the wheel; but I had not returned one particle of his hope, and now he was finished and had never gone anywhere.

Husar reached over and gave my thigh a virile pat; his eyes rested on the roof of the jailhouse below, where the town was laid out in haphazard patches of green, brown, and gold. Behind the jailhouse was a large overgrown yard running into the gardens of Little Italy. "Is the yard part of your property?" I asked, pointing.

"If you can call it a yard. Just a big mess of fig trees."

"Darlene told me you lived in a jailhouse," Mr. Leary said enthusiastically. "I'd like to see it! Hear you really fixed it up inside, you wouldn't know it was a hundred years old."

Husar started the motor without replying, but when we drove past the jailhouse a few minutes later the old man pressed the subject again. "Can't imagine what it looks like inside. I'd really like to see it. Hear you've got all the modern conveniences, air conditioning, TV . . ."

I set my lips, sickened by the thought of his touching anything in that room, but again Husar ignored the hint and from the sudden silence in the back seat I could tell that Mr. Leary was smoldering with anger at this rebuff from someone he had grown to think of as his patron. By the time we parked the car he had worked himself into a state. "Too much to expect any consideration for me," he barked, resisting Husar's attempts to help him out. "The life I lead up there — nothing to do but read the paper, nobody to talk to but her."

"Look," said Husar, "you'll be going back to your son's place pretty soon, he'll have that room finished for you . . ."

The old man shot me a black look. "That's a new one. A lie, every time she opens her mouth. Why do you listen to *her?* Why do you side with *her?*" He was glaring into Husar's face as he was forced to bow under the younger man's strength, and with a final jerk he was lifted bodily from the car. His mouth opened wide with humiliation and fury. "Go off and screw her then, if you want a hag like that . . . I had her too, at least she had looks then . . . but filthy rotten inside . . . a bitch, a blackmailer, they had the law on her . . ."

"Shut up now!" Husar snapped, and the torrent suddenly ended. By the time we reached the house the old man had regained his composure and his face was covered with misgivings. "I'm an old man," he said pitifully as he was put into his wheelchair, "I get upset, Vince, don't hold it against me . . ."

"Get some rest, Mr. Leary," said Husar.

"Call me Pat," he said uncertainly, "you make me feel a million years old with that Mr. Leary business."

"Sure," said Husar.

"And Vince, we'll go out again tomorrow, won't we?"

Husar nodded vaguely but said nothing. Outside on the porch he shook his head at me. "The guy is really vicious."

"Oh, you're wrong," I countered. "That outburst about sex or whatever it was — every time he talks that way I can't believe it's him. You have no idea how it hurts me to see his mind going . . . he was a man of character, he was greatly respected . . ." If as I looked at him my face bore an expression of stoic pain it was due to the effort of swallowing my gorge. But I had convinced him: his annoyance was subsiding under his respect for my patience and largeness of spirit. Once again I had managed to cast a veil of disbelief over the old man's theme of past intimacy.

But as I went back into the house I wondered how long I could keep doing this. There he sat, waiting for me with the look of a man bothered by a practical problem, not even afraid of me any longer. I had no weapon to use against him; the anger that boiled in me must be given no outlet.

"Look here, Rose," he said, "you tell him to forget that little scene."

"And I," I asked carefully, "am I also to forget it?"

"Why not?" he shrugged. "I don't even remember what I said. I just got mad, that's all. It's being carted around like a kid in a baby carriage, never having any say in anything . . ."

"Your enthusiasms are short-lived. Yesterday you were quite satisfied."

"I'm not satisfied with as little as you are. You think I don't know how you've lived all these years? You think Monica never mentioned how you never left this dump except to come to the city once a year? How you looked like a warmed-over cadaver?"

I stepped back from him, realizing how close I was to losing control.

"Running away, Rose? What's happened to your nerve?"

"Let's not have another quarrel, Mr. Leary."

"Who's quarreling? I'm stating a fact. You went off the deep end when that kid died and you never came out of it. And you never will, velvet pants or no velvet pants, and that's O.K. if that's how you want it, but don't expect to drag *me* with you. You won't make a mummy out of *me*."

I heard the last of it from my door, which I slammed shut. To wait a whole week or more before I got my license, to wait that long to do away with him — it flattened my resources, it exhausted me, and except that I had control of myself it would have terrified me. I did not go to Husar's that night, but climbed into bed early, hoping to catch up on my sleep and restore my nerves. But, instead, I dreamed again of Gloria standing on the deserted road, and woke drenched with sweat. Twice now I had seen that small broken face, filled in with cement. It seemed impossible that one could work such cruelty upon oneself, it was as though dreams like that must spring from some alien source and sink in from the outside, like an evil phosphorescence, like the malevolent gleam from the old man's eyes.

Chapter

27

WHEN I ANSWERED THE DOOR the next morning, expecting
Husar, I found instead a woman whom I did not at first recognize as Darlene — big raw bones crated into a peacock blue knit
suit, hair backcombed and sprayed to the shape of a stiff snood,
face heavily powdered and decorated with two coal-black eyebrows, a pair of heels that made her six feet tall. The eyes —
which were her only recognizable feature — looked through me
with regal disdain and she entered without a word.

Naturally the courtier in Mr. Leary was set off like a pin-
wheel. "A sight for sore eyes — a knockout — if I were twenty
years younger . . ." but she brushed it aside with a self-
sufficient shrug and got down to brass tacks. "Notice you've
been going out driving," she said to him. "Thought I'd keep you
company today if you'd rather stay home."

Of course a warm protest — "Hell no, Darlene, you come
along, make it a foursome" — and she accepted so readily that it
was obvious that was why she had come.

"Uncle Patrick is staying home today."

"No, I'm not," he corrected in a glancing aside, and the two of them proceeded to converse as though I weren't there.

"You know," she said, chewing her gum thoughtfully, "I sent my telephone number to your son in my letter, I wonder why he hasn't called yet."

"Oh, you know what I found out? He's building a room onto his place for me, wants it to be a surprise. That's Frank all over, gets all engrossed . . ."

"Well, will you be going there?" she asked darkly.

"I might visit them once in a while," he replied, "but I wouldn't stay on. I hate the city."

Still having it both ways, I thought to myself.

"But if he's building a room for you and all," she persisted, "he won't pay to keep you somewhere else, will he?"

"He will if I say so."

Oh, the believable picture he could paint with such poor material as thin air; it was a rare talent, and she was an eager audience. "You know what I think!" she said all at once. "I think you ought to move down to my place now and *then* tell him. Why not?"

"Because," I said loudly, stepping between them, "you would be laying yourself open to a charge of kidnapping. His family has placed him with me."

"How could it be kidnapping if it was with his own permission?" she asked in a belligerent tone, acknowledging my presence for the first time.

"Because he is not of sound mind."

"Well, we might see about that!" she shouted over the old man's affronted squall, and it was this disordered scene that Husar arrived upon, his face immediately hardening.

"Darlene's coming along," Mr. Leary told him with iron in his voice, having recovered from his outrage. I nodded in reluctant agreement, for I dared not leave them both here. Anyway, there was always the hope that with her to talk to in the back seat he would be distracted from his usual commentaries.

But it was a foul trip. During the first half Husar's face never altered in its grimness; perhaps he saw himself as chauffeur to a crew of backwood misfits to whom he would never have given the time of day in his usual environs. I tried desperately to disso- ciate myself from the two fools by looking back at them through my nostrils and then glancing intimately at Husar, but he did not respond; and all the while there was great hilarity from the back seat as Mr. Leary told off-color anecdotes and Darlene boomed with laughter.

But a nervewracking silence filled the car as I took the wheel. Then it broke: "You're flooding the engine!" Darlene cried.

"She's flooding the engine!" the old man echoed.

"She's jerking it," Darlene yelled. "She's jerking it, Husar."

"Be quiet, Darlene," Husar said, his face the very picture of disgusted forbearance, and yet from his tone I sensed he was slipping into the spirit of the moment, that without malice he was nevertheless enjoying the humorous implications of my mis- takes compounded by my embarrassment and nervousness.

"What's the matter with Mrs. Munck?" Mr. Leary asked his companion. "She's jerking us all over the place. What's wrong with Mrs. Munck?"

"I don't know what's wrong with Mrs. Munck," she replied gaily. "But Mrs. Shotwell's getting carsick. We better stop or I'll toss my cookies."

"Then toss them out the window, you gross imbecile!" I snapped, plunging my foot down on the pedal in order to roar off in a cloud of dust, but succeeding only in flooding the motor once more. I felt so foolish I could have wept, and with my foot shaking like aspic I tried again, and again, as Husar's mouth twitched with restrained amusement.

All the way back I sat in silence, listening to the three of them discuss football. Darlene's fund of knowledge was far greater than the men's and she chewed her gum rapaciously as she rattled off scores, her eyes fastened on the back of Husar's neck. When we got out of the car she followed us back to the house, and flopping down on the sofa heartily accepted the drink Mr. Leary suggested. I was relieved to find Husar looking bored and annoyed all over again, seeking my company in preference to theirs. Sitting down next to me, he sipped his drink gloomily.

Darlene looked at me and said in a voice very soft for her, "You could use a shot, you look tired," and a note of insinuation crept through the solicitude. "You ought to get some sleep at night."

I pretended I hadn't heard, but I could not keep from glancing at Husar, who emptied his glass quickly and got to his feet, his face flushed as it always was after a drink. Turning to me so that the others would not see him, he mouthed "tonight" and went to the door as Darlene broke off her conversation with Mr. Leary and hurried to him. He threw me a helpless look as he opened the door for her with exasperated politeness.

I sat all day at the window with an open book in my lap as Mr. Leary wheeled restlessly around with the morning newspaper, pausing in his bored peregrinations only to abuse the silence with loud unsolicited newscasts. My eyes kept straying to the corner of the jailhouse roof which I could just make out. In the summer the fig trees would be thick with bright leaves and the sunlight would fall through them with a cool green luminescence while the ground beyond shimmered in the heat. A child in a sunsuit played under the trees with a tin shovel as her mother stood talking over the fence to the old woman who was her neighbor. "Yes, a warm day," the words floated through the quiet afternoon. "Come around and have a glass of something cool . . ."

All day this vision warmed me, even after the jailhouse faded in the dusk. I rose from the chair at last, and Mr. Leary, still wheeling up and down the room, came to a standstill. His eyes, in which the morning's fire had dimmed, looked at me almost forlornly as he waited for me to get my coat and go down to Husar's. But now he inspired himself: "You'll be lucky if he has any juice left for you tonight!"

"Hush," I said softly, distractedly, for I knew it was time I cleared away the thorns that littered the path to his death — even if I pricked my hands painfully, it must be done. But, I realized suddenly, if in the process he were, in an uncharacteristic burst of honesty, to finally admit Gloria as his own and his responsibility for her death, I might then be released from the need to avenge his fraudulence. Wandering through the darkening house, I tried to strengthen myself for the conversation I meant to precipitate, and finally, I opened the door to his room.

I turned on the light. He kept the room very neat. Sometimes he borrowed the broom and awkwardly swept the floor from his wheelchair, imperiously leaving the pile of dust in the hallway. Except for the stuffiness — the window could not be opened — the room was pleasant and inviting. Potted violets stood by the window and a summer landscape by Monet hung on the closet door. In the corner stood Mr. Leary's old but expensive suitcase, open, with his shirts and trousers neatly stacked inside like an overnight guest's. On the dresser lay his comb and brush set, heavy silver ornate things, hugged to his chest all these years.

With my toe I pushed aside the clothes in the suitcase, seeing a few odds and ends underneath: his pearl stickpin, the leather appointment book from his office — I remembered it always sitting on his desk next to the crystal inkwell. I bent down and opened it. The paper was yellow, the ink faded; a few business notations and page after page of doodles. Putting it back, I saw a pair of cuff links, big, clumsy, mother-of-pearl, gleaming as brightly as on that St. Patrick's Day morning when he had come to my room and stood there shooting his cuffs and leaning forward on his silver-tipped walking stick, his face flushed raw. I picked them up and put them in my pocket and sat down on the bed, wondering if I had the fortitude to discuss that day.

"Well, just make yourself at home," he said irritably, wheeling in, but I could tell that he was glad I had come in here — perhaps he thought I had decided not to go down to Husar's. He waited for me to speak; I had not spoken all afternoon. But I was gazing at the frayed edge of the suitcase.

"Good quality," he said, following my eyes. "I always had good quality."

I had tin, I said to myself, a tin suitcase whose every dent I once knew by heart. I had gotten rid of it a few years after moving here; I had taken out the notebooks and given it to the Salvation Army store in Martinez. And coming back, I had spent the whole afternoon destroying all sixteen notebooks, feeding them into the stove page by page in order that they would burn thoroughly, following them with the stiff dog-eared covers torn in two. It had taken a long time. When it was done there was a gray mound of ash. I took a deep breath and looked at him. "Tell me, how would you describe your life?"

"Good life. 'Til I had the stroke. Even then it wasn't bad. Dull, though — I'm glad I got away from there."

"Have you ever seen your paralysis in the light of payment, of retribution?" But this was not what I meant to say. I meant to be gentle.

"I see it as a test," he said reflectively. "Like the one put to Job."

"What exalted company you keep."

"Well, you're irreligious. What do you know about God?"

"Not much anymore, I confess. What information do you have?"

"I know I'm His. I know He cares about me. I'm a good man." He raised his brows. "Go ahead, laugh. I expect you to. You're a brittle woman, Rose."

But I doused my smile. I started again. "Tell me about your life with your family. Tell me about Bea, I have always been curious."

He removed his eyes from my face, as though the subject was sacred.

"I heard many good things about her," I said.

"They don't make them like that anymore."

"And yet you hated her," I said under my breath.

"Come again?"

"What about Frank? I suppose he always loved and respected you?"

"I don't know what you're getting at, but he's always been a good son to me. Always stood by."

"I suppose you could look at it that way. He stood by in the wings. Even helped you. Waiting. As I waited." But again I was falling into mordancy, the very thing I wished to avoid.

"What's all this interest in Frank all of a sudden?" he asked. "As far as I know you've only met each other once or twice."

"True, but we have much in common." I crossed my ankles

nervously, knowing I could not forever circle around the subject. The electric light gilded the old man's face so that the hairs poking out from his sparse eyebrows shone like burnished wires, and the sagging eyelids were naked and yellowish under their worn fringe of lashes. He is so very old, I thought to myself — shouldn't that be punishment enough for someone like him? But the afflictions of old age were not earned, but developed naturally and by themselves; they were not meted out by justice. "How do you really feel about what happened?" I asked as a stitching of sweat broke out along my hairline. "I want to know. Will you talk about it at last?"

"I'm not sure what you're talking about," he said evasively, slowly spreading out the fingers of his good hand on the wheelchair arm.

I looked at him for a long while, my heart pounding. "You tell me why I brought you to Port Carquinez."

His hand rose in a gesture of uncertainty. "I don't really know."

I shook my head wearily. "I hoped that perhaps you had felt just a little of what I have all these years. That might have been enough for me. It might have been enough."

He scrutinized my face for a moment, then began to speak rapidly. "My God, it was hard on me, too. How do you think it felt to be mixed up in a child's death? It's not a memory that's easy to live with. Believe me, I felt more than just a little remorse. I still do. It's true!"

I turned away from the watchful eyes. "When does it bother you the most?" I asked. "Late at night when you suddenly awake? Or when you're happy, and then you remember?"

I turned back to him and he returned my look with intensity. "I dreamed of her once," he said with a deep frown. "She was wearing a long black shawl or something, all moth-eaten, and her hands were covered with jelly and pieces of dirt . . ."

A long shudder went through me.

"I suffered," he insisted.

"But not enough. Not enough for a man who killed his own child."

"*A* child," he countered swiftly, and now the fightlust leaped back into his eyes. "And it wasn't me who knocked that junk off. Ah, Rose, Rose," he suddenly sighed, extending his hand, "what good does this do? It all happened a quarter of a century ago."

"And this is the way you remember it?" I asked, controlling my voice.

"It's how it was," he said shortly, retracting the hand. "To set the record straight once and for all. And there was a lot more, too, if you'll recall. There was a little matter of blackmail . . . phone calls, threatening to go to Francis . . ."

"I don't know anyone by that name," I whispered, with a detached curiosity.

"Kiernan! Francis Kiernan, my own brother-in-law, finest attorney on the coast." He narrowed his eyes. "The gall you had, Rose."

"The gall," I repeated softly, testing the word. He was staring at me belligerently, his jaw set. The conversation was over. I had spoken spiritlessly, as though the subject, festering for twenty-five years in its subterranean chamber, had with his arrival erupted like a volcano only to fall back into a thin stream of pointlessness as sadism grew threadbare and murder untenable. That was the impression I could see he had been left with. Perhaps now it was just as well.

I nodded again, and the belligerence on his face was joined by a look of gratified surprise at my sudden capitulation.

"It's true, it seems a terribly long time ago," I said flatly, dotting the final *i*, and suddenly engulfed by self-contempt for having descended to such dishonesty though no lie had crossed my lips.

"Yes. It was a long time ago," he said after a silence, in a final tone.

I felt a strange sense of relief; he had solidified my resolution. There was no turning back now.

And now I knew I must perpetrate another lie; it was like having to swim another mile when you thought you had felt a sandbar under your feet. "I don't know if we'll be going out on our lesson again tomorrow," I said dismally, getting to my feet.

"Why not?"

I gave a tired shrug. "You've been very disruptive in the car . . ."

"Ah hell . . ."

"Well, you have." I looked at him ruefully. "It's so silly of you, this resentment against Mr. Husar," and I let my voice run on as though in private despair. "I'm having a hard enough time facing what's happening without your . . ."

"Face what? What's happening?"

"Nothing!"

"You mean he's like I said . . ."

"He's nothing of the sort!"

"He's just passing time . . ."

"Please don't talk about him," I said crossly. "He's a very fine person, but we . . ." I broke off, as though unable to go on without disclosing some great blow to my pride and hopes, and he sank back with a satisfaction he immediately tried to cover up. "Life's full of disappointments, Rose," he said with a cloying solicitude which I marked as the note I would be hearing from now on. For I had at last painted myself in the undeniable colors of a woman throwing herself at a man who was not responding properly; and the old man was delighted, he positively expanded, his eyes even softened. "Disappointments abound. Yes, they abound," he informed me with feeling.

"We haven't eaten yet," I said abruptly.

"Then let us eat!" he replied, with obvious good appetite.

Afterwards, when I finally got my coat and went to the door, he leveled a pitying look at me, a foolish woman doggedly treading a futile and demeaning path.

Chapter

28

As THE HOUSE RECEDED BEHIND ME, so did the old man and the conversation, everything that tasted acrid, and rising up in their place with every step I took was a hope for something better. "Why not? Why shouldn't I have something out of life?" I asked myself, but as though in answer I felt again the presence of those three figures who had fared so badly at my hands. Drawing my head down with the old shame and sorrow, I whispered, "I am sorry, I am deeply sorry . . ." but those words, so sincerely meant, sounded stale and meaningless, as though I had already said them too often, and the heavy threefold presence remained. A burning helplessness took hold of me, rooting me to the spot, then pushing me roughly forward to the jailhouse, as I felt a great desire, almost a compulsion to propel this relationship that, for all its newness, seemed to me so slow in coming to ripeness.

But I found Husar in a troubled mood and I shied away from intruding on it. He poured us drinks, and we sat down together on that great expanse of rug. I felt the lineaments of my future gathering together in the air around me; I sipped my drink abstractedly, looking into my glass, waiting. Not a sound from the outside pierced the silence of the room. From the corner of my eye — just for an instant — I saw an infant crawling victoriously over the rug, its head raised, its eyes full of concentration and joy. I set the glass down nervously and lit a cigarette with fingers that felt weightless, as if they were filled with laughing gas. Would life never end its preparations and begin its actuality? But I was reluctant to speak, not encouraged by his mood. Nor did he say much, though he looked at me with what seemed a deeper warmth than ever before, unless I imagined it. I pulled my knees up, encircled them with my arms and rocked back and forth.

"I think Uncle Patrick has passed a kind of geriatric crisis." I smiled at last. "I think he'll be no trouble in the car anymore."

But at this Husar made a small grimace. "I've been thinking maybe we should put off the lessons for a while. He's getting to be pretty much of a drag."

I unlocked my arms, my heart skipping a beat. "But . . . I really must get my license as soon as possible if I'm to take him over to Martinez for therapy treatments."

"Ah," he said dully, "I guess he'll be hanging around your neck forever."

"No! Only for a little while longer."

"Then why bother with therapy treatments, driving lessons, all that, if he's leaving so soon anyway?"

"You don't understand!" I snapped, recovering myself immediately, but seething with the frustration of being unable to explain anything. "I just want to. It's important."

"Well, we'll have to skip tomorrow anyway, I have to go over to the city. And when I get back I don't see why we can't wait till next week to start in again. Give us both a rest away from it."

"No!" I protested in an unbidden voice full of tears. Now that I had at last paved the way to that desolate cliff — and at such a cost of my self-respect! — why must he throw in this new impediment? "Please!" I cried, unable to hold back the furious tears, and I clutched at his shirt sleeve, looking at him beseechingly.

"What's the matter with you, Rose?" he asked with surprise and disapproval. Obviously it was not the clinging woman with frazzled nerves he wanted. I removed my hand, wiped my eyes, and collected myself. "Nothing has come over me," I said calmly. "It's true he'll be going back soon, but I thought that even a few therapy treatments would benefit him. I'm certain his son won't bother with such things. You've been very patient and helpful, Vincent, but I understand how you feel. We can postpone the lessons if you wish."

His face had relaxed as I stepped back into character. And now, in fact, he relented a little. "We'll see," he said. "If you say he'll be acting more normal . . . what're you going to do, feed him tranquilizers?"

"We just thrashed a few things out," I murmured. "It cleared the air." I looked up at him, wondering if the evening had been set right again after the little derailing. It seemed to have been, for again I felt those gray eyes kindle with a particular warmth until they were like smoke. And yet there was an uneasiness behind them. He reached overhead and turned out the lamp and we lay back on the rug.

It was a strange kind of love he made that night, a kinetic parallel to the hot smoky eyes with their shadow of unease, and the unease infected me along with the fervor. For a long time afterwards he said nothing, but it was more than silence, it was a kind of breath-holding; I felt it, lying with my head on his chest, and my disquietude turned to apprehension.

"I have to tell you something," he said at last.

I could almost see him bowing his head and stepping into the confession box, and in a flurry of anticipated catastrophe, I grabbed a cigarette, faithful when all else is found wanting.

"I don't want anything to stand between us," he said, caressing my shoulder. "No lies, nothing like that . . ." And he plunged on rapidly, "When I first came here I got mixed up with Darlene for a while . . ."

I was too startled by his choice to say anything, but shook my head with fierce impatience in the darkness; I knew what he was going to say next.

"I can't keep anything from you," he went on. "When we made love just now I know you must have felt a . . ."

"A guilt on your part, yes." And now I remembered Mr. Leary's crude remark.

"I wanted to tell you then, I want to tell you now . . ."

"She came back here with you this afternoon."

"Well, she wanted to have a talk, I couldn't refuse." Silence, and the flare of a match. In the glow of the light his eyes squinted not with self-condemnation but sheepishness. He lit the cigarette and blew the match out quickly.

"But Dar*lene*," I breathed.

"I know, I know, she's not exactly a prize. We had a few drinks, she was all upset. I couldn't help pitying her."

"I see," I said crisply. "You're a sexual humanitarian. I suppose you've visited your blessings on Bobby, too."

"Don't make a joke of it, Rose. Someone like Darlene — she's not like you. I mean someone so lost — they work on your pity."

"Pity? Convenience, condescension, and sloth, passing for pity."

"Well," he said after a pause, "you're pretty cool about it."

"A barbarian needs great coolness," I said distantly, breaking free from his arm and walking across the dark room. I could see that gum-chewing grotesque pulling off her garish suit with those long arms of hers, kicking her shoes across the room, laying that big loud head down on my pillow. And the liquor they had drunk and the crude jokes they had shared and the sudden grunting and sweating. What an insult! What an insult!

He came up and put his hands on my shoulders. I moved away to the phonograph, my back still to him.

We stood for a long while, stark naked, our forced breathing making a somehow ridiculous pattern of counterpoint. At last he said with a helpless stupidity that infuriated me, "You like music. Let me buy you some records."

"Fine," I cried, my voice thrilling with contempt. "You buy me Bach's *Mass in A Major*. But don't bother listening to it yourself, because you couldn't in a thousand years understand it!"

Again he lifted his hands to my shoulders, and against my will I found them warm on my chilly flesh. "I understand your feelings," he said softly, "but I wanted everything to be honest between us. I wanted us to start out with a clean slate. Nothing like that is ever going to happen again, it's all going to be different now. With you everything's going to be different."

"Different?" I said, in my turn helplessly. His phraseology struck a chord of skepticism in me, and yet his tone rang with strength of purpose. I turned around and allowed him to take me in his arms, hoping that he would say or do something to weigh the balance in favor of the future. Suddenly he picked me up and brought me over to the sofa where he sat down with me on his lap; stroking my hair with gentle, soothing regularity, he gave nourishment to that small, steady unspoken need that never left me; whether by instinct or accident, he was for the first time protective, and at the moment when it was most essential. My thighs warmed by his, my head under his chin, I found myself slipping almost immediately into sleep.

When I woke later I was lying on the sofa with a quilt over me; the lamp was on, he was watching television in his bathrobe, a drink at his side. Refreshed, I gave a deep, graceless yawn and put my clothes on. "No, you don't have to turn it down every time I come here," I told him as he reached toward the television knob, and I sat down in the chair with him, snuggling up against the rough bathrobe, exchanging a look with him that sealed the past on Darlene.

On the screen people sat about discussing a kaleidoscope of subjects, drawn out by a man at a little table who would now and then hold out an item — a hair dryer or box of soap — about which he would say a few kind things; then the talk would re-sume, as disconnected, cross-purposed and screech-punctuated as the dream of a mental patient. We both drifted off under the aegis of these excitable raconteurs; waking later, I could envision millions of people throughout the night-shrouded nation, slumped stone-still before their television sets, as though shot dead.

I looked slowly around the room as Husar snored by my side. Over there on the desk lay the two half-finished carvings, a dog that looked like a cat, myself who looked like Benjamin Frank-lin; on the coffee table stood the usual clutter of bottles and dirty glasses, and near them, scattered with cigarette ashes, was the do-it-yourself psychology paperback whose contents were

probably hastily underlined here and there; and here was the
television screen still crepitating with the raconteurs, who were
now on the subject of brassières. And here was I. I remembered
having once written "me" in the place of God, with all seriousness.

Chapter

29

A BELL? A cry? It broke two, three times through my thin veil
of sleep, and stumbling out of bed, I raised the window on the
morning — dark, shaken by sudden gusts of rain. Over the strait
hung a lofty, watery cliff of violet, sheering away from the
heavy clouds at an angle and now and again whitened by the
hidden sun as though by slow lightning. The pipes on the frontage were reflected in dark pools of water, along with equipment, trucks, and workers. They were hammer blows I had
heard; now another one rang out, and then another, until they
blurred together in one unending vibration.

Dressing hurriedly, I went down there, drawn to the clamor
as though to the suddenly exposed source of a mortal illness.

Everyone was there. Sal had popped out of his store in his
green apron, Felix stood under a newspaper which he shared patiently with the mongrel; there was Darlene with some of her
children, none of them dressed for rain, hugging their goose-
pimpled arms; and apart from them stood Royal, glowering at
the workmen he had hoped to oversee; off by herself was Bobby,

dressed in a transparent raincoat scotch-taped up one side, trying to light a cigarette in the drizzle. And there were the old Italians, a knot of dark clothes and weathered faces under a sea of black umbrellas; now and then they turned to each other with a voluble burst of words, but for the most part they just looked on as the others, a shorter more gnarled race, with an older gaze.

I turned away and looked out at the water, dark from the top of the hill but muddy down here, the waves snatching fretfully at the wet rocks. A strong smell of sulphur was carried down the strait from the refineries.

"Hi," said a sad voice at my side. It was Bobby, pulling vainly on her soggy cigarette and looking over her shoulder. Her husband and her usurper had driven up to the bottom of the steps with a U-Haul trailer and were getting out of the car, the woman limping badly. Bobby's usually nut-brown face was colorless, and under its plastic hood her bouffant was carelessly arranged. Her eyes settled on the workers with automatic coyness, but the lids were strained and bereft of eye shadow.

Darlene, on the other hand, vibrated with energy, moving her feet restlessly on the wet gravel, her large eyes flashing; they held a beauty, something fierce and alive, and I felt them fall across mine like a razor slash. I looked down, somehow diminished by the stare of that woman I held in such contempt.

"They're moving today," Bobby said through the noise.

I shook my head distractedly.

"Ah, what do you care about my problems? I see you driving off with Husar every day, gay as hell." She gave a wan smile. "Well, you've got him. I guess education pays."

"That kind of talk tires me," I said impatiently.

Again she looked at the trailer. "What will I do now? Let me come up to your house for a while. Please. I've got to talk to somebody." Though her words were quiet, there was agony on her face, something I hadn't believed it capable of.

"All right," I sighed, giving a last look at the wet glare of confusion. Darlene still moved restlessly, her hand vaguely extended toward her smallest child who had fallen down on the gravel and sat screaming; she looked at her house stained dark by the rain, and at the back of her husband who had turned and was slogging toward it, toward a long stupefied sleep on the couch littered with newspapers and orange peels. Pushing back her wet hair, she pulled the child to its feet and with a bitter scowl started back.

"He's really leaving," Bobby said as soon as we were in the house. She repeated this several times, standing at the window with her eyes clinging to the blue speck below that was her husband's shirt.

"Will you be staying on in Port Carquinez?" I asked.

"No, there's nothing for me here now."

"Then you must decide where you'll go. Can you stay with one of your children?"

"No, we don't get on." She gave me a sidelong glance. "I think maybe I'll move to Crockett . . ."

"That's where they're going, isn't it? You mustn't go there too. Don't hang on to him as though he were an anchor. It's over. You must start a new life."

"You know all the answers," she sighed. But after a pause she added, "Where?" and her eyes filled with tears.

"I suppose you'd better move somewhere you can continue to work in the canneries. What about Stockton?"

"God, it's like stepping out into thin air," she said in a staggering voice. I went into the kitchen and made her a cup of strong coffee and when I returned with it she seemed to have gotten hold of herself. "Maybe I ought to give Stockton a try," she said dully. "You really think it would be a good place for me?"

"I don't know. I only know you can get work there, and it's a large town; you won't be bored as you have been here." My advice rang somehow forlornly in my ears. I thought of the time I had advised that nervous, bony writer — Levin? Levine. Levine of the dark shiny suits and bursts of torment. I had advised, and he had up and acted, and I had gone back to my room to lie in the darkness.

She stood at the window until the trailer disappeared up Locust Street; then with a whitened face she thanked me for the coffee and left.

Mr. Leary did not rise until late. He wheeled in radiating relaxation and self-certainty. "God, I slept like a baby," he yawned. "And in all this racket. What the hell is it?"

"They've started work on the frontage," I said indifferently, already engaged in the next step of my plan. I was walking around the room as though searching for something.

"What are you looking for?" he asked at last.

"Just some road maps," I muttered.

"What do you want them for?"

I did not reply, affecting to be lost in my search.

"What do you want them for?" he asked again.

"Oh, I'm going to see a little of the state after I get my license."

He paused for a moment. "Alone?"

"I won't mind. I'm the solitary type, as you know."

Now he looked at me with an almost offended frown. "What about *me*?"

"Well, I don't know. I've been thinking about it. Let's be frank, Mr. Leary, you haven't exactly been an easy houseguest, and you've been extremely disruptive in the car. I can't really feature driving with you for any long distance. What I may do is have Bobby come up and stay with you."

"You think I want to be cooped up with that dismal jackass? Have a heart!"

"I don't understand you," I said, shaking my head. "First you were climbing over everybody who came here, and now no one's good enough for you . . ."

"O.K., but things have changed. Maybe I was a little high-strung when I first came, but you weren't exactly the perfect hostess . . ."

I struggled to keep a straight face at this delicate description. "It seems that in some ways you've grown more impossible the longer you've been here."

"I need to get out more, that's all. I had a very full life before the stroke, I had friends, I went places. And I still can — I've gotten my strength back here. It's hell for me just to sit around all day."

"Still . . ."

"Look, it'll probably be a few weeks before Frank finishes that room — not that I want to move into it; I want a place of my own — but the point is, it'll be a couple of weeks before he gets in touch. And you'll be ready for your driver's test any day. We could go off for a whole week or two!"

I had not hoped for such overflowing enthusiasm, such rich cooperation. I shook my head uncertainly. "I'd only planned on a few days, actually . . ."

"Whereabouts?"

"Oh, Yosemite, or Tahoe. Tahoe's closer, and I understand it's still nice this time of the year."

"Used to go up there all the time," he said, smiling with the memory. "Had a summer house right on the lake."

"Well, if we go — mind, *if* I take you — it won't be anything so grand as that. We'll probably stay at a motel."

His face broke into a grin. "How'll we sign the register, baby?"

"Just tell them I'm your niece from Chicago," I said dryly.

"God, I hadn't thought of that for years," he mused, thinking back. "We had some good times, didn't we?"

"Did we?"

"Damn, you won't admit anything decent ever happened between us. You're nuts on the subject." But he caught himself with a polite smile. "I'll look around for those maps."

"Yes, do."

The hammer blows continued to ring out through the wet day. I went to my room, stuffed cotton wool in my ears, and tried to busy myself tidying some drawers. Again and again my eyes were drawn to the cuff links which I had placed on top of the bureau — too high for the old man to see from his wheelchair if he chanced to come in. They gleamed coldly at me wherever I was in the room, two alert, unblinking eyes. I found myself constantly seeking their glint to light my way to the cliff's edge.

"Lord," Mr. Leary murmured as I came out, "listen to that god-awful din. Sounds like they're banging the whole town apart. Wonder what they'll have when they're finished."

Standing there, I envisioned something continental — colored umbrellas outside cafés with beaded curtains, a fountain in the shape of a dolphin, palm trees and tubs of geraniums, a host of silent sailboats skimming the blue, their white sails billowing. "It might be quite lovely," I said.

He threw me a surprised look.

"Why not?" I asked. "It's unrealistic to always expect the worst."

For the first time since his arrival we spent an almost pleasant evening together. He worked at a crossword puzzle at the table while I put up the hem of the sheath dress I had bought and did my fingernails. Once in a while he would break the silence to ask for a synonym, his voice faint and preoccupied, like that of a scholar lovingly immersed in his work. It was almost with annoyance that he lifted his head as a knock sounded at the door.

But it was with warmth that he greeted our visitor. "Mr. Husar, what a pleasant surprise!" The warmth was restrained, dignified. Once again Husar seemed to marvel at the old man's changeability, and gave me a look of confounded approval, at the same time handing me a package. From its shape I knew it was a record, and remembering the request I had made the night before, a great fear took hold of me.

"I had no idea you'd remember," I stammered, drawing it out with heavy hands. It was an album of matted dove gray from which a great rose window flared — blue, claret, gold, ruby — the mullions appearing scarcely strong enough to hold the intensity of each segment. The album was bordered in the same fiery gold as the center design of the window. Along the top stood the title, and in one corner was stamped the insignia of the record company and a series of numbers. I must have studied it an unconscionably long time.

"Something wrong with it?" Husar asked.

"No, of course not," I said hastily. "It's very kind of you. I had no idea you'd remember."

Mr. Leary, wheeling over to us, extended his hand for a look at it.

"Don't touch it!" I rasped, and he pulled back his hand as

though it had been burnt, embarrassed and offended. Husar, too, looked at me strangely. Embarrassed myself, and in a sudden storm of emotion, I wanted to knock it off my lap, but I made do with turning the blazing cover over. "Gloria in excelsis Deo," the text on the back read, "Luke 2:14; Glory to God in the highest, and on earth peace, good will to men." The silence swelled until it seemed to crush against the walls.

"Well," said Husar uneasily, slapping his hands on his knees, "I'll be going. I bought some oil painting equipment over there — the whole schmear, easel, canvas, frames — guess I'll go home and see if I can set it up."

I went to the gate with him, apologizing for my mood but quickly reassured by his kiss. Turning to go, he mentioned something about another driving lesson tomorrow, and at my questioning look, he said, "Sure, take him along." Blowing him a kiss as he descended the steps, I turned back to see Mr. Leary's curious face at the window. But when I came in he was as pleasant as before. He could still allow me to harbor foolish feelings for Mr. Husar, since it was obvious from the remarks I had dropped earlier that I was, much to my chagrin, merely a passing convenience.

"We'll be going out for another lesson tomorrow," I told him. "Of course you don't have to come if you think it will be too boring."

"Not at all! Not at all!" he protested, and he bade me a warm good night.

The change I had wrought in him had been so quick and so complete that I felt more uneasy than when we had been at each other's throats, and after turning the key in the lock of my bedroom door, I took the added precaution of forcing a chair under the doorknob.

Chapter

30

BUT MR. LEARY had at last, after all his false starts, burst out in full fig from the past. The tempered aplomb of his old public image, first choked off by years of scabby inertia at the nursing home, and then allowed only a sporadic flickering during his frantic battle with me, now flourished unimpeded. As though a courtship had evolved from the misting battlefield, he took pains with his speech, his manners, the very set of his face. And as I became more and more his confidante — hating the role but not daring to reject it — I learned that he was enmeshed in his plans for the future; that he had decided in which part of the city he wished to have his flat, how he would furnish it, how he would spend his time. He still held membership to his old club, and he would like to go back to those staid, well-appointed rooms, have a drink, chat with old acquaintances, play cards. He wanted to see more of Frank, of his grandchildren, of everyone. Now, in his last flowering, he wanted more of everything. He antici-pated the trip to Tahoe next week as a well-earned vacation be-fore plunging into his new life, and I, as the means, was treated gallantly, appreciatively, with just a touch of regret at having so soon to part, now that we had recaptured some nebulous flavor of the past; while Husar — reduced to a charming opportunist — was given the benefit of every courtesy.

It was a week of such harmony that I gained three pounds, slept soundly, and even broke down and rented a portable television set in order to insure the old man's continued cooperativeness. And as though to increase the harmony, the weather reached back to spring and grabbed a handful of unblemished blue days that turned the hills to brass and cast shadows as dark and sharp as though they were cut from carbon paper. It excited me, this unexpected springlike warmth, burning the fog off and lifting up the spent grass; in the car, for the first time, I felt the sun pouring through the windshield to lie hot on my arms. During these last driving lessons Mr. Leary was unable to bleach the satire completely from his comments, but he kept them at a minimum and the terminology was more refined. Nevertheless, Husar was growing impatient with the drives — partly because of the old man, and partly because he preferred the role of student to that of teacher, for I divined that I was the embodiment of some new knowledge which, like a knife intelligently wielded, was to cut away all the fatty deposits that clogged his habits and render him muscular of mind and spirit. As a project-minded man, he threw himself into this new enterprise with great earnestness — he asked me to make a list of historians, philosophers, and artists that he should investigate (a list so long, I thought, being almost as uninstructive as no list at all); he developed a sudden interest in the background of the town, as though to weight his presence with a sense of the past; and shoving aside his carving, he threw himself into his new interest, oil painting, depending upon my supposedly educated taste to assess his daily development.

My buoyancy grew along with this unfolding evidence of his need for me, but I soon realized it was not my buoyancy he wanted; it was the measured tread, the look of consequence; like all reformed pleasure seekers he distrusted gaiety as shallowness. And so I found myself dissembling the optimism that was honeycombing my customary reserve. It was just as well, for I was not yet able to express such feelings with anything but a foolish awkwardness.

The only thing that marred the week was the eternal noise from the frontage, which had spread from the hammer-blow theme into a great clanking, sawing, grinding fugue. One place alone offered refuge, the jailhouse with its hushed interior, but though Husar asked me to come any time I continued to make my visits late at night when the old man was asleep, and suffered the racket during the day, hoping it would only be a short while before I could avail myself of the silent oasis.

One night as I sat tailor fashion on the rug with a magazine in my lap, reading aloud to Husar who stood struggling with his painting, there was a soft rap at the door. Husar paused at his work. Then a sharper rap, then a thunderous tattoo that lasted a full minute before breaking off abruptly. Husar applied another dab of paint. He had begun a still life of an apple which had quickly dissolved into an abstract.

"Who was that?" I asked.

"No idea."

"Darlene?"

He scraped off the dab irritably.

"I'm not taking you to task," I said. "You can't help it if she won't give up gracefully. The affair was probably never a graceful one."

He had picked up my habit of accompanying his words with a lancelike stare; I had never been aware of this in myself until I saw him doing it — whenever he remembered to — and I found it disconcerting. Now he turned such a look on me. "Affair? I wouldn't call it an affair. When I first came here I was boozing a lot, and I got mixed up with her, that's all."

"Got mixed up with her, because she wanted it," I murmured. "If she'd been prettier and eight children freer maybe she'd have gotten you to marry her."

"Christ!" he sighed, setting down the paintbrush. "It was just convenience — treading water until something better came along."

"How she would tear her hair if she heard that," I said, remembering the passion of those fists on the door. For all her grating lacks she seemed to have a soul capable of the most fierce wants and the most wounded sense of loss. So, even, had Bobby. It was not much, perhaps, to say for such poor wives and indifferent mothers, but it implied a core of life that had not yet rotted. I had been touched by the strength of that core in Steve, the vestige of it in Felix. "She has feelings, after all," I said. "I'm beginning to think many people have."

"What's your definition of feelings?" he asked, turning back to the canvas.

"You always want definitions." I picked up the magazine and continued reading aloud from it. It was a one-page article on the meaning of modern art.

I did not play the record. Husar had taken it down to the jail-house so that I could hear it on his phonograph, but he soon forgot about it and I did not remind him; in fact, I waited for an opportunity to sneak it past him down to the water where I would let it sink to the bottom and settle into the mud with broken bottles and decomposed tires, things that had had their day and now deserved their rest. But now and again I found myself glancing at its slender gold spine among the other albums, and thought of the music from which Gloria's name had with such grave zest been taken. Not a hint of the melody remained in my memory. It was amazing that I had remembered it as long as I had — eight or nine years — considering that I had heard it only once on the old crystal set.

"What's the matter?" Husar asked.

I realized I had stopped talking. I was sitting on the hideaway bed, smoking. "I was thinking of my childhood," I said.

He went on painting — he had abandoned the abstract and was now copying a photograph of a horse from *Look*.

His indifference did not bother me; I did not want to speak to him of my childhood anyway. I tried to think of other things to say, but slowing my tongue was the heavy, gathering memory of the farm — the low cry of the wind, the hollyhocks trembling on their stems; my parents in the field with Tommy, dark figures silhouetted against the massed, glaring clouds; the three of us inside, the wind throttling the windows, booming down the chimney; Pa, taking the pipe from his mouth, starting in again on his ancient musical evening.

Once as a boy he had been taken with his Sunday school class to Alturas to hear some amateur local group perform. How large the group was, what they played or how well, he never said, for the memory was thin with years, and he had no gift for words; his hands opened and closed like mouths as he tried to explain. "Wanted to get out of that there seat, that's what I wanted to do. Wasn't no good sitting, it was like the itch got you in the lung where you couldn't get at it. Wanted to get out in the aisle and have some breathing space. Squirmed around, I guess, that old-maid Sunday school teacher, she cracked me on the wrist, not even breaking off swinging her head around on her neck with that music like she'd had a nip. So that's what I done, swing my head around to that music, and the itch left off. 'Melvin,' I told me, not out loud because of her, 'say, there, Melvin! Melvin!' It was all I know to tell. Oh, it was something! It was like I seen the wind come up and blow the grass when they all got together on them violins at the same time — all the sounds that was floating around coming together in a big, a great big flying one . . ."

But that was all, his face closed as if he feared the moment might be restored to him; and his eyes filled with a dark, confounded self-pity as they lingered on my face . . . it was then Ma came to the fore, the angel of mercy with wings of iron: "Don't fret, Melvin, you need your rest . . . you got a long, hard day tomorrow and you look tired, you look deep dead tired . . ."

I would look away from the two of them, trying to hear in my mind the sounds he had described, never able to until I turned on the crystal set that day and he came thundering in like a speared ox to wrench it silent.

But none of this would mean anything to Husar.

The trip to San Francisco had provided him with more than a set of oil paints; he had come back with an idea. "A store," he said, "in the old warehouse."

"There's already a store there. Sal's."

"No, an antique store. I noticed the other day in the city they're really catching on; I see them becoming a tremendous business in a few years. Listen, Rose, I've been through that warehouse, it's huge, three stories — plenty of room. We could leave Sal and the barbershop where they are, they only take up a third of the ground floor. I've got it all pictured in my mind — everything divided into sections. One section for old sheet music, books, post cards — one for glassware, especially old bottles, they're going wild for old bottles — and so on. No Salvation Army junk, everything in good condition, with some nostalgic appeal. And maybe set a room aside for some local art group to show their paintings. Have a room downstairs fitted out like a frontier bar, but no liquor, just coffee and hot dogs. Have all the clerks dressed in turn-of-the-century costumes . . ."

"It sounds grotesque."

His face fell.

"I mean it's hard to imagine . . ."

"Try to, baby. It would be wild. And this place will be a natural with the marina drawing people in. We could get in on the ground floor, Rose. It's the opportunity of a lifetime."

"We?" I said with a nervous smile.

"You'd be terrific, with your class."

"You don't understand," I said crossly. "I'm a quiet person, I could never stand working in some noisy, cluttered emporium."

"Oh, come on, you think I'd set you to work selling old bottles? No, I mean behind the scenes; you'd give me ideas on what to buy and how to fix up the place. Picturesque — old Tiffany lampshades, maybe a scrollwork sign outside . . ."

I was wondering what this proposed partnership consisted of in his mind. Was I to stay on at my place and continue to make nightly pilgrimages to the jailhouse — just that? Or did he, as he had often implied, actually have something more serious and permanent in mind? If it were the latter, I now realized clearly that I would be forced to countenance things I disapproved of — this store, for instance. But perhaps I had been inflexible too long: I should bend, I should make compromises. Still, it was possible they might not be mine to make. And there was no gracious way of clarifying exactly what he meant, at least not at the moment, for his head was so filled with this new enterprise that he hardly knew I was there.

The subject of my house had never arisen again after our first conversations, but now I found myself thinking about it a good deal — that small, moth-gray house with its sloping porch and sharply peaked roof; the windows with their wavy glass and black screens, the yellowed bathtub on lion's paws grimy between the toes, the floors once painted brown, now worn away in gray patches. Once it had been a refuge, now it was merely a decaying shell. And yet I had loved the little front yard with its geranium bushes, and the backyard with its poppies and big English walnut trees. But they did not outweigh the groaning waste the house had supported all these years, and I could picture its razing with only the smallest wince.

There were, of course, no road maps in the house (if Harley had had any he had thrown them dispiritedly away after the demise of his car) but I borrowed some from Husar. He was not enthusiastic about my trip to Tahoe; he felt I would be too inexperienced to drive so far with only the old man in the car.

"Well, of course you're invited," I told him, knowing that despite his concern he would never put himself in the position of spending three whole days in Mr. Leary's company.

"I'd like to," he muttered, "but I've got a lot of things to do around here." He looked dejected. "Do you have to go?"

I was elated to realize that he was already missing me. "It's just that I've promised him ever since I got the car," I explained, and pausing an instant, I said, "Vincent, I heard from his son the other day, the room is almost finished. When we get back from the mountains it will only be a short time before he goes home."

At this his face brightened.

I waited eagerly for him to tell me what he planned to do now that I would be free, but he poured himself a drink, wandered to the easel to look at the half-finished horse, then flicked on the television. Any other woman, I felt, would have given him a prod; I could see his three wives — the great beauty, then the gourmet cook, then the fine businesswoman — each in succession giving him a gentle, well-aimed poke with her finger, sending him sprawling into wedlock with an after-the-fact decisiveness sparkling from his eyes. But it was not in me to do this; I sat with my hands clasped tightly in my lap, looking at him and waiting. But when he spoke it was to talk again about the antique store.

Going back up to the house past midnight, I was surprised to see the front room windows lit up. Mr. Leary had gone to bed early to watch television until he fell asleep and the house had been dark when I left.

But now he was sitting at the front room table in his bathrobe, all the maps spread out before him, his hand clutching a pencil. "I've been thinking of the times I used to go up there," he said, engrossed and inspired, "been trying to remember places we ought to see."

"But it's late."

"Can't sleep. Can't sleep." He gave me a merry look, "Anyway, you shouldn't talk, old girl. Seems to me you're getting back later every night."

I tensed myself, but he was far too irradiated by his plans and memories for viciousness; besides, his attitude toward my in-volvement with Husar had developed into one of pure conde-scension expressed by a heavy, pitying silence. In order to per-petuate this attitude I habitually affected disconsolate sighs at home and a coolness toward Husar in the car. Fortunately, Husar played into this coolness by being curt during the lessons, for by now they had become an anathema for him — as would be any project that lasted too long, I felt. I could always sense the old man's satisfaction rising from the back seat as he observed this sterile attitude between us and assumed increased boredom on Husar's part and increased resentment on mine.

"Yes sir," he sighed now, turning back to the maps, "you need a vacation away from everything, Rose. Away from ev-erything. This noise, our friend Mr. Husar, the driving lessons. It's all been a tremendous strain on you. You need a good rest. I only wish it could be longer."

"You're really too concerned about my welfare, Mr. Leary. I'll manage."

"Oh, I imagine you'll get along in your way. We'll come back from the mountains, and I'll go back to the city, and you'll go on living here just like you always have. I mean it's not the worst life in the world, but I can just see you going out less and less with all that marina ruckus around you. Even with the car. I just have the feeling you'll make this one trip and that'll be it. I know you, Rose. You're not about to break out of your mold at this late stage of the game, car or no car. Probably use it just to go back and forth to the library." He expelled a deep, tremu-lous breath, "I'd like to leave knowing that you were going to get a little more out of the years you've got left, but I guess I won't have that satisfaction."

I fought down the disgust I felt at all this solicitude rising like an empty froth from his own rich, bubbling plans for the future. "Don't trouble yourself about my life," I said coolly.

"Well, I'll be very honest with you, Rose," he said, tossing down the pencil. "When I first came here I have to admit I hated you for the things you did to me. Then after we straightened everything out, I only felt sympathy. I mean, you've had to live with some terrible memories."

Chapter

31

IT WAS DECIDED that we would go to Martinez for my driving test on Friday. If I passed — and there was no doubt that I would — Mr. Leary and I would start for Tahoe early Saturday morning. During the whole week I had wondered what to do with the old man while I was in Martinez, for if we brought him along it would mean he must wait for Husar during the test; it would mean bringing the wheelchair, unfolding it — extra bother that Husar would resent. Also, the thought of letting the old man loose in a police station set my head whirling. And if I left him home there was the possibility that Darlene might come barging in — for I could not lock the front door without shattering the trust I had built up in him — claiming she had received a call from his son who was coming in a few days and who asked that his father stay with the Shotwells until then; some such irrational and stupid lie with loose ends dangling in profusion, yet shot through with the compelling intensity of her will. It was true that Mr. Leary's esteem for the woman seemed to have sunk even farther this last week, now that he no longer needed her, but I had drawn him into such a maze of falseness that I half feared he had done the same to me, and once in a while as I sat reading a book to the muted sound of the television in his room, I would look up with terror, fully expecting to see the carving knife descending upon me with a swiftness too great to divert. But these moments were rare; for the most part my confidence rose high: and on Thursday my apprehensions about Darlene were put to rest. Bobby called to me from her door that day as we were going back to the house after the last lesson. Though it was midafternoon she still wore a housecoat, and her hair was uncombed. She was smoking with such nervous distraction that she gave the impression of holding several streaming cigarettes in either hand. "I'm leaving tomorrow," she said, "on the eleven o'clock train."

"Well, that's good, Bobby," I said with some uncertainty, for she looked so miserable. "You've made your decision."

"Yeah. Packed. All ready to go. Darlene was supposed to drive me over to the station but her and Royal have to go to a funeral in Oakland tomorrow. Her old aunt. Lived in a big mess of junk, they figure they can sell it." She gave a hard smile, blowing smoke through her nostrils. "If there's an easy buck to be made they'll make it. But it leaves me stranded. Maybe you could drive me over, it's the last favor I'll ask."

"Certainly, we have to go to Martinez tomorrow anyway."

" 'We.' You're lucky."

"We're all lucky in different ways," I said, going down the steps. "You've got your youth." Standing there in her flowered housecoat, her face scrubbed clean, disconsolate though she was, she looked twenty-five. "I'm a hundred years old," she murmured.

"I'm afraid you'll have to stay home tomorrow while I go for my driver's test," I told Mr. Leary, "but it shouldn't take long."

He did not care in the least. His whole attention was riveted on the weather, which had grown cloudy during the afternoon. "What if it rains?" he asked worriedly.

"I'll take the test anyway."

"But I mean the trip."

"Just because it rains here doesn't mean it will rain up there."

"Rotten luck! It's been perfect summer weather right up until now." The other day he had given me a list of purchases to make for him: sunglasses, lightweight summer shirt, straw hat, sandals. He had put everything on and wheeled through the house very happy, no doubt imagining himself sitting at a beach-umbrellaed table on the lawn of some resort motel, sipping a sparkling drink and breathing in the warm clear mountain air.

I, too, had bought new things, but not for the trip: pale delicate cashmere sweaters, nightgowns frothy as beaten egg whites, a satin dressing gown, sheer underwear mostly black . . . a trousseau, I thought, looking at them spread out in my room.

Friday morning I was up early and at the window. The hills were bathed in fog and the leaves dripped with moisture; then as I watched, the sun rimmed the sopping world with fire.

"You see," I said as I prepared to leave, "it will be a fine day."

But I was wrong. As I went down the steps I saw fog and sun still battling, merging in a thick coppery smoke that all but obscured the lead of the strait. I knew the fog would win; it was not high fog but tule fog, and that always won. I prepared myself for an argument with Husar.

"It's stupid to take your test under the worst conditions," he told me.

"The worst conditions are the best test."

He gave in. He did not really care that much, and anyway,

my resolute attitude pleased him, as it always did. With Bobby slumped in the back seat, we drove away across the damp frontage, leaving the hammering and grinding behind us.

Bobby sat quietly, not even smoking. Today her round brown face was meticulously made up, the eyebrows plucked into two Gothic arches, the lipstick artfully extended a quarter of an inch around the edge of the drooping mouth. She wore a tight-fitting red suit and more jewelry than usual. Only her plump, rather dingy hands had been overlooked, and lay with heavy negligence in her lap, one nail-bitten finger absently caressing another. I did not envy her her journey to a strange city of fruit canneries and loneliness.

The visibility grew steadily worse. Tule fog is not like ocean fog, thin and moving, but lies like dead weight across the ground, pressing the grass beneath its belly, squeezing out dark rivulets, filling your nostrils with the still, close dampness of earthen cellars. It will be better in Martinez, I assured myself, it's a little more inland. But I was growing worried now.

Bobby, on the other hand, seemed to be getting hold of herself now. Glancing back, I saw her sit up straighter and take a deep breath. By the time we arrived at the station she managed a smile. While Husar got her luggage from the trunk she lit a cigarette and stared down the tracks. "Well, it's all buttoned up and done with," she said, touching her courageous bouffant in the breeze. Miles down the shore we saw the train emerge from around a curve.

Before climbing aboard, she fumbled for our hands, and as her fingers left mine I thought with fleeting melancholy that perhaps I had just persuaded an unhappy nymphomaniac to be unhappy in another county; she would wander back to search for Rob. But she climbed the two metal steps with a heavy firmness, and her wave was brief and final.

"Funny she wanted to move all the way to Stockton," Husar said, getting back into the car.

"She wanted to start all over again. From scratch."

"Well, I've got to hand it to her. It's the ultimate in creativeness."

"Not everyone is given the chance to start all over again," I said as we drove into town, and I saw with relief that the fog was not so dense here.

"Given," he murmured, "nobody's given anything. You've got to make things happen."

"That's true," I smiled, laying my hand on his knee, but he said no more.

The test, which I had prepared for with such long diligence, was over before I knew it and I was on my way back to Port Carquinez with my temporary driver's license in my purse. But instead of the happiness I had anticipated, I felt an increasing discontent. When I returned from the mountains — and for the first time it occurred to me that I would be returning not in my beloved car, but on a bus or train, or perhaps in Husar's car if he came up to bring me back from the tragic outing — I wanted more than a filmy potential to be waiting for me. Perhaps, I thought, as we drove up before the jailhouse for a celebrating drink, the time had come for me to give that gentle poke. But with the raw turmoil echoing from the frontage and the cliff looming from the mists of tomorrow I felt no gentleness in me, only a savage sense of imminence.

"It's so quiet in here," I said as we sat down. "It's always like being rolled up inside a great soft rose." I lit a cigarette nervously.

"Very poetic," he smiled, pouring out our drinks.

I drank from my glass with the same deep gulps I had found

necessary the first time I had sat here on this sofa, and I felt the burning liquid unclench my nerves a little. Putting down my glass, I said with an attempt at simplicity, "When I come back from the mountains and Uncle Patrick leaves, I may sell the house and move away."

His eyes widened in an astonished stare.

"After all," I continued, "I can see that it would be impossible for me to stay on with all that noise from the frontage."

He took an immesnse swallow of his drink. "I thought . . . well, I thought . . . we had a lot of plans, like the antique store . . . "

I shrugged.

Another deep swallow; getting up, he mixed a new one, and the bottles clinked dully together with an aggravated sound. Sitting down again, he lit a cigarette with a series of jerky movements and snorted out a cloud of smoke. "Don't you see that I need you?"

"Perhaps . . ."

"For the first time, a meaningful involvement . . ."

"Oh, that phrase," I murmured.

"I don't mind using it, it's the truth. Don't you understand that you can't just go off?"

"What shall I do, then?" I asked with a helpless smile.

Another long stare. "What would you like to do?"

Suddenly I was disgusted by the art of poking gently, of drawing out and leading on. It was not my art; I felt humiliated, and the sense of savagery took hold of me again. Perhaps he caught a glimpse of this in my face, for he added quickly, "I mean I'd like you to want what I want — " One more gulp, and then, "To get married."

All at once, peace; as though a harsh buzzing in my head had left off, as though nothing but this moment had ever existed. And as this peace deepened, his enthusiasm grew: "We could build a partition in here for a bedroom — the room's huge, no space problem. And maybe enlarge the kitchen — you know I've never tasted your cooking. And maybe I'll do something with the back section — use it as a lumber room for the store. Baby," he said, getting up, "you make me want to do things — you're a new life."

He sat down by me and took me in his arms. "I love you," he whispered.

And for all its smoke and liquor and jangled nerves, the moment held an exhilaration and a comfort that made me long to remain in it forever.

He suggested that we drive up to Reno right away, but of course it was out of the question. I told him I would return from Tahoe on Monday, Mr. Leary would be picked up by his son sometime that week, and then there would be nothing left to interfere with our plans. As I drove down to the frontage and parked the car, not even the roar of the equipment or the slash of a raindrop across the windshield could mar my joy.

Chapter

32

I HARDLY TRUSTED MY VOICE — or for that matter my tongue — to conceal my news from Mr. Leary; but it would never do to throw him off balance on the eve of our trip, and I opened the door cautiously, as though carrying a Roman candle I hoped would not go off.

I was relieved to find him flying far too high to pay me close attention. There was a small red spot like a live coal on either cheek, and his excitement over the trip was matched in its excess by a maudlin nostalgia for the past; I sensed he had been punctuating his restlessness with nips from the whiskey bottle.

At once he plunged us into an atmosphere that reminded me of two roommates, close girlfriends, preparing for a vacation. "Do you think I should take these or the others?" he would ask, wheeling out of his room with a pair of trousers in his hand. "I always used to wear white ducks up at Tahoe." Or, almost tragically, "I don't really like any of the ties I've got, I think they're all garish."

"Why bother with a tie?"

"We'll want to dress for dinner! We always dressed for dinner up there, just like at home. After all, we're not camping out like a couple of bums, Rose. And some of those motels are pretty fancy, you know. And look . . . don't worry about the expense; Frank will reimburse you when we get back. By the way, you'd better give me the money before we get there, so I can pay. It would look funny for the woman to be paying . . ."

And so on through the day. I acclimated myself to the animated deluge of details and crept back into the warm thought of Husar's proposal. Every once in a while I caught it slipping onto the tip of my tongue and had to hold it back.

In the late afternoon there was a disappointed cry: "Look outside, it's raining!"

"Don't get upset," I reassured him, "it will be fine in the mountains, the humidity is much thinner up there." Whatever that might be worth. But it pacified him. He gave a deep, one-sided stretch and started off again: "You'd better pack some sandwiches for us to eat on the way, there's cheese and bologna left over from yesterday — ah, I wish we had some of those little kosher pickles, the kind they used to have at that place near the office, remember?" He wheeled into his room only to wheel immediately out again. "What time should we start? Is five o'clock too early?"

"No, the earlier we start the earlier we'll get there."

"Good! You'd better set the alarm for four-thirty, then. And fix those sandwiches so we'll be all set to go. Did you fill up the tank? And you'd better drive the car up to the top of the steps tonight."

"Heavens, Mr. Leary, calm down. Why don't you take a nap?"

"A nap! That's for old men!"

It was true he seemed fifteen years younger than when he had arrived whimpering in Frank's arms. His eyes were bright, he held himself so erect that even his sagging left side was lifted; and his voice, as though from intensive use after long silence, had worked back to a fair likeness of what it had once been, low and gravelled. He sat there with three ties hanging rakishly around his neck, cigar smoke streaming up from him in an arrow-straight blue plume, his feet thrust into his new sandals where the toes of his good foot wriggled and stretched as though treading some great open stretch of land.

"You're in excellent shape for this trip," I complimented him, going to my room to pack, and calling over my shoulder, "Why don't you gather the maps together and put a rubber band around them? And then see if you can find a thermos bottle. I think there's one in the pantry."

Closing the door, I packed the few things I was taking; then with a thrill of self-indulgence I gathered together all the clothes I had recently bought and spread them out on the bed like a banquet on a table: smooth satin, soft cashmere, pools of black lace.

Evening was falling, the rain tapped steadily against the window. From the bottom of the hill the rumble and wail of a freight train broke through the patter. I thought of Bobby carrying her suitcase down a rainy street in Stockton.

Pulling down the shade, I turned on the lamp. In the amber light the room was reasonably bearable, almost cozy; and tonight I expanded with peacefulness in the soft glow, gazing at the swirl of clothes, reluctant to put them out of sight though I knew it was unwise to display them like this with the possibility of Mr. Leary wheeling in. Which he did at that moment, holding up the thermos. "It's as old as the hills, and there's a crack in it. But maybe it'll be all right. What'll we put in it, coffee? Or . . ." he lifted his eyebrows mischievously, "a little fire water?"

"I think not," I said, casually placing myself between him and the bed of clothes. "I think you've been at the fire water quite enough already." And indeed, he had reached a disagreeable pitch of intensity. I wished he would go to bed; I longed for the morning; he would put on his new straw hat and grab the bag of bologna sandwiches and we would be off at last. The front door would slam, the car door would slam — beyond that I could hear nothing until the explosion at the bottom of the cliff.

I caught a wide flash of false teeth. "This is nothing compared to what I put away in the old days! They called me Limitless Leary at the club. Could dispose of untold amounts and never turn a hair. Never a slurred word, never a hiccough. Always the gentleman!" Catching sight of the clothes behind me, he pursed his lips in a low whistle. "Looks like you robbed a store," he marveled, wheeling past me and picking up a slip between thumb and forefinger with an expression of comic prudery. "Fancy . . ."

I felt my nostrils flare at the sight of that horny thumbnail pressed into the fragile material. Then he dropped it, only to rest his hand on one of the nightgowns. "What do you want with this kind of stuff?" There was an edge in his voice that broke like a needle through his massed preoccupation with the trip.

I shrugged, and began folding the clothes quickly.

"Look at these," he grunted, poking a pair of black lace panties with his knobbed finger. "See right through them. Like a Mission Street whore." He began to count under his breath. "Six. Six pairs. Four nightgowns. Four petticoats."

"You're behind the times," I said in a bantering tone, "they're called slips."

"I call them petticoats!" he shouted so unexpectedly and with such anger that I drew back.

"He bought you all this stuff!" he accused shrilly. "You're going away with him."

"It's none of your concern what I do." But immediately I bit my lip at this poor reply, which now lent a note of hysteria to his voice.

"You *are* going away with him!"

"No, I'm not going away with him. We're staying on in Port Carquinez." It was useless. Obviously I wanted him to know or I could do better than this. I wanted him to know very much.

"He's not *marrying* you?" he asked with scornful, trembling incredulity.

My silence spoke for itself.

I knew it was stupid and reckless to have told him — especially after all the pains I had taken to conceal Husar's feelings for me — and that he would now be plunged into the worst possible temper for the trip, but the sight of his face was almost worth it. He seemed to have been stricken both speechless and motionless, his only sign of life being a deepening flush as vivid as a bonfire. I had not expected so extreme a reaction.

With an almost epileptic jerk he broke from this trance. "It's a lie!" he cried, straining from the wheelchair.

"As a matter of fact, it's not. But I see no reason for you to be so upset."

"You don't have the right," he whispered. "It's not in the scheme of things. God sees . . . God *sees*!" he cried in a sudden burst of passion. "And He *judges*! He made you alone to punish you! You're to stay alone!" He fell back, breathing deeply through distended nostrils, and striking his fist on his knee he turned his head aside as a tear squeezed from his eye and rolled down the knotted features, which were shaking rigidly.

"Mr. Leary," I stammered, frightened now, "get hold of yourself . . ."

"It's not fair!" he screamed. "I had standing! I could write my own ticket! They were good days!" Breaking off from this non sequitur, he threw his hand up to support his trembling head, sinking the fingers like stakes into the flesh of his face. "You think you can live like other people?" he asked in a sharp sob. "You think you have the right after what you did to me?"

He turned his face up blindly, the eyes squeezed shut in some great remembered outrage. "A nothing! A cheap little file clerk! The gall! The poison! Hounding me, persecuting me, maligning me — dragging me to court! Having to sit there in front of everybody while you threw that slime at me! A clean name I had! A good man!" And in a frenzy he grabbed the wheel of his chair and hurled himself around in a futile half circle, coming to an abrupt stop as his hand once more flew to his face to steady it. "You hexed me! Nothing was ever the same again. Francis never spoke to me after that . . ." There was shocked disbelief in his voice, as if it had happened yesterday. "You turned him against me! Tried to turn Frank against me! My own son!"

"Don't stop," I breathed, filled with an almost painful exultation to see the mask torn off at last, to hear him speak from his store of truth.

"Look at you! You think you can get married, live like other people? I don't care how good you look on the outside — that's just wrapping. Inside you're a disease!"

My hand rose to my throat, where the pulse exploded over

and over under the skin. "You're speaking from jealousy," I whispered.

"Ah, he'll be so puking sick of you when the novelty wears off! You'll come creeping back here all alone. You're going to die alone, Rose . . ." He lifted his head, his eyes wide. "Die all alone. Here. And it's how it should be — because you've ruined everybody you ever got near."

"You can say this?" I asked, my voice suddenly wild in my ears. "You who were the cause of it all?"

"Me? It's always been you and that crazy rage of yours! When you've got it in for somebody you'll go to any lengths to hit back. Look what you did to me! And even ruined that poor slob Harley's life just to stay in the family and get back at me someday."

"And you really think you never did anything to deserve it?" I cried.

"I always tried to help you! But you were too far gone, even then. Maybe you should have been committed then, maybe the doctors could have straightened you out. But it's too late now . . ."

"Shut up!" I cried.

He stared up at me, breathing like a storm. "It's too late now."

"Shut up!" I cried again, and I felt my features were so contorted that they must indeed appear to belong to a madwoman.

"There's that look on you again! Just like the time in Oakland when you didn't care who got hurt as long as you got back at me . . ."

"It was you who knocked the burner over! It was you!"

"No you don't," he said ferociously. "I can still see clear as day that ragged sleeve of that filthy old robe of yours catching on it while you tried to hit me. You murdered your kid. You're not going to pin it on me!"

A raw cry broke from my throat; I fell on him, summoning the reserves of my whole body to stop his voice; but it rose to a crescendo as he fought back, striking at me with the thermos, then dropping it to use the wheelchair as a battering ram against my legs. With unwonted strength I dragged him out of the wheelchair and threw him down on the bed where I pressed my hand over his mouth, pinioning his head down in a froth of lace. Clawing at a scarf, I secured it to his flailing wrist, yanked it to his ankle, and tied it tightly. My knees were resting on a cashmere sweater in its plastic bag; I pulled it out from under me and ripped the bag off, leaning over him with it.

As though his blood had dried and lay like rust in his veins, he stared at me, motionless. "Rose," he whispered, and I jammed the bag over his skull, hearing a long groan. It was much better than the cliff, I suddenly realized, for it was a death I could watch closely. At once he drew in a deep breath that glued the bag to his mouth as to a vacuole, the thin plastic fitting closely to his false teeth. He was too terrorized to realize my presence any longer, and through my mingled satisfaction and repugnance I felt a twinge of irritation that he did not see me. I pressed my hand to his heaving chest, and his wild, drowning eyes jerked to mine, not only recognizing my presence, but with all the life left to them begging me to help him. Slowly, very slowly, I shook my head, and he threw himself back and began to writhe, his mouth open, and so large that it seemed to consume most of his face.

I felt the need to retch, and clamping my teeth together I turned away for a moment. Now the face was paling; his good side jerked with machinelike regularity each time he sucked in a breath.

As I watched, a kind of lassitude fell over me — I felt myself descending into a dusk whose great chill seemed to rise from a group of shapes I sensed huddling around me in a circle.

His body was thrashing now, the head pounding against the pillow, the fingers of his good hand ripping convulsively at the ankle it was tied to.

The dusk deepened. The circle of figures pulled more closely around me until their chill seemed to enter my body, and I gave a long shiver. A memory stung me like a pinprick of light. I thrust it aside, leaning over the chasm of the old man's mouth.

Again the pinprick. Merely the memory of my elbow touching something hard.

"*You!*" I cried at him, as though the death throes were not enough, as though nothing could ever suffice for his punishment.

The prong of light tore wide, filling my brain. It was my elbow in the soiled old robe that had knocked the gas burner off. As direct an annihilation as if I had taken an ax to her head.

"*You!*" I cried again, more feebly.

I had crouched over her and stared into the crushed face.

Peace must be contrived to follow a moment such as that. What was truth when you might have peace? And now I had had a quarter century of peace — the peace of the graveyard. Suddenly as I listened to the fading gasps I knew with a bone-deep sense of shock that their cessation would not set me free, but would chain me irrevocably to the circle of the dead.

As though to flee the figure at my side, I scrambled from the bed and ran to the door — and found myself turning, running back and ripping the bag from the agonized face.

Though he struggled wildly for breath, his eyes remained shut; then the lids split wide apart, and in the instant before they crushed back together again the eyes shot forth a beam of hard, inhuman light, like the glare from stone.

My body was heavy with fatigue, as though I had sat here by him for three hours rather than three minutes. Two or three minutes — that was all the time that could have elapsed. And in those minutes I had come to feel an insanely discomforting heat of wrongness, like a scene in which everything is at an impossible, gravity-defying angle, and either you have gone mad and are seeing with the eyes of madness, or else you have always been mad and have suddenly been jolted sane for the first time and see things as they are. I heard again his words soon after we met: "Once in a lifetime this kind of thing happens, this strong bond, as though it were predestined, and there's nothing you can do about it." And I remembered my response: "There is no bond." He had spoken for the effect of the moment, I with all seriousness, and yet he had been right. Long after he had disappeared from sight I had crouched, hushed, at the outer edge of humanity, fingering my tiny scrap of life, never moving, waiting for his return. And until a moment ago I had been prepared to bury us in the same grave.

His eyes had opened by timorous degrees, as though he were emerging from a sickening dream. Tears slipped down his cheeks in two thin lines. I untied his swollen hand and ankle, and looked at him anxiously. I did not want him to die and I feared that any moment his head would fall limply to one side. I went to the kitchen and made a pot of strong coffee, and when I returned I was relieved to see that he was sitting up against the pillow. His eyes were red with broken blood vessels and his breathing was harsh. He took deep gulps from the cup I held for him, and little by little the trembling in his limbs decreased and his irises cleared of a film that had covered them.

"Get Darlene," he whispered. "Get a doctor. Someone."

"Nothing on the outside can help you."

He cringed, covering his face with his hand.

"I don't mean that. I won't touch you again."

"Get someone," he pleaded.

"There is no one to help you. There is only you."

He stared at me, unaware of my words, only cognizant of their tone, and the tone held a distance like the space between the stars. It steadied him a little; he flexed his fingers, then slowly rubbed the ashen skin of his face.

I looked away from him. "It was I who killed the child," I said quickly.

A faint expression of combined suspicion and relief passed over his features, and he seemed to wait — to wait, almost, for an apology.

"But that doesn't change anything on your side!" I leaned over him and grabbed his collar. "You must admit something at last! You must admit that you were her father. Only that much."

Closing his eyes and pressing his fingers to the lids, he groaned, "Don't you think I would if I could? Could a decent man do anything else?"

I sat slowly back. My enemy was still a good man, still rubbed clean of his past, rubbed to a sliver. As I looked at him he appeared to me as something worn thin, almost transparent, like a votive candle held too long in his own anxious, rapt hands, guttering now toward the long night, but still burning, throwing up a thin white fraudulent flame.

"Why did you run away?" I pursued wearily. "Why did you

lie at the hearing? Everything in the world you lied about. You left me no pride!"

He opened his eyes and glared weakly at me, like a cat held by the scruff of the neck. I shook him violently, demanding an answer.

"I had my name to think of!" he gasped.

"And what about mine?"

Softly, almost sympathetically, he shrugged.

I let go of him and stood up. I wished only for sleep at this moment, and sank into a chair. The room lay in disorder: my new clothes hung, twisted, over the side of the rumpled bed; some lay on the floor near the plastic bag; the empty cup sat on the side table in a pool of spilled coffee. Silence seeped from these objects, as from a stage set after the curtains have closed, a silence made vast by the patter of rain, drawing me toward sleep. But though my body called for sleep, my mind refused it. There was something I must do, now. I could not understand what it was; I only knew that as I sat there I saw Husar's heavy face superimposed on Harley's, asking for yet another compromise, another exile.

When I stood up at last the hands of the clock overlapped at twelve. Mr. Leary had fallen into an exhausted sleep. I walked out of the house, locking the door behind me.

"Rose, what's wrong?"

He had not answered for several minutes, perhaps afraid that it was Darlene. At last I had simultaneously pressed my shoulder against the bell and beaten my fists on the door, and it had opened to a crack. Now he flung it back and urged me in, staring at my wet hair and clothes.

I walked to the middle of the room, which was bathed in the

glow of a single lamp. "Turn on the overhead light. Please!"
The lamp was too soft, and everything it touched with its warm
glow filled me with weakening memories.

With a click the room was illuminated by a clear yellow light.
He stood there in rumpled pajamas, his short hair sticking up in
clumps, yawning and rubbing his eyes. "What's wrong?" he
asked again, walking to the coffee table and bending over the
bottles. "Let me get you a drink."

"I don't want a drink."

"You want one," he said, pouring it. "You're all upset."

He took my hand and put the glass in it. I opened my fingers
and let it drop.

"What'd you do that for?" he asked angrily, as the liquor sank
into the rug, leaving a large oblong stain. "What's the matter
with you, anyway?"

"I told you I didn't want it."

Giving a deep sigh, as though accepting the inevitability of a
scene, he poured himself a drink and stood waiting.

I sat down on the edge of a chair, shivering in my wet clothes.
"I have to talk to you . . ."

"You should take that sweater off, it's soaked through. You'll
catch a chill." As he leaned over to take it, I shrank back.

"What the hell's the matter with you?" he demanded. "This
morning we were all set to get married, and now you come in
here like a stranger, acting hysterical, won't even let me touch
you."

I hesitated. "I suppose it's because we really are strangers.
We don't know each other."

"That's one of the reasons people get married," he explained
irritably, sitting down across from me. "So they can get to
know each other."

"But we would never achieve the depth that's needed for two people to really know each other."

"Oh for God's sake, I see a lecture coming on. I'm too tired for it, baby. You'd better postpone it till tomorrow."

I felt relief that his attitude was making it easier for me to break off with him, and yet I felt disappointment too, for I realized now that I had still harbored some hope when I walked in. But there had only been the usual offer of a drink in the place of concern, and the usual irritated reaction to my showing any lack of self-sufficiency. "I suppose I came here to tell you it's all off," I said quietly.

"All off!" He set the drink down and stood up. "Are you crazy? Why?"

"Because there's nothing but lies between us!"

"What do you mean, lies? I've been more honest with you than anybody else I ever knew."

"For what that's worth! Anyway, I can only speak for myself, and I lied to myself about everything. Do you think I really accept the marina — or the antique store — or those hobbies of yours — or your drinking, or all that psychological jargon?"

"You really hit below the belt, don't you?"

"Hit back then! You don't accept me either, except when I play the role of your muse."

He picked up his glass and looked at it reflectively. "Why don't you just admit you've had another run-in with the old man? Every time he goes off his nut you take it out on me. Look, when he leaves you'll feel better. Forget about that trip to Tahoe. Go home, get some rest instead. Call his son to come for him this weekend, and then . . ."

I shook my head, getting up from the chair.

"Come on, baby," he said as I walked by him, and his hand shot out and clamped around my arm. "Don't leave like this." His voice fell to a whisper. "Get out of those wet clothes. Come to bed, get warm . . ."

I shook my head again, disengaging myself from the thawing circle of his arm. "I left something here. I want to take it with me." I went over to the phonograph where I picked out my record from the other albums. Turning around with it, I looked at him for a moment. "Shall I play it?"

His crumbling patience turned to an exasperated shrug. "What for!"

Opening the phonograph lid, I slipped the record over the spindle and clicked the knob on. I felt sure now, as though the moment were at last right to listen. The record dropped and the arm moved over and settled on the edge of the disk; I lifted the arm until the phonograph was warm and the volume full, then I set it down again.

GLORIA! GLORIA! GLORIA!

"Turn it down, God damn it!" Husar yelled.

I did not touch it, but stood motionless — dazzled by the immense soaring of voices, carried from the room by them. The plain lay clear in noonday light, a mountain of clouds moving over it.

When the music clicked silent I slipped the record back into its album and put it under my arm. Husar had sat down again, his legs flung to either side, his fingers drumming loudly on the arms of the chair.

"This is the whole reason," I said, touching the album with my finger.

"If you want us to break up it should be for a better reason than some crazy whim in the middle of the night . . ." A long exhausted yawn interrupted the words and he got heavily to his feet. "You'd better go home and get some sleep. We'll talk things over when you come to your senses."

"There's nothing more to talk about. It's all been said tonight."

"Nothing's been said! You've just come barging in here and created a scene for no reason at all. I don't understand a woman of your intelligence acting like that."

"How could you understand a woman of intelligence?" I asked.

"Listen, baby," he replied with deadly calm, "I admire your originality and all that — I don't mind your being different — but you go too far."

"Not far enough. I have a lot farther to go, but it can't be with you."

"Christ, I've had it," he sighed, turning around, and then swinging back impatiently. "Did it ever occur to you that you're not the prize you think you are? You can make a fool of yourself if you want to, but you're not going to make a fool of me."

"But I'm not trying to make a fool of you . . ."

"For not trying you're doing a damn good job! Why don't you go home and get yourself together? I'm not taking any more of this crap." He switched off the overhead light, then striding across the room he turned off the lamp and got back into bed. Slipping the record under my sweater to protect it from the rain, I stepped outside and shut the door behind me.

As I walked down the street I looked carefully at everything I passed: the houses of Little Italy, the warehouse, the equipment on the frontage — a mass of cold metal in the dark; then the bait shop, Bobby's empty house, the Shotwell house; and each familiar wooden step, this one sloping to the left, this one to the right, the next one cracked through the middle — fifty-six of them.

Bobby would be asleep by now in a strange room, her suitcase standing open, her ashtray crowded with dead cigarette butts, and the blinding morning before her.

I wished us well.

Epilogue

MR. LEARY WAS STILL ASLEEP on the bed. I turned out the lamp, rolled up the shade, and brought a chair to the window. By infinite degrees the opaqueness of the small hours dissolved, exposing a steel blue sky. He stirred behind me.

"How do you feel?" I asked, turning.

"Get somebody," he whispered.

"I'll drive you to Frank's house tomorrow. I don't want to keep you any longer. He can do with you what he wants."

"You take me to him today," he said, his voice growing fuller.

"Not today. I'm going home today."

"What do you mean, home?"

"My home. The farm, up in Modoc County. We'll leave as soon as it's a little lighter."

"Are you crazy? Do you think I'd go with you?"

"Do you think I'd leave you here alone? I'll feel more comfortable with you in the car."

"My God, my God," he moaned.

"Don't be frightened. There's no reason for you to be frightened of me any longer."

"I can't go on a trip!" he cried. "Don't you realize what I've been through? There's a roaring in my ears . . . my breath comes hard . . . I feel faint. I may be dying . . ."

I studied him carefully. Although I could sense his old toughness standing him in good stead, he still bore the marks of his ordeal: he looked weak, his face was pale, and his breathing was still forced.

"I'll fix you something to eat," I said, "you'll feel better after that."

"I can't swallow," he said reproachfully, his fingers tenderly touching his throat.

But he managed to swallow the scrambled eggs and milk toast I made for him, complaining all the while. After he was fed and washed he seemed to rest more easily. "You'll be all right now," I told him. "You can sleep all the way up there, and all the way back, for that matter. We'll be here late tonight or early in the morning, and in the afternoon I'll drive you to San Francisco."

"Have pity!"

I put the record away, and taking my orange dress from the closet, went into the bathroom and changed; my skin was still cool, cleansed by my walk in the rain. Afterwards, I drove the car up to the end of the old road above the house, and as I parked it I was suddenly overcome by relief that it would not end up at the bottom of a cliff. With some blankets and a pillow I arranged a bed in the back seat for Mr. Leary.

"I'll die on the way," he groaned as I wheeled him onto the porch and locked the door behind us. The rain had stopped and a drizzle fine as mist filtered through the morning twilight. I struggled up the steps with him to the car and opened the back door, but he refused to be settled in. "I'll sit up front with you," he said stubbornly.

"You're in no condition to sit up. Get under these blankets and try to get some rest."

Reluctantly, he allowed me to help him into the back seat but would not have a blanket over him, and lay on his side, wide awake, looking as though he might rise up any minute. After putting the wheelchair in the trunk of the car I backed carefully down the old road, ignoring his apprehensive glances in the rear-view mirror. As I drove toward Crockett I could see him fighting to stay awake, jerking his eyes open when they threatened to close. Gradually he sank down and seemed to sleep, but when I reached the Carquinez Bridge and stopped to pay the toll he suddenly raised himself and opened his mouth as though to cry for help. I drove off quickly, and once again he sank back, this time overcome by exhaustion, and began to snore. A few miles later I stopped and checked him to make sure that he was all right. His color seemed to be returning and his breathing sounded better. I put my fingers on his wrist and found his pulse to be regular. Throwing the blanket over him, I got back behind the wheel and drove on.

An hour or two later I had left the drizzle behind and drove along under a metallic sky that tinted the countryside silver. It was pleasant country, a rolling patchwork of plowed fields marked off by rows of slender trees, but the trees were leafless and the ground looked hard with cold. I thought of my own environs, without a tree or hill to soften winter's encroachment.

By three o'clock the sky seemed already darkening with the approach of night. I could easily reach the farm in another hour or so, but night came quickly this time of year and I didn't want to be cut off by the dark in the middle of my visit. Besides, my eyes were blurred with fatigue. "Look for a motel," I told Mr. Leary, who had just awakened with a loud yawn. "We'll stay over and go on in the morning."

But even as I spoke I saw that the scenery was beginning to transform into the country I had grown up in. My blood quickened and I pressed the gas pedal down, forgetting motels.

"Slow down," he cried, "there's one."

"Good. It has a restaurant. We'll eat. Then we'll go on. I've changed my mind."

"And it'll be dark when we get there," he said ominously. "Who lives there? It's not deserted, is it?"

"Yes, it is," I replied, pulling up before the restaurant.

"Rose," he whispered, "you're going to put me through it all over again."

"No, I am not," I said, getting him into the wheelchair, "just relax and be quiet. Don't spoil this trip for me."

The restaurant was one of those chrome and glass affairs that had sprung up during my exile. As I slid into a booth I thought how strange that there was no wood or cloth anywhere, only metal and plastic. I laid my hands on the tabletop, gray formica embossed with swirls of gold, bordered by a strip of chrome along which I noticed another strip, a black threadlike accumulation of food. A picture of the completed marina flashed into my mind, the littered concrete and hard glare of steel.

My passenger, sitting across from me in his wheelchair, ordered anxiously, his eyes resting with haggard hope on the waitress's face. She returned his look with a doll-like smile and took our orders back to the kitchen, leaving us in a heavy silence. He turned and surveyed the other customers, his chin resting wearily on his chest.

"Cheer up," I said, "tomorrow you'll be all settled in cozy and snug at Frank's."

"Don't treat me like a child," he spat, swinging around. "I may be crippled but I'm a man!"

When the dinner was served he picked at his food, his hand

trembling so badly that he could hardly maneuver the fork to his mouth. "What is it?" I asked in an undertone. "Do you think God is after you with a bolt of lightning?"

The fork vibrated in the air. "God has always watched over me!"

After the meal, as I started wheeling him away, he exploded into a wild, unholy protest that startled me as much as the people around us, and I grabbed at his thrashing arm, embarrassed and furious. The waitress rushed to him with a glass of water which she urged him to drink and which he knocked from her hand, clutching her skirt and pulling her to him. She backed away with a face as red as the underdone meat she had served us, as he cried, "Oh pardon! Pardon! Come back!"

"Please forgive him," I shouted over his cries, "he doesn't know what he's doing when he gets like this . . ." And grabbing the wheelchair, I pushed him out as he twisted around in it, still shouting entreaties.

With a great effort I managed to get him back into the car — into the front seat this time, where I could keep an eye on him. "If you flare up like that again, you'll be sorry," I warned him, getting in beside him. He sat leaning against the dashboard, his eyes glued to the door of the restaurant, and as I drove away he pivoted around to keep it in sight, as though still expecting someone to fling it open and with an encouraging cry come after him.

Soon the scattered farms and houses disappeared; the occasional small hills leveled to a gray waste, though the road was still softened by a line of cypresses. When we passed the turnoff to Alturas I knew I had only twenty miles to go. A few minutes later the trees ended abruptly, the plain stretched unbroken in every direction. Then I was jolting over the long dirt road that led to the farm, and I strained my eyes for the cluster of buildings that had always risen against the horizon like an outcropping of rocks. Gradually they took form, and as we drew nearer I knew that they were in ruins. I noticed, too, half a mile away, something that looked like a small concrete storage depot, which must have been built after I left and abandoned along with the farm.

I stopped the car in the yard and rubbed my burning eyes. "I'm going to leave you in the car," I told Mr. Leary, whose face was set in a dread of the decayed buildings. "Why don't you get into the back seat and try to sleep again?"

He shook his head sharply, still staring at the buildings. I got out, slamming the door behind me.

The barn and plowshed had collapsed and the little willow was gone. The fences had fallen and brought in the wilderness, so that where a crosswork of paths had once existed there was only dirt; even the walls of the house had become a haven for the wind-blown earth, all their pores clogged with gray dirt, their cracks laced with dirt-jeweled webs. The roof did not seem so high as it once had, nor as straight, for the building now leaned to one side and was looking with resignation at the ground upon which it would one day fall.

Stepping through the front door, I stood in the desolate salon where the three of us had spent our evenings, in winter accompanied by the crackle of the wood stove, in summer by the whir, the interminable whir of the fan. Some of the furniture still stood; the brown sofa gnawed by rats, an empty bookcase which had been used as a rack for my father's guns and tools.

I stood for a while, listening. So frail was the old structure that it creaked in the little wind that nosed over the ground outside. The staircase seemed to gasp at intervals. I crossed the room, my feet crunching on the gritty floorboards, and climbed it. Disappearing from the twilight below into the darkness of the upstairs hallway, I slid my hand along the wall for a doorknob, and finally pushed open a door into a cube of gray light — my parents' bedroom, everything gone but a blue speckled chamberpot and a 1945 calendar on the wall. So the farm had not been abandoned until then, I reflected, looking around. It was a small room, though when I was young it had seemed spacious. There in the empty corner had stood the double bed where I was born, and where, I thought, as I returned to the hall, my father had been brought back from the fields after his stroke, and where my mother had slept alone afterwards, with my postcard crumpled on the table beside her.

I found my own room still occupied by the enormous, clumsy bureau that had always stood there, now covered with grit. I worked the drawers open — they had always stuck badly — and ran my fingers over their floors, bringing back little piles of dust, and turning around again. Looking at the crumbling room, I felt a flash of proprietary pain. She had lain on a narrow bed by the window, sprawled there on late summer nights under the small aureole of a candle, reading, or totally still, an arm dangling to the floor, eyes half shut. There were things to keep a pair of sleepy eyes interested for a time: the steady, intricate flight of a night insect; a handful of stones rising from the table like an ant's mountain range; a white robe hanging from a peg and forming a flag, a thunderhead, a departed spirit. Sleep came suddenly, with a close sour smell — this from the old quilt she burrowed into — and the candle burnt itself out toward morning.

The bureau still bore marks where the candle had dripped, hardened, and been scraped off, leaving a small waxy cloud formation on the dark surface under the grit and dust. Wiping the dirt away, I leaned over and laid my cheek against it, looking horizontally into the pitted mirror, and saw Rose's face forming with a strange languor, as though all these years behind its pocked mercury the old glass had sheltered the components of her image.

The room was darkening rapidly; outside the wind was rising, moving the dust over the ground in long drifts and shaking the screen that still dangled from one side of the paneless window. I walked over to it and leaned out. A gust struck me in the face and I breathed in a lungful of air, catching it in a sudden small cry as I stared out across the plain.

Stepping onto the front porch, I thought I heard voices nearby and stood still, wondering if there were tramps here I hadn't seen. Straining my eyes through the darkness, I made out two figures a hundred or so feet from the car, one on the ground and another crouched over it. As I drew near I saw that it was Mr. Leary on the ground. "Somebody came," he gasped, and clung to the figure of an old woman as she tried to lift him. "Somebody came to help me," he said breathlessly.

"I'm Mrs. Hoberg," she said to me. "I seen you drive up from my window."

I glanced at the elderly woman who had once been my neighbor. "I'll take him," I said, throwing his dead arm around my shoulder. "He shouldn't have gotten out of the car."

"I won't go back in!" he cried.

"It's all right," I reassured him.

The woman laid her hand firmly on my arm. "He don't want to go back in the car."

I moved my arm but she didn't loosen her grip. "This here's a scared man," she persisted. "Leave him be for a minute."

"He'll freeze out here," I said, pulling away from her. "He must get back in the car."

"Sure enough, then I'll sit next to him till he calms down. You want me to, don't you?" she asked him, and he nodded vigorously.

Once we were inside the car, the two of them in the back seat, the old woman stated in the tones of an inquisitor, "This is a funny place for anybody to come. I wondered what you wanted when I seen you from my place." She indicated the small concrete structure I had noticed earlier. Lights were burning in its windows now.

"I thought that was a storage depot," I said, starting the motor.

"No, it's my house," she replied, offended. "My husband built it."

"I'll drop you off there, then," I told her, and added, "I'm surprised you built way out here, so far from your own farm. Did you buy ours, here, by any chance? It belonged to my father. Do you remember me, Rose Davies? Melvin Davies's daughter?"

She did not reply until we had reached her house, then she said, "You better come inside."

"No," I replied, "he's all right, we'll go on."

At which Mr. Leary began his clamor again, holding tightly to the arm of his new-found benefactress, who seemed unaware of him as she leaned forward and whispered like an ocean into my ear, "And you'd go on, and never even ask about your mother?"

I looked into her face illuminated by the lights from the windows, a humorless, weathered farm face like hundreds in these parts, with thin white hair stuck back behind the ears and sunken cheeks. In this timeworn, anonymous face my mother's eyes burnished wounded and outraged.

I flung myself around back to the wheel.

"You could go on and not even ask!" she said again.

"I . . . I have often wondered," I stammered.

"Ah!" she gasped, sitting back, and after a silence she said, "It's a greeting I could expect from you."

Mr. Leary had stopped his exhortations and was as silent as my mother, whose eyes I could feel boring into the back of my head. At last she said again, "You better come in."

"No," I murmured.

"*I'll* come in," Mr. Leary told her, "I'm not well, I need to lie down."

And with sudden energy, ignoring me, she began to help him out, her wiry old body equal to the task.

"Get the wheelchair," he said to her in a strained voice. "It's in the trunk, you'll need the key."

"Give me the key, Rose," she said.

"Why? Let us go on."

"The man is sick," she said impatiently, holding her hand out for the keys. I laid them in her palm.

She went to the back of the car and opened the trunk and pulled out the folded wheelchair, dragging it around to where we sat. "I know how to work these things," she muttered. "Hoberg had one."

A few minutes later she got the old man into the wheelchair and pushed him to her door. "Are you going to stay there?" she asked me.

I followed them inside the little cellblock, where Mr. Leary stretched his hand toward an electric heater. My mother stood behind him. She lifted her eyes and slowly, bitterly surveyed me. "Your coat's filthy," she said.

The dirt from my room had rubbed off on it. I took it off, suddenly sweating in the heat.

"You dress like a whore," she said, looking at my orange dress. Then her eyes returned to Mr. Leary.

I looked around at the room. It was spotless, and in spite of being cramped, had a Spartan air. The walls were the same inside as out, rough and gray, and the concrete floor was bare. Through two open doors I saw a kitchen and bedroom, both little larger than closets.

My mother, too, had removed her coat and I saw that she was still wearing the same kind of shapeless print dress that she favored thirty years ago, reaching almost to her ankles. It suited her better now. She was still hovering over Mr. Leary, but now, as though with a sense of duty, she came over and stood before me.

"I never forgot that post card you sent me. A cruel letter like that to your own mother."

"I've regretted the card," I said, looking away.

"You laid a knife between us," she went on in a flat voice. "It can't ever be changed." Then, looking over at Mr. Leary, she said, "I want to know who this man is and why he was acting the way he was."

"He's my uncle by marriage. He's staying with me."

"Mrs. Hoberg," he said, motioning her over, "if Rose is your daughter I don't want to say anything against her, but the fact is I can't stay with her any longer. If I do my health will be ruined."

"What's keeping you from going somewhere else?" she asked.

"She won't let me."

"That's not like you," she told me contemptuously. "You were never no angel of mercy. You must be getting money for keeping him."

"Yes, his son sends me two hundred and fifty dollars a month." Somehow I was pleased to corroborate her suspicions.

Her expression softened as she walked back to him, and she rested her hand protectively on the wheelchair. "Does he have any other clothes?" she asked. "These are damp from him laying on the ground."

"It's not necessary, we're going now," I said.

"I've got some pants of Hoberg's, they'll probably fit. Come on, dear," she said, wheeling him into the bedroom. Too relieved by his rescue to care about being undressed by a stranger, he went without protest.

"We're going to leave," I told her when they came back.

"Hush now," she warned, sitting down near him. "Let him rest awhile."

"Only for a while." Mr. Leary sat quietly, warming himself before the heater. The room was plunged into silence. "Did Hoberg buy the farm?" I asked at last.

"He come into it when he married me," she answered with the cold formality that she had apparently decided was my due. "Alice Hoberg passed about the same time as your pa, and Hoberg was lonely." She got to her feet and went into the kitchen. "I've got some lamb chops here," she called out.

"I don't want anything," I said.

"It's for him. A man gets hungry."

When she had the chops under way she went into her bedroom, emerging a few minutes later with her hair combed, a starched apron tied around her waist, and a pair of carpet slippers on her feet. She bustled around the kitchen and presently set a tray of food on the old man's lap, drew up a chair for herself, and proceeded to cut the meat for him. Laying down the knife, she pronged a piece with the fork and slipped it into his mouth.

"I can manage," he said, taking the fork from her.

"Not yet," she countered, taking it back, and he suffered her solicitude, not looking at her. Her eyes, moist and bright, darted eagerly back and forth from the fork to his face.

"What about the farm?" I persisted.

She was too involved with her feeding to answer, but when she had finished, taking the plate into the kitchen and scouring it, she described how Hoberg had sold his own farm — though in better condition than ours it was much smaller — and devoted all his efforts to reclaiming ours. He had even brought a tractor in.

"The soil was sterile," I said. "Why did you let him sell a reasonably good place to work on a bad one?"

"Hoberg knew soil better than me," she said complacently. "It was his own choice."

His own choice, I thought, you picked up where you left off with Pa; you got hold of poor old Hoberg, and when he came back from the field at night feeling like death you sat at his feet and cooed and waited for him to start shriveling up.

"But he never felt at home on the farm," she went on. "So he built this. He chose this spot because it was the only spot in five miles that had a tree growing on it. Hoberg liked trees — when he run into that little willow by the barn with the tractor and bashed it down, he near cried. That's why he built here, by a tree. Only he built too close to it, the pipes got tangled up with the roots and it died."

"That sounds like Hoberg's luck. He must have been a source of constant satisfaction for you."

"We were satisfied," she agreed. "The last five years he was a puny, ailing man, but I took care of him and it brought us even closer together. When he passed on — here in the bedroom, poor sick soul — I didn't know what to do."

"What have you done?" I asked.

"I've gone on living," she said simply, "the way you have to." Then, fixing me with a hard look, she said, "And what about you? Where do you live? Have I got grandchildren?"

"No."

"Of course not. Well, where do you live? What does your husband do?"

"I live in a small town near San Francisco. My husband worked for a brick company."

"In an office?" she asked quickly.

"No, he was just a factory hand."

For the first time she seemed pleased by what I had said. "You didn't do so good out there, did you?" she asked with a smile. Then the coolness returned. "You talk about him like he wasn't around anymore. What are you, one of them divorced women?"

"No, I'm widowed." But I was strangely bored by her questions, by the malice in them; I no longer felt involved in the bitterness of her life.

Her interest, too, seemed to be fading. She looked at the old man. "You want to lie down," she said, and with unbelievable dispatch she put him on the couch and spread a blanket over him. Straightening up with a current of efficiency, she said, "He can't travel the way he feels. What are you going to do about him?"

"He's well enough to go back with me now."

A groan issued from the couch.

"Do you want to stay here, dear?" she asked, bending over him.

"Permanently?" I interjected. "Because it would be permanent, wouldn't it, Ma?"

"Of course not. He could decide whenever he wanted to leave," she said, tucking the blanket around him.

"He could decide. But would you act on his decision?"

"You're talking in circles, like you always did. He can decide."

But I whipped the blanket back and pulled him to a sitting position. "Do you realize how isolated you are here? That road down there is a dirt road, there's no traffic on it . . ."

"That's not true," my mother interrupted. "Once a week the hired man from Hoberg's old place drives over here and takes me into Alturas to buy my groceries."

"There, that's a good indication," I told him. "You're on the face of the moon here. Listen to me! When I leave, I won't be coming back. You'll rot here, because she won't let you go and there'll be no one to make her. And you — you, with all your great plans for the future — you'll be worse off than in the nursing home. She'll grind you into a jelly!"

"Don't talk about your mother that way," she broke in, "or I'll slap your face."

"You're still depending on Frank," I went on, ignoring her. "You think you'll rest here a day or two, then you'll write him and he'll come for you or send someone for you. For God's sake, will you face the fact that he's not coming? Will you tear that whole web of lies out of your head at last? Frank loved his mother — never you. And he'll never forgive you for what you did to her. He'll leave you here. If you don't come with me now you'll stay here for good."

He looked at me bitterly. "Do you remember what happened last night?"

"All right, I won't expect you to drive off with me alone. Ma can come with us." I turned to her. "Ma, if you're as concerned about him as you seem to be, what would you say to this? Drive with us to Alturas. I'll set you both up at a hotel and pay your expenses. Then you can telephone whomever you want, Mr. Leary — Twin Oaks, Cathleen, anyone — and tell them you're coming back; or you can wait until Monday and call Frank at his office. Ma, I'll pay you whatever you want to stay with him and get him back to his people. We can start for Alturas now, it's still early."

My mother mulled over the question for a moment, sitting down with a basket of mending. "He seems a fine man," she said at last, "and I know his people would be glad to have him back. But I can't see no sense to rushing off like that."

"Mrs. Hoberg has already put herself out enough for me," Mr. Leary said with a cold look at me. "I'd never ask her to go through all that trouble for nothing. Besides, after what I've been through I need a rest."

"Anybody with a pair of eyes could see he's in a bad way," my mother agreed. "He's too much of a man to complain, but he needs to be taken care of, not shipped off on another trip."

"And Frank will come for me when I'm ready to leave," he stated as though in conclusion. "You've always tried to turn me against him, but I know my own son."

"That's how she is," my mother murmured.

"All right," I said, "Mr. Leary's son will be sending his checks to you from now on, Ma."

She plunged her needle through the material and pulled it through, drawing out a long black thread, and did not answer.

"That won't be necessary," Mr. Leary said. "We'll be happy to repay you for your kindness, Mrs. Hoberg, but we won't put anything on a monthly basis since I won't be staying that long."

"You suit yourself, dear," she said, biting the thread in two with her long teeth.

"Where will he sleep?" I asked.

"In the bed, of course. I'll sleep out here on the couch."

"It won't be comfortable for you."

"Have I ever needed comfort? I won't mind. It'll do me good."

"How," I asked, "will it do you good to sleep on a hard narrow couch you can't turn around on?"

"It will do me good to give up something for somebody else," she replied, her eyes candid and at peace. "Without a man to do for a woman goes empty and dull."

"You haven't felt her bite," I informed the old man.

"Hush this kind of talk," my mother overrode me. "You always had crazy ideas, but you got to stop it now and give this man some peace. You don't know how to bring a man comfort. It's what they want."

The great mother, the last of the one-celled animals, crawling along the ground with all its sensory apparatus tuned in for digestible matter. She sewed on with neat little stitches, her feet perfectly aligned on the floor, like someone in church. Her small hands were rough as burlap, her chest flattened, her back curved under the hump of the aged, rigid and hard.

I picked up my coat. "I'm glad I came," I said, looking out the window. "I saw the plain. I always remembered its beauty."

"There isn't no beauty out there," she corrected as though I were feeble-minded.

"There was for me. You called me a freak once, Ma. That was good, that sort of freak I should have stayed."

"You're a worse one now," she ventured, looking to Mr. Leary for approval. "A grown woman talking foolishness."

But he was too sleepy to respond. Though loathe to lose contact with the warm little room and the solicitous farm woman, he was dropping off, his lids slowly lowering. He looked for the first time that day deeply relaxed, and I knew he would sink into a sleep of good dreams.

"You can't keep your eyes open another minute," my mother said to him, putting her sewing aside and getting up. "Let's put you to bed where you can get a proper rest."

I gazed at my old enemy lying on the couch in Hoberg's baggy trousers and remembered him sitting on the edge of my bed in his sober suit and high collar, his pearl stickpin gleaming from his tie, laying his hands all over my body, his eyes closed in a spasm of anticipated pleasure . . .

He gave her a grateful look and nodded, sitting up on his elbow as she brought the wheelchair to him. She had him in it in a minute, her hands very sure, and rolled him past me into the bedroom.

Putting on my coat, I thought of the long return trip ahead of me. When I reached Port Carquinez in the morning I would go to bed and sleep for twenty-four hours, as long as I wanted — the thought sent a shiver of delight through my tired body. Time was no longer my enemy; I could take all of it I required to make my plans and pack the things I would need. Later on I could decide whether to sell the house from a distance or to leave it; and even if it remained, standing for years before it fell, a bitter husk, it would no longer belong to the woman who had lived there.

Glancing through the half-open door, I watched my mother peel off the old man's outer clothing, pull back the covers, and help him in between the sheets. The light in the cubicle was weak, brownish, and turned his face the color of clay. He smiled up at her.

She bustled around, plumping his pillow, straightening the blankets, her carpet slippers slapping against the floor. Then they conversed a moment about his teeth. Did he leave them in at night or take them out? He left them in. But it was better to take them out, she said. It was better to take them out, she repeated softly, and ignoring his feeble gesture of protest she leaned over and removed them. Holding them in the palm of her hand she went across the room, where I heard a faucet being turned on and the clink of the dentures in a glass.

"Have you changed your mind?" I whispered from the door.

His eyes opened slowly, the sockets cavernous in the dim light, and he looked deeply and steadily at my face, as though burning into my mind the triumph of his escape. Only when my mother approached his side did the look end, as he closed his eyes and crushed his face wearily into the pillow. She gazed down at him for a moment and tucked the blanket under his sunken jaw; then with a sigh of completion she picked up his clothes and began hanging them in the closet.

"Goodbye, Mr. Leary."

As the car bumped back down the dirt road I could smell again the fumes that had permeated the cab of the old truck that summer morning twenty-six years ago, and saw again the cloud of dust rising behind us, and Hoberg passed me an orange.